Dueling on the Roof

He'd chased her through the library, up onto the roof. Then he'd challenged her, drawing a power-glyph in the air—and though he wasn't the chief force behind the killings, Di knew the challenge could not go unanswered.

He spread his hands wide, then clapped them together—and she had a split second to decide if the snarling thing with the head of a jaguar and the wings of a bird was real or illusion.

Because if she guessed wrong, she was dead . . .

Mercedes Lackey

BURNING WATER

TOR
HORROR

A TOM DOHERTY ASSOCIATES BOOK
NEW YORK

BURNING WATER

Copyright © 1989 by Mercedes Lackey

Cover art by Maren

A Tor Book
Published by Tom Doherty Associates, Inc.
175 Fifth Avenue
New York, N.Y. 10010

Tor ® is a registered trademark of Tom Doherty Associates, Inc.

ISBN: 0-812-52485-3
Library of Congress Catalog Card Number: 88-51004

First edition: February 1989

Printed in the United States of America

0 9 8 7 6 5 4 3

Dedicated to
Mary Jean and J. R. Holmes,
who gave Diana a place to grow up

ONE ·

LUPE SOBBED HARSHLY, HER VOICE MUFFLED, AS IF SMOTHERED by the darkness all about her. She clawed at the rubble that hemmed her in; her finger-ends were surely raw and bloody, but *she* couldn't see them, and she was too hysterical to feel much pain. All she felt was panic, the panic of a trapped animal—for she was trapped helplessly beneath tons of rubble, rubble that, less than an hour ago, had been the twenty story hotel in downtown Mexico City where Lupe worked as a maid.

Today was September 19, 1985. Mexico City had just experienced one of the worst earthquakes in its history.

Ironically enough, it was also Lupe's birthday.

Less than an hour ago she'd been happy. It had not much mattered that she'd had to work on her birthday; she had known that she was lucky to have this job at all. Less than an hour ago, she had descended the stairs to the cellar storeroom singing. It would only have been a few more hours, and then she'd have been off, free for the evening. There was going to be a party, cake—and handsome Joachim, who worked as a bellman, had promised to come. She had a new dress, red and soft, like rose petals, and Joachim liked red. One of the tourists had already given her a tip for bringing extra towels. And there had been a full, unopened bottle of wine left behind after the party in room 1242. She'd hidden it in her locker, for *her* party. It was going to be a good day, with a better evening to come.

The ashtrays she'd come seeking were kept in boxes next to the stairs; cheap little metal things that the tourists were always taking. Somebody had overfilled the particular box she reached for and several of them had fallen out and rolled under the staircase. She'd had to wedge herself under the staircase to reach them. She hadn't minded; the cellar was well lit, and she was small enough to fit beneath the staircase easily.

That was what had saved her.

For with no warning, the floor began to buck and tremble like a wild horse; the lights sparked and went out. She screamed, or thought she did—she couldn't hear her own voice in the shrieking of tortured metal and concrete. She'd been flung backward and against the wall, and hit her head, seen multicolored flashes of light, then nothing.

When next she could think, she was hemmed in on all sides by concrete and debris; trapped in the dark—a darkness so absolute that there was nothing she could compare it to.

The reinforced staircase had protected her; kept her from dying beneath the crumbling hotel.

She knew at once what had happened; Mexico City had suffered earthquakes before. But she had never been caught inside a building by one; never known anyone who had been buried alive like this.

Lupe had survived the quake. Now as she stared into the darkness, she realized slowly that she faced death in another, more painful form: suffocation, starvation, thirst—

Madre de Dios, she prayed wildly, *I'm only seventeen! I have always been good—I can't die—*

The air in her tiny, sheltered pocket was already growing stale. She panted in fear, and the air seemed to grow thicker and fouler with each breath. The sound of her breathing was a rasping in her own ears, for the silence was as absolute as the darkness. She rested her forehead on the wall in front of her, feeling her chest constrict and ache. How long before the air became unbreathable?

That fear was enough to make her tremble in every limb. But worse than the rock that hemmed her in, worse than the thickening air, worse than any of it was the terrible, menacing darkness all around her.

Lupe was afraid of the dark; she had been afraid of the dark for as long as she could remember. It was a vague fear she couldn't even define, just a feeling that there was *something*—waiting for her. Watching. A something that lived in the dark—no, it *was* the dark.

And it wanted Lupe.

But it was rarely "dark" in Mexico City, even in the early hours of the morning. Certainly it was never dark in the two-room apartment she shared with her sisters; the neon signs of the nightclubs across the street saw to that. Her night-fears had been easy to laugh at until this moment.

Now she was caught in the very heart of darkness; thick, hot darkness that seemed to flow sluggishly around her, seemed to be oozing into her very pores and trying to force itself down her throat until she choked on it.

She could feel it now—

She gasped, coughed, and frantically scrabbled again at the wreckage hemming her in; whimpering and hardly realizing she was doing so. She had barely enough room to crouch; impenetrable rubble formed a tiny pocket around her—like the pocket holding the larvae of a tourist's "jumping bean." But the larvae would grow wings and escape—

She never would. She would die here, and the dark would eat her bones.

She wailed, and pounded at the wall before her with aching hands. Trapped—trapped—

Lupe's mother had had no patience with her child's phobias. The census said they were Mestizo—but Paloma had told all her children that they were truly Azteca, and descended from priests. "Look for yourself, if you don't believe—" she had told them all, and more than once. "Go to the museum and see for yourself." And so, dutifully, they had gone—to see their own high-cheekboned, beaky profiles (so unlike most of their schoolfriends' round faces and snubbed noses) echoed at them from pots, from paintings, from bas-relief. "You are of noble blood, the blood of warriors," she had scolded Lupe when the girl confessed her nightmares. "How can you be so afraid?"

Mamacita, she cried out in her mind, *what good is noble blood when the earth shakes? What good is descent from priests when the dark comes to steal my breath?*

She sobbed, the thick air tasting of her own fear. The smell of her own sweat was rank, thickening the dark further. Her eyes were burning with tears as she continued to beat at the unyielding wall before her. She knew it was useless—but what else was there to do? It was either that, or curl into a ball of misery and die or go mad.

Maybe the Virgin would grant a miracle, and someone would hear.

She forced herself to pound on the wall, while her arms grew weary, and fists numb. Pound—pound—pound—

Then the wall moved.

She started back, hugging her bruised fists to her chest with an involuntary intake of breath, afraid now that she might have triggered a fate worse than the one she sought to escape—a second falling of rubble that would crush her.

When nothing else happened, she reached out with one hand, heart in her throat, and pushed tentatively at the spot that had yielded.

Again it moved—moved outward just the slightest bit. She tried to think, when the movement brought no corresponding descent of stone on her head—what direction had she been kneeling? What lay before her?

Carefully now, she felt along the wall; it was flat, or nearly. Cracked, cracks she could stick a finger in up to the first knuckle, but mostly flat. It must be the basement wall, then, rather than a tumble of concrete. She must be facing the back of the staircase.

Maybe the quake had opened up a hole next to the foundation! Maybe—maybe it was even a way out—

Lupe didn't hesitate any further; the thought of a way out gave her arms a new and frenzied strength. She shoved at the yielding place with all her might, bracing herself against the wreckage that held her trapped; shoved until she thought she was going to tear herself in two. And when the wall suddenly gave way, she was unprepared, and went somersaulting headfirst down a pile of dirt and rocks, hitting her head on a stone and nearly knocking herself out a second time.

She sat up, after a long moment of dazed blinking at the false lights thrown before her eyes by the blow on the head. Then she moaned and groveled in the dirt, for she realized she had merely exchanged one prison for another.

It was just as dark *here* as it had been *there*; the only difference between "here" and "there" was that now she could no longer touch the walls that held her prisoner.

That, in its way, made "here" even worse. The darkness was growing colder with every passing moment; she was somehow certain of that. Colder; and flavored with the taint of evil, like a nest of snakes. She could almost hear something breathing out there beyond the reach of her groping hands. The thing that had always waited in the dark for her was *here*, she *knew* it!

She scrambled backwards, inching a little higher on the mound of dirt, trying to reach the pocket in the rubble of the hotel basement that now seemed a haven of safety and sanity. But the dirt was loose, and slipped and slid under her, and she could get nowhere near her invisible goal.

She became aware of a strange smell; sweet at first, then repellent. Rather like the smell of the old catacombs where her mother had taken them all on the Day of the Dead.

But with the smell came something so welcome she ignored the faint charnel odor.

Light!

There was light out there—

Or was it only that she thought there was light?

She scrambled to her feet, peering hopefully into the no-longer-threatening darkness, clawing sweat-sticky hair out of her blinking, burning eyes. Yes, there *was* light, a dim, reddish glow—and it was coming from somewhere ahead of her.

So was the odor—but she ignored the smell in the rush of elation she felt at the promise of light.

With her hands out before her, she stumbled blindly forward, tripping on rocks she had no chance of seeing, until at last there were no more rocks and the dirt under her feet was level and smooth. Then it was no longer dirt beneath her feet, but stone, smooth stone, that the heels of her shoes clattered against like castanets.

Abruptly her hands encountered stone at eye level.

She squinted, and made out the dim bulk of a regular outline against the dim glowing. She had found the top of a low doorframe. Perhaps—perhaps another part of the cellar; perhaps the cellar of another building. There was no way of knowing what kind of a jumble the quake had made of the buildings. She ducked, and passed the threshold—

And the glow flared up, angry and hot before her eyes. It was like molten iron, red and glaring, so that she cried out involuntarily and hid her face in the crook of her arm.

At nearly the same moment, she felt something slam down behind her, closing off the doorway practically at her heels.

She whirled, going to her knees, and beat on the slab of stone that had fallen down to seal off her exit, seeing only now in the raw red light that her hands were bloody, the nails split to the quick, the skin gashed and the flesh torn and lacerated.

Something laughed soundlessly behind her.

Again she pivoted, plastering her back against the cold stone slab that blocked the door, mouth dry with fear.

She saw she was in a low-ceilinged, stone-walled chamber. Although there was no apparent *source* of light, the chamber was bright enough that she could easily see the colorful paintings on three of its four walls. She couldn't look at them for very long, though; the garish colors and the light that pulsated with every beat of her heart made it seem that they moved. They made her dizzy. The floor was black and crusted—and it was plain that *this* was the origin of the sickly sweet stench. And on the fourth wall—

On the fourth wall, the wall opposite the door, was a block of stone like an altar, and behind it, a statue. The statue, the paintings—they were like the ones she'd seen in the museum, only untouched, undamaged by years of profaning hands.

Things of the Ancient Ones, the Azteca. She seemed to remember, vaguely, that all of Mexico City had been built on ancient ruins, the ruins of the Aztec capitol, Tenochtitlan. And hadn't some of the museum artifacts been unearthed when they had dug the foundations of this very hotel?

The statue was of a dead-black stone that reflected none of the light in the chamber, and pulled at her eyes until she could no more look away from it than escape from this place. She knew, in a way beyond knowing, that the statue was of the rarest unflawed black jade. Priceless, and peerless.

With that knowledge, a voice insinuated itself into her head; it hummed behind her eyes, seductive, hypnotic.

She listened; she couldn't have escaped it even if she'd wanted to. And she didn't want to. It promised, that voice, even if she couldn't yet understand *what* it promised. It soothed; it began to drive out her fear. It was so good to listen to that voice, full of more promises than Joachim's, even. Almost, she could almost understand it. It was telling her—that she was brave, and good, and beautiful. That she was awaited here, long awaited. So good not to think, just to listen—thought ebbed away, and pain, and finally, the last chill of fear.

In the moment her fear left her, she saw that the *statue* was the source of the chamber's illumination; in that moment, the stench of the room vanished, replaced by a subtle perfume. The hurting of her hands and arms ebbed away as well, and she looked down dumbly at her hands to see them not only healed, but flawlessly groomed and soft, as only the hands of the lady tourists were. She looked up again at the glowing statue—and now it seemed to represent the very pinnacle of desire.

Fearful no longer, she approached it; the sweet, hypnotic voice still humming behind her eyes, cajoling, promising.

"Sherry—"

Sherry Bryce Fernandez knew that exasperated tone of voice only too well. She braced herself for another inevitable sample of her husband's sarcastic wit, and winced in anticipation.

"Are you quite finished?"

"Not quite—" she ventured, and Robert sighed dramatically.

"So what," he asked, with carefully measured venom, "makes this tourist trap any different from all the other tourist traps we've gone past today?"

Sherry shook back her straight blond hair, held out the brightly brocaded *huiple* in nerveless hands, and attempted to explain. "This is Tenejapa work, Bob—I had no idea there'd be any this far north—it's the Chiapas women that do this kind of weaving—"

"Never mind," he interrupted, boredom and irritation showing only too plainly on his handsome face, somehow getting past the concealing sunglasses he affected. "Don't get started. I suppose now you're going to spend the next two hours dickering for that rag?"

"You know we don't have much to spend," she retorted, flushing. "And this could be very useful to me."

"All right, all right—don't go throwing *that* argument in my face. I'll see if I can find something worth shooting—" Robert backed out of the tiny cranny of the shop as Sherry turned her attention to the keeper.

It wasn't as if he hadn't been getting plenty of pictures, she thought resentfully, as she concentrated on bargaining the price of the *huiple* down to something she could afford. That was just about *all* they'd been doing on this trip—shooting roll after roll of film, spending hours in the broiling sun until the light was "just right"—it might be April, but April in Mexico was as hot as June in Dallas. This was the first time Sherry had been able to track down anything in *her* area of interest—

She felt an immediate surge of guilt, and tucked a wayward strand of ash-blond hair behind one ear with nervous habit. That wasn't fair—this was supposed to be a working vacation. And it was *Robert's* assignment that was paying for it, not hers. She was just lucky that the magazine had been willing to pay for two plane tickets, otherwise she wouldn't be here at all. And Robert would be the only one enjoying the sights of Mexico City—

And the temptations.

Now it was her turn to fight down exasperation. Robert couldn't help himself; he just wasn't made for monogamy. If he just wasn't so damned good-looking— one of his models had likened him to a "young Fernando Lamas."

And that little slut was right—too damned right. He attracted women the way a rock star attracted groupies.

He had all the smooth moves, too; women practically threw themselves into his arms. *Especially* his models, once they figured out (and it didn't take long) that he wasn't gay.

She stole a glance into the street, and saw that he was totally engrossed in setting up a shot of another vendor's wares; pacing restlessly up and down, trying out camera angles, totally immune to the curious glances of passers-by. Her heart lurched as it always did when she caught a glimpse of that craggy profile, especially now that his sarcastic expression had been erased by the concentration he was maintaining. And God, that body—even after six years and a child, the sight of his muscles rippling as he moved was *still* a turn-on!

She dragged her own attention hastily back to her bargaining, grateful for her fluency in Spanish. To have a blond *Americano* begin a sharp bargaining session in their own tongue usually threw shopkeepers off balance enough to give her a real advantage.

To this day, she still didn't quite know why Robert had married her. God knows he'd gotten everything he wanted out of her without *that*.

Maybe he had been telling the truth when he proposed;

maybe it *was* love. Half the time she was sure it was—half the time she wasn't sure of anything.

This trip had seemed like a godsend, a chance to prove to Robert that she was still just as attractive as she had ever been. Bobby stayed with his grandparents; she'd made a conscientious effort to leave behind every T-shirt and pair of blue jeans she owned; to slough, if only for two weeks, her holdover hippie image. It was supposed to be the honeymoon they'd never been able to afford.

And this was Robert's big chance, too—the chance to get his work seen by everyone who meant anything in the Dallas fashion scene. Granted, he was just out here on spec for *TravelWorld*—cheap airfares and cheaper off-season hotel rates had made their benefactors seem more generous than they really were. But *TravelWorld's* execs had an experiment they wanted to make—their hopefully innovative notion was to take destinations thought to be "overexploited"—like Mexico City—and make them look interesting again. Mexico City was chosen as the test case because it was near *TravelWorld Magazine's* Dallas headquarters, it was inexpensive, and it was probably the *last* destination any experienced traveler would choose. If this test issue generated interest—and income for the advertisers—the project would go into full production.

And Robert—*if* his work passed muster—had a chance of becoming a staff photographer—a chance for a secure position. That was the carrot, the big prize he was really hoping for.

Security—Sherry had never thought there'd come a day when that was something she longed for.

God, it all depended on Robert, and whether he could work enough magic with his camera to make tired old sights seem new and entrancing.

Or so he thought. Sherry had experienced enough disappointment in her marriage to Robert to convince her that this trip was the time to further an idea of her own.

Once upon a time Sherry really *had* been a holdover hippie; her handcrafted clothing outlet had a small, but

devoted clientele, though Sherry had been more interested in the craftwork itself than the money it brought in.
But that phase had ended three years ago. . . .

The whole world and what was important had
changed for her the first time Bobby (poor asthmatic
little baby) had gotten seriously ill. The hospital had
wanted money in advance, and Robert hadn't worked in
weeks. They'd ended up borrowing from Robert's parents (who weren't all that well off themselves), after a
frantic midnight phone call.

It was then that Sherry realized that it had been *her*
money, not Robert's, that had been paying most of the
bills. It was then that she decided to take her work
seriously, and began researching craft techniques and
expanding her circle of customers. She had gotten the
feeling lately that she was on the verge of a breakthrough
—what she needed now was something new and different in the folkloric look to make *her* own name. Research
had convinced her she just might find what she needed
right here.

The ancient Aztec garb of brocaded *huiple* and wrap-
skirt was timeless, practical—and might be just different
enough to provide the answer she hoped for, once
updated for the eighties. The Aztec wrap-skirt with the
double ties and pleats was looser, easier to move in than
contemporary skirts—and far less apt to "get away"
from the wearer. And the *huiple*, a loose, sleeveless
blouse held close to the body in front, but loose in back
to catch the breezes, was—so far as Sherry was
concerned—the ultimate in summer comfort.

She finished her bargaining in a rush, and hurried out
into the street with her purchase clutched under her arm.
Robert was glancing around with a crease between his
thick brows; she knew that look. There was something
not quite right about the shot he wanted to take. He
spotted her coming toward him as she slipped between
two plump, gossiping women, and smiled.

Her knees went weak again. God, that smile—it was
like Apollo parting the clouds and bestowing his blessing. No matter how feckless, how unfaithful, how ne-

glectful he was, all he had to do was smile and she knew she'd never have the guts to leave him.

"Sunshine! You're *exactly* what I need! Go stand over there and look touristy—" he pointed toward a display of Aztec-replica pottery. This lot was rather better than the usual; it looked real. She draped the *huiple* gracefully over one arm and posed artlessly, seeming totally unconscious of the camera. She was an old hand at this—she'd started out as Robert's very first model, after all.

And as usual, Robert was right. Her pink sundress (her own design—*that* might do her some good, too) and long blond hair contrasted nicely with the dark pottery and white adobe, making the scene seem more exotic than it really was. Robert snapped off a dozen shots from as many angles in a few minutes, passed the grinning potter a couple of pesos, and took her elbow with an expression of satisfaction.

"Now where?" she asked. She was perfectly content to be dragged anywhere he wanted, now that he was in a good mood again, and now that she had a prime example of exactly what she was looking for in her possession.

"The ruins, I think." He eased the strap of his camera case a little further up on his shoulder.

"Haven't they been done to death already?"

"Maybe—that's what I want to check out. Maybe some different angles, dramatic lighting—I don't know, maybe I can stage something. . . ."

He went introspective and brooding on her, with one of his typically instant mood-changes, and she knew better than to interrupt his train of thought.

The earthquake had been eight months ago, and parts of the city *still* looked like a war zone. The plunging prices of oil had brought as much economic disaster to Mexico's economy as to Texas—more so, in some ways. The earthquake had just been the mud-frosting on a rock-cake. Recovery was going to be painfully slow—

"Robert—" she tugged at his arm, bringing him out of his reverie. "Over there—quick—"

"Over there," in a courtyard complete with the week's washing hanging out to dry in the hot sun, was a group of eight or ten kids dancing. For the moment, if you couldn't hear the rock beat coming from the ghetto blaster (fortuitously just on the edge of the group), you'd swear they were performing some quaint native dance. For a wonder the girls were in skirts instead of jeans. Granted, they were cheap Cyndi Lauper imitations, but they were also colorful, borderline folky, and rather cute. Robert got half a dozen shots before one of the boys started moonwalking.

"Good eye, Sunshine," he applauded as he waved down a cab. "I'll have to crop the radio out, but that was nice composition."

She couldn't help herself, no matter that he'd probably be snarling at her before another hour was over. For now, she had his approval, and she glowed.

Robert stared at the ruined pyramid as if it had personally offended him, and Sherry sighed. There was *no* shade out here; the sun was bearing down on both of them mercilessly, but Robert showed no signs of wanting to move on. She squinted into the glare; sunglasses weren't helping much. She wanted a margarita and a cool place to sit, badly.

She knew what his reaction would be to her suggestion that they come back later—a sullen snarl. He had taken these old ruins as a personal challenge. He was obviously bound and determined to make something interesting out of them, or die in the attempt.

She shifted uncomfortably on the crumbling stone step, and scanned the few other people she could see, hoping for something interesting. Unfortunately they seemed equally divided between earnest and impoverished college students and pudgy middle-aged American tourists, all of them squinting against the sunlight reflecting off the white stone pavement.

The Ugly American lives, she thought wryly, wondering for the thousandth time why it was that the skinny students wore the jeans, and the pasty, middle-aged monuments to cellulite exposed their thighs for all the universe to gawk at.

She fanned herself with her hat, wishing she could somehow capture the incredible blue of the sky in a dye-lot that didn't look garish. White stone, green vegetation, blue sky—sun so bright it had no color at all, and not a cloud to be seen. It was gorgeous, and looked as if it would make a perfect photo. But that brilliant sun was the problem; any pictures taken now would look washed-out by the bright light.

Besides, they'd look like a thousand other pictures of these ruins. What Robert needed was a setup that would convey the age and awe-inspiring quality these ruins had, without looking contrived or like every other picture of an Aztec ruin. Or worse, come off a poor second to the latest round of adventure-movie stills.

Too bad I can't convince some Aztec ghosts to show up and pose for him, she thought idly, brushing damp hair off of her forehead. *It would be just what he—*

She started as a girl came around the corner of the pyramid she sat on.

My God—

For a moment, she thought the girl *was* a ghost. The features, the profile—she could have posed for any of a hundred paintings and carvings back in the museum. Hair so black that it held turquoise-blue highlights, smoldering eyes that took up most of the upper half of her face, a complexion like gourmet coffee lightened with the smoothest and finest of cream. And her costume—

My God, it looks like she copied it from that painting of Smoking Mirror and his priestesses—

The colorful, elaborately brocaded *huiple* and wrap-skirt were perfect replicas of those in the painting, so far as Sherry could remember. And the workmanship of both made the blouse she carried in her bag seem like the fumblings of an amateur weaver.

The girl moved as gracefully as a hunting cat, carrying herself with a dignity that was totally unconscious. Sherry knew a handful of dancers who moved that way, but not many. She was about to say something to get Robert's attention, when he turned and spotted the girl himself.

He froze; just stopped moving completely. Sherry had been steeling herself for his inevitable reaction to an attractive girl—but this was an entirely new response, or at least one *she'd* never seen from him before.

He might not even have been breathing; he didn't even twitch when an enormous fly landed on his arm. It was like the old cliché of being turned to stone.

His reaction was so abnormal she found herself thrown entirely off-balance by it, so that *she* froze in place.

While they stared like a pair of idiots, the girl approached both of them, head held high, the image of some ancient goddess deigning to take notice of a pair of mortals.

"Señor?"

The liquid sound of her voice snapped the strange trance that held both of them. The girl held out an arm draped with silver necklaces that gleamed in the sunlight —not with the highly reflective glitter of most of the jewelry that had been offered to them, but with a soft, subtly textured shimmer, like antique satin.

Or—like scales.

Sherry was suddenly struck by two strong and mutually antagonistic reactions. Half of her wanted to reach out and touch those bright garlands of metal—and the other half shuddered with revulsion at the thought.

That jewelry—it's like dozens of skinny little snakes wrapped around her arm—

"Silver, señor?" The girl struck a pose within touching distance of Robert, and smiled up into his eyes. "Very fine, very cheap."

"My God . . ." he mumbled; the girl did not seem to notice that he had said anything at all. She simply continued to pose, patiently.

He continued to stare; the girl, strangely, did not seem in the least disturbed by his scrutiny. "My God . . . " he said at last, "you could have come down off one of these walls—"

"Pardon?"

Robert pulled himself together with an effort clearly

visible—at least to Sherry. "Señorita," he said, in Spanish far better than Sherry's, "I will buy your necklaces, on one condition—that you pose for me here—"

The girl regarded him measuringly.

"Señor," she asked, "are you wishing for a model?"

"Well—yes, I suppose so." For the first time in Sherry's experience a woman had succeeded in making him uneasy.

"You photograph for the American magazines?"

"Sometimes—"

"Then," she said coolly, "I make *you* an offer. I will pose for you, and my sisters—all tomorrow if you wish. You need buy no silver. But you must see that important people see the pictures, and know who we are. You must see that we are given more jobs, so that we may have green cards. My sisters and I look much alike—it is our resemblance to the Ancient Ones you wish, no?"

Both Robert and Sherry stared at her, more than a little surprised at the strange turn the bargaining had taken. The girl smiled again, a serene, slightly superior smile.

"You see," she said, "I am no ignorant Mestizo. I have some learning. I know what a camera like *this*—" she gestured gracefully at Robert's hands, the necklaces chiming softly with the movement "—means. We wish to come to America, and as legals; we wish to be models, and rich. You will take such pictures that will make us famous—"

"There—there's no guarantee of that—" Robert stammered.

The girl shook her head, dismissing all doubt. "You will make us famous. *And* yourself."

Now she turned to Sherry, who had been totally ignored until this moment. Her eyes were just as enormous as Sherry's first impression had painted them, and so dark that they looked black. Sherry could not look away from them—and found her suspicions ebbing away. Why—of *course* all this made sense! What a clever girl, to have thought of a practical way to make it into the States, instead of sneaking across the border!

The girl smiled a little more broadly, and Sherry smiled back. There was no reason to distrust such cooperation. There was no doubt that the girl would do everything in her power to help Robert.

"Señora," the girl spoke softly, still staring deeply into Sherry's eyes, "you are a lady who has admiration for the old ways, yes, I can see it. I see that you long to examine the work of my people's hands—" She smoothed the front of her *huiple* with her free hand, a movement totally free of any hint of coquettishness. "I should be gladdened to bring with me more such pieces tomorrow, if it would please you—and I see that it would."

Somehow the girl had taken total control of the situation; in a way that left Sherry bewildered and breathless. There was no doubting her, somehow. She had succeeded in hypnotizing both of them.

"So. I shall come to your hotel."

"The Sheraton—" Robert breathed.

"The Sheraton." She nodded, turned with a grace that would have called up raw envy in a prima ballerina, and began to return along the same way she had come.

"Wait—" Robert called, as Sherry sat, still bemused and unable to think. "Your name—"

She cast a glance over her shoulder, arch and full of amusement.

"Lupe, señor. Lupe."

Robert spent the remainder of the afternoon among the ruins, a man obsessed, talking to himself and scribbling notes at every possible setting. Sherry knew better than to interrupt him. He'd been like this only a handful of times before—but those times had produced some of his best work. If the girl had inspired him to a new height, then *she* was not going to argue about the result. For the first time she began to really believe that he might pull off the hoped-for coup of attaining the pinnacle of a permanent position with *TravelWorld*.

They ate in the hotel restaurant, Robert still scribbling away in his plan-book. He could have been eating cardboard, or a plate of fried bugs, for all the notice he took of the food. And *she* just wasn't there for him. Back in their room he checked over every piece of his equipment, then rechecked, then paced the balcony, muttering to himself.

Sherry hardly felt like herself; found herself able to think of little more than the promise of having *her* goal delivered on a platter. So while he paced, she charted patterns—then, unable to concentrate on anything else, dialed room service and turned on the television.

He was still wrapped in thought and never noticed the arrival of the waiter with the drinks she'd ordered. She offered him his share, but he didn't even look at her.

She was too used to him in this mood to be piqued—and she'd done without for too long to let the pitcher of margaritas go to waste. So she ignored him, and curled up to enjoy the margaritas and a Mexican vampire movie. It was one of the worst flicks she'd ever seen, boasting a professional wrestler as its star. Maybe—probably—she was drinking too much. But to see Robert so *enthused* was such a relief that she wasn't paying as much attention to her intake as she usually did. By the time one of the hero's opponents in the ring turned into a werewolf, she'd drunk so much it seemed the height of hilarity.

When she crawled into bed, more than a few sheets to the wind, Robert was still pacing.

In the morning it seemed like a dream, especially with a tequila-head to conquer. She was more than half afraid Lupe was a fraud; that she wouldn't show up at all, and Robert would crash down from his creative height to spend the remainder of their stay in sullen apathy in the hotel.

But the strange, queenlike girl and her three sisters arrived with the dawn.

And they were incredible, all four of them, two shorter and one taller than Lupe herself, but otherwise nearly identical. As they stood in the lobby, they looked like a quartet of ancient Aztec princesses—and it was their surroundings that seemed disjointed from time, not them. They made the gleaming modernity of the hotel lobby seem tawdry and contrived—poorly conceived and cheaply executed.

The youngest and smallest carried a neatly wrapped bundle, which she pressed into Sherry's arms wordlessly, with just a slow, coy wink of her eye. From the moment her hands touched the fabric, she found herself unable to think of anything else—and her hangover inexplicably vanished.

Sherry's obsessions returned full force and then some, and when she saw the patterns woven into the fabric that held the promised clothing, she could not restrain her impatience to get back to the room. She answered Robert's absent farewell with equal distraction, and did not even wait to see the odd procession leave.

The contents exceeded her wildest hopes; not just *huiples* and skirts of the finest and most intricate brocaded patterns, but an unsewn garment in the first stages of construction. Not only would she have patterns for the brocades and embroideries, but she would have a working pattern to adapt for a modern set of garments. It was more than she had dared dream for.

She had brought her own camera and film; she spent the entire day closeted in the hotel room, photographing every inch of the intricate brocades, the construction techniques, and how the garments were meant to drape. She didn't even miss eating lunch; her notebooks were full of sketches and instructions and she'd used every last frame of her film by the time Robert staggered in the door, sweaty, dusty, and totally exhausted.

"My *God*, Robert—" his appearance alone served to shake her out of the trance she'd been in all day. She took his equipment from him and he stumbled over to the bed, throwing himself down with an utter indifference to anything that might have been in his way.

She glanced out of the hotel window to see with a feeling of shock that it was already growing dark.

"Where on earth *were* you?"

"God." He groaned, and turned himself over. "I think

I've been over every square inch of ruin from here to Cancun. I haven't one frame of film left. God, Sunshine, those chicks were in-bloody-credible!"

"Good?"

"Good isn't in it. That Lupe was right on. If what's in those cans doesn't set both *TravelWorld* and my agency on their collective asses, I'll eat my equipment and go push Big Macs for a living." He sat up, wiping a film of dust from his forehead. "You mark my words, Sunshine —half the agencies in the Southwest are going to be fighting for the right to offer those girls their green cards. And you and I are about to hit the fuckin' bigtime, because Lupe told me they aren't gonna work with anybody *but* me."

"Robert—" The strangely intense, inward-looking expression he wore frightened her a little. "Robert— you've never talked like this before—"

"That's because nobody ever handed me the way to the top on a platter before." He looked absently down at his filthy hands, and seemed to see the dirt for the first time. "God, I look like a pit. Get room service to send up a sandwich while I shower, will you, lover? Oh—Lupe said to leave the stuff at the desk; she'll get it in the morning."

He kissed her with a kind of preoccupied gentleness, peeled off his shirt, and dropped it on the carpet, drifting into the bathroom in a half-trance.

She picked up his shirt, feeling her own bemusement return to make all the questions she wanted to ask him seem irrelevant. After all, she had *her* treasures now—

But later that night, Robert woke her from a sound and dreamless sleep, tossing restlessly in a dream from which no amount of shaking could wake him, and crying out—

Only one word was clear, and that only because he repeated it so often.

"Tezcatlipoca," he cried out as if he were calling for someone, "Tezcatlipoca!"

TWO ·

DETECTIVE MARK VALDEZ IGNORED THE HORDE OF HARRIED travelers crowding up against him and searched the TV monitor for the Amerine Airways flight from Hartford. Thanks to being shoved he managed to overlook it twice before finally spotting the entry.

Every time you turn around, they're changing schedules, changing flight numbers on you—oh great. It's coming in at the other terminal, of course. Halfway across the county. I hate DFW. It was bad enough before, but when they started letting everybody back inside the terminal five years ago, it turned into a zoo. Sometimes I wish they'd go back to the old security system: nobody gets inside without a ticket.

He elbowed his way out of the crowd and trudged along the concourse thinking longingly of a cold beer.

Huh-uh, Valdez. No beer. You're still on duty.

He spotted a concession stand that hadn't a line of customers twenty deep and settled for a large Coke instead. His head hurt, and he hoped the caffeine would do him some good. His feet hurt, too; well, that was par for the course for a cop. Normally people gave cops a wide berth, so he'd have been spared the pushing and shoving—but he wasn't in the uniform. He was plain-clothes division, and good God, he especially wouldn't wear the monkey suit on *this* pickup. So—he'd gotten jostled just like everybody else.

There was a sickly *beem-boom* right behind him, and a mechanical, pseudo-female voice bellowed—

"Amerine Airways shuttle cart in motion. Puh-leez stand clear of the cart."

He jumped, scuttled out of the way with the rest of the shell-shocked walkers, and the cart sailed by. He felt like cussing the driver out, but he was just too tired. His ribs were sore where somebody had elbowed him, and his shoulder was aching because he'd pulled a muscle re-straining the reaction that would have sent the elbower crashing into the wall. That would have been a little hard to explain to the Chief, seeing as said elbower had been an eightyish old lady with blue hair. And *very* sharp elbows.

I hope to hell Di is traveling light. This hasn't been a good day.

He'd been up since four ack emma, so he was tired enough that when he got to the moving sidewalks linking the two terminals, he let them carry him along, squashed over on the right side so that stews and athletic types could pass him. He savored the cool bite of his drink, ignoring the annoyed glares of those who squeezed past him. The echoing and re-echoing of voices along the concourse was enough to drive anybody with sensitive hearing right into catalepsy. And all the crossechos distorted the boarding and arrival announcements into unintelligible gibberish.

Sounds like a bunch of religious yo-yos speaking in tongues. You'd think they'd do something about the acoustics of these places while they're on the drawing board. I think this terminal was designed by a reincarna-tion of Torquemada. God, I hate DFW!

By the time the third walkway terminated, he had finished the Coke down to the ice—of which there had been considerably more than cola. He dumped the cup in an overflowing trash receptacle, and headed for gate eighteen.

He was way early, and found himself a seat in the no-smoking section away from everyone else, loosening his tie and collar as he sagged into the uncomfortable plastic chair. Dallas was experiencing an abnormally hot spell—eighty degrees in January. It seemed rather like they'd gone directly from fall into summer, with no spring, and only a nod to winter. And as usual, the air-conditioning system of DFW Airport was not coping well. In fact, knowing the current state of things, it might not be working at all. Certainly it was hot, damp, and smelly in the terminal—not much different than the atmosphere outside.

He slumped and tried to relax, then sat bolt upright as a horrible thought hit him. He hadn't talked with Di since he'd asked her to come. She'd sent him her flight number—which had changed, of course—but other than that he hadn't heard a word from her. While Diana wasn't exactly chatty at the best of times, he should have heard something more than this—

There wasn't anybody at his gate yet (DFW was so hectic that agents frequently didn't materialize until ten minutes before boarding), but there was an agent manning one of the others nearby. Mark jumped to his feet and sprinted over before she could move away. He pulled out his shield and ID and shoved them under her startled eyes.

"Can you tell me if a Diana Tregarde is on flight 185 from Hartford?" he asked before she could muster a question. Unless you were a cop, dispensing that kind of information to questioners was strictly against airline regs. There'd been a couple of cases of irate wives and husbands showing up at airports with mayhem in mind when they'd found out about certain trips. . . .

But the agent frowned worriedly, almost anxiously—more so than the question warranted—as she punched the query into her terminal.

"Yes sir, she is—" the woman replied after a moment.

"At least she got a boarding pass about five minutes before departure." She bit her lip, and wouldn't quite look at him. "Is—is there something wrong?"

"No, no, not at all," Mark sighed, then smiled. "She's a special consultant, and I wanted to be sure she made the flight, that's all. We kind of got our wires crossed, and then you guys changed all your flight numbers on me, so I wasn't sure if I was making the right one or not."

The woman's answering smile was bright with relief, and she bent her dark, curly head over her keyboard as he turned away and walked back to his chair.

Oh shit, he thought, suddenly having his memory kick in. *I shouldn't have startled her like that.*

Because everybody in DFW was bound to be a little jumpy lately; only last month there'd been a hostage situation. Some crazed Iranian trying a ground hijacking. It had tied things up for half the day, and the whole incident was fresh and raw in the minds of anybody who worked here. Probably they expected bomb scares whenever they saw a shield at this point.

He slouched back into the ill-fitting seat, trying, without much success, to find a comfortable position.

Man, this is the last thing I ever expected to be doing—bringing Di in as occult *consultant, of all damned things. To think that she told me I'd be doing just this years ago—and I didn't believe her.*

He could still hear her final words when they'd last seen each other, as if it had been days ago instead of years.

"*You'll see me again,*" she'd said, giving him that Mona Lisa smile. "*You'll need my expertise some time in the future. You'll call me. Trust me, I'm sure enough to put money on it.*"

Which parting had been a damn sight more peaceful than their meeting. . . .

Mark was looped; Tim, Phil, and Quasi were a good bit farther along than that.

Quasi—short for Quasimodo—was carrying the booze-box, for the reason that he was the only one of them capable of toting that much, drunk or sober. Quasi was built like a gorilla, and just about as hairy.

He was also on a full academic scholarship to the anthro department. Phil claimed it was because he was the only living specimen of Neanderthal and they wanted to study him; Mark knew better—he'd seen Quasi's midterm marks. Impressive.

It was three flights up to Quasi's apartment, and this old wreck of a building didn't have an elevator. Normally, this was no big deal, but half blitzed, it was an adventure. The staircase was lit only infrequently, and poorly; the stairs were worn and slippery. Mark was clinging to the banister with both hands, but frankly wondered if it would stay attached to the wall if it had to take his full weight.

"This," Tim announced to no one in particular, "is 1970. The Age of Enlightenment. The Age of Illumination. This is the dawn—"

"Of the Age of Aquarius, Age of Aquar-i-uuuuus—" Phil warbled. He was, as usual, off-key.

"Shut up, dork," Tim said, glaring at him from under an untamed thatch of thick black hair.

"Sir, yessir!" Phil saluted—which struck Mark as hilarious, since Phil, flatfooted, four-eyed, and a genuine asthmatic, had about as much chance of being drafted as a nun.

"You were saying—" Quasi prompted, shifting the box a little, and pointedly ignoring Mark's snorts of laughter.

"My point is, what the hell are we doing having a seance?" Tim demanded, squinting almond eyes at their host.

"One," Quasi replied amiably, "This *is* Halloween. It is traditional, as it were, and I am *all* in favor of tradition. Two, I'm curious about that 'spell' I dug up. My anthro prof claims he's seen magic work—you know, stuff that had no rational explanation. The way I see it, if a magic spell ever works at all, I'm betting it will work on Halloween. Three, I'm paying for the booze."

"And very good booze it is," Phil agreed, nodding so

hard his glasses slid down his nose. "Well worth a bit of cavorting and chanting."

"Okay," Tim replied, mollified. "That's a good reason."

"Hey, we're here—" Mark interrupted, hauling himself up the last few stairs and getting to the door on the landing ahead of them all. "I want to get this over with."

He held the door open for the other three. Phil had been entrusted with the key to the apartment, and skipped to the front of the group. The hallway was even dimmer than the staircase; Mark suspected that the bulbs in the light fixtures were at best fifteen-watt refrigerator bulbs. It was probably just as well; by the musty smell, nobody had cleaned the hall carpet for years. Mark was just as glad he didn't have to look at it. It might be growing something.

Phil fumbled with the lock while the other three made rude comments, and finally got the scarred and gouged door open. Quasi shouldered him aside impatiently; Mark trailed in behind his three friends.

Quasi had obviously been hard at work earlier today; his usual clutter of Salvation Army furniture and books had been pushed up against the wall. The couch was shoved against the wall next to the door they'd entered. It was absolutely covered with junk. The chairs and orange-crate tables were piled up against each other on the back wall. The curtains were tightly closed and then pinned shut with enormous safety pins.

It was, without a doubt, the cleanest this place had been in weeks.

Drawn on the anonymously brown rug in colored chalk was an intricate diagram. Placed at the four corners of the design were rickety candlesticks apparently salvaged from a church; they stood as tall as Mark's shoulder and held black candles as thick as his wrist. In the center of the diagram was a hibachi stoked with instant-starting charcoal. Beside the hibachi was a sheet of newspaper with a neat arrangement of little piles of unidentifiable flotsam on it.

The three invitees stared at the bizarre setup. Quasi

set the box down on his cracked vinyl sofa and took control of the situation.

"Okay, since you want to get this over with, let's move it. Phil, you go stand in the south—"

"Right." He made a face. "*Which* way is south, Leatherstocking?"

"Behind the candlestick in front of the record player." Quasi cast his eyes up toward the ceiling. "Give me strength."

"If you're gonna raise a demon, you should be looking in the other direction," Tim pointed out.

"How many times do I have to tell you cretins? We're *not* raising a demon, we're trying to contact a dead person. That's what this book says—" Quasi waved a thick paperback at them; the cover said *Voudoun Today*. Mark squinted at the letters, which wavered in front of his eyes.

"Voo-doon? What's that?" Mark wanted to know.

"It's not 'voo-doon,' dummy, it's *voodoo*. Sheesh. You go stand to Phil's right."

"Over here—" Phil flapped his right hand helpfully. Tim took the other open position without being directed.

"Shouldn't we be wearing robes or something?" Mark asked, looking down at his jeans and Grateful Dead T-shirt doubtfully. It didn't seem like the right outfit to be talking to a ghost in—even if he didn't believe it would work. Well—the skull on the front was okay, but the outfit itself seemed kind of—disrespectful.

"Nah—you'll be okay." Quasi dismissed his objection with an airy wave of his hand, and took a healthy slug of whiskey directly from the bottle. "Now, don't move, or you'll ruin the pentacle."

Quasi moved unsteadily around the diagram, closing up lines they'd erased by walking on them, lighting the candles, and giving each of the participants a carefully printed slip of paper.

"Okay, when I point at you, say what's on that. I wrote it down pho-net-ic-al-ly—" he had a little trouble getting the word out "—so just say what's there. If this works—"

"If? Why shouldn't it?" Phil wanted to know. "My sister gets answers on her Ouija board all the time!"

"Well, I didn't have everything, so I had to make some substitutions in the formulas," Quasi admitted. "But I did it logically, okay? So it should work. Anyway, if it does, the ghost will show up in the middle, in the center of that five-pointed star. I'm trying for Julius Caesar—" He lit the hibachi; there was a sharp chemical smell and a sparking line traveled across the surface of the charcoal.

"You wanted me 'cause I know Latin, right?" Phil blinked owlishly.

"I wanted you 'cause you're a Scorpio, okay? Now shut up, I'm gonna start." Quasi palmed the light switch, and suddenly the only illumination in the room was coming from the four candles and the hibachi.

Mark went very cold; with the lights out this was beginning to seem like something other than funny. The Scotch he'd downed had worn off all too quickly, and with it his bravado. He wanted very badly to walk out that door, but didn't dare. He *knew* what the other three would say if he did. He'd never live it down. He was supposed to be studying criminology; it wouldn't look real cool if he couldn't handle a spooky situation.

Quasi, looking warped and sinister in the flickering candlelight, began chanting and throwing various substances on the coals in the brazier. Some of them smelled vaguely pleasant; some stank to high heaven. All of them produced a good deal of smoke, further obscuring vision. Mark could scarcely see when he pointed dramatically in his direction.

He stammered out what was written on the notebook paper, not feeling at all ashamed that his voice shook. This *wasn't* funny anymore. He waited, feeling a cold chill ooze down his backbone, as Phil and Tim said their pieces. Then Quasi intoned a final sentence—

Everything—just stopped. No sound, no nothing. Then Mark's stomach lurched, and every hair on his arms stood straight up. The temperature in the room dropped at least twenty degrees. But that was only for openers.

Without warning a soundless explosion in the center of the diagram knocked Mark right off his feet.

By some miracle, he *didn't* turn over the candle behind him; as he staggered upright again he saw that Phil and Tim hadn't been so lucky. His candle and Quasi's were the only sources of light—

Then something at the heart of the diagram flared greenly; the remaining two candles were snuffed out by the hurricane wind that followed that flare of sickly light. For with the light came a tempest.

Mark dropped back down to his knees and sheltered his head in his arms. There was a whirlwind raking the room; it was centered by a vortex in the heart of the diagram. The wind was sucking anything loose into that vortex—papers, bits of herb, posters torn loose from the walls. Quasi was staring at his handiwork with a face that was panic-stricken and utterly dumbfounded.

There at the heart of the vortex was the source of the evil light—it was—

Mark didn't know what it was, only that it was a dark, amorphous blot that smelled utterly foul and made him sick to his stomach. It had eyes that glowed a vile, poisonous green; eyes that he *could not* look away from.

He found himself rising again to his feet, and realized with cold and helpless horror that he was being pulled toward it.

Phil screamed; an incongruously girlish sound. Mark heard him clearly above the howl of the wind.

And then Mark heard the sound of his footsteps fleeing toward the back door. A splintery crash marked the slamming of the porch door against the wall—then Tim followed Phil, backing out slowly, unable to take his eyes off the apparition. Tim was not screaming, he was giggling hysterically. Quasi held out a few moments longer, but when the thing turned its horrible eyes on *him*, Quasi howled like a mad dog and followed the other two.

Mark fought the fascination as best he could, but found himself taking a slow, deliberate step toward the thing—then another—and another—

He was too frightened to cry out, too terrified even to pray. He could only fight against the pull, and know his fight would be, in the end, useless.

The creature in the vortex chuckled wetly, and Mark felt his whole self become one inarticulate and soundless cry for help.

And—like a miracle—help arrived.

The front door literally exploded inwards, with a force that dwarfed the initial explosion that had brought the thing, and the compulsion and the whirlwind weakened as the thing turned its attention to the newcomer.

Light—light against the awful darkness.

Brilliant, clean white light poured in the open portal. Standing in the light—or had she brought the light *with* her?—was a young woman. A very *angry* young woman.

Some unencumbered part of his mind recognized her as one of Quasi's upstairs neighbors.

Her waist-length hair stood out from her head as if she had taken hold of a static generator. She was wearing ballet slippers, a leotard, and an ancient Japanese kimono that whipped wildly about her in the screaming wind.

She was holding what could only be a broadsword.

The sword *was* glowing. Blue-green flames flickered all up and down the blade. The thing in the vortex saw that, and snarled at her.

The girl sidestepped into the room, slowly; she looked like she knew exactly what she was doing. She was holding the sword in both hands, and Mark had the relieved feeling that this was *not* the first time she had fought this particular battle. She eased along the edge of the diagram until she stood a few feet from Mark—

Then she suddenly dashed the remaining few feet toward him and slashed the fiery blade down into the space between him and the thing, as if she was cutting a line that was binding him and the thing together.

The compulsion to join the thing snapped so abruptly that he stumbled backwards into the wall.

The girl was shouting words that he couldn't quite make out—and didn't really want to—above the howling of the wind and the higher wailing of the apparition in the vortex. He crouched and covered his ears with both hands, unable to look away. She gestured with the sword, drawing fiery lines in the air between herself and the creature, lines that glowed and continued to hang suspended before her long after any afterimage should have faded. The thing's wailing grew in intensity—and so did the sucking wind. Mark huddled against the wall, his heart pounding with absolute panic.

Then the girl changed her stance, balancing the pommel of her sword in her hand as if the whole massive piece of metal was nothing more than an oversized throwing-knife.

Mark stared at that; the back of his head was insisting that you couldn't *do* that, but his eyes were telling him that she was, and logic be damned.

She held it that way for only an instant—then cast it, throwing it as if it had no weight at all, aiming it at the darkness between the thing's eyes.

There was a third explosion and a flash of light that left Mark half blinded and half-deafened, and not a little stunned.

When he finally came to himself again, the electric lights were back on. There was an awful stench filling the apartment, like burned and rotting meat.

There was nothing in the middle of the room except a blackened spot in the center of the rug, a spot that had a sword sticking out of the middle of it. Mark stared at the blade with a slackened jaw; it had buried itself into the floor for a depth of at least two inches. He couldn't imagine how the *hell* she had tossed it that hard.

The girl was again standing between him and the spot where the thing had been, surveying the wreckage with her feet slightly apart, and her hands on her hips. As he stared stupidly at her back, she turned to face him.

She was *not* happy.

"Well," she said at last. An angry frown marred her otherwise pretty face as she grabbed the hilt without looking at it and wrenched the sword from the floor with an audible *crack*. "You sure blew *my* study plans all to hell. I'm not too thrilled about having to drop everything to rescue an almost-damned fool. What have you got to say for yourself?"

"Uh—" He swallowed hard. "Thanks?"

She stared at him for another long moment, then began laughing.

So it was that Mark Valdez, criminology student, and Diana Tregarde, expert in the occult, first met.

She never did let me off the hook for interrupting her midterm studying, either, Mark reflected wryly. *Recruited me for her ghost-hunting squad before you could say "poltergeist." Lord—ghosts, phony mediums, the Celtic Nightmare—half the time I thought I was making a mistake in letting her boss me around like that, in letting her railroad me into her Spook Squad. I should be, I am, just as glad—now. She told me once that she always helps if anybody asks—that she has to—and unless my instincts are all wrong, we need her, and badly.*

"Amerine Airways flight 185, service from Hartford, Connecticut, with continuing service to Phoenix, now arriving gate 18. . . ." The announcement broke into his recollections and brought him to his feet, pushing forward with the rest of the modest crowd awaiting passengers from the plane.

He had to watch for her carefully—even after all these years he was *still* vaguely amazed at how tiny she was. She'd certainly been impressive enough when she'd rescued him; she'd seemed ten feet tall, no matter what her true physical size was. But for all that she loomed large in his memory, she scarcely topped five feet, about the height of the average ballet dancer. She looked like a dancer, too—or at least she used to—

He saw her finally; nearly the last one down the jetway. She had a pair of turquoise nylon carry-on bags and a hefty purse slung over her shoulders, and was wearing an outfit that he remembered was almost a uniform for her, a black leotard and jeans. She waved at him and eased her way gracefully toward him through the throng of embracing relatives and friends.

She hadn't changed a bit; still wore her long, silken

brown hair waist-length and unbound, still had the same piquant, heart-shaped face with her high, prominent cheekbones and brown eyes so huge she looked like one of those stupid velvet paintings of big-eyed kids—and she still had her dancer's grace and dancer's figure.

"Hello, love!" She dropped her carry-on bags, threw her arms around him, and gave him a very thorough and shamelessly hearty kiss.

"You had me worried for about five minutes," he said, when he'd recovered from the inevitable effect. "I realized I hadn't heard from you since you told me your flight number, and for one long moment I wasn't entirely sure you were going to be *on* that plane."

"Oh ye of little faith," she chuckled, picking up her bags and indicating with a nod of her head that he should lead the way. "I'm sorry; I was smack in the middle of a particularly tangled love triangle, and I had to get it sorted out and in my publisher's hands before I left. I literally finished the damn thing at the last minute. I *did* drop the FedEx package with the final in it at the pickup box at the airport. Good thing I have an account with them, or I *wouldn't* have made it."

It was Mark's turn to chuckle. Diana took no compensation for her occult work—and being unable to live on air, had a perfectly non-arcane way of paying the rent and grocery bills.

She was a writer—but not of horror or even books *about* the occult, as might be thought.

She wrote romance novels. Sentimental, wildly entangled, and blatantly melodramatic romance novels, with never an unhappy ending in sight.

"So what was it this time?" he asked, taking one of her two bags and leading the way to the baggage-claim carousel.

"Regency." She laughed as he made a face. "Oh, you might have liked this one. The heroine was a tomboy, the hero was a smuggler, and the complication was a duke."

"A dastardly cad, no doubt."

"But of course, aren't they all? You're looking for turquoise-blue rip-stop nylon, like the rest of my gear."

She shrugged at his raised eyebrow. "Hey, it was a bargain, and it's certainly easy to see in a crowd."

He spotted and retrieved the appropriate bag—and he almost suspected her of a little spell-casting, it came off the plane so quickly.

He gave her a long sidelong glance, and she laughed.

"Don't give me that look—you *know* I don't work that way," she admonished.

He continued to give her a teasingly skeptical stare.

"Honestly, some people—work it out for yourself, Sherlock."

"Huh?"

"Lord, I thought you were supposed to be *good* at figuring mysteries out. I told you myself that I was in a hurry, so much so that I posted the FedEx package at the airport. Ran on the plane at the last minute. Simple airline procedure, silly. Last baggage on is first off. No hocus-pocus needed. Except maybe a little nudge at the handlers to make sure my stuff got on at all."

"Okay, okay, I believe you." By way of apology he relieved her of one of her carryons. "After you—" he gestured grandly.

They headed out the door, to be met by a blast of heat, light, and noise.

"Good *Lord!* This is like walking into the ninth circle of Hell!"

"Welcome to January in Dallas," he shouted over the screeching of tires and the roar of motors. "So you were up to your eyebrows in love triangles right up until you left, huh?"

"Uh-huh. The best is yet to come—I wangled an advance on a five-book contract, all five to be set down here. That's who *paid* for these plane tickets, m'lad. I am ostensibly doing research even as we speak."

He shook his head with admiration as they approached his battered little red Karmann Ghia. Diana handed him her burdens silently, then said, very softly, and with just a faint hint of mockery—

"I wondered how long it was going to take for you to call me. I've been keeping track of your weirdo killer in the news items. That's the reason I went after that contract in particular—I was about ready to call you up and volunteer."

Mark sighed. "If it had been up to me, I'd have called you in sooner."

She waited until he unlocked the passenger door before replying. "Why don't you pretend I don't know anything about this and start from the beginning. What I've gotten so far has been what's hit the national news, and it's probably pretty distorted."

She waited quietly for him to organize his thoughts, while he negotiated the Ghia out of the parking garage and onto the superhighway. A quick glance to the side told him that if she was feeling any impatience she certainly wasn't showing it. But then, she rarely displayed signs of emotion; she kept her feelings, like her private life, to herself.

"Like I said," he told her, finally, "if it had been up to me, I'd have called you earlier. The feeling of the whole area has been *real* weird for the past month or so."

"How so, weird?"

"Off—just—off. Unsettled, and not in a good way. You know I'm not real sensitive, that's the best I can tell you. But we've been getting all those signs of 'bad ju-ju' you always told me to watch out for—"

"Increased violence at mental institutions, an upswing in the number of nasty cultists coming out of the woodwork, an increase in psychiatric admissions?"

"All of the above. And the fourth—an increase in certain kinds of people finding excuses to bug out of the area."

"Like?"

"Most of the Rom are gone. Flat *gone* is what Bunco tells me. So far as we can tell, the great majority of our regular gypsy population pulled out and headed north last September. And we're down to half the usual population of 'psychic advisors,' and it ain't 'cause Bunco is busting 'em. It's getting so that Bunco can't even find them. I figure the real ones left early, the marginally sensitive bailed out this month, and all we're left with now is the flimflam artists, or the ones too desperate poor to leave."

She pursed her lips, looking thoughtful. He hit the brakes as a pink-beige Cadillac with a vanity license plate saying TOMMY H and an "I love Tulsa" sticker cut right across his front bumper.

"Asshole," he muttered under his breath. "I heart Tulsa. Jerk."

"Accident looking for a place to happen," she supplied, absently.

Then, a fraction of a second later, the look of abstraction vanished—and she seized the steering wheel and yanked it violently right, sending the Ghia careening across three lanes of traffic with a shriek of tortured rubber. Behind them came the sound of frantic horns and the scream of brakes—

And at exactly the same moment, the driver of the Cadillac that had cut them off made a fatal misjudgment.

He tried the same maneuver that he'd inflicted on them a moment earlier, only this time it was with the semi-rig in the far left lane. Unfortunately, the driver of the semi chose the same instant to accelerate.

The semi clipped the rear of the Cadillac, sending it spinning right across the slot they'd occupied until Diana had wrenched the wheel over.

Before Mark even had time to blink, the Caddy spun across their lane behind them, rolled, rammed into an overpass, and burst into flame.

"*My God—*" He started to pull over; the automatic reaction of any cop. Diana, face as white as skim milk, forestalled him.

"Go—just go," she choked. "He—you won't help him."

After one look at her deathly pale face, he obeyed.

He had forgotten that—among other things—Di was an empath—sensitive not to thoughts, but to feelings and emotions.

My God—she must have felt *the whole thing—*

Silence reigned for so long that he finally reached over and turned on the radio, unable to stand it any longer.

"Ah—" After a song-and-half she shook her hair back and massaged her temples; her color was returning. "That was *not* good. That's what I get for unshielding on the highway."

"Yeah, well." He negotiated a tricky bit of driving to get around an elderly Buick doing forty. "I'm glad some of your other talents are still working."

She grimaced. "Not as well as I'd like, nor as predictably."

"You—" He took another glance at her. She looked okay, now. Pretty well back to normal. "You ready for the debriefing again?"

"No—but go on, anyway. Instinct says I'm late getting on this one as it is."

"Okay. So far as the Chief is concerned, this whole mess started about three or four months ago—"

"I take it you think differently."

"Uh-huh. I think it began about eight or nine months ago. We started to get the cattle mutilations about then, and I'm convinced that they're related."

Now she looked at him, quizzically. "There's something you're not telling me. About *why* you're convinced. Confession time."

He blushed. "One of the ranchers getting hit was an old rodeo cowboy; you know, the oil economy isn't the only thing that's in trouble down here, the ranchers are having problems with keeping their spreads. This guy—damn it, I felt sorry for him; he spent half his life risking his neck just so he could save up for a place of his own—then these sickos start wrecking his herd. Well, I couldn't get anyone to stake out the place, and I had the feeling this was more than just the work of a garden-variety sicky, so I snuck out there on the full moon—"

"And?" she prompted.

"I—I warded it." He could feel his face burning. Good Catholic boys didn't go around casting pagan magic. Good cops didn't either.

"Well?"

"They never hit *his* place again."

"Hmm. If it looks like a duck—"

"Yeah. It *wasn't* just some sicko; a sicko wouldn't have cared squat about a warding, right?"

"A sicko wouldn't have noticed it, right. He might even have been caught by it; that's the thing about the warding I taught you bunch of refugees from the loonybin, it's a little like a watchdog. If somebody sensitive comes, it warns them off; if they come in anyway, it bites them; if they're wearing armor or just don't notice it, it raises hell with the master. If it had just been a nonsensitive sicko, the minute he crossed the boundary with ill-intent, your cowboy would have felt a pressing need to go visit that pasture—armed."

"Well, we've had animal mutilations before, just not so close to Dallas or so many; the Chief was inclined to let the county mounties handle it. But then it escalated, and we started getting dead people."

"Ah. So our weirdie upped the ante."

"They," he corrected, pulling off on his exit ramp. "What we've been seeing is too much work for one person alone. And—I know you told me that my main psi-talent is mediumism and not sensitivity, but—well, I've been *feeling* something around the murder sites. Something—I don't know—"

"Evil?"

"I guess. Something *I* don't want to touch, anyway. Makes my skin crawl, and frankly scares the shit out of me."

"How's the shielding I put on you holding up? Any chance you could be getting leakages? That might account for it. Violent death tends to make for violent spirits. And you *could be* a very sensitive medium if you ever unshielded. Spirits could just slide into you like they were coming home. That was why that critter was targeting *you* the night we met, not one of the others."

He shook his head. "No way; that's the first thing I checked for. Shields are as good as when you put them on me right after that Halloween party. Anyway, that's when I talked to the Chief and managed to get him to agree to your coming in on this."

"Not under my true colors, I take it?"

"Are you kidding? I don't want you burned on my lawn! This's Bible-thumper country; one hint of the stuff you're *really* into, and we'll both end up covered in tar and feathers if we're lucky. No, you're an 'expert on modern cults.' That double major of yours in anthro and psych helped convince them you had the credentials. They still think this is just another Manson thing."

"Gah. I wish. Not by all *my* preliminary investigation. Yeah, it's cult-related, I'm sure of it—but I'm also sure there's a purpose and they know exactly what they're doing. But I was hoping it would just be one person. Group-minds are a lot harder to pin down, and a lot better at covering their tracks."

He shook his head. "Sorry. All our evidence points to at least three."

"So your department is feeling out of their depth, huh? They must be pretty antsy; a little bird in the Hartford PD told me they'd been making inquiries." She grinned. "I suspect they liked what they heard."

"Liked it enough that they're going to put you on a retainer. Your rep for never getting involved with the press or blowing your own horn helped."

"God—" she shuddered. "No thanks. I have enough problems without getting followed around by Astral Annies. Good; at least they're going to be predisposed to listen to me. Now, how big is this retainer? *You* know I'm not exactly rich."

"Hey—what about all those books?"

Her face was shadowed for a moment, and her eyes darkened with unmistakable sorrow. "I—I've got some very expensive things to take care of."

Then she brightened again, though he had the impression that it was a forced brightness. "Expensive—honey, I got expenses you wouldn't believe—have you seen the price of crystal balls recently? Things *I* need you *don't* find at K-Mart. *And* they don't come cheap. And I *still* have to eat and pay the rent. So what's my retainer, hm?"

"Well—we're under a budget crunch. Not real big. It'll cover a hotel bill or food. Not both."

He pulled into an old residential neighborhood; houses that dated back to the mid to late 1800s—which for Dallas, was old. The street was tree-lined, quiet; a considerable relief after the highway.

"I have a couple ideas, though."

"Hm?"

"I've got an old maiden aunt that takes in student boarders, and one of her 'girls' just headed out for overseas study last semester. She's got a room free. And she's a darn good cook. I already asked her—she said she'd be happy to have you. My apartment isn't too far from here—it's in the Rose Point complex. She'll give you bed *and* board for the amount of the retainer."

"Okay. Or?"

"You could stay with me. But I've only got a studio. One bed."

"Uh-huh. And I don't think you picture either of us sleeping on the floor." She shook her head. "No, I don't think so, love. I'm not the one you want, so I'm not going to settle for being the one you're with."

His mouth dropped open. "I—uh—" he felt himself blushing again, this time all the way down to his toes. Despite the earlier reminder, he'd completely forgotten that picking up odd information about people's emotional states—apparently out of thin air—was one of her most unsettling habits. Her *primary* psychic talent, the one she relied on most, was empathy—as she had so amply demonstrated back on the highway. It was a very useful gift, but did tend to cause some consternation among her friends.

Especially when she blantantly *said* things like that.

"Uh—okay, well I kind of figured—Aunt Nita is pretty much waiting for us."

He pulled into the driveway of an enormous Victorian home, painted light gray with darker gray trim, and genteelly shabby. The lawn was the usual withered brown of Dallas grass in midwinter, but was showing some signs of reviving in the unseasonably warm weather.

The driveway was obviously a relic of earlier times; it was cobblestoned, and barely wide enough for the Ghia. Mark would never have wanted to pull a standard-sized vehicle in here.

His aunt—as he could have predicted—had been watching for them. As he and Di got out of the car, a white-haired old woman in a gray, lace-trimmed dress opened her front door and descended the steps of the porch with the same dignity and poise Queen Elizabeth exhibited when treading the steps of Parliament—and with a good deal more grace than most monarchs ever displayed.

Mark waited respectfully; Aunt Nita was not a woman that anyone treated lightly. She was a ramrod-straight, iron wand of a woman of aristocratic *hidalgo* blood. Her parents and grandparents had held *rancheros* the size of counties. Her great-grandparents had been virtual monarchs.

All that had vanished, either at the hands of greedy Texas politicians, or in the Depression. All that was left her was her dignity, her pride, and this enormous house.

"Aunt Nita," Mark said, "This is the young lady I told you about, Diana Tregarde. Di, this is my Aunt, Juanita Valdez."

Di offered her hand with a smile whose warmth surprised Mark. He was even more surprised to see that his aunt was wearing a smile of identical warmth.

"I believe I have read one of your books, Miss Tregarde—*Blood and Roses*—"

"Good heavens, Miss Valdez! I didn't think *anyone* had bothered to buy that one!" She smiled ruefully at Mark. "That was one of my rare attempts at a serious historical—and it was a total failure. *I* thought it was a natural, it was set during the Spanish Campaign of the Napoleonic Wars, and done from the Spanish viewpoint. I guess I didn't get enough fainting and ravishing in it."

"It may have been an economic failure, Miss

Tregarde," the white-haired lady admonished, "but it was an artistic success."

Di laughed. Mark wished she'd do so more often; it was such a musical laugh, like a clarinet arpeggio. "If you're going to praise me so extravagantly, Miss Valdez, you've earned a friend for life, and you're going to have to call me Di."

"In that case, you must give me the pleasure of hearing you call me 'Aunt Nita,' as Mark and my young ladies do. Would you care to come in and see your room? You *are* staying—"

Mark sighed. "Yes, Aunt; Di's staying. Her virtue is safe."

Di gave him a warning look, but his aunt merely smiled.

"Has Mark told you why I'm here?" she asked, as they climbed the stairs of the ornately carved wooden porch.

"You are some sort of expert in the occult, and he thinks you can help with these dreadful murders," she answered, obviously surprising Di.

Di looked back over her shoulder at Mark, who was following with the luggage. By the look on her face, she was no little taken aback.

"Aunt Nita's a believer," he said. "She actually tried to warn me about being too open before I went off to college, but I had no idea what she meant."

"A believer, but not a practitioner," his aunt agreed. "Poor young Mark was so puzzled—he thought I just meant that he was too trusting!"

"Anyway, she knows a good bit about you—"

Di sketched a pentagram in the air and looked back at him with an inquiring expression. He shook his head negatively.

"In that case," Di said, turning back to his aunt as they climbed the staircase to the rooms rented out to the boarders, "my work will be a little easier. I might do some odd things from time to time—I might ask you some odd questions. I promise that whatever I do or ask, I won't compromise any of your beliefs. If you feel any doubt or any discomfort at all, just say so."

"That statement alone confirms my welcome to you," the old woman replied, as Mark heaved a mental sigh of relief. They were hitting it off just fine. That had been his only worry.

After all, both Di and his aunt were very strong-minded individuals. "Alpha bitches," was what Di would have said. There could have been only two endings to this meeting—mutual respect or mutual antagonism. It was, thank God, mutual respect.

"Whatever else you are, dear, you are certainly on the side of the angels. I'm certain my parish priest would be shocked, but my people spent a great deal of time among the *indios*. There is good, and there is evil, and whatever other differences there may be are window dressing."

Mark smiled. This was going as well as he could possibly have hoped.

The old woman led the way down a white-painted hallway; the wood floor was highly polished, and bare of rugs. She paused before the door at the end.

"This will be your room, my dear, for as long as you care to stay," she said, unlocking it and handing Di the key.

Di just stared. "Oh—my—"

"It is rather nice, isn't it?" his aunt said, pleased at her reaction.

Mark dropped Di's bags just inside the door. He had seen all the rooms at one point or another; he'd known this was one of the better ones. The furniture was all antique; sturdy stuff that had been handmade by local craftspeople. It was of the dark wood and simple style found in most of the early *rancheros*, but having seen originals like these, no one would ever be content with the copies. The walls were painted white, with Indian rugs carefully mounted on them. The tall, narrow windows were curtained with loosely woven beige material. The bureaus and desk held fine examples of Indian and Mexican pottery.

"Aunt Nita is fairly careful about who she takes in," Mark said wryly.

"I trust my instincts," his aunt replied, just as dryly.

"With one exception, most of my young ladies are graduate students in classical music and anthropology. They appreciate a good environment."

"What's the exception?" Di asked, plainly amused.

"I rent the basement to a young lady who is a dancer with the Fort Worth Ballet. She has a studio set up down there—which, she tells me, you are welcome to use."

Di grew immediately thoughtful. "That's very welcome; I'd rather not do my karate exercises around all these antiques. I suppose—" now it was her turn to look wry "—Mark told you about that, too."

"Good guess," Mark grinned. "You'll find you don't have a lot of secrets Aunt Nita doesn't already know."

"I won't even try to keep any, then. Why waste energy?"

"I save the best for last," Aunt Nita said with a smile full of mischief. "And I had intended to use this as an inducement to tempt you to stay here instead of risking your 'virtue' as Mark would say, with him. That door there is the closet, but the one next to it is your own bathroom."

"Oh, Aunt Nita—you know your sex only too well!" Di laughed. "Given the choice between having my own bathroom and sharing one with *anyone*—much less a man, who is likely to leave the cap off his toothpaste—what would *any* sensible female do?"

THREE ·

MARK WAS STILL A LITTLE FLUSTERED BY DI'S TOO-ACCURATE reading of his emotional state. As he watched her unpack, he thought about the mess with Sherry, and wondered if she'd mind giving him a sympathetic ear on that one, too.

He decided, given that *she'd* brought it up, even if obliquely, that she probably wouldn't mind. And he wanted badly to talk to her about it. Di had a way of asking the right questions that let you at least get a new handle on things.

So he waited for her to finish getting her things put away, and, watched patiently for the right opportunity.

It didn't take her long at all to get settled in; Mark noted that she still tended to travel light. Jeans, underthings, the ubiquitous leotards—one good suit, the fancy shirts and gear that went with it.

There really wasn't much that was out-of-the-ordinary in her wardrobe; none of the trappings of occultism so beloved of movies and bad novels. No dark, hooded robes or strange costumes, although one of the things she'd brought with her—the lab coat—raised his curiosity. She had everything neatly stowed away in less than an hour. The only bag she did not unpack was the smaller of her two carryons. He remembered that she had never allowed him to take it. What *that* signified he had no idea, although it did suggest that she had come prepared for trouble of a nonphysical nature. Certain of her "tools" were very sensitive; things of that ilk she generally kept at home, where she could be certain they would remain uncontaminated. To have brought them with her proved that she was taking this whole problem with deadly seriousness.

That unopened bag went into the closet, still packed.

"Well," she said, folding her arms and pivoting to face him as he lounged on the room's short couch, "I don't know about you, but I'm hungry. I'm not sure what it was they were serving on that plane, but I doubt it was ever alive. I have the feeling that my so-called Reuben sandwich had been on enough planes to earn a frequent-flyer trip to Hawaii before I ever saw it. What are my options?"

"Aunt Nita will feed you breakfast and supper—lunch will be on the department, and probably either hot dogs or our godawful cafeteria slop. But tonight—how about Italian? My treat."

"You're on—" Her purse was lying on the bureau by the door; she grabbed the strap and slung it over her shoulder in one smooth motion. On the way out she turned to check the door as she shut it behind them to make certain it had locked.

Then she dug briefly in the purse and came up with a vial of colorless liquid. Dipping her finger in it, she traced a wet line around the doorframe, then drew an invisible but intricate diagram on the door itself.

She accomplished the entire bit of rigamarole in something under thirty seconds; if he hadn't been standing right there and watching, he probably wouldn't have guessed she'd stopped long enough to do anything.

She glanced over at him as she stoppered the vial, and grimaced. "As they say—'just because you're paranoid, that doesn't mean there isn't anyone out to get you.'

When I get back I'll do a more thorough job and include the windows—but the patterns on those ceremonial rugs will be enough to keep 'things' out for the short time we'll be gone."

"The—*what?* The rugs?"

She grinned. "That's what you get for being a medium instead of a sensitive. Or else you're so used to the vibes you don't notice them anymore. More of your aunt's instincts, I suspect—those aren't just any rugs on the walls, those are medicine blankets. Good ones, too. I'd give a pretty to know how she got them."

"They were mostly given to her grandparents by the local Indians," he said, slowly. "They were pretty enlightened for their times, and unusual in the way they treated the natives—like equals."

"I bloody well guess! There must be an interesting story there—damn! I *wish* I had more time—"

"You could always write her and ask when this is all over," Mark pointed out. "Aunt Nita is one of the old-fashioned type of letter-writers; for her, six pages is short. She'd love to correspond with you."

"Good thought." Di brightened. "Well, I think I hear a lasagna calling me—don't you?"

Mama Antonia's was a little family-operated place; Mama cooked, Papa was the waiter, three of the daughters were waitresses. It was a longtime favorite of Mark's. Papa welcomed him with a sly grin when he saw that Mark wasn't alone, and showed them to a table in the back corner, hedged in with ferns and lit mostly by candles.

"The lasagna is a good bet, provided you aren't worried about gaining weight."

She shrugged, and tossed her hair over her shoulders. "You'll be running it off me, I have the sinking feeling. Lasagna it is."

"Two—" Mark told hovering Daughter Number Three, a pretty, plump little child of barely seventeen, named Angelina, "and the house red."

One dinner and half a bottle of wine later, Mark felt the last of his reticence vanishing. Di sipped her own wine and looked at him with amused expectation.

"You have, I suspect, a personal problem?"

"I've got a question for you, first."

"Shoot."

"You're holding out on me." He'd known that from the way she'd clouded up when she'd talked about having heavy expenses. "Something's into you for a chunk of your income; I'd like to know what it is."

She looked uneasy and uncertain. "I—"

"C'mon, Di, I'm a friend. I'm *also* a cop. Maybe I can help. You being blackmailed or something?"

"No." She looked at him, long and hard, then seemed to make up her mind. "No—I've got—a sick friend. Too sick to work anymore. He's got major-medical, but I'm covering his nonmedical bills for him. Lenny's done me some pretty hefty favors in the past; I figured it was my duty to do the same. So I am. Besides, like I said, he's a friend, and right now, he hasn't got a lot of those."

Mark put two and two together, and made the jump to twenty-two. "AIDS, huh?" he said, making it a statement.

Her eyes widened. "How did you guess?"

He shrugged. "Put 'male,' 'friend,' and the fact you were pussyfooting around the subject together. I've got no argument with that—not like I'd have if somebody was putting heat on you. You do for friends, but you damn well don't pay danegeld."

"Well it'll sure help if I can get as many of my expenses paid for as possible."

"No sweat; I'll figure a way to squeeze as much out of the department as I can. Like—we're good for long-distance calls so long as they're partially business, okay? And if you need to FedEx something, we can probably put that on the account."

It seemed he had relieved her of a certain stress with his matter-of-fact acceptance of her situation. "Very okay. Now—what about that problem of yours?"

He sighed. "It seems pretty trivial stacked up against six corpses."

"But you'd like to talk about it anyway." She looked at him sharply, and bit her lip, as if to hide a smile. "Mark Valdez, I do believe you are in love!"

"Yeah—I guess so—" he said gloomily, and stared at his half-empty wineglass. "Problem is, the lady is married. *And* has a kid."

"Oh, boy—" She raised an inquisitive eyebrow.

"I do *not* go around seducing other people's wives." He glared at her, daring her to challenge him.

"I never suggested that you should."

He traced around the squares of the checked tablecloth with his finger. "The other problem is who she's married to. An old friend of mine—going back to when I could barely toddle. He's a professional photographer, Robert Fernandez."

"The *wunderkind?* I'm impressed. You can't open a magazine without seeing his models these days." She gave him a second, sharper glance. "Mark, you are *miserable*, aren't you?" She shook her head sympathetically.

"I guess so."

"How long has this been going on?"

"Oh—almost a year. Since he hit the bigtime. Back before then, I'd never met Sherry—I knew about her, but I'd never met her. Robert—well, he wasn't doing real well. I used to get him freelance work for the department when I could—I fed him lunch about three times a week. Then he went off on that Mexico City trip, and came back with a portfolio full of gold."

"The travel spread. I heard about it—set the Dallas sportswear mavins *and* the tourist business on their respective ears. Even made *Time*, as I recall. I've got a friend who has a travel agency—those photographs more than doubled her Mexico bookings, and she told me it was the same across the country. Those four girls are just incredible—"

"And they won't work with anybody but him, so he's

got it made. He's banking enough to keep him comfortable from now until the end of the universe, even if he never works again. So he decided to start paying me back."

He laughed, but his heart wasn't in it. "Took me to—you wouldn't know the name—a fancy restaurant. The only reason I didn't get thrown out was because I was with him. I've never been so uncomfortable in my life. Rob figured *that* wasn't going to work, so he started inviting me over to his new place in the Bear Creek complex for dinner and drinks, and for the parties he's been throwing. That's when I finally met Sherry."

He sighed, and chewed his thumbnail.

"How often are you seeing them?"

"A couple times a week; she's got a thing about being the gracious hostess. It's driving me nuts—and I can't seem to stay away."

"Hm. I've heard that excuse before." When he looked up, the velvety brown eyes that met his over the candle flame were cynical.

"Yeah, I know." He sighed again. "It's just—when I'm there the girls aren't. Rob's a real Don Juan; I know he's sleeping with all four of them, because he told me himself. Sherry knows too; it's making her wretched. She still loves him."

"One wonders why," Di remarked dryly, playing with a bit of candle wax. "It doesn't sound to me like he's worth keeping, money or no. I still don't understand why *you* keep inflicting mental pain on yourself by hanging out around her. Last time I looked, you weren't a masochist."

"Because the girls never show when I'm invited. Whenever I'm over there, Sherry can forget about the girls for one evening, pretend they don't exist. It may be driving me insane, but it gives *her* a break, so I keep coming. Gives Bobby a break, too—poor little guy. They keep wearing perfume and stuff that he's allergic to, and he's asthmatic. I think he's picking up on the tension between his parents; Sherry says he's been having really bloody nightmares every night. I like the little house-ape,

anyway, and he knows it; thinks I'm better than Magnum
P.I. And Rob sure doesn't pay much attention to him.
Shit, I'm not sure Rob's even sleeping in the same room
with Sherry anymore. But I won't take advantage of the
situation, dammit, I won't!"

Di echoed his sigh. "Lordy—it's as bad as one of my
novels. What a mess! I wonder— "

She suddenly broke off the sentence to stare out the
window, brow creased with puzzlement and something
akin to pain.

"Di—"

"There's—something wrong." She frowned, her attention focusing inward, eyes plainly not seeing him.

"What?"

"I don't know—it's too nebulous—but—Mark, I
think we'd better be leaving, and fast—"

Dwight Rhoades *should* have been a happy man. He'd
been promoted to DP manager of Ransome Internation-
al just this past year—the goal he'd been aiming at since
he'd hired on. Data Processing had assumed an extraor-
dinarily high level of visibility since the new director
took over. The new man on top was convinced that the
DP department was the one likely to make waves and
save money in the future. So Dwight was in a position to
make his mark.

He closed and locked his gray office door, and shuddered. The way things looked now, the only mark he was
likely to make was a blot when he hit the sidewalk.

The grey carpet muffled his footsteps as he passed the
row after row of identical cubicles that held his staff
during the day. If only he could make them over the way
the corporate planners had made over the DP complex
—take away the spouses, the kids, the outside interests;
make them into perfect servants of Ransome. Take
everything away from them except a need to spend
sixteen or twenty hours out of every twenty-four sitting
in those little cubicles and producing the miracle that
would save him.

Because it was going to *take* a miracle to save him.

He shouldered open the outside door, stepping out into the balmy evening. It slammed shut behind him of its own weight, the *thud* of its closing echoing across the parking lot.

It had a very ominous sound, like the lid slamming shut on a coffin.

He headed for his car, his own footsteps echoing in the silence.

Damn the new tax laws! That's what had gotten him into this mess in the first place. He'd agreed to a deadline set by guess and then undercut, a guarantee to get them into the system, a reckless deadline that had made the director's eyes light up—the programmers had tried to tell him it wasn't possible, but he knew better. He'd seen them, seen the way they worked. They were too used to taking it easy, too used to putting in their eight hours and heading home. They thought they could put one over on him because he'd been in data management, not programming. But regs said salaried personnel weren't entitled to overtime pay, and that compensatory time off was up to the discretion of the manager. And *this* manager had had every intention of showing them what it was like to hustle.

Besides, jobs were scarce in Dallas, what with the oil business bottoming out. He had wagered they wouldn't dare revolt if they wanted to keep getting their paychecks. So when things began to get tight on the schedule, he'd just handed them the appropriate ultimatum— put in the overtime, or look somewhere else for a job.

But now the project was weeks behind, every new body he'd hired had either quit ("You can take your six hours a day of uncompensated overtime and shove it up your wazoo," one had screamed at him, throwing his resignation on the desk) or gotten transferred. The director was beginning to wonder why he had such a high rate of resignations, and why the DP department had suddenly become such a hotbed of discontent. Antimanagement cartoons were showing up on bulletin boards—and little signs and stickers ("Poor planning on your part does not constitute an automatic emergency on mine," read one) were appearing in the director's interoffice mail. The old employees, the ones who had too much time in to quit, had come up with a new twist—they were getting "sick" as soon as five o'clock came around—migraines, allergies, nothing catching, nothing you could or couldn't prove. They went home "sick," and didn't "recover" until eight the next morning. And since they weren't getting "sick" during regular working hours, none of the regulations intended to keep salaried employees from pulling "sick-outs"—like forcing them to come up with doctor's notes proving they were *really* suffering from some infirmity or illness—could be enforced.

And as one told him insolently—"You want to force me to work when I'm sick? Go ahead and try—my lawyer says that would make me very rich."

Somehow, somewhere, he was going to *have* to find somebody to blame for this mess—before the director landed the blame squarely on *him*.

He was so involved in trying to think of a scapegoat who was high enough in the hierarchy to be credible (but low enough that when it came to claim versus claim, the higher rank would win out) that he never heard the footsteps behind him and never felt the blow that knocked him out.

When he woke up, the first thing that he noticed besides his aching head was that he was terribly cold . . .

He opened his eyes slowly, and moved his head just enough to look down at himself. He discovered that he had been stripped of all his clothing. He dropped his head back down; he'd been left lying on his back. He found himself staring up into a lacework of naked tree branches against the starry sky.

My God—I've been mugged—

He started to lever himself up into a sitting position; his head throbbed so painfully it was all he could do to roll over onto his side. For a moment he couldn't even see; his eyes fogged over and his stomach churned sour bile.

When his vision cleared, he realized that it *wasn't* an ordinary mugging.

He could see quite clearly in the moonlight. He was

wearing—something. Not much. And *not* his underwear. A *loincloth*, the kind TV Indians wore; some
strange jewelry. When he moved his head slightly, he
realized there was something fastened on it, tied under
his chin. He felt along his head, and encountered feathers. He grabbed the feathers and pulled the thing off—it
was some kind of weird headdress that would have
looked about right on a Las Vegas showgirl. He dropped
it on the sandy ground beside himself. There were more
feathered things on his upper arms and on his ankles, but
he ignored them since they weren't bothering him.

He tried to get his feet under him, and felt a tugging at
his right ankle. That was when he discovered that one of
the feathered ankle things concealed something else. He
was tethered by his ankle to an enormous boulder beside
him.

He felt his stomach contract with fear, and ignored the
throbbing of his head to sit up and seize on the tether. He
tugged at it, with no result; it wouldn't break or pull
loose. He could feel the knots, but the thing was made of
what felt like leather, and he couldn't even get the knots
to loosen. He looked around the ground next to him for
something to cut it with, but there was nothing there, not
even a shard of glass or a sharp rock. The ground for as
far as he could reach had been literally scoured. There
were four sticks with feathers stuck along the edges lying
next to him, but nothing useful.

He cast about frantically for help—or whoever had
put him here. This place looked like a park—

And parks were patrolled. The cops went through
every park in Dallas once an hour.

"*Help!*" he yelped, so scared his voice jumped an
octave. He got halfway to his feet, clawing at his tether.
"Somebody—help! I've been mugged—somebody help
me! Police! Fire! Help!"

"No one will hear you," a deep voice said behind him,
startling him into silence, "or heed you if they heard
you."

He wrenched around on his knees, the sandy soil
grating against his skin.

Out of the shadows beneath the trees behind him stepped a figure so strange Dwight was halfway certain he must be hallucinating it.

The man was wearing a loincloth a bit longer than Dwight's. His armbands and anklets were made of flowers instead of feathers. He must have been wearing forty pounds of elaborate metal jewelry, jewelry that gleamed silver in the moonlight. And his eyes peered out from the shadows cast by a bizarre helmet-like headpiece, like nothing Dwight had ever seen before. It seemed to be shaped like a snarling cat's head, with the man's face coming out of the open mouth.

He was carrying sticks like the ones lying in the dirt beside Dwight—except that instead of feathers, the edges were set with bits of something dark that glittered in the moonlight.

"What—what do you want?" Dwight stammered. "I'll give you whatever you want, anything you want. I've got money—I've—"

"I have what I want," the man interrupted, with heavy calm.

"But—"

"You are here for another purpose. You are a man in a position of power; you must have had courage to fight your way to that position. You are here to prove that courage."

"What—"

The man moved to the edge of Dwight's patch of bare earth, his sandals making a grating sound in the sand, and toed the feathered sticks.

"Take up your weapons," he said, "and defend yourself."

Dwight scrambled backwards until his back encountered the cold, smooth boulder. He edged into its protection, mouth dry and heart pounding with fear.

My God, I've been caught by some kind of nut—

"I—I—" he stuttered.

The man came toward him and struck him lightly with the stick he carried. The blow looked almost playful—but Dwight felt sharp pain and looked down, startled, at his shoulder. There was a long gash there, and blood welling up and glittering blackly in the moonlight.

Suddenly it began to hurt—a *lot*. He nearly vomited. His stomach turned over, and he gasped as he swallowed down the bile of fear.

"I said to defend yourself." The man hit him again, opening up another gash to match the first. "Comport yourself with honor."

Dwight whimpered, and cowered into the shadow of the boulder.

The man's eyes glistened wetly in the moonlight, and he smiled. It was the most terrible smile Dwight had ever seen.

Terror overcame him. He flung himself, groveling, at the man's feet, blubbering like an hysterical child, begging for mercy.

"Please—" he wept shamelessly, "Please, I've never done anything—I don't know how to fight—I've never hurt anyone—"

He ignored the nagging memories of the careers he'd destroyed—or tried to—to get his current position. He pushed out of his mind the recollections of the hours he'd stolen from the private lives of the people beneath him—

That wasn't hurting anyone. That was just good business; good management. Any good manager would have done the same.

The warrior spat at him, impassively. The blob of spittle struck his cheek; he winced, but he was too frightened to wipe it off.

"Dog. Son of dogs," the man said. "You shame your family; you shame your gods. If you will not delight the Great One with your courage, then you must pleasure him with your pain."

He made an abrupt summoning gesture, and from out of the shadows behind him ran four wildly garbed young women, bedecked with flowers and feathers, wearing headdresses even more astonishing than the warrior's cat-helmet.

My God, it's a Manson-cult—

Before Dwight had a chance to react, they had seized his arms and legs, and were dragging him back to the boulder, sand grating in his cuts and getting into his eyes and mouth.

He tried to fight them, but they were far stronger than they looked. He accomplished nothing more than getting more dirt into his mouth.

They dragged him onto the boulder, and it scraped the skin from his back—

They stretched him out over the top of it, one on each limb, pulling his arms and legs so far apart he thought he was going to scream. They had him pinned, back bent over the rock; spread-eagled, unable to move enough to see anything except sky and tree branches and the heads of his captors.

The warrior loomed over him; in his right hand there was a knife-shaped object that glittered blackly in the moonlight.

"What—" that was all Dwight managed to get out.

The man studied him for a long moment, then reached out with the glittering thing, and drew it in a slow, deliberate line down the middle of Dwight's chest.

After that, all he could do was scream in agony.

Mark felt vaguely sick. *This is number seven—and it doesn't get any easier with repetition.*

Diana had gotten into his Ghia and—tranced out, was the closest Mark could come to figuring out what she'd done. It was a funny kind of trance, though; not like anything he'd ever seen her do before. She was sort-of "there" and sort-of "not there."

She'd told him, in a foggy, preoccupied voice, to start driving. After about ten minutes she'd told him "left"; then "right." He'd gotten the idea in fairly short order. Any time he'd ever been with her in the past, she'd always *known* where she was going. This time, she was evidently having trouble pinpointing her goal. So she had turned herself into some kind of detector; circling in on whatever she was sensing.

That had been a couple of hours ago; about the time

that *he* figured out that Bachmann Lake Park was probably their destination, they'd gotten an "all points" on the radio in his car.

He and Diana had arrived on the scene at about the same time as the first squad car.

There wasn't much doubt in his mind that the victim had—quite literally—been sacrificed. What was left of him was lying spread-eagled and stark naked across a huge flat boulder—a boulder whose shape made it a kind of natural altar. In due course his belongings—all of them, including wallet and pocket-change—were discovered neatly folded and stacked, under a nearby bush. So robbery was out as a motive.

Mark figured he either died of shock or blood loss. Either would have done the trick. He had been mutilated with some incredibly sharp instrument, and with an almost artistic precision. Only "swimming" through a vat of broken glass could have produced lacerations so extensive.

The coroner agreed with Mark about the lacerations, but disagreed about the actual cause of death. *He* felt that the poor fellow had still been alive when his heart had been neatly removed from his body. Maybe even conscious.

The heart was lying in a little depression in the boulder, next to the victim's head.

The park patrol was a couple of rookies—more used to dope dealers and muggings than anything like this. One of them was still over in the bushes, throwing up. Mark had taken charge as soon as they arrived on the scene, much to the intense and obvious relief of the two patrolmen. He had made sure that the area around the body stayed unmolested until the arrival of the Homicide squad and the coroner. Once they arrived, Mark stayed out of the way. He was *not* a Forensics man; his forte was legwork. These days even detectives specialized.

The boulder and its burden were the center of a pool of glaring white light now, light so bright that the entire scene looked phony, like a movie setup. Mark found it easier to think of it that way; he wondered with macabre curiosity what the Parks Department was likely to do about the boulder. It was sandstone and the victim's blood had soaked into it so deeply that there would be no removing the stains. Would they leave it for the curious to gawk at, or would they break it up and remove it?

Mark had seen more than his share of ghastly corpses in his time; it was only the tortured expression branded on the man's face and the extent of the mutilations that disturbed him. He was somewhat queasy, but under control. The same could not be said for some of his colleagues—several of those who had arrived before the Homicide squad had joined the first officer in the bushes.

What rather surprised Mark was that Diana—except for a pronounced pallor—seemed about as unaffected by the grisly scene as he was. Once he had established the appropriate perimeter, she had gone straight to the edge of it and begun examining everything as minutely as she could from the distance permitted her. Mark watched her for a moment, trying to figure out just what she was up to.

She stood carefully and quietly at the border of string that marked the point-past-which. She made no attempt to get any closer, or to touch anything—but she spent long minutes studying the body, what portions of the boulder she could see, then finally getting down on her knees and examining the ground with the same care as the Forensics experts.

They had regarded her with some suspicion—but when she made no moves to interfere, and no comments —and when, in fact she had unobtrusively pointed out a bit of something they had overlooked—they began to regard her as—possibly—one of their own.

About that time Mark's boss arrived on the scene.

He was a balding, overweight man, incongruously dressed in a Hawaiian shirt and jeans. He looked far more like a particularly dull and dense redneck county sheriff than the owner of one of the sharpest minds Mark had ever worked under. It was an image he took pains to cultivate. Being consistently underestimated gave him a hell of an edge in interdepartmental politicking.

After making his own examination of the body and the

proceedings, he wandered ponderously over to Mark's side.

"That your pet expert on wackos?" he asked, nodding in Diana's direction and taking out a cigar. He did not light it; he was trying to quit smoking, and claimed that just holding the thing in his teeth helped curb his craving for tobacco.

"Yes sir—"

"Huh." The cigar migrated to the other side of his mouth and he nodded, thoughtfully. "More brains than I'd'a thought, just to look at 'er. Got sense enough not t' touch anythin', and not t' get in th' boys' way."

He watched as Di made a close examination of the mutilations on the victim's legs. "More guts, too. M' wife'd been halfway t' the Panhandle by now."

"She didn't get where she is by being squeamish," Mark felt compelled to point out.

"Yeah, Hartford PD sets pretty high store by 'er." The Chief clasped his hands behind his back, and continued to watch her. "I was kinda disinclined t' believe everythin' they told me, them bein' damnyankees an' all, an' her bein' a Yank too—but I think I'm changin' my mind."

Mark thought about what *he* knew about her. "Diana has that effect on people," he agreed.

At that point she got up from the ground beside the boulder, and walked slowly toward them, one eyebrow rising inquisitively when she saw that Mark had company.

"Diana Tregarde," Mark said as soon as she was within earshot, "Chief of Detectives Samuel Clemens Grimes."

She took the outstretched ham masquerading as a hand with no sign of hesitation, and Mark could tell by the slight widening of the Chief's eyes and the slow smile that she had returned his attempted squeeze with interest.

"Any relation to Mark Twain?" she asked as he released her hand.

"Somethin' distant on m' mother's side; she slapped it

on me t' annoy some uppity aunty of hers back East," the Chief replied with perverse pride. "Well, missy—you bein' the imported expert, what y'all think?"

Diana gave Mark a look that held just a hint of amusement and that said quite clearly, *I'll tell you more, later.*

"I have absolutely no doubt that this was a ritual sacrifice, with all that implies," she said slowly—so slowly that Mark got the distinct impression that she was choosing each of her words with utmost care. "I think it was very carefully planned and executed, possibly with this specific individual in mind as the victim. I also would judge that it wasn't timed randomly—I think whoever did this had some specific goal in mind."

"Like what? What th' hell good's a stiff t' anybody? Unless y' think this ritual stuff's a cover-up fer a paid hit."

Diana looked at the Chief, measuringly. "Try to think like someone who'd do this sort of thing for a moment—there are any number of traditions that place a very high power value on a ritual sacrifice carried out with precision and according to a ceremony as involved and elaborate as a Catholic High Latin Mass."

"Huh. So—why?"

"If you think of magical power as a tangible force—and these people *do*—you want to accumulate as much of it as you can *without* having to give anything up yourself." She made a half shrug. "There are two traditional ways of raising power, both involving sacrifice. The first is *self*-sacrifice: abstinence, chastity, the accumulation of power by *not* using it for the pursuit of pleasure. That's the kind of thing that a Buddhist monk, a Shao-lin priest, or a *real* yogi would do. And that's the hard way; it isn't in these people to do anything the hard way. So the other way to get power is to take someone's power from them. The easiest way to do so is to murder—with as much pain inflicted as possible."

"So you don't think this was just some isolated nut?" Mark prompted. He knew that, like himself, the Chief was convinced that they were dealing with a group, but it was interesting to see how he was taking what Di told him and integrating it with his own suspicions. Mark could almost see the wheels going around in the Chief's head.

"No—nor do I think this is some cult that's sprung up on its own," Di replied soberly. "Everything points to a group with an established and elaborate ritual to complete."

"Like—what? What's tippin' you off?"

Di waved her hand at the boulder and its burden. "Just about everything over there. The mutilations, for instance; they're absolutely symmetrical to fractions of an inch; the order in which they were made argues for following an established pattern. The area around the boulder is completely clean of *any* sign of footprints; they obviously cleaned up after themselves. There were a couple of flower petals—I couldn't identify what kind— and bits of feather in the grass beyond the dirt, which leads me to think that the victim was decorated and the decorations removed to avoid their being traced. The petals were fairly fresh, so they probably weren't from anything brought into this area during the day, and there's nothing in bloom around here, so it looks as if whoever did this brought them *and* remembered to remove them. That's the kind of thing amateur Satanists and the like don't think of doing. They tend to be very sloppy—and sometimes they even leave things behind on purpose, since one of their goals is to terrify the believers and nonbelievers alike. It's part of their power trip to frighten people."

The Chief chewed on the end of his cigar, thinking furiously. "All right, missy," he said after a long pause. "I'll buy what you're sayin'. You do seem to know—"

"I've made something of a study of it," Di said modestly. "I managed to point the Hartford cops in the right direction once or twice, anyway."

"Okay—then you tell *me*—*is* this Satanists an' witches? We got some kind of coven thang going here?"

Mark choked, and quickly turned it into a cough as both of them glared at him. Di had told him the very night they met that she was a practicing witch. "Fam-trad," she'd said, "Which means 'family tradition.' I was trained by my great-grandmother; the psi-senses skipped two generations in my family. It was kind of funny; Mom was raising me as a good little Episcopalian, and Grandy was giving me another sort of education altogether—and although it may seem to be a contradiction, in her way she was as devout as Mom. Grandy's generation kept everything as secret as in the Burning Times. Well, witchcraft is about the only way *I* know of to train psychics; at least they're the only folk around with a fully developed course of education."

Di did not seem in the least discomfited by the Chief's question, nor did she read him the same lecture she'd given Mark when he'd confused witchcraft—"Wicca" she called it—and Satanism. "It doesn't correspond with any ritual of dark witchcraft or Satanism that *I've* ever heard of," she said, shifting restlessly from foot to foot with an unobtrusive swaying motion, the only real sign that she was deeply disturbed. "For one thing, it's the wrong time of the month; both types of cult would have set this at moon-dark, and we're halfway between full and last quarter. For another, both place a great deal of emphasis on binding a blood-victim, and the only place I saw the mark of tethering was on his right ankle."

"What if they're mavericks?"

She shook her head, tucking a flyaway strand of hair back in place. "I told you, this kind of sacrifice *has* to follow strict formulas, or the practitioners consider it ineffective. Blood-sacrifice *has* to take place at the dark of the moon, otherwise the power just isn't released properly. Now there *is* a superficial resemblance to certain Druidic rites—but—"

"But—" prompted the Chief.

"Well, the sacrifice in *that* case either has to be a willing victim, in which case he would have been a member of the order, and he'd have been drugged to keep him from feeling pain—"

"Well, that sure don't match this."

"—or he's an oathbreaker, a violater of the laws—

which again would mean that he would also be a member of the order. They just don't do this sort of thing to nonmembers."

The Chief looked speculatively in the direction of the corpse, now shrouded and soon to be taken away, and shook his head with a little regret. "No sign of that; Mr. Rhoades was a good Freewill Baptist boy, an' what time he didn't spend in church or with 'is fam'ly 'e spent at work."

"Well, there's also something like this in Norse ritual—a punishment for someone who has truly made an implacable enemy of a cult-member."

"Now that sounds promisin'," the Chief said, nodding. "From what I make out, Mr. Rhoades wasn't too well liked by his people. Seems he's been pushin' 'em pretty close t' the breakin' point."

Di sighed and shook her head. "The problem there is that if he had angered some practicing Norse pagan cult, they'd have either hung him from an oak, or performed something on him called the 'blood eagle.'"

"Which is?"

"Are you sure you want to hear this? Don't say I didn't warn you—the victim is put on his stomach, not his back—slits are made between his ribs, and his lungs are pulled out through them. He is left that way until he dies—which is usually hours to days; basically, until he dies of shock or his lungs dry out."

The Chief was taken a bit aback by her matter-of-fact recitation. "Whoa—nice people. That *is* a little like this 'un, ain't it?"

Again she shook her head. "I told you, these people are absolutely serious and absolutely fanatical about what they do. This just doesn't match the 'M-O,' as you'd say. The closest I can come—and what I'm going to be following up on if you want me to—is this is something like the rites Aleister Crowley developed. Or maybe— just maybe—some outlawed Hindu cults. The thugee cult in particular."

"Who's this Crowley? Can we get aholt of 'im?"

"Well, his followers would say 'yes,' but I have severe doubts about their sanity." Di managed a wan smile. "I'm afraid he's been dead for a good long time."

"But he does still have followers?" The Chief pounced on that bit of information.

"As they say, 'there's one born every minute.' Yes, Crowley still does have followers. The main difference between what we have here and Crowley's rituals, is that Crowley left the sacrifice alive, rather than cutting out the heart as a grand finale—presuming the poor devil he'd been slashing didn't bleed to death. It was the spilling of blood that was important, not the death. The Hindu cult of Kali is almost a better bet; they *did* cut organs out of their victims, they *did* tend to torture before killing, and they *also* decorated their sacrifices. Trouble is, I haven't heard even a rumor of a single *thug*—that's what they're called—in the entire United States."

The Chief carefully removed his mangled cigar from between his teeth and smoothed it between his fingers while he looked Diana up and down.

"Well," he said, canting his head to one side, "you seem to know what you're talkin' about, anyway. Tell me somethin' missy—can you take orders? Take 'em when they're given, and not go asking questions until there's time fer questions?"

Di nodded emphatically. "Of course," she replied. "You don't joggle an electrician's arm—and you don't ask questions when you might be under fire."

The Chief grinned and stuck the cigar back in his mouth. "Missy, you got a good head on you fer a woman an' a nut-case expert. I'm thinkin' we're gonna get along. All right, boy—"

For the first time in this conversation he acknowledged Mark's presence.

"—your little lady here is on; no holds barred, she's ours, she gets what any critter on the squad gets. I want you two in my office 'bout ten ack emma. I'm thinkin' this case is gonna need some special handlin', and I'm thinkin' I'd better set somethin' up now t' do that, 'fore it's too late."

"Yes sir," Mark responded. "Ten A. M. it is."

The Chief wandered off to see to the removal of the body. Feeling that they had been dismissed for the evening, Mark gave Di a quizzical look.

"In the car," she said, shortly. "This place is literally making me sick."

Since the Ghia was parked only a few yards away, it wasn't long before Mark's curiosity was satisfied.

They sat, side by side, in the silent car, until Di cleared her throat and began to speak, hesitantly.

"I've seen uglier corpses, love," she said, staring out into the darkness beyond the windshield and rubbing her hands along her arms as if she felt chilled. "This was more than just an ugly death. Everything I told your chief was true—this *was* a ritual of power. It was more than that. It was a ritual of invocation."

"Invocation? Of what?"

"I don't know; it doesn't correspond with anything I've ever run into before, either myself or by hearsay. I can get a general sort of picture just from the power currents that have been set in motion, but every time I try to get something more than a generality, I just pull a blank. This is just one of a series of rituals, I think; there have been some before, and there will be more unless we can put a stop to them. They will *all* be blood-rituals culminating in death, and intended to bring *something* into full manifestation. What—I don't know. But the manifestation—it's close; it's very close."

She regarded him with troubled eyes, light from the parking-lot lamp contrasting with shadows in the hollows under her cheekbones.

"There's something else bothering you—and I think I know what."

"Hm?"

"I've been with you on other hunts; you've never had problems pinpointing bad vibes before this. You're good; you may be the best I've ever seen, inside or outside the law. So why did you have so much trouble even *finding* this place—especially with the amount of emotional anguish that must have been here? Why was the trail so cold to you? *That's* what I think bothers you the most."

"Bingo," she said soberly. "Right on target. This thing has me badly worried because—even though this must have released a tremendous amount of *power* as well as the emotional turmoil—I didn't pick up a thing. Not a glimmer. I tracked this by a snatch of precognition and a 'dead' spot that shouldn't have been here."

Mark whistled. "Good Lord—whoever they are, they're shielding like crazy! Then that means they really do know what they're doing!"

She nodded unhappily. "Exactly what I told your chief. These people—whoever they are—are for real. And because they're for real, they are far more dangerous than your chief realizes."

After they had watched the Homicide and Forensics crews clean things up and shut the operation down, there didn't seem anything more that either of them could do. Di wasn't being particularly talkative, and it was getting late. . . .

"I'll tell you what," Di said finally, "I think my best bet would be to start at the beginning. Why don't you get me all the records on 'John Doe' homicides and animal mutilations for the past six months—no, make that a year—"

"Sure," Mark agreed, stifling a yawn with the back of his hand, and turning the ignition key. "Just—Di, I've been up since 5:00 A.M., can't it wait until tomorrow?"

"Where's your stamina?" she teased. "You used to be able to do better than this!"

"Darlin'," he drawled, "Let me tell you a simple fact of life. After thirty, the warrantee runs out. After thirty-five, parts start falling off. And I need some sleep—before my radio runs my battery down."

"Okay, okay. Can you stay awake long enough to get me back to your aunt's place?"

He backed out of the parking slot and sent the Ghia sedately on her way. "I don't have to—the Lady in Red already knows the way. You know, just like old times."

Di shuddered theatrically.

As he'd half expected, his aunt was waiting up for them. Mark suspected that she was not at all certain that Di's presumed virtue was safe in the hands of her nephew. She opened the front door before Di could get her key out of her purse.

"Heavens, you're awfully late," she said, with a world of unspoken questions in her eyes. "I thought you'd just gone out to eat."

"We did—but Homicide found what looks like one for us at Bachmann Lake Park," Mark answered. "You know I've got a radio receiver in Lady. We've been out there most of the night."

Aunt Nita ushered them both into the entryway; Mark was about ready to fall over, but he answered all of his aunt's questions with fairly good humor. After all, now that she'd found they'd been out examining mutilated corpses, and not assuaging Mark's lust, she was rather embarrassingly relieved.

"Not that I was worried, mind," she said, realizing that her concern had been a bit too obvious and attempting to cover herself. "But—"

"It's all right, Aunt Nita," he said, too tired even to tease her. "I should have warned you that we might be keeping some really oddball hours. I just didn't think that it was going to start this soon."

"Heavens, here I am keeping you standing around in the hall—Mark, would you like some coffee, tea—"

"Something with enough caffeine in it to get me home safe would be right welcome about now," he admitted, as she led them back into the kitchen. "Di?"

"Tea, I think," she replied, "If it's not an imposition. I've got some research to do before I hit the hay—I wish I could have brought more in the way of books with me than I did, but I can at least make a start."

"I wish you'd been able to finish your degree work,

Mark," Aunt Nita said wistfully, as she started hot water for tea. "I know you do a lot of good where you are, but I wish there had been enough money for you to have become a lawyer like we planned."

"Is *that* what your original major was?" Di asked curiously.

Mark shrugged, and selected a teabag from the assortment his aunt offered. "I'm not certain now I would have gone through with it, especially not after getting involved with your little group. As it was, instead of detective work I *almost* went into Bunco—"

"You'd have been wasted there," Di admonished, spooning honey into her tea.

"Maybe—but I would have been able to separate the phonies from the few with real abilities, and see that we hustled the ones that deserve being hustled."

"Small potatoes," she replied, as Aunt Nita dropped into a third chair at the table, plainly fascinated. "Just because we rousted out a couple of phony mediums at college, and it seemed like it might be interesting—you can take it from me, it gets old real fast, Mark."

"One of those phony mediums was a *real* killer!"

"And who was the one that pegged her? 'Twasn't me. You're where you belong, love." She turned to Mark's aunt, tapping her spoon against her cup to emphasize her point. "Your nephew has a real gift for sensing things wrong, Aunt Nita. That was why he called in the Hartford cops on that wretched creature back in college. She was preying on sick little old ladies, first running the usual seance scam on them, then getting all their portable wealth away from them under the pretense that she needed it to keep the 'contacts' going. She'd take everything: cash, jewelry, even the family silver. Well, that's not unusual, as Mark could tell you, but when she'd taken them for all they had, this lovely lady gave them farewell cups of foxglove tea before anyone found out she'd milked them dry."

"Simulated heart failure," Mark nodded. "And Hartford PD hadn't seen the connection."

"That's because they weren't working our end of it,"

Di pointed out. "They hadn't known the old dears were even *seeing* a medium. We were the ones who saw them coming and going, and it was *you* who noticed how many of Madame Thelma's clients ended up on the obituary page."

He shrugged.

"And I have the feeling," Di continued doggedly, "that it's going to be connections where no one else has noticed connections that is going to hand us the answer to this one. It may be my knowledge and my gifts, but it will be your ability to put chestnut hulls together with feathers and see a stuffed and roasted goose."

"Maybe—" he yawned again. "But if I don't get some shuteye, I'm not going to be able to tell the chestnuts and the feathers apart."

FOUR ·

THE PHONE RANG.

Mark was nearly half awake; he tried to ignore it, to bury himself somewhere in the middle of his mattress, but it wouldn't *stop* ringing.

"Go away," he growled at it. "Shut up!"

It didn't shut up. *Somebody* was very persistent.

Cursing Alexander Graham Bell and all his descendants unto the ninth generation, he reached for the handset on his nightstand, missed, reached again, and got it finally on the third try.

"If this is a siding salesman," he mumbled, "I'll be sending a hit man around to take you out in one hour."

"It's Di, Brighteyes." The voice in his ear sounded far too alert and cheerful for his liking. "Having conquered the intricacies of the Kabala and the twisted philosophy of the mad Arab, Abdul Alhazred, I have crowned my career by mastering the Dallas bus system. I'm down at the stop at the entrance of your complex. I figured I'd better give you warning before I pounded on your door. You *might* have shot me."

"I *still* might," he grumbled.

Her only reply was a trill of laughter as she hung up.

He fumbled the phone back into place and peered at his clock. Seven A.M. The Chief wanted them in his office at ten. Gag. Better go stand under the shower for a while.

After five minutes of hot water followed by one of cold, he was feeling somewhere around the level of *Homo erectus*. With a transfusion of coffee he might reach *Homo neanderthalis*.

Clothing.

He'd managed to find everything but his shoes—and more important, drag the clothes on over his weary body—when Di tapped on his front door.

He knew it was Di before he even got within five feet of the door, and not by any paranormal method, either.

"Pardon me, sir," came a high-pitched, squeaky voice, only partially muffled by having to pass through an inch of wood, "but I'm working my way through Gramarye School, and I wondered if I could interest you in a complete set of the translations of the *Necronomicon*? Bound in genuine simulated humahide with fourteen-karat goldlike tooling? A priceless heirloom designed to be passed down to future generations, should you live so long?"

Less than ten hours ago the owner of that voice had been kneeling at the side of a very mangled corpse, doing a valiant job of not throwing up. Now she was making jokes . . .

Damn, she's got the same defense mechanisms cops do, Mark thought in surprise. *Which tells me she has been poking around some pretty grim situations the past few years. Well. She always was tougher than she looked—I think I can stop worrying about her taking care of herself—*

"Does this translation include the commentaries and footnotes by Robert Bloch?" he called back.

"I—don't think so, sir. August Derleth, but not Robert Bloch."

"Not interested." He opened the door.

Di was leaning up against the doorframe, an impish grin transforming her face to pure gamin. "Well, how about some Gargoyle Scout Cookies, then?"

"Only if they have caffeine. Get in here, before my neighbors start to talk."

She skipped inside and he closed the door behind her. "You mean they don't talk now?"

"Of course they do—but if wholesome types like you start showing up, making me get up *early*, they just might think I've gone respectable."

"Good God, we can't have that." She took a quick look around the living room; there wasn't much to see. Mark's one extravagance was his entertainment center; the rest was Salvation Army tables, foam flip-chairs, and futons. "Lord, Mark, you're slipping—this is cleaner than my place."

"Don't look in the bedroom; there's things growing in the corners." He staggered into the kitchen to start the coffee maker; she followed noiselessly behind him.

"Well now," he asked, before she crossed the threshold, "How is the one love of my life?"

"I trust you don't mean me—"

"Bite your tongue," he replied, scooping up a small, furry handful of delicate charm from the middle of the kitchen floor and turning back to Di. "You forfeited your claim on that position when you called me at 7:00 A.M. Di, meet Treemonisha."

"What a love!" she exclaimed, holding out her hand for the cat to sniff. Treemonisha, a dainty sable Burmese that Mark had found in an alley one night, examined the proffered fingers with aristocratic care. She determined that Di was appropriate company for Mark, and bestowed her approval with a tiny lick and a rub of her head.

Mark put her down on the floor and filled her bowl with chopped chicken from a bag he extracted from the refrigerator. The acknowledged queen of the household resumed her stately progress toward breakfast, a progress she'd interrupted when the doorbell rang.

"Getting to be a real homebody, aren't you? Furniture, cats, microwaves—"

"Bite your tongue. Coffee?"

"I don't suppose you have it in IV? No? Black, sugar."

Ten minutes later he was feeling alert enough to deal with Dallas traffic, and they were on their way to headquarters.

"Had any inspirations since last night?" he asked, as they pulled onto the freeway, figuring he might as well get the ball rolling.

She shook her head. "There's nothing in any of my books that even bears a superficial resemblance to what we saw last night except the Kali cult, and I have a hard time believing I wouldn't have picked up on *thugee* moving in. What I want to do now is to winnow out the deaths and mutilations that really *are* the work of our cult—"

"Can you do that?" he interrupted.

"Oh sure, that's not the problem. That aura I picked up last night will *still* be lingering around the sites; I'm a good enough empathic clairvoyant to pick it up off a map or a photograph. You don't wipe away the stain of something like that in a few months, not even in a big city. No, the problem will be coming up with a good rationalization to give your chief about *why* I'm going to pick that particular set of cases as our string. I *hope* that between us we'll be able to find the common link to satisfy him. I want him thinking I'm doing this scientifically, not by esoteric means."

"Tall order." He sent the Ghia flying for the exit ramp.

"I never said it was going to be easy," she pointed out. "My work is a lot like yours—I've learned bunches from the Hartford PD about investigative procedure. All right, once I do pick out the cult-kills, I'm going to try to fit them into some kind of lunar/solar/stellar pattern. I *did* bring full ephemerides with me, and a sort program and astrological database I developed with the Hartford PD on diskette. If I can find a pattern, that might tell us something about what tradition the cult is working in."

He pulled into the HDQ parking garage. "Sounds good to me. I'll drop you off with the Records people; I've got paperwork to do on the murder last night. I'll come get you in time for the meeting."

* * *

"She's in the back," Sara told Mark in a nasal Bostonian accent, looking up at him over the rims of her bottle-bottom glasses. "I thought she'd be a real flake, but she's okay. Knows the retrieval system, so I just gave her the spare terminal and a laser printer and let her rip while I check out this program of hers and see if it's compatible with our system. It should be, both us and Hartford have nearly the same setup, but you never know. When are *you* gonna get computer-literate, goat-roper?"

"As long as I have you around, why should I?" he asked over his shoulder, as he headed to the back of the Records Room. "That's what damnyankees were created for."

"One of these days, Valdez—the *least* you could do is buy me lunch sometime!"

"Sure—the day you learn to appreciate real food. Chili, *chimichangas*, and *fajitas*—not sushi and tofu."

"Get *real*."

"I happen to like sushi," Di admonished, not looking up from her terminal. "Although tofu isn't on my all-time favorite list. Looks too much like Styrofoam."

Mark shuddered. "Woman, the day the Pope told us we didn't have to eat fish on Friday anymore was the happiest day of my life—and why anybody would eat the stuff *raw*—"

"It isn't raw, it's marinated; you only ruin the flavor by subjecting fish to heat. You've just burned out all your taste buds with jalepeño peppers, that's all." She shut the machine down, turned it off, and spun her chair around to face him. "All right Daniel, let's go beard the lion in his den."

"A li'l bird down in Records tells me you been puttin' in a good mornin's work, Miz Tregarde." The Chief regarded her thoughtfully over his loaded desk. "'Specially since we ain't payin' ya'll jack."

She spread her hands deprecatingly. She had the good chair; the one with wheels that stayed on when you moved it. Mark stood, rather than chance the other.

"You asked for help," she said. "When you ask *me* for help, you get it; I don't do a job halfway."

"Uh-huh. Mark, I gotta tell you, I gotta allow as how this young lady is comin' off mighty impressive. I didn't think much of the notion when y'all talked me inta it, but she didn't lose her cookies last night, an' she ain't gone flappin' her beak t' the newsboys—I didn't necessarily trust them damnyankee cops, but she's been livin' up t' what they told us."

Mark was a little uncomfortable with the Chief talking about Di as if she weren't there, but the amused wink she slipped him eased his embarrassment somewhat. "She has a tendency to surprise people, like I told you last night."

The Chief chuckled. "Damn well told! Okay, I done some thinkin' on this mess; you ain't the most senior, but you got a better feel fer this thang than anybody in the department. I got a gut feelin' this ain't gonna get solved real quick. So you an' Miz Tregarde are on special assignment as of right now. I'm puttin' you on detached duty; y'all report straight t' me fer the duration. Y'all are on free rein; take as long as it takes, an' I'm figgerin' on months. I'll have a reg'lar team on this too, somebody t' give th' newsboys somebody t' watch and nag at. Maybe we'll break this thang the reg'lar way, but I ain't bettin' on it. Y'all are my ace in the hole. An' I ain't gonna admit y'all even exist."

"Thank God," Di said fervently. "The *last* thing I need is to have some yazoo from *National Enquirer* climbing in my bedroom window. Trust me sir—"

"Y'all might as well call me 'Chief.' "

"If you'll call me Di. Chief—I don't want to be known for this any more than you want me attracting attention. If nothing else, I have a living to make—I assume you know I don't do this as a career. I can't write if every time I get into a juicy love scene the phone starts ringing and it's some jerk who wants me to find Judge Crater or something. I've had friends who ended up on the scandalrag sourcebooks as 'experts in the occult.' They had to change their names, finally. Those bozos *won't* take 'no' for an answer, not even when it's backed with a club."

The Chief chuckled again. "Okay, Miz Di. Now what I'd like from you right off'n the bat, is t' check out th' fruitcake angle. I don' wanta mess y'all up if you got a lead—"

"Not yet," she said, shaking her head. "I'm just getting organized. I don't see a problem; mind you, I told you last night that this probably *isn't* the work of some known fruitcake, but it *will* help to be able to eliminate them right away."

"Fine—I'll get you the makesheets on 'em an' send 'em on down. The first one's th' head somethin' of the Church of Satan—he's been pretty mouthy 'bout the homicide last night, denyin' his flakes had anythin' t' do with it 'fore anybody could even ask 'im. The second, he's got a porn palace; goes in for the leather an' whips an' chains bunch. Vice tells me he's got some other stuff in th' back that ain't strictly porn, stuff that looked pretty spooky t' them. Mark, Ramirez sez he ain't goin' back there without seein' his parish priest first if that tells y'all anythin.'"

"Maybe, maybe not; Ramirez spooks pretty easy since Vice broke up that cathouse with the voodoo woman for a madame."

"Maybe he's got a good reason to be spooked," Di put in thoughtfully. "This might tie in with voudoun; I hadn't thought about that here, it isn't the territory for it. Louisiana, Florida, I'd expect—Texas, no."

The Chief raised his eyebrow. "You kin check for yourself, I reckon; see what th' ol' boy has on his shelves. I kin tell you this much—when y'all spouted names at me last night, I checked with Vice; their report sez this ol' boy has got a lotta stuff by that Crowley fella."

"Now *that* is interesting; it wouldn't hurt to see if the killings fall anywhere around where this guy lives. The archives and the computer could tell me that fast enough. By the way, you wouldn't mind my adding a little program of my own to your base, would you? Sara said to ask. It could end up being useful on other cases like this one."

"Depends. What is it?" the Chief asked suspiciously.

"Just another search program; this one is based on moon cycles, seasonal cycles, and star charts. I told you loonies like this try to do things to match patterns—this program will help you find out if there are any matches."

"Jes' make sure t' check it out with Sara; if she says it's okay, then it's okay by me. I gotta tell you, Miz Di, I was right pleased t' find out you was down there with your nose in th' archives. I figgered out a helluva lot more cases doin' snoopin' and pryin' than I did playin' Dirty Harry. People round here get touchy when you start leanin' on 'em wrong—an' you go wavin' a piece at 'em, they're likely t' wave a piece of their own right back at you." He warmed to his subject; Mark stifled a sigh. He'd heard this all before.

"You start actin' like some yoyo on th' tellyvision, you ain't gonna get nowhere. . . ."

Mark could practically recite the monologue in his sleep—not that he disagreed with the Chief on any of his points. It was just that you got a little tired of hearing it after a while.

And there were times when it was *so* tempting to forget the Miranda decision ever existed—

Then again, from what he'd read about the late Mr. Dwight Rhoades, it had probably been *real* tempting for his former employees to create Rambo fantasies. That was why *he* didn't think it was an employee, current *or* previous, and not just because there didn't seem to be a tie-in to some of the other cases. If *he'd* had Dwight Rhoades for a boss, and *he'd* gone around the bend, Mark knew what *he'd* have done. He'd have gotten himself a nice legal semiautomatic rifle and filled Dwight Rhoades with so many holes he'd have looked like a lace tablecloth . . .

He shook himself out of his reverie. Di was still looking attentive, but the Chief was winding down.

"Anyway," he finished, "Y'all know what you need to

do, so I ain't gonna get in your way. When you think you can go give those loony-tunes a look-see?"

"Tomorrow soon enough?" Di asked. "By then I'll have my data together, and I can put a preliminary report in your hands."

The Chief whistled. "Miz Di, I wasn't expectin' anythin' in writin' *that* fast—"

She smiled as she stood up and Mark got ready to leave. "Chief, I have one real advantage over your staff—I *write* for a living. I may not be a detective, but I'm hell on wheels over a keyboard!"

He laughed. "Lady, you better not let any of th' other boys know that! They'll kidnap you, an' never let you see th' light of day again! Hellfire, *I* might—what's a felony when I got somebody t' do all my paperwork?"

"All right Yankee, how do you like your hot dogs, and how many?" Mark asked as he and Di pushed open the door to Records.

"Two and everything. Large diet cola, easy on the ice. Sara, what do you want?" Di said before he could interrupt, smiling sweetly. "Mark's buying."

"Like hell; the Department is buying, and—what the hell, I'll pick up the tab this time. Four-eyes?"

"The same, wetback. Di, I've been looking over that correlation program of yours, and I don't see any problem; if it ran on the Hartford mainframe, it should . . ."

Mark made his escape while he could; technese was worse than Greek to him.

When he returned, Sara was involved in a search for somebody from Legal, and Di was back at her terminal in the rear. Mark dropped Sara's lunch on the desk— careful to leave it in a clear place; he'd never forgotten the day he'd left a coffee cup on one of her precious little disks—and headed for the rear.

Di was just sitting; the terminal was mostly blank, with a tiny *running* in the upper left-hand corner. He touched her shoulder and she jumped.

"Lordy—I shouldn't have let myself blank out like that—"

"Any results?" he asked, plopping down into a chair beside her and starting on his own lunch ravenously.

"Here." She tapped a pile of folders to one side of the terminal. "I got hard copy because I figured we might want to consult some of the data when we're away from here. Everything else I looked into was either copycat or garden-variety loonies. Either one you'll catch eventually; they'll slip. Our cult—they're too careful. We'll get them only by being smarter than they are."

He picked up the top folder and began leafing through it. By the time he reached the bottom of the pile, he had noticed one thing: there were no dates earlier than April of the previous year.

The cases had not been arranged in any particular order. On a hunch, he sorted them in order of the dates of occurrence.

He felt a line of cold run up his spine when he saw that there was a second pattern—

The incidents started with the mutilation and killing of a single animal; the next was like the first, and the next. Then came the slaughter of half a dozen animals. Following that one was a similar slaughter, but this time the carcasses had been carefully laid out in a pattern afterward, and the mutilations on their bodies had been very precise.

Then came a series of single "John Doe" murders: winos, addicts, bagladies. The pattern with the animals was being repeated—first simple murder, killing that almost looked as if it had come as the result of a fight. Then something more elaborate. Then mutilations before death—

And now, tonight—

"Is it too much to hope that this is the end of it?" he asked Di, praying that the answer would be yes.

"No, I'm afraid this is likely to be just the beginning of a new phase for them," she replied thoughtfully. "And it looks to me like *I* am going to be in trouble. I'm running the correlation program to make sure, but take a look at the dates, and compare them with the chart I made from the ephemeris."

Mark put the dates of the incidents on a timeline, then compared it with Di's hastily scrawled chart. He stared at the result, chewing the end of his pencil as he tried to find a pattern.

"If there's a correlation there, *I* can't find one," he admitted finally.

"Me neither," she replied, surprising him. "Nor can the computer, I'll bet, though the job isn't finished yet. There isn't any pattern following any cycle that I've ever worked with—yet there *is* a pattern of self-consistency within the incidents; they are all about three weeks apart until the end of the animal series—then they're about every day. There *is* a ritual being followed; I have no doubt of that whatsoever. You'll notice the other pattern—"

"Increasing violence," Mark said grimly.

"Exactly. It goes from simple death to real atrocity with the animals—then starts the pattern all over again, but this time with human beings."

"The last couple of John Doe killings have been groups of two and three—until this one."

"Now we get the elaborate ritual murders." She sighed. "Everything I can see points to more to come."

"No," Mickey's mother whined, "You kids stay out here."

Mickey stuck his lower lip out and pouted. "I wanna book."

Robin and Lisa jumped on that. "We wanna book! We wanna book!" they chanted, jumping up and down and pulling on their mother's arms.

For once their mother didn't cave in. "There *aren't* any kids' books in this store. Besides, I thought you wanted some G.I. Joe stuff."

Mickey stuck to his guns. "I wanna book. I wanna book *too*."

"You just *stay* out here and play. I'll get you a G.I. Joe book at K-Mart."

"But I wanna book—"

"Mickey—" His mother got that pinched, angry look

around her eyes. The one that said she was about to forget her EST and nonviolent parenting and smack him one. "You wanna live to reach nine?"

Mickey hadn't made it to eight without learning the danger signs. Mommy would be real mad at herself for smacking him, but he'd *still* get smacked. He shut up, and dragged seven-year-old Robin and six-year-old Lisa with him. Their mother vanished into the bookstore, heading straight for the romances.

Mickey walked away from the bookstore, and looked for something new to try. Experimentally, he shoved at a big metal cylinder three stores down. It didn't take him long to figure out that while one kid couldn't knock over the big freestanding ashtrays, three kids working together could. The stainless steel tubes made a clang you could hear all over the mall when they hit the floor, and they flung sand and cigarette butts out in a spectacular shower of white that reached for yards.

Now *that* was exciting!

They got a total of three turned over before Mickey spotted the rent-a-cop hurrying down from the upper level. He led the other two on a fast end-run around to the play area.

There were about a half-dozen other kids in the play area, but no mothers. That was a good sign. Only two of the kids were playing together; that was good too. It meant that the three of them could take it over, easy.

They pushed the two kids on the teeter-totter right off; one of them ran away crying, the other looked ready to fight until Mickey sucker-punched his stomach. The ones on the swings took one look at this junior Mafia and left to find their mothers. The one on the slide wasn't so easily intimidated; they had to follow him around for nearly five minutes, glowering and muttering threats, before he gave up and left. They never did see where the sixth one went, or when she left. She just vanished when they weren't paying attention to her.

That left them the complete masters of the play area. With no strangers around to intimidate, their unity fell apart, and they began fighting with each other.

They finally decided that wasn't such a good idea when Mickey managed to tear the whole sleeve off Robin's jacket.

"Oh-oh—" Lisa said, as he stood looking at the sleeve in his hands and trying to figure out a way he could blame someone else for doing it without having Robin tattle on him. He looked up, and saw trouble.

There, sniffling kids in tow, were two mothers with determination in their step and fire in their eyes.

Time to make a quick exit.

They scrambled out of the play area before the adults could reach it, and headed for the escalator at a dead run.

Once on the second level, Mickey remembered he had two dollars in his coat; enough for some hot pretzels. The pretzel place just happened to be right by the top of the escalator, and Mickey knew from experience that if you were buying something or had just bought something, adults left you alone. Especially if it was something to eat.

Six pretzels later—and in the wake of the pretzels, a trail of mustard on the coats of unsuspecting grownups —they were at the far side of the mall wondering what to do next.

"Mommy's gonna be in there a long time," Robin whined. "An' they won't let us in the toy store here anymore."

No kidding. The clerks in the toy store knew Mickey and his siblings by name, and had orders to chase them out if they came without an adult.

Lisa sat down in the middle of the concourse, forcing everyone to walk around her. "I wan' somethin' t' *do*," she sniveled. "I'm *borded*."

Mickey thought, knowing he had to figure out something or Lisa would start to howl. That would bring an adult, or worse, the cop. Then he heard a strange sound, like a whistle.

He glanced up, looking for the source. The sound resolved itself into a peculiar song, one that sounded a lot like it was being played on one of those weird whistles they had for music class—"ocarina" his teacher called them. The kids called them "sweet potatoes," 'cause that was what they looked like.

The teacher never let Mickey play one of those. She never let him play the drum or the cymbals, or even the triangle. All he ever got to play were the notched sticks and the blocks with sandpaper on them. And not even the blocks since he'd tried to sand Jimmy Kreske's face with them.

But the kids at school never got any music like that out of their whistles, not even nerdy Elen Atkins, who was taking clarinet lessons. It was weird—but real neat.

He finally spotted the player, and was amazed that he hadn't seen her before. She couldn't have gotten to the middle of the mall without passing them at least once. It should have been pretty hard to miss someone dressed like that, in a kind of coat or cape made out of bird feathers. It was wild, like something out of a Conan movie, and like the music she was playing. Mickey wanted a coat like that—he could just imagine what the other kids at school would say when he swept in with it over his shoulders.

The flute player had painted designs on her face and looked like a punk rocker. Mickey liked punk rock. Maybe this girl had a band! Maybe she'd want him in the band!

She sort of nodded her head at him when she saw he'd spotted her, and stopped playing.

"Wow—" said Lisa in awe, scrambling to her feet. "*I* wanna look like that—"

The girl tucked her whistle away somewhere out of sight, nodded at them again, and vanished through the door behind her leading to a service corridor.

Robin pulled Mickey's sleeve. "You think she wants us t' go with her?"

Mickey was certain of it. This was just how neat things happened in cartoons.

"What d'you think? Come on, or we're gonna lose her!"

The three of them scrambled after the girl; when they

got to the alcove she'd been in, the door to the service area was closed—but it was also unlocked.

"See?" Mickey crowed with triumph. "What I tell you guys? Let's go!"

"Hey wetback?" Sara called from the front, her voice echoing hollowly in the nearly empty room.

"What?" Mark answered absently.

"I'm off—but you might get some bodies down here. We got a couple of missing kids—"

"Every time the weather gets warm we get missing kids, so what's new?" Mark stared at his map, and frowned.

"These have been gone a while. All from the same family. Dan Rather even picked it up. Big-time stuff."

Mark grunted something in reply. He was trying to see if there was a pattern to where the cult-killings showed up on the map.

"Anyway, third shift may be busy, but Chief reserved that terminal for you guys, so don't let them bully you off of it, okay?"

"Fat chance," Mark replied, replacing the pins that represented single kills with ones with blue heads, to see if anything stood out that way. "But thanks for the warning, Yank."

"Just buy me lunch again."

"On *my* salary?"

"It's bigger than mine." Sara sailed out the door, he heard it *thunk* shut behind her, and Mark promptly forgot her.

Di was keying more data into her astrological database after a quick trip to the public library. The 'normal' cycles hadn't come up with any more of a match than could be accounted for by chance, so now she was trying some more esoteric ones.

"If this doesn't work," she muttered at Mark, who was switching pins around again, "I'm going to *have* to make a long-distance call. A couple of them, actually. One at least to my voudoun contact in New York to establish some credibility for me with whoever's local. Probably

one to my house sitter if I can find a modem; I need more
stuff from my database."

"I didn't know you knew so much about computers—" he looked sideways at her in surprise.

"I don't, actually," she said, keying like one possessed.
"The real work was done by my house sitter. André is
very good, and since he has a lot of time on his hands *and*
knows what my 'other job' is, he set me up a number of
programs and databases."

"Hm. Boyfriend?" That was news. Di had always been
pretty much of a loner.

"Sort of. Off and on. More me being flaky than
anything else; I don't really see where I can settle down
right now."

He chuckled, and leaned back to see if he could see a
pattern from a distance. "I have a hard time picturing
you with a hacker."

"God forbid!" She actually took her eyes off the screen
for a moment to glare at him. "I have better taste than
that! André is just good with computers. He's 'just good'
at a lot of things—he plays violin very well, he's a damn
good dancer—"

"Ah, but can he *cook*?"

"He burns jello. Can you?"

"Burn jello? With the best—look, do *you* see any
pattern here?"

"No," she said finally. "Have you tried a chromatic
from blue with the oldest kills first?"

"No—" he bent over his map.

It was hours later, Sara's warning notwithstanding,
when they were interrupted.

"Mark?" came a call from the front of the room. "You
guys still at it back there?"

"Yo, Ramirez," Mark called back, his voice fogged
with fatigue. He craned his neck to see over the low wall
of the work station. "What's up?"

A short, thin, intense young man in faded jeans
wormed his way back through the desks and terminals to
their position. "You guys up with the news?"

Mark stretched, feeling his shoulders pop. "Couple

kids missing?" he hazarded. "Sara said something before she left."

"Three," said Ramirez grimly, "And dead. Chief sent me after you. He thinks your nut case just became a baby-killer."

"Ah *shit*," Mark cursed; his tone, if not his words, conveying anguish—the anguish a cop was supposed to stop feeling after a while. The anguish he couldn't help feeling when a homicide victim was under twelve. "Man, I *hate* it when stuff like this happens."

Ramirez just nodded; he felt it too.

Mark couldn't force himself near the site; just couldn't. Couldn't handle itty-bitty shapes under those olive-drab sheets. It made his gut twist up inside; made him want to go pound on something. Made his eyes sting—

So Di had gotten her clearance and was with the Forensics team without him.

This time the location was a half-abandoned ranch just outside the Fort Worth city limits—well outside the range of any of the previous human deaths that they knew of—but within the range for the cattle mutilations. Mark made a mental note to ask the Narcotics boys if they'd been finding any John Does out here since April.

The kids had been found in an old cattle tank, a tank that the caretaker swore on his life had been left dry, with the drainhole unplugged.

It wasn't dry now. It was full to the rim, and the water was fresh. It wasn't rain water, either; there hadn't been enough rain in the past week or two to put more than a couple of inches on the bottom of the tank.

Somebody had come out here and deliberately filled the tank; and they'd have had to fill it by hand, bucket by bucket, from the tap fifty yards away. Somebody had gone to a lot of work—and done it undetected, unseen— so that somebody could drown three kids here this evening.

Again, undetected, unseen.

They'd taken the old caretaker away about an hour

ago; Mark hoped they'd reached the hospital in time. The shock of finding the kids had thrown the former ranch hand into a heart attack.

"Hey Valdez—" one of the Forensics boys hailed Mark, who waved him over. "Look, this is none of my business, but what makes you guys sure that this is the same loony? The kids weren't slashed up or anything—"

"This—" Mark held up an envelope that Melanie Lee, one of the other Forensics folk, had given him. There was more than enough of the flower petals this time to go around. "We looked back over all the records; nine times out of ten you guys found plant stuff, and I suspect the tenth just meant the cult was either real good at cleaning up after themselves, or there was already native stuff in bloom on-site. None of the copycats or the lone loons left flowers behind."

"Weird." The Forensics man shook his head. "I like that chick you guys brought in; you never know she's there unless she finds something—then she just points it out and waits for us to deal with it."

"Yeah, she's okay," Mark admitted. "She find anything this time?"

"Naw. Look, if this is gonna help you—it'll be on the coroner's report, but I can tell you now. This is real bizarre. It doesn't look like anybody laid a finger in violence on these kids until they put 'em away. Doc thinks they were maybe drugged; he'll be looking for that in the autopsy. I figure they *had* to be—see, before they were croaked, somebody painted 'em with rubber cement."

"With *what?*" Mark hadn't seen the pathetic little corpses, so this took him by surprise. Ramirez, who had, just nodded.

"Honest to God, thick rubber cement, or something a lot like it; painted 'em about half an inch thick everywhere except their mouths, and I mean *everywhere*. Like that old story about the gal who got painted gold—kids would have died from that if they hadn't been drowned. Whoever it was sealed everything shut with the stuff, in fact, before it dried; eyes, nose, genitals, the works, all but the mouth. Thing is, it wasn't messed up much; they really don't seem to have struggled."

"Which bears out the drugging. Prints?"

He shook his head. "Just like all the rest; partials only, damn near worthless, and what little we get doesn't match any files. We've sent 'em to the FBI, but—"

"Yeah, I know, even if our birds have passports or were in the armed forces, *those* records aren't on-line. Means searching archives."

"Which could be months."

"No shit. And even then, working only with partials we're gonna match half of Texas." Mark shook his head. "Man, I wouldn't have your job—at least I can make some motions like I'm doing something."

"Yeah, well I wouldn't have yours. I'd just run in circles. In the lab I can maybe figure something out." The Forensics man nodded, barely visible in the gathering darkness. "Luck, Valdez."

"Thanks. Same to you."

Mark and his colleague watched the Forensics crew begin breaking things down in silence until Di separated herself from the rest and made her way across the dusty stockpen to them. In the near-dark after sunset she looked like a thin, wispy ghost.

"Mark, I need to—" She stopped, noticing the third person.

"Sorry, I didn't have time for formal introduction before. Ramirez, this is Di—Di, Alonso Frederico Ramirez, fellow slave in the department; was Vice, now with us—Homicide, I mean. Us guys with names that end in *z* gotta stick together."

Ramirez smiled thinly. Until lately, that hadn't been too far wrong. Then the Chief had been made Chief— and things had gotten better. The old fart hadn't given a fat damn about affirmative action—but when he saw potential being wasted, he saw red, and did something about it.

"He's currently clawing his way up despite the efforts of the rest of us to keep him down."

Ramirez grinned a little more genuinely.

Di gave him a long appraising look. "So what's that got to do with creative esoterics?"

"He's cool, Di—he was on that voudoun cathouse bust, and the madame cursed him."

"Made *me* a believer, let me tell you," the young man said fervently. "Ended up taking a vacation across the border, looking for an old-time *brujo* to get it off me."

"Did you ever find one?" Di asked, curiosity evident in her voice. "In my experience you have to fight like with like."

"No—no, I got lucky. Dispatch hired in a little bitty gal from Baton Rouge. Ran into her in the hall one day—she took one look at me, freaked, and practically bludgeoned me into accepting a date with her."

"*You* sure freaked when you found out that the date included her *and* her granny. . . ." Mark could still remember the sour look on Ramirez's face when he'd confided the details to Mark.

"And a soon-to-be-deceased rooster and a mess of other shit. Damn good thing for me her granny was visiting."

Di chuckled. "Damn good thing for you that she and her granny have a soft spot for cops. A lot of voudoun practitioners won't even *talk* to cops."

"Yeah, well, maybe I did 'em a little favor or two, like passin' on down the grapevine that the old lady is okay and maybe Baton Rouge Bunco shouldn't hassle her."

"Well, I need a favor; I want to do a full unshielded probe and some other things, and do it without attracting attention. Can you two keep me standing up and pretend to talk to me for about five minutes?"

"You gonna go limp or rigid?" Mark asked.

"Rigid."

"No prob. Ramirez, grab her elbow—okay Di—"

One second she was "normal"—the next, stiff as a corpse; eyes staring, teeth clenched. Mark and his companion pretended to make small talk, watching covertly for anyone approaching them, but no one did. Four or five minutes later they could feel her muscles relax, and she was "back."

She leaned up against Mark, shaking. "Oh *hell*. Mark, I hit problems. Feels like I've been run over. I—nasty stuff. Worse than the last time."

"Get anything?"

"In general, yes—it *is* the same bunch, and this time I got enough to identify five signature auras. But in specific, no, I got hit in a major way. In very specific— they know about me, and they're blocking me."

"Huh?" Mark was startled out of speech.

"They know the Chief's brought in an expert," she replied grimly, "And they are actively working to prevent me or anyone else from pinpointing what tradition they are working in. I could *feel* it; I'd get a clue, start to get close to identifying them, then I'd hit a booby trap, and it would be gone. Knocked right out of my mind."

"You sure it wasn't, you know, the 'on the tip of my tongue' phenomena?"

She shook her head, and her long hair brushed his sleeve. "No—and it wasn't just that floaty forgetfulness you sometimes get in trance. This was deliberate—first redirection, then getting forced off the track, losing the entire train of thought. Then sabotage when I got *too* close. Multiple times. Mark—they're good. Frighteningly good."

"Good enough to beat you?"

She sighed. "I don't know. They were good enough to sucker me—and I'll tell you more about that later."

· FIVE

THERE WERE NO JOKES THE NEXT DAY.

Di called from the bus stop again, but Mark was already awake. He hadn't slept much that night; he'd spent most of the night hours wondering what he could have done to prevent what happened. When the phone rang he was lying on his back, staring at the ceiling, feeling every muscle in his shoulders ache with tension.

This was the first time *his* work, *his* assignment, had involved dead kids. He'd been feeling wretched: and not only miserable and torn up inside, but unaccountably guilty as well, even after getting home last night. It had taken a double shot of bourbon to put him to sleep, and his dreams had been nightmare-haunted.

He headed for the shower after Di gave him his wake-up call, hoping, somehow, to wash some of the depression away. It didn't work. But at least he was showered, shaved, and dressed by the time Di rang his doorbell.

He let her in; she looked just as blue as he felt. She followed him to the kitchen without a word, moving as quietly as Treemonisha at her sneakiest. She took a seat and watched him feed the cat. They brooded at each other over coffee until she finally broke the silence.

"It isn't my fault," she said grimly, "And it isn't yours. It happened, it could happen again. If we can prevent it, fine. If not—well, dammit Mark, we're *trying*. If we've got to lay some guilt, let's put it on the bastards who drown little kids! We shouldn't *have* to be protecting every innocent creature in Dallas."

"But—" Mark tried to articulate his own guilty feelings. "Di, we're the only ones who really know what's going on. Doesn't that make us responsible for preventing things?"

"No, dammit," she replied, strain in her voice. "Okay, we're the best shot the law has at catching these lunatics —but there's only two of us, and the bad guys are at least as good as I am. That's gonna make it harder; we'll do it anyway. But we aren't going to do anyone any good if we wallow in guilt that we don't deserve."

He thought about that; thought about it hard. They *were* trying; doing the best that they possibly could. Finally he nodded, slowly. "Okay," he replied, "You're making sense; you're making sense to my gut as well as my head. I think I can deal with that."

She sighed as his tension eased, and the line of anxiety between her eyebrows faded. He gave her a questioning look.

She shrugged. "One of the problems with being an empath is you get caught in positive feedback—I felt wretched all last night, and once I got inside your influence it was worse. And we can't let this stop us—that's exactly what 'they' want."

He nodded. "Okay, changing the subject. Tell me something, you said you were being 'blocked' last night. Shielding I understand, but how can anybody block a thought?"

"You *would* ask about theory at seven in the morning, wouldn't you." She stirred a little more sugar into her coffee and contemplated the dark fluid for a minute. "You never used to be interested before—it was always 'Don't tell me, I don't want to know—just tell me what to do.'"

"People change; I've been getting curious."

"Okay, on your head be it. You want theory—you're going to get chapter and verse from now on. This is crazy stuff, so get ready to suspend your skepticism," she said. "I'm going to give it to you like it's fact—I don't know if it is or isn't fact, it's not provable, but it works this way for me, and in magic, that's what counts. The whole of the way I work is a half-baked combination of my Wiccan tradition and some of the parapsych experiments they're doing now, *and* a little tad of particle physics and of traditional psych."

He raised an eyebrow. "Strange bedfellows."

"In spades. It goes like this—Jung was almost right. There *is* something like a collective unconscious, sort of a human database. Only its 'memories' don't go all the way back to the cave, like Jung thought—they're only as old as the oldest human alive. Got that so far? There's another 'historical' memory that *does* go back that far, but that's not what I was after last night, and I have to go through a whole song-and-dance act to get at it. Still clear?"

Mark nodded again and sipped his coffee. "Think so."

"Okay; I can tap into the current memory bank, but I can do it consciously, deliberately. It isn't telepathy; I'm not a telepath—it's—something else. I think of it as data retrieval, and that's how it works for me. Most anybody can do this, you do it yourself when you dream, I just do it on purpose. *But* if you know what you're doing—*and* if you're dealing with a very small area of collective knowledge—you can also lay roadblocks in the collective mind. Essentially that's what I hit. When I'm dealing with something arcane that I don't recognize, I generally take a dive into the collective mind and trace back what clues I do have to the source. Except that this time—"

"You hit the roadblocks," Mark supplied.

She sipped her coffee before answering. "Exactly. Now comes the tricky part; behind the roadblocks were traps, traps I sprung on myself when I tried to get around the blocks. You know that 'tip-of-your-tongue' phenomena you were talking about? Where you *know* you know something, but the harder you try and work to get it, the farther away it wiggles? Whoever is doing this knew that an occultist was going to be called in, and laid a trap to do just that to any similar knowledge the occultist in question possessed. They can't really wipe it, the way I implied, but they made it damned near inaccessible to me."

She looked angry and frustrated, and Mark didn't blame her one bit.

"I am royally ticked off at myself for not anticipating traps. Now the only way I'm going to figure out what magical system they're using is to come at it from the side, find it by process of elimination, or get hit in the face with a clue so broad the trap doesn't work."

Mark polished off the last gulp in the cup. "Well, where do we start?"

She managed a wry quirk of her lips. "The hard way. We spend long enough at HDQ for me to work up that report I promised the Chief and for you to collect the preliminary on last night from Forensics. I called André last night; we aren't going to chance a modem because I might lose data to the phone lines—he doesn't much like the quality of the lines down here, he told me. He's arranging for a package of books and some dump-down diskettes to come to HDQ via FedEx. I assume I can arrange for that to get billed to the department? You said I could, and I warned you I'm not exactly rolling in money."

He nodded. "We've got a little account for stuff like that, I'll warn the mail room that it's coming."

"Good, thanks." She bit at a hangnail, eyes dark with worry. "After that, we'll get the files the Chief promised on that Satanist and the other jerk, and go check them out. By now André has called my New York voudoun expert—"

"And if I know how these things work, you should have a contact here by nightfall?"

"I think so; depends on how paranoid the locals are

getting." She sighed. "If I were local, I'd be either gone or hiding so deep it would take a backhoe to dig me out."

"You want me along?" Mark asked, when they pulled up outside the former massage parlor that was now the First Dallas Church of Satan.

"How unobtrusive can you get?" she asked. "How good is your poker face these days?"

He considered that question for a moment, staring through the windshield. "I think I can probably still manage the 'Mr. Nobody' routine we used to use. The one where I'm your wallpaper boyfriend—"

"Then it wouldn't hurt to have you along, although I really don't expect much of anything. Put out your antenna for a minute, and you'll see what I mean."

Mark did his best to get the "feel" of the place, even though he wasn't nearly as sensitive as she was. "Nothing," he reported. "Not a damn thing."

Di smiled wryly. "That's because there's nothing there. High Priest Azarel, alias Thomas Harden, is about to conduct a Black Mass in there right now. He has a full weekday lunch-hour congregation—all seventeen of them—and if there was ever going to be any power being built even *you'd* feel it now. Fact is, there's not a thing there to be sensed. It isn't shielding, either. There isn't a person in that building that could magic their way out of a wet paper sack, or shield against *you* on your worst day."

Mark snorted. "But I'll bet they've convinced themselves that the world is trembling in fear of them."

"Bingo. Well, come on. If you can keep your stomach steady and keep from laughing your head off, we'll go play eager converts."

The Black Mass was about as exciting as a Knights of Columbus luncheon. The nude female serving as the altar looked as bored as Mark felt; by her garish blond hair and makeup, and a certain feeling that he'd seen her somewhere, Mark guessed she was one of the local stripper-cum-b-girls from one of the clubs in the neighborhood. The congregation of middle-class, middle-aged businessmen and housewives did appear to be enjoying the "thrill" of doing something wicked, though. Mark wondered how long it would take to wear off.

He and Di were the only people in the entire room under the age of forty. Di's exotic good looks were drawing a lot of attention from the male contingent and one of the ladies; for that matter, there were a couple of the hausfrau types that were watching *him* out of the corners of their eyes.

Probably wishing this was the Saturday night orgy, and not the weekday ceremony, he thought, finding himself rather grateful that it *wasn't*. One of that lot looked like she'd enjoy devouring him whole if she got the chance. He edged closer to Di, and caught disappointment in her expression before she turned away.

The founder of the cult had stolen from just about every ceremony he could lay hands on. The form was almost a parody of the Catholic Mass; the main differences lay in the philosophy as well as the ceremony. The nude woman as a living altar was the most obvious. Substitution of deity was another. But the main point of the ceremony was exaltation of the flesh instead of the spirit, and selfishness instead of selflessness. The entire thrust was toward "do whatever you want, whenever you want"—the old sixties "let it all hang out" credo dressed up in semiliturgical costume and taken to its furthest extreme.

The congregation stood the entire time; Mark wasn't certain if that was part of the ceremony or if it was because Azarel was too cheap to buy chairs. Mark was fairly certain that beneath the various robes, which were as motley as those who wore them, they were also nude. Full nudity was reserved for Saturday night, Di had told him.

In the light of day the congregation looked like a bunch of moulting crows.

The weekday "mass" was mercifully short. Afterwards Di grabbed his elbow and hauled him with her to accost the High Priest before he could pull a vanishing act.

"Mr. Azarel?" she asked breathlessly, "I'm Sally Bradey, the one who called earlier—"

The "altar" had already done her vanishing trick. The man's face had brightened the moment he saw an attractive young lady hauling Mark along towards him—and if he was disappointed that "Sally" had a male companion, he didn't show it. He was altogether a rather pathetic little man, Mark decided after a moment's perusal. Thin, short, and balding, with a bit of a pot belly; he was trying to grow a moustache and goatee in imitation of the founder of the cult and failing miserably. His "robes of ceremony" were only too obviously salvaged choir robes with moon-and-star appliqués sewn to them. His watery blue eyes reflected a lifetime of not-quite-failing. Mark decided that he was sorry for the little nerd.

Just exactly the kind of jerk who'd get taken in by an operation that was founded by a flimflam artist. Poor geek. Probably believes everything they told him.

"—would you like to come around to my office, Sally?" the little man was saying, in a kind of faded baritone. "I think we can probably answer all your questions in an hour or so."

"Oh *wonderful*," Di gushed. "We were afraid you wouldn't have any time—I'm sure you must be *terribly* busy."

The Dread Azarel smiled smugly. "We always have time for worthy converts. Back through there, Sally, the door on the right; I'll join you in a minute."

The "office" was decorated in floor-to-ceiling bookshelves. The shelves themselves (the inexpensive board-and-bracket type) held not so many books as a plethora of other junk. It looked like a bankruptcy sale at the demise of a horror-movie company. The shelves were crammed with plaster skulls, "voodoo dolls," odd and badly executed statuary, black candles, incense burners, and the inevitable inverted crucifixes. The place reeked of cheap incense and low-grade pot.

Mark felt his lip curling with contempt. It was all so tawdry—like a tired old stripper in a carny geekshow, doing the 'Ugha the Ape-Girl' act because her stretch marks showed too much for her to work the peep shows anymore.

"Priest Azarel" made a would-be dramatic entrance, flinging back the worn velvet curtains at the rear of the office and striding through. He was no longer in his High Priest costume; he wore black pants and turtleneck, both polyester, and an inverted crucifix around his neck. He didn't look sinister—or even worth a second glance on the street. If anything, he looked like a burned-out old hippy who wouldn't let the sixties go.

Within a few moments it was plain even to Mark that neither Azarel nor his followers could have had anything to do with the killings.

For one thing, he knew less about them than had been printed in the papers. For another, despite his boasting about how much power he and his followers had raised through "evil," his idea of "evil" seemed to consist of holding weekly orgies spiced with a little grass and coke, casting "curses" on the enemies of those within the congregation, and pulling petty "acts of vengeance" on those so-called enemies that were somewhat on the level of teenaged pranks. Sugar in the gas tank; slimy, fecal things in the garden.

Then Di pulled the last trick they'd planned on him.

"Do you mind if I smoke?" she asked, reaching into her purse without appearing to look. Mark knew what she was up to, though, and was not surprised when she cursed and pulled her hand back out with a cut across the thumb.

"Dammit!" she exclaimed, holding the freely bleeding thumb out before her. "My damned *mirror* broke! I don't suppose you have a Band-Aid in your desk?"

Azarel stared at the blood, and paled; the kind of greenish pallor that accompanies nausea.

"N-n-o," he stammered. "I—"

He gulped and gripped the edge of the desk.

"You're going to have to leave," he said unsteadily. "You're in danger—I feel myself under psychic attack from my enemies, and they would feel no remorse at striking at *you* as well—"

Di squealed, and stood up hastily. "Psychic attack! Oh

how *horrible!* Thank you Mr. Azarel, we'll leave right now! Will you be all right?"

He tried to look haughty as Di waved the blood-smeared thumb practically under his nose. He succeeded only in looking sicker. "Of course. I am far stronger than they—it is only that I have to extend myself to protect you—"

"Then we'd better go—" They practically ran out of the office door—their haste due mostly to the fact that they didn't want to blow the game at this point by laughing in the man's face.

"What a wimp!" Mark exclaimed with contempt when they got to the haven of the Ghia.

Di gave a little snort of disgust and agreement. "Why anyone would bother with that turkey—" She fished in her purse for the razor blade she'd used to cut her finger, wrapped it and put it back into a little plastic box so that it couldn't bite her again. "Well, at least we've got a good solid reason to write him off."

He nodded. "I doubt even the Chief will want us to bother with him after we tell him about the way Azarel nearly threw up when you cut your thumb."

She grimaced, and sucked daintily at the cut. "The things I do in the line of duty! Ah well—let's go check out Jorden MacKever and the House of Dark Desires."

The House of Dark Desires was in Fort Worth, not Dallas; thirty minutes as the crow flies, but it took them slightly more than an hour to wind their way through all the back streets. It was in a neighborhood similar to that surrounding the Satanist Church; an area of porn purveyors, stripper bars and pawn shops.

"Ho boy—*this* I did not expect."

Di stared at the front of the shop with a look of startled surprise on her face. Since the storefront was nothing more than black glass with the name ornately lettered in gold, Mark didn't think her surprise was caused by the decor.

"What is it?" he asked, as the bucket seat creaked with his efforts to get a better look at the store.

"This *isn't* one of the five signature auras I picked

up—but this guy knows at least something of what he's doing," she said, turning to him with an utterly sober expression. "No, don't unshield, take my word for it—I'd rather not chance you getting caught by what he's got going. He's got what we call a 'glamour' on the store; it will attract anyone with psychic gifts, unless they know enough to see through it. This is a hunter, Mark; and the store is his trap. And I think I know why and what he hunts."

"*Could* this be our pigeon? Could the others—the signature auras you talked about—be involved with him?"

She shook her head. "I don't think so; what he's done is a little crude by my standards, and it certainly lacks the finesse of the traps I ran into. If this were the number-one person behind the killings, he should have more subtlety. Besides, one of those five auras had an incredible feeling of power and the lust for power in it; and I can't see *that* person playing number two to anyone. But this guy is *not* a nice man, and if we can find something to hang him with, we should do it. *If* he's into Crowley, and it feels like he is, he's drawing in unawakened psychics, using their potential, and throwing them away when they're drained and ruined."

Now Mark was worried. "You want me in there with you? You think you can handle this by yourself?"

"Near at hand, but not *with* me, okay? If two of us with shields come in at once, he might spook. If just one comes in, he might figure they're unconscious shields, and he might bite." Her expression firmed into determination. "This isn't our prime target, but I *want* him, Mark. He's been using people—using them up. In some ways, that's worse than killing them."

Mark nodded. "All right then; I'll be right outside if you need me."

Diana edged her way into the porn shop, feeling her skin crawl with every step she took. The man who owned this place—and the people who frequented it—were genuine sadists. No masochists allowed. At least not here. In the back room—that was another story.

Power through pain—as long as it isn't mine. Maybe the ultimate in self-centeredness.

And at least some of those people—the owner included—understood the theory and practice of raising occult power by the infliction of pain far, far better than she did. They were doing as others before them had done; draining the power of unawakened innocents for their own uses, and throwing away the husks afterwards without a backward glance. A psychic, even one who'd been abused physically and spiritually, *could* recover from that kind of ethereal rape—but it wasn't easy, and they had to find expert help right away. Too often the wounds just festered until the psychic ended up on a couch somewhere, trying to explain things no classically trained psychiatrist would believe.

The aura of the place made her nauseous. Like a fish tank when the gravel has been stirred; the psychic atmosphere was muddy, murky, and tainted.

"Can I help you?"

Dressed all in black, he—appeared—from between two rows of high bookshelves. He had meant to surprise, even frighten her; she locked down her startled reflex before it could betray her. With eyes half-lidded and feigned boredom she said, "I suppose you might. I was told I could find a copy of Crowley's *Moonchild* here—"

He could have posed for a recruiting poster for the SS; though middle-aged, he was in superb physical condition, from his black-booted feet to his blond crewcut. Blue eyes, pale as watered milk, seemed to bore right through to her soul. She strengthened her shields a bit as she felt him probe at her. This was the kind of creature High Priest Azarel only dreamed of being.

His eyes narrowed as she resisted his probing. "Are we playing games, little lady?" he asked in a near-whisper. "I know what you are."

She dropped all pretense. Since he'd seen through the act, perhaps she could startle truth out of him with bluntness. "No games, not today. Not unless you had anything to do with three dead kids."

"Those children on the news last night?" He shook his

head. "We don't do children. Only consenting adults here, white-knight lady. We don't kill, either; that isn't the Way."

She got a flash, then—from him, there was no doubt of it; it reeked of his aura—full of emotions. First of fear (another's), then of sexual arousal, then fear (his own). Then a picture, carried to her by the emotion, and a name. A woman—

And she heard herself saying, "Then what happened to Dana Grotern last week?"

Oh hell, she thought belatedly, as his cool surface vanished. *That's torn it! Some day I am going to have to put a governor on my mouth!*

"That was an accident, bitch—" the man was snarling, "but I doubt that much matters to you—"

She put up full shields just in time; he hit her with a psi-bolt that would have knocked Mark to the ground. She gave a little with it, judging his strength, then recovered. She had his measure now; if this was his best, then he was far below her level of expertise.

The first bolt was followed by two more, equally ineffective; she could see them hitting her outermost shields and dissipating in a shower of sparks.

He wasn't slow on the uptake, though, not this one; after three levinbolts it was obvious that she was stronger than he—so he rushed her, hands poised to strike, his multiple shadows cast by the many overhead lights rushing crazily with him.

Tai Kwon Do, she recognized with the back of her mind. The front was preparing to meet his attack.

She ducked under and around the strike; she made her own, felt her foot connect solidly, the side kick making her miss a breath.

Bad form—sensei *would have your hide, fool! Tighten up; balance, center your* ki, *dammit*—

But she did send him reeling into his own bookshelves with sore ribs. The shelves went over in a crash of splintering wood; he went with them. Using the momentum of the kick, she spun around to face him as he scrambled up out of the wreckage of books and wood.

Unfortunately, since he'd been moving in the direction of the kick, she hadn't done him any real damage.

He circled her warily, his boot-soles making scuffing sounds on the linoleum as he moved, looking for an opening. Behind her she heard the street door slam open, and then close; she heard the sound of running feet—she went alert for an attack from behind, then recognized Mark's step, and dismissed the need for wariness in that direction.

But Mark stopped just outside the combat area.

There was no further sound from him; after a moment, she realized there wasn't going to be.

That creep! *He's going to stand around and* watch! *I'll* kill *him*!

She gave Jorden a sucker-opening. He took it. *This* time he wasn't moving in the direction of the force; but even as she delivered a neat chop (*Good! Solid!*) that must have numbed his arm to the shoulder, he got in an unexpected blow of his own. He missed her throat, but got her eye—with the side of the hand, thank the gods, not a thrust.

Agh!

She hissed in pain; her head rocked back. She danced away, her sneakers squeaking on the floor; seeing stars, and getting mad. She felt the blood rushing to her face, making her flush with outrage, and making her eye throb.

Lock it down; you know what the sensei *says. The one who brings anger into the circle is the one who will lose. . . .*

With an effort she shoved her anger back into its proper compartment, felt herself cool, and faced off her opponent again. He was grinning with satisfaction at having scored; she locked down another surge of anger called up by that insolent grin. She could feel her eye starting to swell, the tissues puffing and the vision out of that eye narrowing to a slit.

Dammit, that hurts.

That hurt and that loss of vision would put her at a little disadvantage.

Not as much as he thinks, though. . . . I wonder if I can sucker him twice? Well, nothing ventured—

She faltered a little, shaking her head, though it made her eye hurt and throb to do so, feigning that she was having trouble seeing. The second time she did so, he rushed her; *exactly* the way she wanted him to.

She ducked, came up in low-line—foot to the stomach —he folded around it, then started to unfold—then she executed a spin, and foot to the crotch.

Both hits were clean; felt absolutely solid, and looked textbook pure as she connected. She felt a little more redeemed for getting the black eye.

As he bent over, mouth open in a silent scream, she finished him off with a chop to the base of the neck.

Forgive your unworthy pupil, sensei. *I don't want to kill him,* sensei—*I just want to hurt him. I want to hurt him a lot. I want him to know what it feels like to be hurt instead of inflicting the hurt.*

He went down on his face and didn't get up again.

From behind her came the sound of applause.

"Thanks a bunch, Magnum," Di said sourly, as Mark applauded the end of the fight. "You're always there when I need you."

"You were doing okay," he replied with a grin, still leaning against the bookshelf. "It didn't look to *me* like you needed help."

"This ain't chopped liver," she retorted, gingerly touching the edges of her rapidly blackening eye. "Ah— this is going to be a bad one. Put the cuffs on that jerk and go call the office, huh?"

He pulled the cuffs out of his back pocket and walked over to bestraddle the body on the floor. "What're we charging him with?" he asked, bending over the unconscious porn peddler and snapping the cuffs on his wrists, locking them behind his back.

"Assault, for one; he came after me. I'll be perfectly happy to press charges. You might even get him on assault with a deadly—I don't know how they view martial arts in this state, and he's had more than a bit of

Tae Kwon Do. I've got more than that to pin on him, though. You might want to talk to your friends in Vice; there'll be a gal named Dana Grotern in a coma in one of the hospitals—he put her there. She was playing M to his S last week, when they had a little accident. Seems he didn't bother to find out she had allergies before he gagged her. She was choking, he thought she was acting."

"Huh," Mark said, shaking his head as he gave Jorden a quick pat-down. "Yeah, we look hard enough, we can probably find enough to get him on that. Any link to our cult?" He stood up.

Di's eye was becoming rather impressive. "No, worse luck. This lot follows standard Crowley, right out of the book. I got some empathic flashes from him, and I'd know the signs of that backwards and blindfolded. It ain't our bunch."

"Okay, I'll get on the horn, then I'll take you back to Aunt Nita. You look like you could use some TLC."

"And I'll tell her," Di replied, both amused and annoyed, "That *you* are the one who did this to me!"

Crazy Jake followed Timbuktoo into the no-man's land of the old railyard with a mixture of hope and disbelief. Timbuktoo claimed he'd found this stash—

"Cases, man, cases! Just waitin'! Man, I'm tellin' you, cases!"

It was a bum's dream—Jake just hoped it wasn't a dream.

Timbuk said he'd found this stash of wine in the culvert under the abandoned S&P rail line. He'd spent last night trying to empty it by himself, but reason and guilt had got the better of him, and tonight he'd invited some friends to help him polish it off. Crazy Jake, Tonto, old Dusty, and Pete.

Certainly Timbuk had been *somewhere* last night; he hadn't shown up to panhandle the johns on porn row, and he hadn't shown up at the mission to crash. And he smelled like a distillery right now; his walk unsteady, his hands waving expansively as he talked.

Jake didn't have a thin dime to his name, and he was starting to get the shakes. Before too long he'd start seeing them snakes. He shuffled along last in line, and hoped that Timbuk wasn't seeing snakes of his own; he *needed* a good snort, needed it bad.

They trudged single file down the abandoned right-of-way, weeds higher than their heads in places. Jake could remember when nothing would grow on the right-of-way. He could remember bumming on the S&P freighters that had come roaring out of here under great clouds of steam. He could even remember back to where all the bumming had started, the Big One, the Great Depression. Kids these days didn't know what a real depression was. A real depression was not walking too close to tall buildings, 'cause somebody might be taking a notion to jump. A real depression was meeting bankers on the bum. A real depression was finding a kid dead of starvation 'bout once a day along the line. Nobody starved in the US of A these days, unless they were too damnfool stubborn to get help. A lot of folks starved back then. A lot of folks froze to death, up north, Chi-town way, where Jake came from. Nowadays, someone froze, it made national news.

The weeds rustled, and out of habit Jake started, looking over his shoulder. He scolded himself afterward. No railroad bulls, not here, not these days. Nobody here but five worn-out old bums, hoping for a boozy miracle.

"Down here—" hissed Timbuk through the gap in his teeth, and he led his buddies on a skidding slide down the top of the embankment and into the culvert. The weeds crackled and snapped as the others plowed through them as best they could.

It was dry down here this time of year. Dry and sheltered from the cold winds. Of course, the weather had been real weird this year; hot as summer, it was, hot as hell. But you never knew when the weather was going to turn, and when it did, it was no bad thing to have a tidy shelter lined up.

Especially nowadays. All these kids, all this fallout

from the itty-bitty depression they were having now. These kids, they were taking the good spots away from the regulars; taking the bridges, the underpasses in town. And they were too healthy, too young to fight. It wasn't fair. It wasn't any damned fair. An old bum oughtn't to have to fight for the place he'd always been able to claim as his own. An old bum hadn't ought to turn up at the mission to find all the beds gone.

Jake was last; he slid down the slippery grass to land beside the feet of the other four. They were staring at the darkness beneath the culvert, jaws dropping. Jake's eyes followed theirs, and he felt his jaw drop in imitation of his fellows.

"Ho-lee shit—" he mumbled, gazing with benumbed satisfaction at what was under the plastic tarp that Timbuktoo was holding up. Timbuk was grinning from ear to ear, the gap in the front of his mouth wide enough to drive a truck through, his whole body saying "didn't I tell you?"

"What I tell you guys, huh?" he crowed. "What I tell you?"

"Timbuk, ol' buddy—you were *not* wrong," Dusty hacked.

Beneath the plastic tarp were cardboard boxes, each one holding twelve big beautiful bottles of vino. It was gonna be a cracklin' rosie night for sure. There were— Jake counted—six, seven, *eight* cases. And that didn't include the case already opened, that Timbuk had started on last night.

"Oh *man*," Jake said reverently. "Oh, *man*!"

"Help yourselves, boys," Timbuk said magnanimously. "Drinks is on me."

Before Timbuk could change his mind, Jake had a case open and had grabbed up four bottles. *Twist-off caps too—oh man, the livin' don't get any easier than this.* He found himself a nice, comfortable spot in the culvert, opened the first bottle, and poured it down his throat as fast as he could gulp. The shakes were hitting pretty good, and he had to steady his bottle with both hands— but he didn't spill a drop, nossir. He waited for the booze to hit; as soon as he stopped shaking, he relaxed into his chosen spot and began sipping at his second bottle.

The third brought a pleasant buzz to his thoughts. The fourth brought oblivion.

So he never saw the five barbarically clad figures step into the culvert to see what their baited trap had caught this time.

Pablo tossed back his beer and waited, sullenly, for the stranger to speak. He couldn't see the man's face in the shadows of the smoky bar; he had no idea who he was talking to. The note with the folded bill had just said that he wanted to talk, not what about.

But fifty bucks buys a lot of attention in the *barrio*.

The clothes were okay; loose white suit, like about any other dude. The color of the hand holding the beer bottle—which was all he could see of the man—was okay. Of course he wouldn't have gotten past the door of *this* bar if he hadn't looked like he fit. Pablo remembered last year, when some yuppie gringo reporter had tried to get in. Broken jaw don't do a dude much good on the six o'clock news.

Maybe the man was in dope, looking for runners, dealers, protection. He didn't smell like "cop" to Pablo. But if the man was new in dope, Pablo was going to think hard about turning him down. The big boys wouldn't deal nice with somebody pushing in on their turf.

Then again, maybe Pablo *would* deal with him. There was a power about this man—a power Pablo wished he had. This man could hold your attention just by sitting there drinking a beer. Somehow Pablo knew that when the man spoke, he would *listen*. He would have to. Like a puma, the man was; like a jaguar. Which was a good sign; Pablo's gang was the Jaguars.

"I hear," the man spoke at last, "that you *hombres* think you're pretty good, you Jaguars. I hear other people think the same."

Pablo had been right about the voice. It was deep; you felt it as much as heard it. It was a voice that could issue a command and be obeyed without an argument. It was a voice that would put chicks on their knees. *Power*, said the voice to the back of Pablo's head. *I have Power. More Power than you dream.*

"We're okay," Pablo shrugged, not indulging in any of the usual bullshit. You didn't bullshit a man like this one. "We got a good turf, and we hold it."

"I hear you don't take anybody but *Mestizo*."

"You hear right." He toyed with the beer bottle, making little wet rings linking together into a chain on the tabletop.

"You got a reason?" the man asked—and Pablo knew he'd have to tell him.

"We're the first people; we were here before anybody," he said, becoming more passionate with each word. "Everything we had got stolen from us; first by the Spanish, then the whites. So—we're takin' some of that back, the Jaguars. Takin' back what's ours by right."

"So." The man leaned forward, and Pablo got a good look at him. He nearly died of envy. The man—looked like a movie star, a statue, a god! That manner, that voice—and now that face! What couldn't *he*, Pablo, do with a combination like that?

"I hear passion in you, *hombre*. I hear a heart, I hear guts. I hear a warrior. Tell me something, man—you interested in *doing* something about this, something real? Something *big*?"

Oh man—give me a chance— Pablo thought, and said, as level and cool as he could, "Try me. Try *us*."

The man smiled; predator's smile, jaguar's smile. "You ready to go back to the old gods—the warrior's gods? You ready to give them what they need? You gotta pay for power, *hombre*. You think you can come up with the coin? Warrior's coin?"

Pablo nodded, but before he could answer, the man rolled on, his own words hot beneath the ice-cool of his tone.

"You think you can handle yourself smart—be a warrior *and* deal with the new world? You think you can deal in the big time? You think you can handle more than a gang?"

"Like?"

"Like maybe an army?"

Tuf couldn't figure out where he was. One minute he'd been following this chick—oh man, *that* had been an armful, long black hair, round and soft in all the right places, a come-on look in her eyes, and a promising wiggle to her hips—the next minute, *bonk*.

No idea who hit him; never saw them. Now he was waking up cold and confused, and God knew where.

It looked like a warehouse, or something. He was just about bare-ass naked except for a single strip of cloth. He was lying on cold cement, and his head hurt like hell.

Whatever it was, wherever he was, the building was empty; there was real dim light coming from a couple of exit signs, but that was it. Enough to hint at a high ceiling, far-off walls. The echoes when he moved told him *empty*.

He started to get to his feet, and found that one of his ankles was tied to a support beam. He tried to get the knots undone, but they were too tight, and he didn't have anything to cut the rope with. He swore and struggled, but only succeeded in ripping one of his fingernails off.

Suddenly—light.

Blinding light from a fixture directly over his head struck him with an almost physical blow. The light was so bright that it threw everything outside the circle it delineated into absolute darkness. Tuf cringed, and shaded his eyes, but with no result; he couldn't see the rest of his surroundings anymore.

Footsteps; sound of bare feet scuffing against cement. Into the circle of light stepped an old enemy.

Pablo. Chief of the Jaguars. Tuf suddenly recalled that he'd been on Jaguar turf when he'd been coldcocked.

Better brazen it out.

"Say hey, Pablo." Tuf was trying to be cool, but it wasn't easy. Pablo looked rigged out for some kind of costume party; fancy loincloth, ropes of flowers on his wrists and ankles, for chrissake; some kind of helmet shaped like a big cat's head under one arm, about a ton of silvery jewelry. He should have looked stupid—he didn't. He looked *mean*.

"Say hey, Tuf." Pablo sounded cool; sounded amused, like he was laughing at Tuf. He moved a little, and Tuf could see his other hand come into the light. He was carrying what looked like two sticks.

"What th' hell's all this, man?" Tuf asked, trying to sound casual.

"Like, you're my enemy, man. I caught you on Jaguar turf, fair an' square. Like, I coulda killed you, but I'm gonna give you a chance."

Tuf snorted. "What chance, man?"

Pablo just grinned and threw one of the sticks at Tuf. "Like we fight, man. You an' me, *mano-a-mano*." He pulled on his helmet, and his eyes looked darkly out of the big cat's mouth, shadows within shadows. "Like you haven't got a choice, man. You fight me, or you die."

Tuf had caught the stick almost reflexively, and took a good look at it. It was flat, polished wood, and along both edges were set feathers. Feathers?

"I'm s'pposed to fight you with *this*? For what? Turf?"

"Honor, man. For the gods. For the old ways." Tuf did not much like the way Pablo's eyes were burning down in the deep shadows of the cat's mouth. "We fight for Burning Water, man—or you die for Burning Water. You take your pick."

"With a stick? What if I lose?"

Pablo laughed. "You die, you just die quick. You don't fight, you die slow. 'Member that dude they found down to Bachmann Lake? Like him."

Tuf swallowed fear. "And if I win?"

"I die; you kill me, you take my place." Pablo sounded as if it were a matter of supreme indifference to him.

"Who says?" Tuf asked belligerently.

"Burning Water." Pablo nodded at the area outside the circle of light to Tuf's right. *Something* stood there, or somebody. Dark and shadowy—and powerful. Even from here Tuf could feel the power—like the power of a black sun.

"So who's this Burning Water dude? Huh?"

Pablo's eyes shone with fanatic devotion, and his face was transformed by a vision only he could see. "He's gonna make us free, man. He's gonna make us *warriors*. He's a god; no lie, an old god. He's gonna wipe out the white man, he's gonna give it all to us. I'm tellin' you."

The smart-ass retorts on the tip of Tuf's tongue died before he could speak them. Somehow—that vague shadowy power seemed capable of all of that. That shadow was the shadow of Fear—of a hunger that could eat the world. Tuf could feel the force of that hunger, and it was squarely behind Pablo.

"You gonna fight, man?" Pablo was sneering, "Or you gonna die like a sheep?"

Tuf took a better grip on his stick, his hands slippery with the sweat of new fear, and went into a fighting crouch. This was no more than a fool's chance, but it *was* a chance. And whatever—*he* was not going to go down without a fight. "What you think, man?" He gestured with his fist, and Pablo laughed at the obscenity. "Come on, man—I ain't waitin' all day. You gonna rumble or not?"

And only when Pablo stepped fully into the circle of light did he notice that where the edges of *his* stick were inset with feathers, the edges of Pablo's glittered with something dark and sharp-edged.

And knew, with despair, exactly how much of a fool's chance he'd been given.

·SIX

FLIES, FAT, LAZY AND ENGORGED, AND NOW DISTURBED IN their feeding, rose in clouds from the end of the alleyway.

LaRoss took one look at what they'd been feeding on and nearly lost his lunch.

"My God—" Greeley whispered.

You don't patrol the barrio *without getting a tough hide,* LaRoss thought, holding off shock and sickness at a desperate arm's length, *But this—this isn't death, it's carnage. It's like a slaughterhouse.*

"I'll call in—" he gulped. Greeley just nodded wordlessly. LaRoss assumed the nod meant "okay," and got out while he could still control his stomach.

He left Greeley at the entrance to the cul-de-sac; his partner had gone pale, but it seemed like he was taking the sight better than LaRoss. But then Greeley had seen a fair share of mangled bods in 'Nam and maybe he could handle this a little more calmly than a guy who'd been too old in the sixties to draft.

LaRoss did not walk to the car—he ran. Without really thinking about it, he found himself reaching for the radio handset through the window of the squad car. He spoke a few words into it—not really conscious of what he was saying, but it must have been the right thing, since he got the promise of more help on the way. He couldn't really concentrate—kept seeing the pile of bodies—

—*just like carcasses at a packing plant, just piled up on top of each other. Cut up like they'd been rumbling with razor blades and hopped on PCP at the time. But my God—those eyes; those punks, they saw Hell before they died. God help them.*

There was a buzzing near his face; absently he brushed it away, then with a shudder of realization of why the insect was so lethargic, smashed the fat fly against the hot, shiny enamel of the squad.

Can't leave my partner alone back there, he thought, and shuddered again. *It's not the first time we've picked up after gang fights. Pull yourself together, man!*

He made himself return to the cul-de-sac, feet dragging. "Must have been hopped up for sure," Greeley said casually, as LaRoss forced himself to look at the pile of bodies until numbness settled in. "Get dusted bad enough, you don't feel nothin', you know? Buddies must've been just as high."

"Buddies?" LaRoss replied dumbly. There were only six or seven bodies, but his mind kept multiplying them.

"Sure, how d'you think they got here? Had a rumble somewhere else—not enough blood around here— winners hauled the losers off and dumped 'em for us t' find. They gotta know we always check this alley."

Greeley's calm was infectious; LaRoss felt his stomach settling, his mind taking over. "Last night, you figure?"

Greeley shook his head. "Huh-uh; I'd figure some time around shift change."

Now LaRoss was focusing enough to take in the insignia on the back of the jackets, disfigured by blood and slashes though they were. "Hey pard—you notice something else, something weird?"

Greeley nodded. "They're from at least two, three different gangs."

"Must have been a *hell* of a rumble!" LaRoss brooded. "With that big a rumble, wonder how come we didn't get wind of it?"

"That," Greeley seconded, "Is exactly what I've been thinkin'."

Mark stood a little to one side and watched Di wading in like a trooper—and wondered how in hell she had managed to cover up that black eye of hers. The swelling had gone down, but it had been a real beauty last night when he'd dropped her off. He was able to keep his stomach under control as long as he was thinking about that and not too closely about the reason for the all-points.

The Forensics team had welcomed Di like one of their own when the two of them had responded to the call; now Mark knew why she had packed a lab coat. When she was sure of her reception she'd gone back to the car for it—and with the coat on she looked just like one of them; just melted into the crowd. Which was no bad thing for someone who was trying *not* to be noticed by the press.

"Look at this—" Di muttered to Mark, pulling up the cuff of one corpse's jeans with a pencil.

"Holy—rope burns—"

"And just on one ankle," she replied. "They're all like this."

"Like the stiff at Bachmann Lake. You were right about coming out here; these have got to be ours. You picking up anything?"

Somewhat to his disappointment she shook her head as she rose from her crouch. "Nothing strong; certainly no signs of any of my five signatures."

He stood, crossed his arms, and thought. "So I'll ask a dumb question. Can psychic traces be wiped out?"

She stared at him, and her eyes widened a little. "Not so dumb; I didn't think of that. The answer is yes—but only—only if you are very, very good. I can't do it."

He nodded; he was no telepath, but he knew what she must be thinking, because he was thinking the same thing, with a sinking spirit. *We could be getting out of our depth fast.*

Before he could say anything else, he heard one of the Forensics people swear under her breath.

It was a welcome distraction, and since she was practically at his elbow, he looked over in her direction. "Problems, Jean?"

"Just the arrival of a chronic pain in the ass," replied the curly-haired technician. "See that blond?" She nodded in the direction of the gathering of vultures behind the police barricade. "German reporter; thinks he's God's gift to journalism. Making a prime pain of himself, and we've been given orders to make nice with him."

A throaty chuckle from his other elbow sent his head swiveling in Di's direction. "But *I* haven't been given any such orders," she said. "Would you like a demo of my foolproof way of getting rid of snoops?"

Jean's mouth quirked a little, and she raised her eyebrows. "Is the Pope Polish?"

Di rose to her feet, and began walking toward the barricade, making notes on her clipboard. Predictably, the blond reporter intercepted her as soon as she got within grabbing distance, catching her by the sleeve and erupting with questions.

They were too far away to hear what she said at first—but then she pulled paper containers out of the copious pockets of her lab coat and began waving them under his nose—her voice rising with every word.

"—fecal samples!" she enthused. "I tell you, it's plain as day! It's all here, in the fecal samples!"

The German backpedaled so fast he nearly ran over another ghoul.

"I'll be *happy* to show you—" Di pursued him, still waving the containers.

"I—I do not think that vill be required, Miss—" he gasped, eyes darting this way and that as he searched for an escape route to get away from this madwoman. "I haf enough information now, thank you—good day!"

For just at that moment he saw an opening—and all but ran out of the crowd. Di contrived to look disappointed, shoved the containers back into her pockets and returned to Mark's side.

If the situation had been less gruesome, it would have been hilarious. As it was, Di was greeted with a mixture of relieved, grateful, and approving looks.

"If we dared," Jean whispered, "We'd give you a standing ovation. Lady, you can work with us any day!"

"Any sign of flower petals or feathers this time?" Di asked, getting back down to business.

"Not around the bodies or in the clothing—but yes, flower petals stuck in the dried blood and actually *in* some of the wounds," one of the others replied. "And it looks, at least superficially, as if some of these boys were reclothed after they were killed. We won't know until we get the bodies back to the lab and map everything, but the lacerations in the clothing aren't always matching the lacerations on the bodies."

"Huh." Di folded her arms around her clipboard, and frowned with concentration. "Now *why* bother to put clothes back on them?"

"Red herring?" Mark suggested. "At least a temporary one? Make it look for a little while as if this *wasn't* one of the cult killings?"

"Buying them time for something—could be. Could be." The look in Di's eyes told Mark enough—that what the cult had been buying time for was to wipe out psychic fingerprints *and* psychic backtrails.

"I don't like you going out there alone," Mark protested, as they levered themselves into the Ghia.

"Mark, one look at you and my sources are going to smell 'cop' and spook on me," Di said, a bit of an edge of exasperation creeping into her tone. "And I won't be alone; you'll be within yelling distance. Besides, the first few are safe; my voudoun contact has been vouched for and knows I'm coming, and after that I'll be talking to people who can 'read' me. They'll know I'm on the level—and unless one of them is a renegade, I'm in no danger from them."

There had been an unexpected bonus; Di's voudoun

practitioner lived within blocks of where the bodies had been found. And Mark could tell that she wanted *badly* to know if anyone sensitive to such things had sensed any otherworldly stirrings last night.

"I still don't like it," Mark grumbled, turning the ignition key. "Why voudoun, anyway? Why not some nice innocent Druids or something?"

"You don't know much about Druidism—if you think they're *innocent!*" She gave him a sidelong glance and shook her head. "Oh, I might as well level with you. Two reasons. One—those who work with blood magic tend to be sensitive to it. Two—I have *no* ties into the pagan network here. I work solo too much—and a lot of the pagan net frankly doesn't trust strangers much. You said it yourself; this is Bible-thumping country, they might end up out of a job or worse. *I* will have to be vouched for by a local, and the only local contact I have now is Noble Williams."

"Okay." He did not immediately pull out into traffic when the Ghia had rumbled to life; Di cocked her head at him quizzically.

"Something else wrong?"

"Are we biting off more than we can chew?" he asked somberly.

Her lips thinned, and she turned away from him, staring broodingly out through the glare of sun on the streaky windshield.

"Well?" he prompted.

"Possibly. Very possibly," she admitted after a moment of reluctant silence. "I've been trying to think of all the ways I know to eliminate psi-traces. Using running water to wash them away; that's out, obviously. Working insulated so that there never *were* any traces is *probably* out, it's too hard to maintain good insulation, and all it would take is one leak. That leaves one alternative that can be worked a half-dozen ways: using pure, raw power to blank any individual signatures. A kind of psychic bleaching. And that's something *I* can't do. If they can—I'm not sure I want to think about that too hard."

Mark gripped the steering wheel hard enough to turn

his knuckles white, feeling real, honest fear. Fear like he hadn't felt since that long-ago night in Quasi's. This was exactly the reason he'd gotten Di involved in the first place; to have his *expert* out of her depth was enough to leave him gut-clenched. "Should we—think about pulling out of this?" he asked slowly.

"Let me counter that with a question of my own: Dare we?" she returned. "So far these people have killed ten victims *that we know of*, and three of those were little kids. Do *you* want more deaths on your conscience? I don't." She swallowed, and bit her lip. "I do this probably for the same reason that you became a cop, Mark—there are things out there that people need to be shielded from. Since I have the talent and the knowledge—it's almost a duty for me to stand in the line of fire. And unfortunately I *don't* know of anyone better equipped than I am who isn't already out fighting fires of his own."

"Unless I'm very much mistaken, this could get fatal."

She nodded, and twisted a strand of hair around one finger. "It could. We have one advantage going for us, though—"

"And that is?"

"That everyone who's been killed has been attacked *physically*, not by magic. And between the two of us, I truly do not think that there is anything *physical* that we can't handle."

He nodded, and forced his hands to unclench. "Okay, I'll grant you that. Can you shoot—" he bit off the rest with a blush of chagrin.

"How quickly we forget," she replied with a hint of irony. "The more appropriate questions would be, What can you get me in a hurry, and can you manage a permit for me to carry concealed?"

"You're asking a Dallas *cop?* When you're working for the force? What do you *want?* I recommend against a howitzer, they're awfully hard to hide." He put the car in gear and eased it into traffic.

"My current personal is a Colt forty-five; a revolver, I like to keep things simple. And button that lip on any smart comments about it being too big a piece for me to handle; I *happen* to have stronger wrists than you do, and I never fire it one-handed. I did *not* bring it with me—I never thought I was going to have to contemplate putting holes in people, and I've always figured that traveling with a firearm is a Very Bad Idea, since you never know who is going to be able to get at your luggage when you check it through. And you are not heading for my voudoun contact."

"No, I'm heading for HDQ. We are going to get you armed right now; you're *already* dangerous." He accelerated and squeezed the Ghia into a gap between two pickups. "What we have mostly are Browning nine-mil autos; that's close enough to your forty-five for you to make the transition."

"I'll take your word for it. I should warn you, there are going to be some situations where I will refuse to carry the thing."

"It's your skin." He hit the freeway on-ramp and piloted the Ghia into the traffic flow with the ease of an Indy 500 driver. "I'll feel better knowing you've got it. Now answer me true, lady—what do we do if we get in a situation where we *are* out-magicked?"

"*You* run like hell. And don't argue; if our positions were reversed, I'd run while you covered me. In a case where I'm the expert, don't you try to be a hero."

"Agreed. But what am I supposed to do if you get put out of action permanently?"

"Now that," she replied, so softly he could barely hear her over the traffic noise, "is something you will not have to worry about. If I go—and I swear to you by all I hold sacred that I *can* do this—I take whoever's behind this *with* me."

It was late afternoon when they headed back out; Diana was now armed, checked out on the police range as being competent, and equipped with all the appropriate permits for the weapon now clipped to her waistband over her right hip. With her jacket on, even Mark had a hard time spotting it.

And that was weird—because a Browning nine mil is not an easy gun to hide.

"Now I feel a little better——" he admitted. "It isn't rational, but I do. Now tell me how in hell you're making it look like you're not carrying anything bulkier than a fat wallet!"

She smirked. "Trade secret."

"You *could* walk."

"Creep."

He growled threateningly; she winced and ducked. "Okay, okay, I'll tell you. I'm projecting harmless innocence; as an empath I'm very good at that—your mind doesn't expect Snow White to be packing, so it refuses to see the bulge."

"Huh." He shook his head, not sure whether to believe her or not. "Is that how you're hiding your black eye?"

"No. I'm using the same stuff they use to cover strawberry birthmarks. Would you like to know the color of my underwear too before you let me out?"

The sharpness of her answer told him how much on edge she was, so he kept the retort he'd wanted to make behind his teeth. "Where do you want me to wait for you?"

"Halfway down the block." They were approaching the address, which proved to be a tiny storefront on the corner. Late afternoon sunlight glared off the window, and Mark couldn't quite make out what was painted there.

"What is this place, anyway?"

"An herbalist—which around here is *admitting* you're an arcane practitioner."

Mark contemplated the denizens of the area, and felt a twinge of serious mundane misgiving as he parked the car. "I don't want to sound racist, but aren't you a bit pale to be wandering around this block?"

"I would be," she replied, slipping out before he could stop her, "except that they aren't going to see *me*. They're going to see only what they expect to see. Watch. . . ."

And sure enough; as he watched her saunter off, he could see that not only was she attracting no attention, but the glances of the loiterers and passersby actually seemed to slide right off her.

He sighed, and scrunched down in his seat, making himself comfortable. *If she could bottle that*, he thought, *we'd make a fortune.*

Di sighed, feeling some of the weight of the need to stay constantly under shields drop from her shoulders. She had known from the moment that she stepped in through the door of the tiny, fragrant, shadowy shop that she was in the presence of a friend, even though she had never met Noble Williams in her life. And the silver-haired, wizened, ebony man behind the counter had responded to her hesitant self-introduction as if she had been a long-absent relative, locking the shop-door, pulling down the shade that said Closed and ushering her into his own sitting room in the apartment behind the shop.

Before she had time to blink she was enthroned in a wicker chair and plied with a very impeccably British tea.

The shields he's got up on this place— she thought, a little in awe. *Granted, he's been at this game twice, maybe three times as long as I have, but still—you could hit this apartment with a psychic nuke and not penetrate.*

And the atmosphere within the shields was genuinely welcoming and friendly; as an empath she was doubly sensitive to things like that. It was the first time since she'd arrived in Dallas that she felt *safe.*

As she sipped her tea, she smiled at her host across his tiny hardwood table. "I must say," she told him, "that of all the things I was anticipating, that very *last* was a Mahatma Gandhi clone with the voice and accent of Geoffrey Holder! Noble, I could listen to you read the phone book and enjoy the experience to the hilt!"

"You are far too kind," Noble Williams laughed richly. "But my dear Miss Tregarde," he continued in mock protest, "our surprise was mutual! From my colleague's brief description, *I* was expecting a six-foot-tall Amazon warrior, wielding a mighty flaming sword— only to be accosted by—what? A music-box ballerina in blue jeans! Do have more tea, won't you?"

"Please—" She held out her cup, deciding that if *he*

wasn't going to mention the Browning—which he had *most* certainly noticed—neither was she. "And—this room—something tells me you've really *read* all these books, and at least twice each!"

For the room was wall-to-ceiling bookcases, everything from books Di had in her own arcane library to Shakespeare to Tolkien to *War and Peace*.

He laughed again. "It is a hunger with me, books. I had rather read than eat, I do think."

"How on earth did you ever meet up with Marie? I didn't think the Haitian practitioners and the Louisianans even spoke, much less kept up a regular correspondence."

He let his eyelids droop, stirred another spoonful of honey into his tea, and smiled slyly. "My dear child, we aren't going to tell you *everything*, you know! We must keep *some* secrets!"

She returned the smile. "I have been rebuked. I'm just glad you were willing to talk to me. This is turning out to involve a lot more than I thought it would."

"Indeed." He set his cup carefully down on the saucer and steepled his fingers thoughtfully, his puckish expression turning serious. "But—you remind me, rightly, of business. This present situation calls for a great deal of cooperation among *all* the blessed. Ask—I shall answer with honesty, and with as much information as I possess."

She set her own cup down, and looked into his depthlessly dark eyes, allowing the last of *her* shields to drop completely. "By now you've heard what turned up a few blocks away—did you, or anyone you know, *sense* anything last night? Or any other night, for that matter?"

The voudoun priest shook his graying head regretfully, a genuine regret she could feel quite strongly. "No. Nothing at all. And it is a source of wonder and concern to me that we have not. Those of us who *are* in tune with feelings have only experienced the fear and sickness of those discovering the bodies of the victims. None of us have sensed the deaths themselves, which *surely* must have been horrible."

"You've felt *nothing*? Not even anything like a power-point where there wasn't one before?"

"No—we have felt threat, and strangeness. But what we have had is a feeling of growing—not *evil*; it is hard to quite describe what we have felt. It is a kind of hunger, a kind of violent, and very angry hunger. And—" he hesitated a moment before continuing. "The *loas* have been warning us of danger for some time now."

Di sat up a little straighter at that. "So *they* knew of something. Danger to your folk specifically?"

"Again, no." His eyes looked off somewhere into the far distance, to a place far removed in time and space from the pleasant little sitting room. "No, they have only warned us of places to beware of, and times when it would not be wise to be alone. I trust you have deduced that all the victims *were* alone?"

"Except for those three children—"

"Who were scarcely able to protect themselves; I think they could be counted as being 'alone.' And again, they were not—as the old phrase of my childhood went—'persons of color.' Have you not noted this also?"

"No," Diana replied, blushing with chagrin at missing something so obvious. "I hadn't. You're saying there's a connection—"

"One I do not yet understand," he said, looking vaguely puzzled. "It is subtler than I am stating; I feel sure of this. But this much I do know; there is a powerful anger, a hatred that this—being—has, and it is *not* directed at the black population. For once in our lives, *we* are not the target of rancor. If this thing were to take one of us, it would be because, like Mount Everest, we happen to be there. We are not immune—but *we* are not the preferred targets, either. Given a *choice* between a black and a white, this thing would slay the white and allow the black to move on unmolested. But this is not anything of ours, either; I can swear this to you. I *do* swear this to you, by all that I am."

Di let out the breath she had been holding in a soft whistle. "I believe you. But *that*—the hatred for whites —is not only interesting, it's something I didn't even consider. So *that's* why you haven't buttoned up, like the 'readers,' or run off, like the Rom."

"Not all the Rom have fled," Williams told her, shifting a little so that the wicker of his chair creaked. "And that may be significant as well. It is certainly significant that the Gitano, who normally do *not* wander, have left the city. Yes, the few Gitano we had are all gone, and the Kalderash with them, and *most* of the Lowara—"

"But not all?" If there were still some Lowara—the Lowara *owed* her. It might be time to collect.

"But not all," he agreed. His eyes now seemed to be looking inward, not outward. "Miss Tregarde—"

"Diana," she said firmly.

"Diana," his voice deepened, and took on a heavier coloration of accent—and a firmness of tone that almost *forced* her to believe every word she was hearing. "You are in most perilous danger. Believe this. There is present threat, and peril to your life."

She went still, almost frozen inside. Power moved here; had moved in so subtly that she had not noticed it until it was there. What was speaking now was *not* Noble Williams.

"This thing has the scent of you—and while it is *now* in the position of the quarry, it may well turn hunter, especially if you press too hard. It knows you, and it can find you if it chooses. Be wise. Do *not* walk anywhere unshielded, or unarmed. Keep all your weapons about you at all times. Guard your back."

A chill of fear threaded down the length of her spine, for she *knew* that it was the height of stupidity to ignore that advice. Especially from a *houngun* whose *loa* was Ogoun, god of war and warriors—and statesmanship and craft.

"Yes?" she breathed, making of the word a hesitant request for further help.

"Until now it has walked in the shadows, in hiding— but the sunlight does not weaken it, and it does not fear the day. It is as strong in sun as in moonlight, so do not presume to think that daylight will protect you."

"What *is* it?" she pled, not really hoping for an answer.

"We do not know," came the bleak reply, "We do *not* know. It is nothing we have ever known—but it is very old. Old in blood and old in death; old in strength and old in cunning. And it has never known, never wanted peace. You must keep it from making a home here for itself, Diana—or it will make of this city a Hell of blood and pain. For *every* living thing." And the far-off gaze faded from the old man's eyes. At her mute look of inquiry, he shook his head.

She sighed, and forced her shoulders to relax, telling herself that she would not give in to the fear and feeling of utter inadequacy until she was forced to. But she wanted to cry so badly that her throat hurt with the effort of holding the tears back; wanted to go running back to Hartford and André and forget she'd ever heard of Dallas. Wanted to pack it *all* in and let someone else take over.

But she knew that there *was* no one else to take over. She was all there was; she and Mark were all that were standing between a city full of innocents and something a major Power feared enough to warn her against.

I'm not good enough for this. I'm just a troubleshooter; a competent magical hacker This it's out of my league. I can't handle this—oh gods, and I have no choice, I have to.

But she was careful to let none of that show. She swallowed a sip of tea, exerted the iron control that had gotten her a black belt in three years, and forced herself to regain an outward calm.

"Well, that was more than I expected, anyway. Every scrap of information helps."

He picked up his teacup and stared thoughtfully into it for a moment. "I believe I can give you another contact," he said finally. He rose before she could say anything and flitted silently back into the shop. When he returned, he had an index card with a handwritten name and address on it.

"One of my occasional customers," he said, as she copied the address into the notebook she dug out of her purse. "I doubt that she has fled the city; I do not think her purse would permit it, nor her employer. If my own judgment is anything to go by, I would say she is practiced, though not as practiced as you."

"Which means she is pretty well entrenched in the local neo-pagan movement?" Di hazarded, since the name on the card was a simple "Athena."

"I believe so," he nodded. "If you will give me a day or two to contact her, I shall try to smooth the way for you."

Mark relaxed when he saw Di emerge from the herb shop and sprint for the Ghia. He was beginning to have uneasy feelings whenever she was out of sight. "Got anything?" he asked, as she pulled the door open and slid in beside him.

"A bit," she replied, as he drove off, noting that the neighborhood denizens *still* didn't seem to be giving him, Di, or the car a second glance. "Whatever, whoever it is seems to have it in for Caucasians. And I was told that it is 'very old'—which could mean a lot of things. But it *isn't* voudoun killings; Noble said not, and I believe him."

"You think he'd fink on his own people?"

"In this case—yes," she said firmly. "We *might* want to look into Middle Eastern or Asiatics though, after all. I'm sure as hell not infallible—there's a lot of room *there* for nasty surprises, and those are not areas that I know much about. I mean, despite that I thought not, we could have a new Kali cult going; the heart-cutting-out certainly fits *that* profile, and it fits the pile of bodies in the alley—"

"But not the drowned kids?"

"I don't know; I told you, I'm just not familiar with that brand of occultism. The flower petals *would* fit, though."

"Okay, what else did you get from this guy?"

"I've got a contact into the local neo-pagan network, but Noble wants to warn her I'm coming, first. And there's another 'but.'"

"Which is?"

"That I really do not think this thing has any ties into the neo-pagan movement. It just doesn't feel right; it feels independent."

Mark whistled tunelessly for a moment, squinting into the late-afternoon sunlight reflecting off the windshields around them. "Okay, I had a pair of thoughts myself while you were in there. One of them actually dovetails with your feeling. Thought one was that there is a fourth way to do things without leaving psychic fingerprints."

"So?"

"Use tools. In this case, human tools."

Di hit her forehead with her palm. "Oh *hell!* The oldest trick in the book, and I *forgot* it! My God, that's Crowley's old trick—*and* the Kali cult's, *and* a dozen others'! How could I forget?"

"Did you?" he countered. "Or were you led to forget? Couldn't this have been an effect of one of those 'traps' you sprung on yourself?"

Silence from her side of the car as he shifted gears and dodged around a double-parked cab. "It could have been," she finally said, sagging a little. "Only the gods know what blank spots I've got in my memory now. It's enough to make me want to throw in the towel and hang it all up. What the hell good am I? What *use* am I?"

"Don't," he said forcefully. "Don't say things like that. And don't blame yourself. That's exactly what 'it' wants you to do—you told me yourself how easy it is for you to get caught in a downward spiral. We'll just realize you may have gaposis, and deal with it. Okay, thought two was—maybe we ought to check on a couple of the maverick tea-leaf readers. The ones that don't feel right, you know? There's still a couple with their shingles up; not many, and all on this side of the tracks, but a couple."

"And?" she prompted, looking very interested.

"And there *are* a couple that give me the willies—but Bunco's never caught 'em out on anything. Like—there's this medium not six blocks from here. . . . You game?"

"M'love," she said slowly, "That is *not* a bad notion."

Diana stared down the barrel of a gun, tasting fear—cold fear—in the pit of her stomach. The business-end of the thing looked as long as the Lincoln Tunnel and twice as black.

It was a .357, to be exact. It was pointed at her midsection, held in the hand of a *most* nervous gentleman who was not, and had never been, a medium.

She refocused from the weapon to the man behind it; thin, very dark—Cuban, she thought. Little scraggle of moustache; crewcut. Hyper to the max. She could feel a trickle of sweat down her back as she tried to think at lightspeed.

I can't pull my piece. He's too far away to jump.

She kept her eyes fastened on the man's face, knowing that his eyes would warn her before he pulled the trigger—

Sensei says I'm good enough to dodge bullets, but this isn't how I wanted to find out!

She froze her expression into a mask of total fear as her mind ran through the position of every stick and exit in the room. The sour reek of mildew and the dust in the air almost made her sneeze—which she didn't dare; that would *surely* trigger him to shoot.

"Please," she whispered in Spanish, pleadingly, "I don't understand. . . ."

The man spat something in *Cubano* dialect so thick she couldn't make out the words. Something about informers, she thought—

There was the door behind him; a window behind her.

If I could throw myself backwards—no, it's barred on the inside.

To right and left, two cheap dinette chairs, aluminum and red vinyl. One had been hers, one his. Nothing else but the table—just bare board walls and rough wooden floor, sagging in the middle. The chairs?

Not heavy enough to stop a bullet.

Between Di and the gunman, there was only the table draped with a stained red velvet tablecloth. On the table lay something other than a crystal ball.

A sealed baggie of white powder, to be precise. *Not*

what she had expected—and her face had given her away.

Smack. Gods help me, a heroin dealer. Where in hell is Mark? Never mind that; you're an empath—project, dammit!

She oozed innocence, helplessness, from every pore, projecting with every erg of energy she had to spare.

Hey man, I'm nothing but a stupid chick looking for a fix on the future, not a drug fix. I just walked in here by dumb accident. I look just like your airhead kid cousin—

She held out her hands, empty, imploringly. The gun wavered. The man's thin face turned puzzled, then predatory.

Good—oh good, I hit a nerve. C'mon, sweetie, remember how you used to want to get into your cousin's pants?

She turned down the innocence, turned up the sex. "Please," she stammered, "I'll do anything you want—"

It was working. She could read it in his eyes, in the flavoring of his emotions. He was *still* going to kill her—but now he was thinking that he was going to have some fun, first.

Mark, where the hell *are you?*

The man grinned; his teeth were stained and yellow, and too large for his thin face. He looked like a horse, truth be told. An *ugly* horse.

The muzzle of the gun moved a little aside; it was no longer pointing at her, but at the floor to her left. The man was relaxed now, his finger easing a bit on the trigger—

And there was a familiar *presence* at the window behind her.

Mark!

She waited; prayed he'd see the opening she had created. Held her breath and felt the tension behind her arc to a peak.

A welcome shout. "*Down!*"

She obeyed, throwing herself to her right, rolling on her shoulder, and coming up with her own gun in her hand as three shots crashed through the window to take the drug pusher in the head, neck, and chest.

The man was thrown back by the impacts, jerking with each hit—his face and torso blossomed into ruined meat. The last shot sent him sprawling on his back in the doorframe. The body twitched, then stilled.

She fought down nausea. *Oh gods—I can't—I—dammit, I've seen plenty of bodies before, I—oh gods.* She swallowed, tasted bile, swallowed again. *I've got—calm, calm, back to balance—* She managed to distance herself for an instant; it was enough—

She started to holster her own gun with hands that shook, then thought better of the notion.

That bastard might not be alone. Just because you don't feel anybody in the house—

So she stayed right where she was, crouched in the darkest corner, ears alert for any sound, however small.

It seemed an age before she heard a footstep she knew, and Mark's whistle.

Di sprawled on the passenger's side of the Ghia, half in, half out, holding her hands out in front of her with a look of exhausted concentration.

Both hands were trembling like cottonwood leaves in a high wind.

The block had been cordoned off and Narcotics was dealing with the mess inside. There must have been ten squads parked, and half as many unmarked cars; the place was swarming with cops, uniformed and plainclothes. So far as Mark was concerned, he was overjoyed to have them around.

"Well that's a new one," Mark mused, as Di slowly brought her shaking hands under control. "A pusher setting up as a medium—"

"I'm not too surprised he gave you the creeps," she replied, her voice dulled with fatigue. "My god, what a scam. You just trot up to the door, and say you need help—that got you in the door. Then you say that Angelita sent you. That got you to the table. *Then* I guess whatever your 'problem' was told him how much and what you wanted."

"And you just stumbled on the code words—here—"

Mark reached behind the seat of the Ghia, took out a thermos, and poured her half a cup of lukewarm coffee. She took it from him, and managed not to spill any.

"Not quite—I was extended and feeling for trigger phrases. Sometimes I can do that if my subject is pretty hyper—"

"Considering he was dipping pretty heavily into his profit margin, I should *figure* he'd be hyper!" Mark replied, looking up to see the shrouded body bag being carried out to the ambulance. "He was heavy into coke. From what I found in the other room, he'd done two, maybe three lines before you came tapping on his door, and *his* stuff wasn't cut much."

She shuddered. "That—gods. That's the closest I've ever come to getting ventilated, honestly. Arcane danger I can deal with but—I swear, Mark, if I'd had any idea what was going on in there I never would have walked into that one. That was *not* a job for me—that was for the pros. Gods, it was worse than *anything* occult."

"Shit, *I* wouldn't have let you walk into that. But you did okay, spooky," he said softly, sincerely. "You did okay. You did everything exactly right, like we'd practiced it. Narcotics is real happy with both of us right now."

She glanced over at him, and he saw that the makeup covering her black eye was beginning to run. She managed a wan smile. "We pick up some points, partner?"

"More'n a few. You about ready to call it a day?"

She sighed and handed back the thermos top. She'd drained it so dry there wasn't even a hint of liquid left in it.

"It's a day," she said.

Sherry woke before Bobby's moans of fear grew loud enough to really *hear*. But she heard them—as she usually heard them.

Mother's instinct, she thought, feeling what was shamefully close to relief when she realized that the other half of the bed was as empty as when she'd gone to sleep. At least Robert wasn't back yet; he was more hindrance than help when Bobby was in one of these states, growling at him that he was being a baby and that it was time for him to grow up—

She slid out of bed without bothering to turn on the light, using only the dim illumination from the readouts of the various high-tech goodies in the bedroom to see by. As she hurried down the hall, the carpet warm and soft beneath her bare feet, Bobby began to cry.

She sat on the edge of the bed and began stroking his forehead, waking him gently. She'd found out the hard way that waking him at once left him dazed and petrified with fear for nearly an hour, and that turning on the light made things worse.

She murmured his name, softly, as she gentled him— and finally the dull, weary crying stopped. "M-m-mommy?" he faltered.

"I'm here, baby," she said, only now taking him into her arms. "It's okay, you just had another bad dream."

Thank God this dream hadn't been as bad as the ones of the past three nights—where he'd woken up drenched with sweat and screaming about blood. He was just a little warm, and clung to her with trust rather than the despair he'd shown then. She hugged him close, breathing the soapy-clean scent of his hair as he tucked his head under her chin.

"Better?" she asked.

He nodded a little. "Mommy?" he asked, finally, "When's Mark going to come over again?"

"I don't know, munchkin," she replied, wishing that she did know the answer to that question, and shifting a bit so that the bedsprings creaked. "What brought that on?"

He sniffed, and she felt him scrub at his eyes with the back of his hand. "The Mean Ladies," he said, finally.

"Is that who you were dreaming about?"

He nodded again, his hair tickling her chin. "They don' come over when Mark's here."

Perceptive little lad, aren't you? she thought, startled. Two of the three models *had* been over after dinner this evening; Lupe and the youngest, Conchita, the one with the come-hither eyes and the air of a girl who'd trip a man she wanted and beat him to the ground. . . .

Sherry stroked Bobby's hair and schooled herself not to tense up; he would read that, he was *very* good at body-language. No doubt, that was what had kicked off tonight's nightmare, his picking up the tension between herself and Robert.

The initial tension, anyway; once Lupe had decided to exert her charm, she'd succeeded in lulling all of Sherry's ugly suspicions away until she and her sister had left with Robert—ostensibly heading for the studio.

But once they had gone, the suspicions returned.

Bobby went limp, which told her he'd fallen asleep. She eased him back down into the bed and tucked the covers around him, carefully and slowly, so as not to wake him again. But when she returned to her own bed, it was to lie wakefully staring into the dark.

Robert had gotten so—strange—since last year. Yet the personality changes she thought she was seeing were hardly fitting any pattern. Some might have thought them positive. He'd become almost a workaholic—sure, he was playing around with the girls, but a good many of those photo sessions really *were* what they were supposed to be; Robert had the photos to prove it. He hardly slept more than three or four hours a night anymore; the rest of the time he was out—at the studio was what he said. . . .

But—the relationship he had with the girls went far beyond the flings he'd had before. The five of them seemed to be able to communicate without words, and to be wrapped up in some secret project or other that obsessed all of them. It was a relationship that left Sherry totally on the outside, and feeling like a stranger.

She longed for the times when Mark appeared for an evening; then Robert went back to his old self, laughing, joking—relaxed, with no signs of the cold intensity that frightened her so much.

Mark was such a *good* friend; so compassionate, trying so hard to be the buffer between Robert and herself. He was giving Bobby the male affection he needed, the affection Robert couldn't seem to show. But then Robert was an only, with an ultra-macho father, and Mark came from a huge family, all of them used to showing their feelings openly. It was too bad Mark's family had scattered all over the globe—parents in California, one brother in Minnesota, one in Vermont, two in the Navy, and the sisters in Seattle, Chicago and Florida. Only his aunt remained—

But Mark's loss was Sherry's gain. She didn't think she'd have been able to cope without his help, now that Robert had gotten so strange.

She turned restlessly, and stared at the glowing numbers of the digital clock without really seeing them. She wondered where Robert was tonight. He never bothered to tell her where he was going anymore.

But it wasn't as if he was being cruel—it was more that he was preoccupied with whatever was obsessing him.

She suddenly wondered if the girls could be getting him involved in some kind of cult—

It would certainly fit the symptoms: the preoccupation, the personality changes, the way he behaved when he was with the girls, like they were all part of some in-group.

If it was a peyote or mescaline cult, that would make even more sense. It would account for the reason he was sleeping so little, and for the incredible energy he seemed to have these days. Psychogenic drugs had caused positive personality changes before this—but if they were giving him delusions of grandeur, that would account for the way he'd been distancing himself from Sherry and Bobby—

In the next moment the notion seemed stupid. Robert had *never* been interested in any sort of religion, not even back in the sixties, and he'd been loudly and impatiently scornful of those of their friends who'd been into the drug scene. She couldn't see any reason why he'd change now.

Maybe it was her.

Maybe—maybe she had just gone dull since Bobby was born. She used to share in what he was doing, even to helping in the darkroom; she hadn't done that in at least a year. In fact, she'd closed *herself* off from *him*—letting her jealousy of the girls drive her out of the room when they appeared, dismissing shots of them with a feigned boredom. She'd been closing herself into the workroom more and more—and God knows Robert had always found her craftwork yawnacious.

Maybe it was her fault that they were drifting apart.

She wished she could talk with Mark; he always listened so patiently. And when he did give advice, it was generally good. And she could always count on him to be honest; if this was her fault, he'd tell her. And maybe he could tell her how to get Robert to show a little affection to his son—

Dear, sweet Mark, she thought, as she finally became tired enough to drift into sleep. *He's always there when I need him.*

· SEVEN

THE WINDOWLESS ROOM WAS DARKENED, SHADOW-SHROUDED, and echoingly empty. Oddly shaped metal structures, like robotic mantises, were pushed into one corner. Dim reddish light came from somewhere behind a massive chair, the only piece of furniture in the room. There was a man in that chair, a man hardly more than a deeper shadow within a shadow.

The door opened, then closed softly again, and a woman stepped into the barren room, her footsteps echoing from the pale, blank walls. Her name *had* been Lupe. Now it was Chimalman; fitting, for that had been the name of a great woman warrior—and she was now a warrior of a different sort.

She had come straight from the street without pausing to change into more suitable garb. Although it was not fitting, she was clothed as these northern invaders were. She hurried to the thronelike chair, and once there, prostrated herself at the feet of her lord and god.

He brooded, unspeaking, his shadows and silence taking on a palpable weight, that his priestess might feel the ponderous bulk of his power before he acknowledged her presence.

Her costume did not please him; she knew that—he

had more than once rebuked her for appearing before him in such clothing. He was making her feel the weight of that disapproval before he would move on to the business that had sent her out into the street.

"Speak," he said at last, in the old tongue. The single word filled the room.

"The witch is still baffled," the girl replied, not daring to raise her head from the floor. "But she is not deterred. She is more stubborn than I had anticipated—and the man—"

"What of the man?" Some vague emotion sharpened his tone, and she trembled.

"He is clever—and he is working *with* her, warrior with warrior. He is as much of a danger as she—"

"No!" The god leaned out of shadow, and his servant, now gathering her courage enough to raise her face a trifle, could see conflicting emotions at war within him by the subtle clouding of his eyes.

"Lord?" she replied tentatively. When the god warred with himself, sometimes it boded ill for his handmaidens.

"No." He settled back into his seat, back into the shadow. "No, the man is not to be tampered with. Nor, for now, the witch. So long as she remains baffled—"

"And if she does not?" she ventured tentatively.

"Witches—" he pondered that for a moment. "They are chancy to deal with at best. I do not know the powers of this one—and this land is *her* home. I know not who or what she may call upon. The wise warrior does not waste his strength. She could cost us more than we can afford at this early stage. Yet she is only one—hear me; if she sniffs too closely upon our trail, warn her off in a way that she cannot mistake."

"And if she will not heed the warning?"

"Kill her."

The priestess sat back on her heels. "To your glory?"

"No," he replied, "That is too dangerous. Kill only."

"But the man, lord—"

"Enough, leave be." The impatience in his tone made her prostrate herself again. "Without the witch, he is of no importance. I say you shall leave him alone. Let us seek another, more easily obtained sacrifice."

It was sunset, and Ben Bronson whistled as he headed up the cement walkway to the ultramodern glass-and-steel RemTech building; he was feeling very pleased with himself, and looking forward to a few pleasant hours *away* from his wife and kids. He'd headed over here as soon as supper was over. Remtech was more home to him than his house was—especially with the youngest teething. Julie seemed to think *he* should help out with the kids when he was home. Fat chance; that was woman's work. He hadn't married her just so he could become a babysitter. There were lots more important ways to spend his time than in fooling around with a drooling little brat. Kids were for showing off when they were clean and acting intelligent, not for hassling over when they were being pains.

"Hello, Ben." The voice made him jump.

Lanky, nerdy Steve Barrigan materialized out of the door-alcove, letting the door close and lock behind him. Ben sniffed in annoyance, and reached for his keycard; after startling him like that, the *least* the jerk could have done was to hold the door for him!

"Steve," he responded shortly.

"About those enhancements to the Pancyber project—"

"I told you I'd get back with you on that." Barrigan *would* bring that up. Ben had hoped he'd forgotten. He pushed his way past the tech into the alcove.

"Yeah, you did," the tech replied, pushing his glasses up on his nose. "You said they were probably not going to want my enhancements. Funny thing, I found out tonight that you took all my programs and implemented them with your initials on them. Is that why you got a raise this week and I didn't?"

Ben jerked his head around so quickly his neck nearly snapped. "How—"

"You forgot, *I'm* the one that coded the production protections, you lying bastard," Steve said pleasantly. "I can track anything I need to—and I figured it wouldn't hurt to check up on what *you'd* been doing lately. Glad I did." He held out his clenched hand, and opened it. Pieces of cut-up keycard fell to the cement with tiny clicking noises. "By tomorrow morning everyone else will be onto you, too. I added a little warning to everyone about you on the sign-on bulletin, one you can't get rid of. I don't think you'll be able to get away with that trick again. By the way, you'll find my resignation on your desk. *If* you can get in."

"What do you mean if—" Ben was too stunned by the tech's revolt to really take in more than the last sentence.

Steve had started to walk into the gathering twilight, but turned just long enough to answer. "You also seem to have forgotten that I used to work on the security systems. They never took away my access. So Ben, ol' buddy, the lock don't recognize you no more. Bye."

Then he was gone. And Ben jammed his keycard repeatedly and with growing anger into the reader— with no more result than if he'd used his MasterCard.

Finally he began circling the building, looking for someone to let him in, trying to think of ways to *get* that arrogant little sonuvabitch.

I'll see he never gets another job in DP again—he's gonna be washing dishes for the rest of his life!

He found lit windows—and beyond them, a cluster of two or three people from another department—he knew them, vaguely. He sighed with relief, and pounded on the window.

They looked up—and must have seen him, seen him clearly. But they acted as if they *hadn't* seen him, and went back to their discussion, ignoring further window-pounding. Ben's temper and blood pressure rose.

They were all in this together, the jerks! By God, he'd have them *all* on the carpet!

If he could just get in.

There were lights on in inner offices, but no one came to see who was making the noise. And by the time he'd circled back to the office where he'd seen those three Judases, the lights were off and they were gone from view.

After circling the building fruitlessly until it became

full dark—after calling every number he could think of inside and getting no response, he finally gave up. He was so angry he could hardly think.

He was certainly too angry to hear the soft footsteps behind him as he headed for his car.

This "Athena" was not living in luxury accommodations. The bus had passed through a pretty dubious neighborhood to get to hers; Mark would not have been amused. As a matter of fact, Di rather doubted that Mark would have let her come here at all if he'd known where she was going.

But this was going to be tricky enough without having him along, bless his pointed little head. She'd left her gun behind, knowing that if the woman was good enough to spot it through Di's disguises, she'd freak at worst, and clam up at best.

It had taken an hour and a half by bus to get this far, and she still had six blocks to walk. She huddled in her denim jacket and concentrated on being invisible. But there was a palpable aura of *hunters* all around here, an aura she could taste, a hint of hunger in the back of her mind. She felt as if she was swimming in a pool filled with sharks.

The address was one more battered little stucco house, surrounded on all sides by similar buildings. The only real difference between this place and the ones to either side of it was that Athena's house didn't have three cars up on blocks in the scrap of front yard, or growling dogs chained in the back.

Di picked her way across the cracked sidewalk and up to the porch. There had been some effort at keeping the weeds and lawn under control here, as opposed to next door. There was no doubt in Di's mind just where the "threshold" of the house was; as soon as she climbed the pair of crumbling concrete steps and got onto the porch she could feel the barrier—

No bad idea; extend your threshold out a little beyond the house walls, and maybe people won't break in, she thought with surprise and approval. *I'll have to try that one myself.*

There was a tiny, faded, hand-lettered sign tapcd over the doorbell—"please knock, bell does not work." She tapped lightly on the metal frame of the storm door, and almost before she brought her knuckles down for the third time, the inner door cracked and a single blue eye peered out at her from around the doorframe, a security chain stretched tightly just above it.

"I'm Diana—" she said to the eye. "Noble said that he was going to call you about me."

"Yes—I've been expecting you. Just a minute, please—" The door closed for a moment and Di heard the scrape of the security chain being undone. Then the door reopened, and a slender, short-haired blond woman beckoned her to enter.

The living room was furnished mostly in floor pillows, brick-and-board bookcases, and books. Hundreds, thousands of books. There was New Age synthesizer music playing softly from a cassette deck, and the lighting was entirely by candlelight. Di took it all in with a single glance, and turned around to face her hostess.

The young woman was perhaps three or four years her junior; she was slender, but fairly strong-looking, with the kind of balanced grace that told Di she was no stranger to the martial arts herself. Her eyes were so intensely blue that there was no doubting their coloring even by candlelight, and her pale blond hair, styled almost in a crewcut, was plainly that color without help from Lady Clairol. She was wearing a faded blue T-shirt and equally faded jeans. She was, to Di's eyes, teetering on an edge between fear and nervous curiosity.

"I don't bite," Di said with a chuckle. "At least not often, or hard."

The young woman echoed the laugh shakily. "Well, pick a spot," she said. "Noble did call—he said you were to be trusted, and he told me what you wanted."

"But you're still not terribly sure of me. Don't blame you," Di replied, seating herself cross-legged on one of the nearer pillows. "I could be anybody; I could get you fired for having a weird religion."

The woman's eyes turned bitter as she took a seat herself. "No, that you can't do. I've already been fired, because I wouldn't take the nightshift. Shit, it's bad enough on graveyard when everything's normal—but now—Lord and Lady, if I put myself out on the street when *that*'s prowling—"

"You've precoged?" Di asked quietly, "that you're in danger after dark?"

Athena nodded, flushing. Di's immediate acceptance of the situation—and her easy familiarity with paranormal talents—seemed to reassure her.

"Some. But not clear enough to *do* anything. I mean, I know I'm on the menu if I go out after certain hours, but I can't tell when *it*'s going to hit, or where. But to go out night after night, during the prime time for *that* to be hunting, I'm going to be narrowing my odds to the point of suicide! But they didn't give me a choice, and they wouldn't listen to my arguments. It was my turn on third, I had to take it or get fired. I'm—I *was*—junior computer operator, low man on the totem pole."

Di frowned. "You've got grounds for a protest—"

Athena shook her head. "Unfortunately not. I'm fourth *dan* black belt; I could probably protect myself better than some of the men if this was just a slasher or a rapist. This neighborhood isn't that bad—it's only if you have to take the bus that you go through *its* hunting areas. And I would be, coming and going. There's one place where it's hunted over in the *barrio*, and another near the industrial park where I work. That's where some of the victims came from, those two places. Mass transportation isn't real good around here. You know where the bus stop is—I didn't hear a car so you must have taken the bus here. The other end for me is still a mile from the center. But when I protested, they just told me to get a car."

"Lovely." Di said sourly, as she lowered her shielding a bit. "Real caring folks, your ex-bosses. So terribly concerned about the welfare of their employees."

"I'm *trying* to save up some cash—and I don't make enough to buy anything but a junker, anyway nothing reliable, nothing that wouldn't eat me out of house and home with repair bills. So what do I do, say that I *know* if they put me on third, the local bogeyman'll get me?" Her eyes were defiant, but her mouth showed despair. "We aren't union; the only lawyer *I* could afford would lose, and I'd be out twice. Look, this isn't what you came for—"

"No, it isn't," Di agreed. But she was now beginning to have a stirring of certainty that meant she'd been brought here for a purpose. Not what she'd thought to come for—"But maybe we can help each other."

Athena looked askance at her. "Well—I can tell you right now that nobody's getting anything, and we've done Work to try and pin this bastard down. I'm talking major circles here, several groups working together. All we get is warnings. Everybody that could afford to, left. The rest of us are trying to keep our butts down. What happened to your eye?"

"My what?" Di was startled by the abrupt change of subject.

"Your eye—" the woman began, then shrugged. "If it's none of my business say so—but my Prime isn't precog, it's healing."

The blackened eye sent a dull stab of pain through Di's skull. "When you turn over rocks," she replied wryly, "things tend to crawl out. One bit me. The one that owned House of Dark Desires."

"Old Creepy-Crowley-Clone?" Athena exclaimed. "I hope you gave as good as you got!"

"I think so—"

"Look," the woman said abruptly, "I'm being rude to keep interrupting you, but I can't help it, it's the way I am. I can't see things like that eye without reacting—can I fix it for you? It's driving me bats, staring at me and hurting."

Di raised a surprised eyebrow, and cautiously let down the rest of her shields.

She was startled again by the depth of what she sensed.

Ye gods, what is a major healing talent doing wasting away out here?

"If you really want to—" Before she could finish the sentence, Athena had stretched her hand out across the space between them, and was holding it less than half an inch from Di's injured eye. Almost immediately she felt the area begin to grow perceptibly warm—

—then hot—and it began to throb, but not painfully. Di had been on the receiving end of psychic healing before, but this was *strong*. And it argued for a substantial energy base.

"Don't tell me; you're an HP, right?" she asked.

"Well—sometimes," Athena replied absently. "My group tends to share high priestess duties around. I guess you could call me that."

Which means she's the best information source I could have found—and if she doesn't know who our quarry is, then it probably isn't anyone in the movement here. Oh well. Di closed both her eyes and relaxed, setting her mind on "blank."

Some timeless span later she felt a little internal signal that said that whatever had been done was over, and opened both eyes again. Athena was shaking the hand she'd used vigorously, as if getting rid of something.

Di felt the eye that had been blackened, gingerly. It was just a scant bit more tender than the other. No swelling, no real soreness. She knew that if she looked in a mirror, she'd see only the faintest of bruises.

Well—She stretched out her empathy again. *Still waters run deep. I wonder—I wonder if I've been given something here for my other problem?* She allowed herself a trickle of hope.

"How likely are you to get another job soon?" she asked before she could change her mind.

"Not. The economy is depressed." Athena looked about ready to cry; from what Di felt from her, she'd been on the verge of it for a while.

What was she *doing as a computer operator? She was damn well wasted on those jerks! Hm—I would lay odds she was confessor and counselor to half her co-workers. And peace-spreader. Bet they find with her gone that everybody is going to be at each other's throats. Serves them right.*

"Considered moving?" she asked quietly.

"Sure. To where? With what?" Athena bit her lip, as if

to bring herself under control. "Sure, I'd move if I could. I've got no real ties here, I'd go about anywhere, but—"

"One more question;" Di took a deep breath. This woman was something very special; all she trusted told her that Athena was worthy of anyone's faith—dependable, reliable—and something more. Compassionate far beyond the norm. She didn't get *feelings* this strong very often—and when she did, by the gods, they never proved out wrong. So Di asked The Question. "Would you be willing to take on something—not a job, but it would get you moved out of here without costing you anything—that meant being constantly exposed to someone with active AIDS?"

Athena looked at her with eyes gone round. "I wouldn't go making love to anybody with it—but—I *am* a healer. What I was saving for was med school, and the whole AIDS thing was what started me on it. I mean, here were all these MD jerks refusing to treat—*somebody* has to! Maybe I haven't taken the Hypocratic Oath, but what I am is oath enough. And when somebody's in pain, I *have* to help."

"Listen—I've got a friend, he's—" Di swallowed the lump in *her* throat. "He's got it. He's sick, he's alone; his family disowned him, his lover died a year ago. He needs somebody to take care of him."

It was hard, at first, to reveal her secret; the words had to fight to get around the lump in her throat. But as she told Athena about Len, and the woman's compassion reached over into *her* heart, the words came faster, easier, until they were almost spilling out of her.

"I hadn't been a real *good* friend until all this happened, but—when Keith got sick and Len was diagnosed positive, it seemed like everybody bailed out on them. I—couldn't do that, I just couldn't."

"You'd have been awfully petty-souled if you had," Athena replied heatedly.

The wave of sympathy and care Di sensed flowing from her was so incredibly deep that she hardly dared credit it. "I was always closer to Len than Keith, so for a while I just sort of hung around, being there. Len wasn't showing any symptoms until last year, so he was taking care of Keith. They were basically coping until Keith died. Then Len fell apart—then he got too bad to work. That's more or less where I took over."

"This isn't meant to be crass—but how's the money situation?"

Di shook her head. "It's not—I know what you meant. It's something that you have to think about. Medical for both of them was covered by insurance, and I'm handling the other bills. I've got it to spare—and I'll tell you the truth, with what I get into I rather doubt I'm going to have to worry about old age, you know? So I can't see anything to save for, frankly."

It was to Athena's credit that she did not make empty noises meant to comfort. "Not if you go around chasing after things like—what's out there now. Someday something is going to be too good for you. . . . Okay, so where do I come into this? I hope to hell you don't think I can cure him—I could probably ease some of his pain, but anything else—"

"No." Di shook her head. "No, I'm not asking for miracles. It's that I can't always be there physically for him—like now. I've got other things I *have* to do—like you, I sometimes don't have a choice. He mostly needs not to be alone—to have somebody to care, to talk to. Somebody of the same religious persuasion, like us. And a stranger might be better at this point than a friend. He can be scared, be angry, break down with a stranger, where with me, he's trying to keep *me* from breaking down. Would you—consider—"

Athena touched Di's hand lightly, and the compassion she had felt earlier was nothing to what she felt now.

"How could I not?" she said simply. "Being what I am, how could I refuse, and still call myself a healer, a true child of the Lady, or even a *human?*"

Di bent her head to hide the tears. It was a few minutes before she could control her voice enough to ask, "Can I use your phone?"

Two hours later, and a substantial number of charges on her credit card, and the arrangements were all made. Athena would be flying out tonight; André would get her at the airport and take her to Lenny's. Di had known from Lenny's voice when she called him that it had been a bad day—he nearly made both women cry with his gratitude when Di told him she'd found him "a companion" and introduced Athena over the phone. He frankly sounded as if he would have welcomed the company of a drug-crazed mass-murderer, much less someone like Athena.

A moving company would pack Athena's gear and ship it off to her later this week, after picking up her key at a friend's house.

And Di's bank balance was going to be lighter by a couple thousand dollars.

She didn't care; it was money she was glad to spend. For once she could make a problem a little better by throwing money at it. That kind of solution was rare.

And the last thing on my conscience is taken care of. If I go down before Len does—he's got my insurance money, and *somebody to lean on.*

She knew Mark was puzzled; though he was sympathetic, he still couldn't understand *why* Len was so important to her. And how could she tell him? How could she explain all the times she'd felt that she'd failed other friends—how *this* time she was determined that she would not?

The last thing they did was painstakingly copy Athena's contact list into Di's notebook. Di wasn't figuring on getting a lot of information from the locals— but maybe somebody would have noticed more than Athena and her circle had.

"Just the psychics—" Di said—then amended even that. "Just the *real* Talents. Not the ones who play at it. I don't care if they're flakes, but they've got to be in practice, or they won't be able to distinguish a power-drain from a potassium imbalance."

Athena had cracked a smile at that. "Well that first narrows you down to about a tenth of the neo-pagans in Dallas, and the second to half of that," she replied. "Maybe less. Amazing how easy it is to let the mental muscles go as flabby as the physical ones, isn't it?"

It was nearly eight when she put Athena and baggage into a cab, and headed back to the bus stop.

No solutions, but—*Well, I didn't get what I came for—but I found what I needed.*

She was thinking so hard about Len that she forgot to stay alert. The streets were very quiet, almost like Hartford; it lured her into a false sense of security. She didn't notice that she was being followed until it was too late to do anything about it.

It was the sound of several pairs of sneakered feet in her wake that finally woke her to danger.

She risked a glance over one shoulder, and saw a handful of young men, all in ornately decorated jackets, following about half a block behind her. They *felt*—yes, they were after her. Predators. Hunters. And a quick probe ahead told her that there were more of the same lying in wait around the corner.

Oh, shit. No, don't run, that'll just set them off. Cross the street first, see what they do.

Half of them followed, the other half moved up to parallel her. She stumbled over broken concrete, cursed under her breath, and thought furiously.

Great, now I'm cut off in all directions. Okay, confrontation time; that's not what they're expecting, it'll buy me delay.

She stopped dead where she was, and whirled to put her back against the wall. Broken glass and trash scrunched under her feet; the brick was rough under her hands. They stopped, and milled uncertainly for a moment. She used the time to think.

Okay, no gun. I'm no karate champ; I can't take out all of them. Any help around?

She risked a glance up and down the street. It was deserted in both directions, not even a stray car in sight. And the streetlight nearest her was out.

Ain't nobody likely to even look out to see why the yelling's going on if I start raising cain. Oh hell. That leaves just one option. Now are they sensitive enough, or hopped up enough to be sensitive?

She dropped shields and touched at the surfaces of

their minds. It was like touching rotting wood and cobwebs. No doubt about it, they'd been doing *something*. That was in her favor.

Gah. They're sensitive enough. Here goes nothing. Boy, I am going to regret this in a half an hour—

She gathered the power within as they regained their gang unity and began to move in on her from both sides, laughing and spitting obscenities at her. She waited, feet slightly apart, arms down at her sides, and hands clenched, until they were just about to rush her—the moment that they were most off-balance.

Then she struck, grateful that there *were* no witnesses.

It was a two-pronged attack; she flouresced her aura in the visible range, bright as a photo-flash, and followed that by psi-bolts to the minds nearest her.

Three of those she hit grabbed their heads and collapsed, moaning. Those of the rest that had been looking straight at her yelled in surprise, temporarily blinded.

She cleared the path for escape with a couple of handstrikes and a kick to those disabled, and ran—

Behind her she could hear commotion, but it didn't sound like anyone was going to follow immediately.

Oh gods, don't let me fade out now!

She ran as fast as she could manage, her breath rasping in her throat, her feet uncertain in the half-dark on the street; her side hurt already, drained as she was by the energy expenditure. It was three blocks to the haven of the bus stop.

She stumbled, recovered, stumbled again. Two blocks —she could see it up ahead, brightly lit, with three or four people waiting wearily for the last bus of the evening. And they looked like cleaning ladies, gas-station attendants, not crazies.

Thank you, Lord and Lady.

One block; was there pursuit yet? She touched back— not yet, but they were thinking about it. But she was almost out of breath, lungs and side on fire. She had to take a break—she let herself slow, her sneakers making slapping sounds on the pavement.

She staggered the last few steps, reaching for the side

of the bus-stop shelter blindly, and sagged against the stanchion. She was well into the lighted area, but totally winded, panting like an exhausted hound.

The four—yes, four—other would-be passengers looked at her curiously, but said nothing.

Just don't let those punks get their courage up and follow, please—

A hand touched her arm; she yelped and jumped away, ready to defend herself.

And felt like a real fool, staring into Mark's disapproving eyes.

"Now that you're finished proving you can do without me, you want a lift home?" he asked quietly.

She blushed, knowing she'd been an idiot this time. But she couldn't say anything; just nodded, and followed him docilely to where his Ghia was parked down the block.

"You could have gotten yourself in big trouble, and *not* just from the you-know," he said angrily when they were out of earshot of the bus stop. "This is *not* a neighborhood to be wandering around in alone at night. You could have asked—you could have told me where you were going. I found out from Aunt Nita that you were gone, and I had to call up that voudoun guy and get the address out of him. And it *wasn't* easy. He made me go meet him in person so he could check out my vibes first."

"Mark, I admit it. Mea culpa; screwed up—" she said, exhaustion making her voice dull and lifeless. "Honest, I'm sorry. I won't do it again." The Ghia was within a few steps; she'd never been so happy to see a car in her life.

He snorted, then unlocked the car door and held it open for her. She literally fell into the front seat.

He climbed in on his side, and took a good look at her. "What in hell have you been doing, running the marathon?"

"Almost," she managed. The inevitable reaction to using that much power without preparation or proper channeling was setting in. She did not want to move, think, or talk much.

"I think I'll take you home, and leave the lecture for tomorrow," he said abruptly, turning the ignition key.

She felt the psi-bolt backlash headache beginning to start, just behind the middle of her forehead, and figured he *might* just have saved his own skin with that statement. . . .

Bridger was heading back to his camp under the bridge in a sour mood. Panhandling had been none too good today; he'd be sleeping with an empty belly if he hadn't found that half pizza in the trash. As it was, it wasn't gonna be easy to get to sleep; his teeth hurt and the pepper on the pizza was still burning down in his guts. The sunset was glorious; he couldn't appreciate it.

No money, no booze, he grumbled to himself. *No jobs, either*. He'd take a job if he could find one, not like some of the other bums out here. He only drank enough to keep his teeth from hurting so damn much. If he could get 'em fixed, he wouldn't drink at all.

No work for a roughneck, 'specially one that can't read but his name, he gloomed. *Maybe I oughta take them Bible-thumpers up on that offer.* . . .

He considered it, then shook his head: *Naw. Can't stomach listenin' to 'em preach at me every other minute. I'll go get mad, an' maybe sock one of 'em, an' be out on the street again.*

He sighed, longing for the smell of petroleum and dust and sweat that was the oilfields at full production. *Never thought I'd miss that in a zillion years.*

He trudged on, feeling the rocks through his thin bootsoles, so lost in melancholy recollection— interrupted from time to time by his aching teeth—that when he saw Jimbo and Billie waiting for him by the bridge in the blue half-light of dusk he half thought he was still daydreaming.

He only realized that he wasn't when they spotted him, gave a whoop, and rushed him.

Seeing his two old buddies was enough to make him forget his teeth hurt. They cussed, and pounded on each other, and carried on like lunatics for a good five minutes

before he got calmed down enough to talk sensible to
them.

"You jerks, you lookin' good—I never reckoned I'd'a
missed you bums—" He suddenly remembered why
they weren't supposed to be in town. "Hey, I thought you
boys had a job—"

Billie shook his head, his hair flopping down into his
eyes the way it always did. "Didn't pan out; some
wildcatter, I guess. Went bankrupt about the time we hit
the site. They gave us 'nough bus money t' get back here,
an' that was it."

"Well, shit."

"Big ten-four," Jimbo agreed, scratching a two-day
beard.

"Hey, I ain't got but a mattress but—"

"No man, that's what we came lookin' fer *you* for,"
Billie interrupted. "Hey, you et?"

"Could stand some more, iffen y'all got it."

"Lissen—you got anythin' back there in that hole you
want?" Jimbo asked suddenly.

Bridger thought, and shook his head. "Naw. Anythin'
any good got stole a long time ago."

Billie was wearing a backpack that Bridger didn't
remember. He pulled it off and rummaged in it. "Here,
when the chick gave us eatin' money, she tol' us t' get
what we wanted, and I thought I'd pick up somethin' fer
you—" He held out a cheap plastic thermos-cup, the
kind they gave away in convenience stores, and a slightly
squashed hoagie. "Triple cream in th' coffee, an' turkey
an' mayo. You an yer touchy gut, gah. Do I ferget my
friends, or what?"

"Oh man—" Bridger did *not* snatch at the sandwich,
but he did bolt it and the lukewarm coffee so fast the
others had hardly time to grin. "—Billie, you are a
helluva buddie, that's all I gotta say," he managed,
wiping his mouth on his sleeve. Already the mild sandwich and the cream in the coffee were calming the storm
in his gut. "Now—what chick? You find a soft touch, or a
bleedin' heart or what? Hey, you lookin' to be Midnight
Cowboys or somethin'?"

Jimbo grinned. "Shee-it, no. Ugly suckers like us?

Gimme a break. Naw, we hit somethin' better'n that; we got us three real live jobs."

Bridger snorted. "Pull th' other one."

"No shit," Billie insisted. "We was sittin' at the bus stop, tryin' t' figger if we got 'nough to pick up a burger or if we gonna have t' hit the Bible-pushers. 'Long comes this car; fancy one, man, a Caddy. Chick drivin'; stops, pulls over, asks us if we're roughnecks."

"We said yeah," Jimbo took up the story. "She says, 'You wanta try drillin' fer water steada oil? Boss's lookin' fer men useta bein' on rigs.'"

"Well, we figgered, sure. But she give us a card, said t' meet her over by White Rock Lake Park t'night 'f we're innerested," Billie continued. "She give us some eatin' an' bus money, an' that's when we thought, hey, maybe this's okay, y'know? Like, she just *gave* us the bread. She weren't wearing no fancy suit, but she weren't wearin' no bluejeans, neither. Looked like some gal might work outa an office."

"She said no more'n three," Jimbo finished. "That's us an' you, we figgered. An' we looked th' card up in th' phone book. It's real, man. Real comp'ny, real rigs."

Bridger just stared. "I—"

"Yeah, no shit, feel th' same," Billie nodded. "Look, it ain't that far, last bus's due, what say we head out? Nothin' else, we c'n maybe sleep in th' park, and we et—"

Bridger laughed. A *job!* A real, live *job!* "Sure, why the hell not! Maybe our luck's finally changed!"

"I am *not* taking you back to Aunt Nita in the shape you're in now," Mark said, trying to keep one eye on Di and the other on his driving. "She'll have my hide!"

"I'll be all right in a bit," Di mumbled, sunk in the seat next to him, with both hands over her eyes. "I just need a few minutes to rest."

"Looks to me like you need more than a few minutes—" he dodged a car running a red light, and swore at the driver under his breath. *Dallas traffic gets more like a demolition derby every day.* "I'm gonna take you home with me whether you like it or not—we'll see if some sugar, protein, and aspirin can't straighten you out, huh?"

"Bananas," she replied from behind her hands.

"Is that a commentary or a request?"

"Request." Sounded like her words were coming through a strainer. "And Gatorade."

Supermarket—supermarket—where do I find a supermarket around here—ah! He spotted a lit sign and changed lanes so fast he probably left swearing drivers in *his* wake. He pulled into a vacant slot; fortunately it was too late for there to be much in the way of customer traffic. He had his booty and was back in the car so fast that Di nearly socked him one, evidently thinking he was a stranger.

"Jeez, some gratitude!" he complained, handing her the paper sack.

"Sorry." She rummaged in the bag at once, the paper popping and crackling, before he even had the car started. She emerged with the bottle and pried the top off like a wino with the shakes and a new bottle of Thunderbird.

He stared in awe as she downed nearly half the bottle before pausing for a breath.

"Good God, how can you drink that stuff *straight?* Yech! There's aspirin in there too."

"Don't ask." Without another word she finished the bottle, using the last gulp to wash down a couple of aspirin.

She sank back into the seat with a sigh, some of the pinched look gone from her face; put the empty bottle on the floorboards, and fished out the bananas.

"Monkey food?" she offered, handing him one.

"Don't mind if I do," he replied, accepting it. "Now, you mind telling me what happened out there?"

"I was stupid. I mean really stupid. I put myself in a situation where I had to use real live magic to get away—and I wasn't ready for it. Then to add insult to injury, I sprinted three blocks. Blew my electrolyte balance all to hell. Gave myself an instant morning-after without a night-before."

"Huh?" Mark replied, a little baffled.

"TANSTAAFL, my friend. 'There ain't no such thing as a free lunch.' Magical energy has to come from somewhere, just like physical energy. Guess I never told you that, huh? Well, I didn't have the right gear with me for self-defense against normals, only against paranormals. And if I'd been thinking I would have taken that gun with me, and taken the chance on Athena spooking. It's only the fact that I'm used to shooting from the hip that gave me *anything* to use in self-defense. So I squeaked out, but I paid for it. Give me an hour and a couple more bananas, I'll be okay. And I am *not* going to do that again."

He shook his head. "I hope the trip was worth the cost of the ticket."

"Hm. Well, it was worth it to me, personally, but not to the case—no, I lie. This contact was entrenched well enough in the neo-pagan community that she'd have known if our group was in that net—and they aren't. She couldn't identify them either."

"You said," Mark reminded her, "That we might have to go at this by process of elimination."

"I did. Okay, so tomorrow we go cruising. We're going to be talking to some more folks like my contact, more of the sensitives in the neo-pagan network; and while we're at it, we're going to be looking for two things—"

"Shoot."

"One—we'll be checking the Middle Eastern enclaves for 'protections'—amulets in windows, designs painted on alley walls, that kind of thing. If it's coming from there, the folks of those nationalities will know about it, and be actively warding against it. Like a Kali cult—neither devout Hindus nor Sihks are real fond of the cults that distorted the worship of Kali. These folks might not be willing to talk, but I'll know what to look for."

"And number two?"

"We're going trolling for gypsies. Noble told me that not *all* of them were gone—and as it happens, I have a hole-card. I did the Lowara Rom a big favor a while back. Big enough that it's an embarassment to them, and they'd like the scales evened up. I think it's time I called it in."

· EIGHT

IT HAD BEEN AN EXHAUSTING SEVERAL DAYS, AND MOSTLY fruitless. More than once Mark had thought longingly of visiting Sherry—

But no. He contented himself with calling Robert— timed for an hour when he knew *damned* well Rob wouldn't be home—and gave her a vague sort of rundown on what was going on. And why he wouldn't be dropping by for a while. They'd talked for a lot longer than he'd planned, nearly two hours. Rob seemed to be burying himself in his work, and Mark frankly couldn't tell her if that was good or bad, or even if it was likely to last much longer. All he could do, really, was be an ear for her. The disappointment in her voice when he told her he wouldn't be by for at least a couple more weeks almost broke his resolve—

But work came first.

Chasing down the list of neo-pagans this "Athena" had given Di had proved more bewildering than anything else. They were a real odd lot—some about as ordinary as a dictionary; people Mark would never have guessed had odd tastes in religions. Certainly not the kind he would have picked as being psychic. Computer people, teachers, clerks—real suburban types, complete with station wagon and kids. But some—

Some were as weird as snake shoes, and as flakey as granola. Mark found himself wondering—if this was the "cream of the crop," what were the *rest* like?

There was the tiny, bespectacled lady with a house full of reptiles, including a twelve-foot python, which she fed while they were there—Mark would rather not have had that particular educational experience. He really had not seen the need to know how pythons ate. But that wasn't all—she *talked* to them. She kept a big lizard on her lap, petting it, the way anyone else would pet a cat. She had actively, *sadistically* enjoyed Mark's uneasiness, too.

There was the long-haired guy in the Grateful Dead shirt and hat who was composing music for whales—or so he said. Mark wasn't sure if he meant he was composing it for them to *hear* or that he was composing the music on their behalf, like some kind of cetacean dictation machine. The guy hadn't been real clear—his conversation tended to wander down strange little side paths. And even when he wasn't going on about the vibrations from the neighbors, he kept changing the subject back to his music, to the point of insisting on playing them bits of it. Thank God it had at least been easy to listen to—the guy may have been weird, but he was a decent musician. Mark had more than a suspicion that the guy was on something—acid maybe, or mushrooms; he sounded like it and looked like it. But what the hell, he was Homicide, not Narcotics, and the guy was looney, but he wasn't hurting anybody but himself with that stuff.

There was the couple in purple robes with little pyramids *everywhere*—even suspended over the bathtub. Mark was ready to run for the car after five minutes in their presence. They were as bad as all the crazed maiden aunts in the world rolled up into two bodies. They *could* not be kept to the subject. They kept trying to get both of them to drink weird herb tea, stuff that smelled like a moldy meadow. And they had no interest in discussing the cult-killer. Instead they practically held the both of them down by force, and gave them long, rambling discourses about their own past lives, going all the way back to the caves.

Then there were the ones that looked like they'd just gotten off the set of a sci-fi movie—a group of five wearing identical silvery leotards; they looked and acted like clones, finishing each other's sentences—who said they were Atlantean ambassadors. Mark didn't have to deal much with them. They ignored him totally, as if he was invisible. If he wanted questions answered, he had to relay them through Di. It was a rather unnerving experience.

The *real* spooky ones were the ones—about a half a dozen altogether, all solitaries—who kept talking to their crystal pendants. It was hard to act normally when they were asking the crystals' opinions, and including the rocks in on the conversations.

But none of the weird ones bothered him down deep the way some of the "normal" ones did. The ones who wouldn't talk with him around at all; who seemed as frightened of him as if he were the representative of the Holy Inquisition. He felt uneasy, and obscurely ashamed, as if *he* was the one directly responsible for whatever had happened that made them so frightened of real-life authority. Living in fear like that—their fear almost made him nauseous.

And that fear seemed obscurely familiar. It was a while before he remembered where he'd seen a pathological fright equaling theirs in the past. It had been in the eyes of an old Jewish woman who'd survived the Holocaust.

Homicide had been wanting to question her about something she might have seen—but a uniform, *any* uniform, sent her into a state of panicked paralysis. He'd been in plainclothes, so he'd been yanked in to talk to her. *She'd* looked like that, before he took her away from the uniforms that called up old, bad memories of the SS and the concentration camps, and gotten her out into the open air and a park bench. He certainly had never expected to see that same fear in the eyes of people his age and younger, born and raised in the "land of the free."

That he *had*—that depressed him. And made him angry, though his anger had no target. And he wasn't sure how to deal with the situation, or the emotions it had raised. . . .

But while he wrestled with uncomfortable thoughts, Di questioned all of them, even the fruitcakes, with apparently unlimited patience.

Mark could understand her thoroughgoing care with the "normals," but not with the others. But when he asked her why she was bothering with a bunch of folk who obviously didn't have all of their ducks in a row, she just shrugged.

"You just happened to be *damned* lucky, Magnum," she'd told him. "Your particular sensitivity didn't show up until you were old enough to handle it. That isn't always the case. Think about what *you* might have grown up like if you'd gone mediumistic when you hit puberty—"

Mark gave that some thought. "I think I would have ended up in the school shrink's office," he said finally. "Or else—gotten a rep as a real looney."

"And when kids get a rep for being looney— frequently they decide subconsciously that it's easier to give in to the rep," she said sadly. "Then, if they're lucky—and usually around college age or later—some of these so-called 'looneys' find the neo-pagan movement. And they find out they really *aren't* crazed. Only—by now they *are*, just a little, as a result of living to that stereotype that they were stuck with as kids. But at least they're happier, and they've found somewhere where they're accepted. So if they live out a few gentle fantasies, where's the harm?"

"None," he admitted. "But—"

"No 'buts.' They may be odd—they may be living in a world that's half fantasy; that still doesn't make their talents any the less valid," she interrupted firmly. "If there's anyone who has *any* inkling of who's doing all this, I'm going to find that person. And there's only one way to do it."

He'd sighed. "Legwork; and among the whole lot of them."

"Roger." She smiled. "Just be glad Athena weeded out all the marginals and the ones with no psi at all. We could have been at this for months."

He shuddered.

Then there was search number two.

Mark had been in and out of more weird little stores in the past week and a half than he ever dreamed existed in Dallas. Thai groceries, Pakistani herb stores, Indian sari shops—it was fascinating, if tiring, but it hadn't been entirely pleasant. Not *unpleasant*, though he'd discovered the hard way that there were a number of spices and incenses he was allergic to. He was prepared now, but always a bit dozey from antihistamines.

Search three was getting nowhere; they had yet to find a single sign of the Romany.

He was ready to call this off; Di seemed inexhaustible.

"Not another Indian restaurant," he groaned, when Di gave him the address. He put the car in gear and sent it off down the back streets, the sun glaring off the pavement in front of them.

She sighed with a certain understanding. "Relax, you don't have to eat anything, you don't even have to go in this time. Just pull around through the alley in back. There—that'll do."

Mark echoed her sigh and obeyed, yet again grateful that the Ghia was tiny enough to squeeze through alleys lined with dumpsters. They had the windows down; it was still damned hot. The odor of garbage was flavored with weird, spicy overtones. He felt a sneeze coming on, and suppressed it. The racket of the engine bounced off the brick walls and called up vibrations in the metal of the dumpsters.

Di was scrutinizing the graffiti on the walls—but the

scrutiny seemed almost automatic. Mark got the feeling her mind was elsewhere. So far *he* hadn't seen anything in any of these alleys that looked like protective signs. It was all the same; spray-painted filth and gang-signs, and the name of an occasional rock group.

"Penny," he said, finally, cutting around two dumpsters jacknifed across his path.

"It's been real quiet," she replied. "Three days of massacres—now nothing. Fits the pattern we established, but I still don't like it. And it makes me wonder—what do they do if they can't find any victims when they need them?"

He eased his foot off the gas for a moment, and took a look over at her; she was broody-eyed, a sign that she *was* worried and disturbed.

"Maybe they store them up, like mud-dauber wasps store spiders," Mark said jokingly. Then felt a cold chill as he realized that it *might not* be such a joke. *If I were raising power with blood-sacrifice, it's what I would do. You can't always be certain a wino or a punk is gonna be in the right place at the right time. And if they can block us from even knowing what rite they're practicing, surely they could hide a few drugged-out street people from us.*

Just then they pulled out of the darkness of the alley into the sunlight. The sun bounced off the hood of the car and into his eyes; Mark reached for the sunglasses on the dashboard with a little haste. *God, it might as well be summer.* It was still so *damned* unseasonably hot—with no sign that the weather was *ever* going to turn. The weathermen had been making vague explanations about the jet stream—which meant they didn't know why it was happening either.

I wonder if they have anything to do with the weather being like it is, too?

It was an idle thought; lost as Di turned and resettled herself in her seat.

"I wonder if we had ought to check out missing persons logs," he mused out loud, as he waited for a gap in the traffic passing by the Ghia's nose. "I wonder if they *are* stocking a larder."

"Me too," she replied grimly. "And I think maybe we'd better."

"This one—"

Rubbing her temple with her free hand, Di held out one picture—just one out of all the hundreds they'd looked at. Mark took it from her. It was a fairly bland color photo, obviously an enlarged copy of someone's driver's license picture. Some guy who looked like any other desk-jockey, except for a certain petulance around the mouth and a shiftiness about the eyes.

I wouldn't buy a used car from him, that's for sure.

"Why this one?" he asked, putting it flat on the table in front of him, propping his chin in both hands, and staring at it as she keyed up the file on the terminal next to her.

"I can't 'find' him. There's a blank where he should be; it isn't a 'dead' blank and it isn't a 'gone to Rio' feeling either—that wouldn't be a blank, it would be a 'not there,'" she replied absently. There was a crease between her eyebrows that told Mark she was on the verge of a headache. "And I *can't* get inside the blank; there's protections on it I don't want to chance springing. Ah—here's two more reasons for you in the files, reasons you can give the Chief. One, he didn't pull any cash out of the bank before he vanished—"

"Hm, yeah—" Mark agreed. "When a guy is dumping his family or running from trouble at work, he usually cleans out the bank accounts."

"Exactly—which bears out my feeling that he's not on some beach somewhere. Two, though—that's very interesting. The last place he was *seen* was at RemTech, by an employee who'd just quit. Athena told me that one of the places 'it' hunted was the industrial park where she worked. Guess where RemTech is—"

"Begins to add up," Mark replied soberly. "Adds up to a total I don't like. Now how the hell do we find him if they've got him? This isn't like an ordinary kidnapping —they don't *want* to contact anyone, they've *got* what they want. What are we gonna do?"

"Well, I'm pretty sure he's probably drugged—it would be the easiest way to keep him quiet and controlled. As I said, there seems to be a kind of blank where he should be, but I can't localize it at all and I'm afraid to trance out and try anything trickier for fear I'll be triggering something. We need a better clairvoyant than I am to do that."

Mark frowned, drumming his fingers on the table. "I have the sinking feeling we're going to go back to one of those fruitloops we've been talking to."

She glared at him—and there was some real anger and resentment in that glare. "If you insist on putting it in those terms, yes. But I would like to remind you that *they* are doing *us* a favor by even talking to us. And some of them will be putting their safety and maybe their lives on the line if they work with us. You *could* be a little more open-minded."

He flushed; she was annoyed with him, and was within her rights. None of these folk were under subpoena; none of them had insulted *him*—unless you counted the "Atlanteans'" studied refusal to admit he existed. "Sorry," he mumbled. "I'm spoiled. The Spook Squad was so—normal. I mean, we were *organized*. We may have been a little bozo, but we were real careful about doing reality checks. I keep thinking everybody that's a trained psychic should be that professional."

"Welcome to the real world," she said. "Let's get to it." She stood up, shoving her chair back, and taking the photograph back from him. "We'll need this. I think our best bet might be Marion." She picked up her jacket from the table, slung her purse over her shoulder and was out the door of the Records room before he could react.

"Which one was that?" he asked, grabbing his jacket from the back of the chair and running a few steps down the echoingly empty hall to catch up with her.

"One of the ones that was scared to death of you," she answered, lengthening her stride a little so that he actually had to stretch to keep up with her. "The one with the thirteen cats and the boyfriend that wouldn't come out while you were there."

He remembered that one after a little thought, a pale, washed-out thing; no-color eyes and hair, and slightly overweight. A face so round and bland only a cop would be likely to remember it—and then only because it was *so* unlikely to be memorable. "Why her?"

"Because she and her boyfriend are much better clairvoyants than I am—and I'm better at defense than anyone in this city," she answered over her shoulder as they slipped out of the cool of the building into the hot, white sunlight. The heat blasted up at them from the baking asphalt of the parking lot and down from the cloudless sky. "We're going to need both."

Di made him go back to Aunt Nita's first; she ran inside and came back out with the carry-on bag he remembered. The one she hadn't unpacked. He got an involuntary chill, seeing it.

She was bringing out the Big Stuff then. Things were about to get very serious.

She left Mark down in the car for a long time when they got to the girl's apartment building—an old place; brick, four stories—too old for central air, and heated with steam radiators, a structure probably built between the wars. When she came back, she looked deadly serious—and asked him in a very quiet, almost toneless voice to follow her lead *exactly*.

He nodded agreement, and followed her up to the back apartment on the fourth floor.

There he was left in exile with the cats on the sun porch full of plants and candles and catboxes. They closed off the french doors into the living room and wouldn't let Mark in until the room had been—so Di told him—consecrated, cleansed, and warded.

He was just as happy. Warding he understood; he was fairly certain that *he* would not have been comfortable around a neo-pagan ceremony of "consecration and cleansing"; there was just too much Catholic still in him. In the past the few times Di had needed to do something like that she hadn't taken him along. The cats were all friendly enough company; they were overjoyed to find someone who'd drag a string around for them to chase. The windows were open and there was a really nice breeze coming through them. Each of the five catboxes had its own little wooden "house"—you hardly knew they were there except when one of the cats decided to use one. So the "exile" wasn't all that bad.

He played with the cats until his arm was tired. He was rather amazed to find how well they all got along together; he knew how Treemonisha would feel about sharing *her* space with any other cat! And she'd have taken her pique out on *him*.

Finally one of the curtained doors opened, and Di beckoned him inside.

He rose and obeyed; she shut the door behind him, the light filtering through the yellow muslin curtains on the doors was dim, but enough to see by. Marion and her nameless boyfriend were seated inside a small circle chalked on the rug. The boyfriend was dark, rather shaggy, and wearing just a pair of jeans—the girl had on a T-shirt and jeans, but nothing more. But *both* of them were scrubbed so clean they practically squeaked, and smelled faintly of herbs.

When he turned to Di, he could see that her long hair, usually free and flowing, was bound up into a knot at the nape of her neck and still damp—she smelled of the same herbal mixture.

He glanced back at the pair inside the chalked circle; they were holding hands now, and the photograph was on the floor between them.

Di was still armed; gun on the left hip, and the sheath of a knife on the other. She was wearing a heavy silver pendant with a large moonstone in the center; other than that, she looked pretty much as usual, which was a relief. He *still* kept expecting lurid lighting and bizarre costumes.

Di steered him wordlessly over to a floor pillow and shoved him down onto it. He seated himself obediently, cross-legged. The rest of the room's scant furniture had been shoved against the walls, all but a tiny table that had two knives, an incense burner, a cup, a little dish of what looked like salt, and a lighted candle on it.

Di sketched a circle in the air around him with her knife-blade, muttering under her breath as she did so. He *felt* something then; he hadn't expected to detect anything, not really—but there was something like a faint feeling of an invisible wall around him.

"*Don't* move," she told him in a fierce whisper. "No matter what happens. If you're tempted to break the circle, just sit tight and concentrate on the idea that you *aren't* there. If we're attacked, whatever comes after us is going to try to frighten us into bolting from our protections—because it won't be able to see us until we do. So *don't* break cover."

Then she left him, and knelt beside the other two. "All right, Marion—give it your best shot. If we can't find this guy I'm dead certain he's going to end up like the others—"

The girl just nodded; she and her boyfriend ignored Mark's presence completely. They let go of the hands nearest Mark; each rested the fingers of that hand on the edge of the photograph. They looked deeply into each other's eyes—and then closed them, almost as one.

And nothing happened. The dim light and stuffy, incense-scented air kept conspiring to put him to sleep. It was, frankly, boring. Mark kept looking at his watch, trying not to doze off, and trying not to fidget; Di hardly moved at all, and as for the two clairvoyants, Mark could scarcely tell that they were breathing.

Then, without any warning at all, the room was plunged into complete darkness.

Mark stifled a cry of alarm; a cold sweat broke out all over him, and he fought down the urge to jump up and head for the door.

It was a hot, stifling darkness, a darkness redolent with a metallic-sweet smell. It was nothing like the sharpness of the incense; after a moment Mark recognized it—in the small part of his mind that wasn't trying to flatten him to the floor in panic—as the odor of fresh blood.

He felt the building of a blind, unreasoning fear. It felt as if he was all alone in this endless night. Alone—

Not quite. There was something *in* that darkness, and it was trying to find him; Mark could feel the searching eyes peering blindly in his direction. Hot, hungry eyes. Eyes that wanted to find him; that *would* find him. And an intelligence behind those eyes that wanted him, wanted him badly.

I'm not here, he thought, his pulse roaring in his ears, the taste of blood in his mouth where he'd bitten his lip. *There's no one here. Nobody at all. No one here.* . . .

Anger was there, an ancient anger as sharp as broken glass. And that hunger kept searching for him.

From a thousand years and a million miles away, he could hear Di, singing something. He felt a pressure building—a *real*, physical pressure; he had to pop his ears when it began to get painful. The heat lessened just a little, and the smell; the angry hunger seemed to turn the hunt away from him.

Then it was gone, the heat and the odor with it, and the light came back to the room.

The two in the circle were huddled together; arms around each other and the picture lying forgotten and crushed under their knees. Di was on her feet beside them; with her hair come loose and flying about her, her hands over her head, palms together, the knife between them. She looked—like an outraged warrior-princess; angry, and tired, and frustrated all at once.

Mark realized at that moment that he *had* flattened himself to the carpet—still inside the invisible-but-not-unfelt boundaries of *his* circle. He slowly levered himself to a sitting position, feeling not in the least ashamed of himself. Whatever that thing had been—it had *not* been imagination, and he did *not* want to meet it again, not until he had some kind of weapon that would work against something like *that* in his hands.

Di took a deep breath and lowered her hands, slowly. She made a cutting motion beside the two next to her, and walked over to Mark and repeated it.

He felt the invisible "wall" vanish.

Di returned to the couple, who were untangling themselves from their fearful embrace.

"Anything?" she asked Marion. "Anything at all?"

The girl shook her head, tearfully. "Only th-th-the barrier, and that he's alive and in there," she stuttered. Her eyes were still dilated with fear, and she was shaking like a leaf. Her boyfriend was in the same shape, except that he couldn't even seem to speak. His back was shiny with the sweat of fear.

"I c-c-couldn't get anything else," Marion continued, unconsciously hugging herself. "Not where he is, or who has him. I got close, but—"

"He was guarded and we set off the alarm, so don't feel bad," Di replied, frustration giving an edge to her voice. "You did the best anyone could, love—you gave it all you had and there's no way anyone could fault you. Damn them anyway! Well, at least the Hunter didn't find you, or this place; I managed that much. Me, he knows about already; it'll be no big surprise that I'm still on his tail. You'll be safe enough, just like I promised."

The girl nodded; there were tears spilling now from those frightened eyes. "I tried—I-I-I r-r-really did—"

"I know you did," Di said, a little more gently. "It wasn't your fault—"

"You said 'he,'" Mark interrupted, getting clumsily to his feet.

"What?"

"You said," he repeated doggedly, trying to shake some feeling back into his benumbed legs, "'he.'"

She sheathed the knife in her belt next to her gun, and began taking the jewelry off. "So I did—" she mused. "There *was* a masculine feel to that guardian."

"I got that, too," Marion offered timidly.

"If you picked up 'male' too—then it's a damned good bet. And—that thing had the same flavor as the strongest of the five signatures I picked up. Well—that gives us a little more than we had before." She looked a little less frustrated.

"One man, four women?" Mark hazarded.

She shook her head. "No, I can't be sure of that. The

chief of this group is male; that much I'm certain of now, but the others—neuter feelings, could be male or female."

He sighed. It seemed like for every gain they made—

She nodded, her eyes bruised-looking, and rueful. "No kidding. Two steps forward—"

"One step back. And we still have no idea of where Ben Bronson is." He sighed. "Helluva haystack."

"And a damned small needle."

"Mark *stop!*"

Mark hit the Ghia's brakes; she squealed to a dead halt in the middle of the street. Di's shout, coming on top of the events of the last hour, had elicited from him a reaction even faster than normal. Fortunately there hadn't been anyone behind them—

"What—"

It was already too late.

She flung the passenger door open and was darting across the street across the Ghia's nose almost before the car stopped moving forward. This little area of fading and empty storefronts was nearly deserted under the late afternoon sun. There was only one thing Di could have been interested in—her goal could *only* be the brightly garbed woman wearing voluminous skirts who was standing in front of a little storefront. An odd storefront; it wasn't untenanted, but it had no sign, and curtains had been strung behind the empty display window.

Holy—that's a Rom—he had just enough time to think before Di reached her.

The woman suddenly seemed to notice the stranger sprinting toward her; she looked startled, then looked for one moment as if she would run away—then Di had her by the arm.

And then Di spoke a single word; spoke it too softly for Mark to hear.

But whatever that word was, it had an electrifying effect on the woman.

Her eyes went round. She stared, licked her lips nervously, and ventured a short question. Di shook her head. The woman scuffed her feet, fidgeted for a moment, and motioned to Di to enter the store—obviously a fortune-telling setup, now that Mark thought about it. Di shook her head again and pointed at Mark, still sitting stupidly in his car, blocking the (fortunately nonexistent) traffic. The woman frowned, gesticulated, argued with her for a moment. Di remained firm and stubborn, and gestured again at Mark. The woman then gave in, grudgingly.

Di sprinted back over to the car, and leaned in at Mark's window.

"Find a place to park and meet me inside," she said hurriedly. "They've agreed to talk; at least the woman has. She'll have to check with her man, but I doubt it's going to be a problem. They're Lowara, and like I told you, the Lowara *owe* me in a major way."

"They know you?" Mark asked, amazed. "They really do?"

She nodded, and pushed a bit of hair out of her eyes. "Oh yes," she answered with grim satisfaction. "There isn't a Lowara Rom that doesn't know at least the name of the Starchild. That's what they called me—after."

Before he had a chance to ask "after *what?*" she turned and sprinted back to the faded shop. Mark perforce swallowed his mystification and looked for a parking place.

He found one about halfway down the block, fed the meter, and plodded back to the storefront. The door was unlocked—he'd halfway expected the woman to lock it against him, she'd glared at him so. A bell over the door tinkled as he opened it. It was dim, the red curtains filtered most of the light; it was like being inside a reddish tent. It was cooler in here; a relief from the heat of the street outside. When he peered through the red gloom of the tiny shop, he could see that all of the walls had been draped with more fabric like the curtains, increasing the tent-impression—there was probably a door in the rear, but it was curtained off. There was just the standard round table—covered by a red velvet tablecloth, of course—and four chairs that looked fragile but proved to be wrought iron, or a good imitation of it. Di was sitting at her ease in one of the spindly little chairs beside the table. "Take a seat," she said, waving at an identical chair. "She's gone for her man."

At almost the same moment, the curtain at the back of the shop parted. A stocky, heavily moustached man with gold earrings and a kerchief around his neck stepped through. He was as dark as gypsies were popularly supposed to be; he was wearing a white, short-sleeved shirt open at the neck, and dark, heavy trousers or jeans. His face—and most particularly his eyes—looked wary and worried. He was followed by the woman, who looked quite frightened.

The man began to say something; Di held up her hand to halt him, replied, and turned to Mark.

"We're going to be speaking Romany," she said apologetically. "I'm sorry, love, but there's a lot we'll be talking about that's secret, so Yanfri wants to make sure you can't understand it. I'll translate what it's all right for you to know."

He nodded reluctantly. He didn't like it—but these weren't *his* secrets, and it wasn't his territory. Di turned back to the gypsy and indicated that he should continue. They spoke for several minutes before he nodded with reluctant satisfaction, said a few words to his lady, and vanished back beyond the curtain again.

The woman, looking a little calmer, took a third chair and placed it on the opposite side of the table from Di.

Di turned back to Mark. "What happened was that I established my credentials. Yanfri is satisfied that I am who I claimed and that what I get now will constitute a quit-claim on the Lowara; now he's turned us back over to Dobra."

The woman seated herself and began to speak, nervously. Her voice, though timid, was very musical. Mark found it quite easy to listen to her and watch her. She was really quite attractive; as dark as her man but more delicate, with a dancer's grace—though not a dancer's figure—and expressive eyes. Di listened . . .

"She says," Di said finally, "that she is afraid; that

they came here last week before anyone could pass them warnings. I assume you know that the Rom post special signs for other Rom to read—?"

Mark shook his head. "Not my department, but it doesn't surprise me."

The woman, who evidently *understood* English quite well, nodded and continued.

"She says that every Rom *kumpania*—that's a kind of extended family group—in this area is leaving; and they are *supposed* to be leaving signs and warnings on all roads out of town. She says that there is great danger."

Di turned back to the woman, and this time she spoke in English herself. "*Drabarni*, do you know from where the danger comes?" she asked. "Do you know its face, its land?"

The Rom licked her lips and spoke, softly, the words tumbling out over one another. Di listened carefully.

"She says that you and I should leave; that no one with sense will stay. She says that those of us with *draban*—that's 'magic'—are especially vulnerable, that this thing seeks those with it. It wants people like us—needless to say she's picked up on the fact that we're both psi. She says that this thing is evil, very *old* evil—"

"We already know that," Mark said. "And you know —surely *she* must know you and I can't leave. We have—"

He turned to the woman, and spoke directly to her for the first time. "We have a *duty*; if you know something of what this lady does, you must know she can't deny that duty. Please—anything you know—would be more than we have now. If we have to work crippled, it would be like sending a wounded dog to pull down a wolf."

Di broke in, her brows creased with concentration. "*Drabarni*, please—you know that what this man says is only the truth. If you know anything we don't, you must tell us!"

The Rom woman trembled at that; she clenched her hands on the table in front of her and spoke in a hurried whisper.

Di started. "*Drabarni*," she whispered in turn. "Tell me if I have mishcard you—"

She turned back to Mark with a look of grim achievement. "She says that the evil is very strong because it *belongs* here. Mark, I think she's saying it's *native* to this continent!"

They both looked back at the gypsy woman who nodded, slowly. And shivered with an absolute and undeniable terror.

By day the building was just another warehouse; empty, deserted. The company that had used it was bankrupt, the company that owned it having no luck in renting the space. The building was just another victim of the boom that had gone bust . . .

By night—

The Jaguars had always met here; Jimi had an older brother who knew a guy who'd had a job and a key to the place—and had never turned the key in when the job went down the tubes with the company. Nobody bothered to check when he'd told them he'd lost it. After all, what was there to steal in an empty warehouse? So every Jaguar had a key; it was as secure a meeting place as a Moose Lodge.

But now, since Pablo had first met Burning Water—it was more than a meeting-place. It was a temple. And now and again—like tonight—their deity would deign to visit.

Pablo prostrated himself at the feet of the god. Burning Water was seated beneath the single overhead light that they had turned on, ensconced in a throne made of old packing crates and stolen fur coats. Under the one light, the throne had a certain rough splendor. Burning Water needed nothing special; he shone with his own power, a power that made itself felt all the way across to the door of the warehouse, where two or three new recruits were huddled in slack-jawed awe. The handsome face was transformed by that power into something clearly more than mortal.

Pablo was wearing his full regalia, the outfit that marked him as Burning Water's champion (embroidered loincloth, silver and jade pectoral, and feathered armbands and headpiece), with an almost overweening pride. Tonight was the first night that the god had permitted him to wear the regalia when not actually in ritual combat. Burning Water was pleased with his champion, and Pablo was ready to dance with joy.

The god was not alone tonight; he had brought all four of his handmaidens. That meant that certainly he intended to convey something especially important. They stood, garbed in *their* full regalia, two on either side of the throne. There was Quetzalpetatl, the eldest and most serious of the four, and vacant-eyed Coyolxauhqui on his left, and sexy little Coatlicue and the chief handmaiden, Chimalman, on his right. They were like princesses, all of them, in the headdresses of quetzal feathers, their gold and jade jewelry, and their brocaded skirts and blouses and feathered capes. Even Coyolxauhqui's pale skin and slightly glazed stare (brought on by a little too much mescaline, Pablo thought privately) could not detract from the dignity she wore as naturally as she wore her cape. They stood utterly silent, and utterly graceful; not even the slightest stirring of a feather showed that they moved. And the power of the god showed, ever so slightly, in *their* eyes as well.

The concrete was cold, but Pablo hardly felt it. His excitement was more than enough to keep him warm. He trembled, not with chill, but with anticipation. He kept his eyes fastened upon Burning Water's face.

"Tomorrow," the god said at last, the power of his voice making even the simplest words full of portent, "begins the feast of Xipe-Totec."

"Yes, lord," Pablo responded, struggling with the harsh syllables of the Old Tongue. He *was* learning it—but it was harder for him; the magic of putting the words into his mind didn't work quite as well for him as for some of the others, for some reason. He'd been severely depressed about it until the handmaiden called Chimalman told him it was only because he had been gifted with the strengths and skills of the warrior rather than the scholar. Hard-faced Quetzalpetatl had undertaken to tutor him the hard way then; she was the scholar of the four, not much of a magician, her beauty a little more brittle than theirs, but brilliant with words and facts. She would, undoubtedly, become the Lord's chief minister when they ruled this land again, as Chimalman would be his chief warrior, Coyolxauhqui the seer, and Coatlicue—she would do what she did best. "Lord, we are ready. We have the ones for the burning—and have found the place to trap the ones for the feasting—"

"And We shall deal with the other sacrifices of the third day," the god replied, frowning. Pablo shivered again, wondering what could have caused that frown. "But—there is, perhaps, a problem."

"Lord?" Pablo asked, bewildered. He didn't think that there could be *anything* that could cause the god a problem.

"There is a witch," the god said slowly, his eyes darkening with thought. "She seeks for Us. Already she has probed the edges of Our defenses. She is strong, and it would not be wise to rouse her to attack at this time. Therefore We desire you to warn her."

Now Pablo was truly bewildered. "Warn her, lord? How do you mean?"

"We wish you to follow her—then strike. Strike and kill. Strike close enough and in such a way that she knows it *could* have been she you took."

For the first time Chimalman moved. She leaned close to the god, her eyes blazing with emotions Pablo could not fathom. "The man, lord," the chief handmaiden said viciously. "it *should* be the man—he is a danger as long as you let him live. I, your right hand, say this to you!"

"We have said once—*the man is not to be harmed.*" The god's eyes flamed red with anger, and Pablo cringed. *He* would not have dared to anger the god that way.

"Come—" Burning Water beckoned imperiously, and Pablo inched forward until his head nearly touched the god's sandal. The god leaned forward a little; Pablo closed his eyes and felt the light touch of the god's hand upon his head, then felt the power of the god pour through him.

A picture formed against the darkness of his closed lids; a young *gringo* woman; tiny, big-eyed, long-haired. Pretty piece. For a *gringo*.

"The woman," said Burning Water.

Another picture took her place; a man, Hispanic, handsome, with more than a little Mestizo in him by the nose and cheekbones.

"The man that you are *not* to harm," said the god, forcefully. Chimalman sniffed a little; for her sake Pablo hoped that it was not in derision.

The god's hand lifted from Pablo's head, leaving behind a tingle of power that filled his whole body with a rush better than the best coke. "Do you understand what you are to do?"

Pablo lifted his head and his eyes to the face of his god. "Yes, lord," he said, filled with elation that Burning Water had chosen *him* for this important task.

The god settled back into his makeshift throne with a smile of satisfaction.

NINE ·

MARK PULLED HIS DIMINISHING ATTENTION AWAY FROM THE heavy, dusty book in his hands, sneezed, and rubbed his blurring eyes. He glanced up at the disgustingly cheerful clock on the kitchen wall, and felt even more tired when he saw what time it was.

Three ack emma. My God.

The harsh fluorescent light illuminated the mess in the kitchen and their own overtired faces without pity. The room was as deadly silent as a morgue; silent enough that the buzz of the fluorescent fixture was loud and very annoying. The only sign of life was the red light on the coffeemaker; Treemonisha had abandoned them to go curl up on Mark's bed, disgusted at the lack of attention they paid her. The sink was full of unwashed cups and plates, there was water puddled on the gray linoleum floor and coffee sprinkled over the white Formica counter. The white plastic trash can overflowed with pizza boxes and the wrappings from microwave sandwiches, some of which had missed the container and were piled around the foot of the can. The gray Formica table was crowded with the books piled between them and stained with spilled coffee and brown rings from the cups.

Di was still deep in *her* book, a frown of concentration

on her face, one hand holding a forgotten cup of coffee. She looked bad; shadows under her eyes, a prominence to her cheekbones that spoke of too many meals missed at a time where she was using every energy reserve she had.

We've been living mostly on coffee, I guess—half the time I never get her back to Aunt Nita's in time for supper. Tonight included. She's got to be running on fumes, and I'll be damned if I know how she's concentrating. Especially on this stuff. I never realized the Plains Indian tribes had so many creative ways of killing people. . . .

They'd gone from the fortune-teller's storefront straight to the university library, using Mark's credentials to cart off as many books about local history and Indian lore as they could carry. Since then they'd been poring through the books, furiously taking notes on anything that seemed relevant, stopping only long enough to microwave a couple of sandwiches and fix more coffee.

Mark shut his book and leaned his head against his hands, closing his burning eyes. Things had been nagging at him—and not just this case.

Dammit, we're at a stalemate. And too tired to make any further headway tonight. So; I've got something else I'd like to talk about. Might as well bring this out into the open before it eats at me any more.

"Di—" he said, hesitantly, prying his eyes open to look at her.

She shut her book, noticed the cup, frowned, and put it to one side. *Then* she focused on him—and her frown deepened.

"Mark—*don't* tell me you're having a crisis of conscience—"

"Huh?" he responded cleverly, then continued with dogged persistence. "Di—tell me—give me a good reason *why* everybody in the case that's a good Christian seems to be a real asshole, and everybody that's *your* kind is a good guy—"

Her lips tightened, and her puffy eyes narrowed a little.

Uh-oh; looks like I hit a nerve—

"Just one minute there, fella," she said sharply. "Let's have some definition of terms, shall we? Just what do you mean by '*your kind*,' hm?"

"Hell—*you* know what I mean—"

"No, dammit, I *don't* know!" she snapped, her patience obviously exhausted. "I'm a *lot* of things, I'm female, short, a yank, a psychic, a martial artist, a writer—and I just *happen* to be a pagan along with everything else! I *do not like* that particular phrase, 'your kind.' Seems like every time it gets used it's meant to *exclude*. And I should bloody well think that somebody who's been on the receiving end of discrimination could be a little more sensitive!"

He flushed, first with anger, then with embarrassment.
Shit, she's right. That was a pretty crude way to put things.

"I'm—sorry," he faltered. "But—it just seems like—I just don't understand some of the things I've been picking up about people's attitudes while we've been tracking down what's been happening, and—Di, I don't like what the implications are."

Di cast her eyes toward the ceiling. "*Why?*" she asked, "Why are these things always at 3:00 A.M.? And why is it always *me*? Since when do I qualify as a teacher? Nobody ever handed *me* the credentials. I never *asked* for the job."

Then she looked back at Mark, no longer angry, just weary. "Mark, *why* did you have to be different? Why didn't you go through this in college like everyone else? I'd have been happy to tell you. I sure had a helluva lot more time for three ack emma discussions back then, and a lot more energy."

"Because—I guess because I always figured I knew what I was doing, then. Now—I'm not so sure," he said, admitting now through his tone of voice that he was profoundly troubled. "You never really took me around with you like this much back in the old days. You kept the fact that you were pagan so much in the background that I was able to forget about it. And back then, the few times you hauled me with you to deal with psis that weren't on the Spook Squad—I was one of your people. Now I'm not. Now I'm The Man, and it seems like I'm a potential enemy."

She sighed. "Didn't like what you saw, hm? Okay. *Use* that brain, Magnum. In 30 A.D., who were heroes, the martyrs, the saints? And *what* was the major religion in the civilized world? The positions are just reversed, and for the same reasons. Established religion gets stodgy, mired in laws and bureaucracy, and repressive. The 'new' religion attracts the free thinkers, the ones who aren't afraid to ask questions and challenge the so-called holy writ. And those *tend* to be the humanists, too. Okay so far?"

"I guess—"

"Established religion is like established anything else. It's *easy*." She looked off into space, and paused for a moment, seemingly gathering her thoughts. "It—offers answers you can get prepackaged and predigested; right off the shelf and the same for everybody. No thinking required, much less hard thinking. Like a board game; follow the rules, you go to heaven. *That's* why established religion gets the assholes. They *aren't* 'good' Christians, Magnum—do you think for a minute any of those yuppie middle-managers that ended up as victims ever sacrificed so much as their convenience for *any* cause? No—I rather doubt they ever gave up a thing they valued for any reason or anybody. People like that aren't good anything. What they believe, they believe because it's 'appropriate,' it's what everybody believes, because it's 'the right thing to do'—in short, it's easy. Our way isn't easy—oh, we get assholes too, but they usually give up and get out or get it knocked out of them."

"Huh. I guess that makes sense. Because somebody who's really a fat-cat jerk won't get into anything that is going to give him grief—"

"Right." She nodded slowly. "As to why those so-called good Christians ended up as the victims—my opinion is that it was simple enough. I would guess it was *because* they were idiots, just like that jerk on the highway. Accidents looking for a place to happen. They lived their lives thinking they were so wonderful and invulnerable that *nothing* could happen to them—unlike *my* people, who know damn good and well that most hands are against them—so they ignored dangerous situations *my* people knew better than to walk into. And finally the odds just caught up with them."

"Okay, I can get behind that. It makes sense—they're the same 'this can't happen to me' bunch that I've seen on cases before. But—"

"But that's not all. Spit it out before it chokes you."

"But why did *you* get into this? *Why?* You told me that you were raised Episcopalian—so why did you change? I trust your judgement, Di—what is it about this pagan thing that's got *you* doing it, instead of working within the C of E the way your great-grandmother did?"

"Lord and Lady. I swear, Mark, you pick the weirdest times to go into seeker mode," she groaned. "Damn, I *wish* you'd sprung this on me back when you were on the Spook Squad."

He just waited expectantly. She caved in.

"Look, I'll tell you what I told the folks who asked the same question back then," she replied, almost angrily, pushing hair out of her eyes. "You get no *answers* from *me*, buddy. I don't give answers, I'm *looking* for them. You want the Tregarde Creed? You *really* want it? It isn't comfortable and it isn't easy, and all it's going to do is raise more questions—"

He nodded anyway.

She sighed. "All right, you asked for it. First commandment. *There ain't no such thing as 'one true way,' and the way you find is only good for you, not anybody else, because* your *interpretation of what you see and feel and understand as the truth is never going to be the same as anyone else's.* Second commandment. *The only answers worth having are the ones you find for yourself.* Third commandment. *Leave the world better than you found it.* Fourth commandment. *If it isn't true, going to do some good, or spread a little love around, don't say it, do it or think it.* Fifth commandment. *There are only three things worth living for; love in all its manifestations, freedom, and the chance to keep humanity going a little while longer. They're the same things worth dying for. And if you aren't willing to die for the things worth living for, you might as well turn in your membership in the human race.* That's all there is, so far as I know or care. The rest is just ruffles and flourishes."

Her shoulders sagged, and she rested her chin on her hand. "Mark, I am not out to disturb anybody's faith. *I* happen to be happy and comfortable with a belief system that has a dual deity and operates on a lunar schedule. It suits my needs. If *you* happen to be happy and comfortable with a belief system that features a single masculine deity and operates on a solar schedule, *fine.* I don't give a fat damn. What matters, Magnum, is what you do, not whose name you do it in." She picked up the coffee and took a large swallow, evidently forgetting that it was cold.

She made a sour face, and Mark had to suppress a nervous chuckle. "Look," he asked, "what about changing established religion from within? From what I've seen of the C of E, it's not that hard to get them to accept new things—"

She snorted. "You're asking for *my* opinion. Kid, that's *all* this is—my opinion, which is that history proves that in general, people that try to do that fail and end up breaking off anyway. Look at the record. Start with Christ—move on to the Greek Orthodox schism, followed by the Albigensians, the Huguenots, the C of E, Luther, the Quakers—Lord and Lady, I could go on forever. They all tried to change from within, and ended up splitting off. This is the lesson history told *me*: when a religion gets so mired in bureaucracy that compassion takes second place to the *law*, and the law is iron-bound and iron-clad and has no room in it for exceptions, then it's no longer a religion for humans, it's a religion for paper-pushers, painted saints, and marble statues. So I didn't bother to try working from within; I looked until I found what worked for me. That's my way and my truth—you go find your own. End lecture. Happy now?"

"No. But I didn't expect to be happy, I just wanted information."

She nodded, and quirked her mouth in a half smile. "You're learning, Magnum."

He sighed, beginning to feel all the tension of the last couple of weeks knotting up his shoulders. "You know, we don't need any more caffeine. How about a nightcap instead? Scotch and soda? Then I'll take you home."

She managed a real smile. "I won't say no."

"Moutainhawk!" Mark called, spotting someone he'd been subconsciously watching for all morning. "Charlie!"

The uniformed patrolman with the carved-cliff profile stopped dead in the hallway and peered in Mark's direction. Mark waved; Charlie waved back, and waited for Mark to catch up to him.

Charles Mountainhawk had been one of Mark's fellow cadets at the police academy; when their stint as rookies was over, though, Charlie had elected to stay on the street while Mark grabbed his chance at Homicide. Charlie was a good guy—but more important than that, at least at the moment, he was a full-blooded Cherokee.

And he had a brother who was a political activist. So Charlie had ears in places where Mark had no hope of going.

"So, what's new—besides the rumor that the city is paying you to drive a pretty young lady all over town?" Charlie asked, grinning fiendishly as Mark got within easy conversational distance.

"Well, the rumor's true for once," Mark replied, returning the grin and the slap on the back. "How many scalps you lifted this week?"

"Three; got me a dope dealer this morning. How come you get all the luck?" Mountainhawk set off back down the corridor with an easy stride.

Mark kept pace with him. "Largely because she's on the big one, and I was the guy that suggested we bring her in on it. And I dunno about luck; remember that smack dealer Narco hauled out in a sack two, three weeks ago? We stumbled over him, and he just about ventilated us.

But yeah, mainly you're right; you know good and well this sucker's gonna be mostly legwork, and it's no bad thing doing it in attractive company."

"Huh." That grunt and the sideways look Mountainhawk gave him were all that showed his surprise. "So that rumor's true too."

"Which one?" Mark asked.

"I just got off. Got time for coffee?"

Bingo—I think I just hit paydirt. Charlie wants to know something—which means I can trade favor for favor.

"Sure—"

"Outside?"

Ah ha. He doesn't want anybody to eavesdrop. Big bingo.

"Try again," Mark countered. "It's raining cats out there."

Mountainhawk made a sour face. "Been in here filling out reports for the past two hours. Hell, it figures. Where can we get some privacy?"

Mark thought for a moment. "Hey, about that back staircase over by the evidence room?"

Charlie shrugged. "'Bout as good as any, I suppose."

A few moments later they were perched on the linoleum-covered stairs like a couple of kids, coffee cups in hand. Mark almost chuckled; Charlie looked pretty odd sprawled over the stairs in his uniform. At least he was wearing jeans—

The staircase hummed with machine sounds and the whisper of the air-conditioning plant, but this area was so seldom used that the landings had storage cabinets stacked on them. It would be a good bet that they wouldn't be disturbed here. Mark waited for Charlie to make the opening move.

It would take someone who knew him to tell, but Mark could see he was fidgety. "Okay," he said finally. "Rumor has it that this pretty thing you've been chauffeuring around is an expert on the occult."

"Cults?" he replied innocently.

"No, the *occult*. Ghosts, monsters—like—" he looked

sheepish and embarrassed. "—she's a bigtime Medicine Woman."

"Where'd you dig *this* up?" he asked quietly.

Mountainhawk looked even more uneasy, as if he was trying to decide something. "Okay, it's *not* a rumor," he finally sighed. "It's—something I was figuring, and I asked Pancho Villa about it—you know, your buddy, Ramirez. The way he hemmed and hawed, I figured I was right. Look, Mark, you can level with me, I believe in this stuff, my old grand-dad is a Medicine Man himself."

"You're right," Mark replied softly. "The Chief doesn't know it, but that's the *real* reason why I was pushing to call her in. She is kind of an occult expert, something like a Medicine Woman, I guess. Di and I go 'way back, and I used to help her out when we were both in college. When I knew this was something other than a Manson-type lunatic, I started pulling some strings to get her here however I could. She's tracked this sort of thing before—only by what we've hit so far, she says she's never dealt with anything this powerful before. This thing is a-one major bad news—"

"Yeah, I was wondering—" Mountainhawk replied unhappily. "See, my grand-dad back in Oklahoma's been writing me, telling me to cut out, take a leave of absence or something."

"Oddly enough, from what we've uncovered so far, you might be one of the safest—it seems to prefer WASP victims—"

"Huh-uh; that's not what grand-dad meant. He thinks if I stay it's gonna get around to recruiting me." Mountainhawk's face twitched a little. "You gotta promise not to laugh—"

"Word of honor."

"I see things."

"Like what? Things happening at a distance, or things not visible to ordinary sight?" Mark asked seriously.

"The second—grand-dad calls it 'spirit vision.' Hey, you—you know what I'm talking about!" Mountainhawk was clearly surprised.

Mark shrugged. "How the hell do you think I met Di

in the first place? At a church picnic? Yeah, I know—I
got a touch of that stuff myself, but don't spread it
around. I get ribbed enough as it is." He thought for a
moment. "Tell you what, Cochise, I'll trade you favor for
favor. If you can get your brother to keep his ear to the
ground for us, *I'll* get Di to fix it so this thing can't see
you—or at least, can't get at you. She put what she calls
'shields' on me a long time ago, or I'd probably be taking
a rest cure right now. What *I've* got can get you locked up
if it gets out of hand."

Mountainhawk considered that for a moment, looking
greatly tempted. "First, tell me why, and what you want
to know."

"We've got a hot tip that this thing is a power native to
this continent. The way I've got it figured, that won't stay
secret for too much longer among the activists—if it's
even a secret now, at all. So—maybe we can get at it
through the native grapevine."

"Okay, Johnnie can go for that. He's into screwing the
white-eyes with lawyers, not chopping 'em up on rocks."
Charlie smiled mirthlessly. "Probably he'd say that they
don't suffer long enough if you just chop 'em up."

"There are times when I'd agree with you," Mark
replied wryly.

Charlie looked Mark over with a thoughtful eye. "Hey,
Cisco Kid—you know, *you* could pass as one of us with
the right person vouching for you. Johnnie just might be
willing to do that, too—if you want."

Mark didn't even have to think about it. He was
getting pretty weary of not being able to do anything on
his own in this case. *This* would be right up his alley, if
Johnnie Mountainhawk could be talked into it. "Hell
yes, I want. I'm beginning to feel like nothing more than
a driver or a bodyguard."

"Okay, I'll see if Johnnie will front for you."

"I'll pay off my half of the promise now; Di's at my
place. I'll take you over right this minute, if you want."

Charlie stood, and dumped his plastic cup in the
ashtray fastened to the wall as he did so. "The sooner the

better. Grand-dad notwithstanding, I can't afford to take a leave. Too many car payments, and a new baby on the way."

Well—nice to have a piece of good *news for a change!* "Hey, you old so-and-so, why didn't you *say* something!" Mark exclaimed as they headed for the parking lot exit and the pouring rain.

Mark gave the recognition yell—which today was "Encyclopedia salesman!"—as he unlocked the door. Di had taken to keeping her piece close at hand, since they weren't feeling much like taking chances. Standing in the rain was like standing under a shower at full blast, and he didn't feel like waiting around for her to answer the bell. He and Charlie piled through as soon as he got the door opened, since his apartment was one without a sheltering overhang. Cops tended to choose places that didn't have anywhere for a would-be ambusher to lurk.

"My God, you look like somebody tried to drown you!" Di exclaimed from where she was crouched over five books spread open on the floor of the livingroom. "Who's your handsome friend?"

"Charlie Mountainhawk, and he's married," Mark replied, as Charlie blushed. "Charlie, this is Di Tregarde. Di, he wants to trade favors."

"Darn, the good ones are always taken." Di stood up, cheerfully dusting off the knees of her jeans. Charlie blushed again. "Name the favors; I'm easy, but I ain't cheap."

She grinned insolently at the both of them, as Charlie did his best to figure out if he should be embarrassed or amused.

"Charlie's going to get us some info from the activists if you shield him."

Di immediately went into "serious" mode. "Problems?" she asked. "I like to know what I'm dealing with."

"Nothing yet," Charlie said slowly, "But—I've gotten warning that this thing you're after may try and haul me in as a draftee. I figured the only thing that was going to stop it was distance, but Mark claims you've got a better solution."

Her eyes widened, but she asked nothing more; Mark suspected her reticence was something along the lines of "professional ethics." "I can see why you'd want shielding—but if what I do is going to run counter to your beliefs, the shields won't take," she warned, twisting a bit of hair around one finger. "Are you really *willing* to let me work white man's magic on you?"

"I don't think anything you do will conflict," Charlie replied, slowly. "I'd like you to try. The warning's been pretty pointed, and it's from a source I trust."

She nodded gravely. "Mark, why don't you two go dry off; I'll be ready by the time you get back to the living room."

Mark took his friend back into the bedroom and pulled out some dry clothes for the both of them. Charlie and Mark were pretty much of a size; he managed to squeeze into a pair of Mark's bluejeans without too much problem, and an old T-shirt stretched enough to get across his brawny shoulders, which had always inspired Mark with raw envy. By the time they'd toweled off and changed, Di had, indeed, gotten what little she needed ready.

She'd put her hair up in a knot again—she was wearing a plain silver choker and matching rings on each hand. "You sit there—on the floor in front of me, with your back to me," she directed, as she seated herself carefully in the chair just under the north window. "Just like I was going to massage your shoulders." Charlie obeyed her, sitting cross-legged at her feet with his back to her. "Mark, turn out the electric lights, would you? I don't want any other fields being generated while I do this."

He obeyed; now she was lit only from behind, by the gray, uncertain light that came through the window.

Huh—Mark thought with surprise, *Now that's peculiar. Very peculiar. They should look faded out—but they don't.* He looked closer. *If I didn't know better, I'd say she looks like she was sitting in sunshine—not in my living room!*

She held her hands about five inches away from Charlie's head, and her eyes went unfocused. Mark forgot the peculiar quality of the light around her, and watched all this with curiousity and interest—he'd been in Charlie's position the last time she'd done this.

There *did* seem to be a faint sort of light linking her two ring fingers—but when he tried to focus on it, it faded out.

"Okay, Charlie—" she said, after a moment. "Before I start, I would like to ask a question, and I promise you that it's relevant. Do you have what they call—uh—I think it's 'spirit vision'?"

Charlie started, and his eyes looked surprised. "I—uh —yeah," he admitted.

"There's a reason for my asking; since you do, you're going to see all of what I'm doing and you can actually tailor the shields to suit yourself. They'll 'take' better if you do. Poor Mark had to make do with what I made up for him." She smiled at Mark, and wrinkled her nose.

"Hey, they're okay, I've got no complaints," Mark countered.

"So what do you think of when I say I'm going to put protection on you?" she asked.

Charlie grinned sheepishly. "Promise not to laugh?"

"Promise."

"A force field, like Star Trek."

"Good image," she approved, nodding. "Easy to work with. Okay; relax if you can, you're going to see just that kind of force field forming up around you in a minute. Um—it'll probably be blue; that's the primary color in your aura. Once I've got it in place I'm going to shrink it down so it's contiguous with your skin. Leaves less of a target that way. The way it'll work is to make magic slide around you, rather than stopping it or absorbing it. Ready?"

Charlie nodded, and she held her hands out, one just above either shoulder, and again, about five inches away from him.

Mark hadn't really expected to see anything of the shields going up, so he was rather surprised to notice that Charlie seemed to be blurring a bit. He blinked, thinking that it was tired eyes, but Di and the furniture behind him remained in sharp focus—

Except those sections that were behind that five-inch distance; those were blurry as well. It was a bit like the heat-distortions above hot asphalt. And at the border of the distorted area was a thin line of the faint light, only this time it was bluish.

Mark was fascinated.

Charlie was evidently seeing something a bit more elaborate, as his eyes were wide with the greatest surprise Mark had seen him show in a long time.

Just when Mark thought he *might* be seeing a bit of a glow running all through the distorted area, Di flexed her fingers slightly, and the distortion seemed to sink into Charlie's body.

Charlie held out his hands in front of himself and stared at his fingers, quite dumbfounded.

"Is that—it?" he asked, hesitantly.

"That's all there is," she replied, wriggling her fingers, then standing up and stretching for the ceiling. "End of dog and pony show."

"I didn't mean it that way," he told her, craning his head backward to look at her. "I meant—wow, that was pretty impressive from in here!"

"Does it feel any different?" Mark asked. "It sure as hell did for me."

"I'll say it does," Charlie exclaimed, getting to his feet. "Like—the difference between driving my Bug and Johnnie's four-by-four. Or—no, something heftier. A tank."

"Something like," Di grinned. "When I do a job, I don't do it halfway, and I rather *like* armor-plating."

One more crying baby or pass from that drunk in first and I think I'd have killed someone, Mary Johnson moaned to herself, loosening the collar on her uniform and pressing her aching head against the glass of the window of the shuttle van. *Bad enough the hour delay on the ground in Frisco. Then we ride a roller coaster all the way here. But* then *to end up waiting two* more *hours on the ground because we can't get at a gate*!

The Amerine Airways shuttle van was crowded far past its intended capacity of ten. Mary and everyone else had their luggage on their laps. She was just lucky to have gotten a seat at all, much less a window seat, and knew it.

My God, it's almost 2:00 A.M. *Thank God I just went illegal, or I'll bet they'd call me in for the 5:00* A.M. *New York shuttle. I think I'd rather die.*

Thanks to three tornadoes on the ground near DFW this afternoon, virtually every flight in and out had been subject to a delay of at least an hour. DFW Airport was a madhouse; kids crying, babies screaming, weary, angry passengers in every terminal—and *of course* all the restaurants and concession stands had closed down at their normal hour of ten and *of course* the computer-driven terminal environmental controller had turned off the air-conditioning at the same hour and *of course* no one knew how to turn it back *on* again.

You could pretty much count on it—any craft that had hit the gate after midnight had left about half its passengers stranded for the night. The gate agents were equally divided between ready to commit suicide and ready to commit mass murder.

And there wasn't a hotel room to be had at any price. She and the rest of the crew were *so* tired they were just about ready to pool their cash to get one of the VIP suites—there were enough couches in one of those things to make sure everybody got some kind of bed, and there were the hot tubs and saunas—

But even those were gone.

So they were catching the shuttle out to the flight academy. Thank God for *that*. The rooms were all dorm-style and not exactly high-class, nor exactly cheap if you were just bunking down overnight and not there for training—but right now all Mary wanted was a shower, a flat space, and a pillow and blanket.

It was as black as the inside of a hat out there; the

darkness had that peculiar quality it sometimes had down here after a rain when the sky was still overcast; it seemed to drink all the available light and give nothing back. Mary was glad she wasn't driving; it would be a bitch to see anything tonight.

"Anybody want off at the gate?" the shuttle driver called out. "You could probably walk to the dorm faster than I'm going to get there. I've got priority stuff for every building on the route."

Mary considered the amount of luggage she had—not much—and concluded that the walk might be just what she needed to settle her nerves.

"Me," she called, "And I'm right on the door."

Her seatmates sighed with gratitude and relief. "Don't use up all the hot water," Captain Forster said, from somewhere behind his carryons.

"Serve you right if I did," she answered. "You should have diverted to Houston—at least we could have gotten hotel rooms there."

"Bitch, bitch, bitch," the Captain retorted. "*I* got us a powercart so I could keep the a/c on. You *could* have been baking back there."

"More like steaming—and I was already," she replied, carefully working herself and her gear out of the van door. "If that jerk in First had put his hand up my skirt one more time—"

Her fellow attendants groaned in sympathy. "I'm black and blue where he kept pinching me when the beverage cart stuck," Lynn Jeffers seconded.

"Y'all had it easy," drawled someone in the front. "*We* had us a buncha drunk Shriners from Vegas—an' we was so low on fuel the cap'n had to kill the a/c *and* most of the lights while we was waitin' on a gate. Talk about your animals!"

The horror stories continued as Mary got herself out of the van and onto the roadway, and as the van rolled away she could *still* hear them at it.

Why did I ever think that being a flight attendant was glamorous?

She was right under the streetlight, so the first thing,

the *very* first thing she did was to open her suitcase and extract her old, comfortable running shoes, changing them off for her pumps. Her feet stopped hurting for the first time in hours.

It was cool, but not too chilly—in fact, as overheated as she was, the cooler air felt wonderful. It smelled pretty nice too, all clean, the dust washed out by the rain. It was too bad that it was overcast; the stars would have been nice tonight.

She shut her pumps into her suitcase and stacked everything back onto her wheelie and strapped it all down, then peered around into the darkness beyond the cone of light from the streetlamp.

There's a jogging path around here somewhere, I know there is—hah! One thing you had to say for old Amerine; they'd put some really nice paved paths through the wooded grounds for runners. Bless their flinty hearts.

She headed off down the path for the dorm, feeling a little more like a human being and not so much like a sardine with sore feet.

One of the shadows beneath the trees on the right side of the asphalted pathway detatched itself from the rest and moved off after her.

"Mark—" Di said, looking up from her book.

"Hm?" he replied, just as happy to set down his own. After sending Charlie home, they had elected to stay in the living room tonight; actually *reading* some of the books that seemed relevant, instead of just skimming through them. They'd moved two of the foam flip-couches over below the good reading lamp so they could share it, and Mark had some nice soothing space-music on the stereo rig. It was a pity the situation was so serious—this would have been an enjoyable evening if they weren't having to think about the guy that was going to become a corpse if they couldn't find him soon.

"Do you remember what Ramirez said when he was talking about trying to get that voudoun curse off him?"

He stretched, and shifted position on the couch. "About the girl in Dispatch?"

She shook her head, and chewed on the end of her finger. "No, before then."

"Huh. Give me a minute." He sat in silence for a moment, Treemonisha purring her approval of his choice of position from the pit of his stomach where she'd curled up. She was a lot better pleased that they were lounging in the living room instead of crunched up against the table in the kitchen. She hadn't been able to get into Mark's lap when they'd been using the kitchen.

"He said—" Mark replied after running the conversation through his mind, "that he had gone across the border trying to find an old-time *brujo* to try to take it off—"

"Yeah! Yeah, that's it! That's what I was trying to remember! That's the one set of practicing magicians we *haven't* checked out—*brujos* and *brujas*!"

He scratched the side of Treemonisha's nose, feeling a bit dubious. "Well, I guess it could be nasty enough. Aunt Nita used to tell stories that could curl a kid's toes. Is it *native* though?"

"According to this book it is—" She held up the heavy volume so he could see the title—*Superstitions and Folklore of the Southwest*. "Although this lot doesn't know as much about it as I'd like; they've got it mixed in with a lot of other traditions that I *know* are separate entities, like the mescaline ceremonies. At least they admitted they didn't know too much. But—that's what was nagging at the back of my mind. Now that you've jogged my memory, I'm remembering that someone in a position to know told me a long time ago that all the aspects of the Virgin that the *brujas* invoke are really Christianized versions of some of the traditional Amerindian goddesses."

"So that would qualify as native, all right," he agreed. "But I hate to tell you this—I know less about where to find a *brujo* or *bruja* than you do."

"*You* would not likely ever find a *bruja*," she replied, smiling a little. "They're rather down on men. And I'll have a hard time convincing one to talk to me—they're equally down on Anglos. But I'll have more luck than you will, I bet, especially since I can point out those three kids that were victims. And I bet I know who can get me pointed in the right direction."

"Who?" he asked.

"It's right under your nose, Magnum."

He shook his head, still baffled. She laughed.

"Your own Aunt Nita."

"This is as bad as when I was in high school." Julia pulled away a little and complained, as John fumbled with the buttons on her blouse. "Hell, we don't even have the back seat of a car—"

He pushed her back against the bark of the tree they were under. "You know why we can't rent a car—what if your husband or my wife found the rental record?" he said with exasperation. "And we couldn't *get* hotel rooms tonight to save our souls—"

Julia squirmed on the blanket she'd filched from the flight academy dorm room, trying to find a position where there weren't as many rocks under her rear. "We could have tried out in the boonies. Nobody else was bothering. We could have rented *two* cars."

"And have somebody turn up the fact that it was only the two of us out there and not the whole crew?" He had her half undressed now; the flight in had been a bad one—the plane had been hit twice by lightning on the way down. Bad flights, so Julia had learned, tended to make Captain John Powell horny as hell.

"Why are you so paranoid, O Captain?" she asked a little acidly. "I have just as much to lose as you do."

"Look I'm already paying out alimony to one ex—if Angie ever found out about us she'd take me to the cleaners. And I *think* she's got a PI checking up on me."

Julia would have asked some more specific questions at that point, but about then things were rapidly coming to a boil—and she didn't want answers any more. Bad flights frequently had the same effect on her as they had on the captain.

Beneath a stand of bushes was a clot of shadow. Within that shadow, a darker shadow watched them, and waited.

Tommy (his real name was William, but he hadn't gone by that in decades) Thomson was rather proud of himself. He thought he'd been real clever, sneaking on that Amerine shuttle van—

He, along with several hundred other passengers, had been stranded for the night when his flight from Florida missed the connecting flight into Chicago. The Amerine personnel refused to do anything for him, claiming that because the delays and missed connections were due to weather, they were free of obligations.

Hah. You can't get away with treating a vice-president of marketing that way. I know all the dodges.

He'd ranted and raved in his finest managerial style— but he'd only been one voice among hundreds—and nothing he'd tried had produced so much as an apology, much less the hotel room he was demanding.

They kept trying to claim that weather delays were "acts of God" and that they weren't liable for anything. Turkeys. I'll fix them.

Since trying to penetrate the bullshit of the underlings had gotten him nowhere, he'd decided to bypass the peons, and deal with the bosses directly.

The question was, how to get *at* them.

Then he'd overheard one of the stews talking about getting a bed at Headquarters, and had followed her. When the shuttle van with its inconspicuous Amerine Airways card in the corner of the windshield had arrived, he'd bullied and pushed his way on board, cutting out one of those uppity stews and leaving her to wait for the next van. He'd figured out a while back that if you acted like you were in a position of authority—if, in fact, *you* started making the demands—people tended to assume you had the right to push them around.

It had worked like a charm. Nobody had questioned him, challenged him, or even asked to see his employee ID.

He'd figured that in a bad situation like they had over at the airport, there were *bound* to be some honchos around. But they wouldn't be *at* the airport, they'd be at Headquarters, where they could monitor the situation, but nobody could get at them to confront them. It was easier and a lot more comfortable and convenient to work that way—it was the way *he* used to work.

So old Tommy was too clever for them; he knew all the end runs and the slick moves, and was ready with a counterplay.

He'd bitched and moaned about the van, the heat, and the driver all the way to the Amerine complex. After all, that's what an exec did. The rest of the van's occupants had gone silent after the first few minutes, and he figured he'd pulled a slick one on them all.

When the van driver had announced "Headquarters," he'd popped out of that van like a horse out of the starting gate. No one else got off, though—there had only been someone waiting at the stop for a package that the driver had handed him. By the time Tommy had gotten himself straightened out, that person had already vanished into the bowels of the building.

Tommy had found himself shivering in the cool damp air. He hadn't brought his coat with him; just left it stuffed in the locker where he'd shoved his suitcases. He was in front of a huge glass-and-chrome building, illuminated against the overcast darkness by floodlights all around it. The Amerine logo was carved into a stone monolith set into the sidewalk about ten yards from the front door.

And sure enough, just as Tommy had figured, there were lights on in some of the offices, and people-shadows moving between the lights and the glass.

Tommy strode confidently up to the front door—his every footstep echoing with authority—seized the chrome doorhandle, and yanked it open.

Or tried.

It was locked; nearly took his arm out of the socket when he pulled and nothing happened. He frowned, and tried again—rattling the door as hard as he could, but all to no effect. Then he tried all the other doors in the entryway.

No good.

It was only then that he noticed the magnetic keycard reader, and realized that *nobody* was going to get in or out of the building without a key.

Or the help of somebody already inside. If he could find someone with the right card, he could surely bully them into letting him in.

He pounded on the door, hoping to get the attention of at least a night watchman, but no one came.

Angry and frustrated, he turned on his heel and began the long hike to the nearest lighted building.

It was dark under the trees, dark and cold and damp— and the wind kept shaking showers of drops from the leaves down into his head. He was regretting his coat; almost regretting the whole idea. He needed to find some *people;* people he could deal with. Mag-card readers and closed buildings wouldn't yield to his skills.

The nearest building proved to be the flight academy dorm. There were lots of people there—and not a card reader in sight.

But he was also accosted immediately by a hatchet-faced old man in a rent-a-cop uniform who demanded to see his employee ID. He got downright surly when Tommy didn't produce one. He threatened to call the Dallas cops and have Tommy charged with trespassing on private property. He looked like he'd do it, too.

And in that mess of tired, irritable stews and crews, there wasn't a single *sign* of anyone likely to be able to give him satisfaction. Nobody was in the least sympathetic to *his* plight—he was invading *their* territory. He was the interloper here, and not at all welcome. They had no reason or desire to be polite or helpful to him.

Tommy beat a hasty retreat back out into the dark, mumbling about leaving his badge in the car. That seemed to satisfy the old man at least enough so that he was not pursued. . . .

But now he was lost somewhere on the grounds; he'd started following a path he *thought* would get him back to where the shuttle van had dropped him off, but instead it only took him deeper into the landscaped wooded area. By day this would have been no problem. But by night, on a moonless, starless night when he couldn't tell one building from another, he was baffled.

So baffled and preoccupied with his own predicament that he never noticed the footsteps that echoed his own along the path behind him.

·TEN

Mark was hiding in the darkness, but the dark would not conceal him forever. Somewhere out there, somewhere past the boundaries of his tiny sphere of protection, was the Hunter.

The thick dark was stiflingly hot, and the very air seemed to cling to him, clogging his throat as if he was breathing wads of damp cotton. If he moved, he might be able to find someplace cooler, someplace where he could breathe freely.

But if he moved, the Hunter would find him.

He could sense it searching the realm outside his safe little bubble, piercing the darkness with eyes of fire. He was not sensitive, not an empath like Di, but he could feel its anger, its scorching hatred, its insatiable hunger.

Much blood had already been spilled to feed that hunger. More was fated to be shed, for the more the Hunter consumed, the more the Hunter hungered. But somehow Mark knew that if the Hunter found him, he would find himself meeting a destiny other than serving that hunger. The Hunter had another purpose in mind for Mark—

And if that purpose was fulfilled, there would be nothing left of "Mark Valdez"—at least, nothing recognizable.

The Hunter moved closer; now Mark could "see" it, a sullen red glow that did nothing to illuminate the darkness. His breath caught in his throat, for it was nearer to his hiding place than it had ever come before. Surely it could sense him, even through his thin walls of deception and protection. Surely it knew he was there.

It came closer still, and now he could see its eyes, its eyes like smoldering coals, and feel its hunger beating inside his head, keeping time with his pulse. Those hideous eyes swept the darkness like searchlights, and he cringed as they passed over him; he expected at any second to be discovered.

His instincts all screamed at him to run; his better judgment told him to remain where he was. But those eyes continued to probe the blackness all around him, coming nearer, nearer, until—

Something screamed in his ear.

He didn't so much jump as spasm, his heart pounding hard enough to tear out of his chest, his throat closing so that for one long moment he literally couldn't breathe. Then the sound came again, and this time he recognized it for the phone tucked into his headboard.

It was as dark in his bedroom as it had been in his dream, only the red eye of the digital clock glaring at him from a few inches away from his nose broke the blackness. He was still stuck in his nightmare, and the red numerals of the clock seemed to be extensions of the red eyes of the Hunter. For a moment he was paralyzed, unable to move or even think, completely frozen in fear at the sight of the strangely shaped red "eyes."

Then the phone shrilled again, and the spell was broken.

He groped for it, still almost in a state of shock. He shivered as the air hit his arm and realized vaguely that he was literally sodden with sweat, from his hair to his ankles.

"Valdez," he said into the receiver, trying to tell his heart that it would be a really good idea if it slowed down a little. *God, it's still night—this can't be Di! Or if it is—I'll kill her twice. Once wouldn't be enough.*

"Haul your li'l ass outa bed, boy." With another jolt, Mark recognized the Chief's voice—and it sounded grim. "Git that yankee gal and haul yerselves on over t' th' Amerine Airways headquarters. Our ol' buddies fin'lly woke up again, an' we got one *damn-all* mess."

Damn-all mess was an understatement.

There was blood everywhere; the first victim—there was more than one, though Mark didn't yet know the exact total—had been killed right on the pristine white sidewalk.

Maybe because they couldn't find a suitable rock? Mark wondered.

At any rate, it was pretty ghastly. No elaborate mutilations this time—they hadn't stripped the girl, either. Just torn the uniform open at the chest, and cut the heart out.

Lord, that was enough. The Amerine people were nowhere to be seen, which wasn't surprising. Likely the only time any of them saw blood was when they cut themselves. This must have messed their minds up for certain.

There was another difference in this kill. This time the girl's heart hadn't been left neatly beside the body. This time it was missing.

The sun still wasn't up; the site was lit by three floodlights, the poor girl sprawled faceup on the sidewalk, eyes open and staring sightlessly at the dark branches of the tree over her head, mouth frozen open in an eternally silent scream. Her face was distorted into a mask of absolute terror and pain. The trees continued to drip down all over everything and everyone, and directly over the corpse what they dripped wasn't always rainwater. There was blood splattered for several feet in every direction. In no way could the murderer have avoided getting it on him. In no way could he have gotten past anyone without their seeing the bloodstains that had to be all over him.

And no one had seen a thing that was suspicious—other than a businessman type who'd shown up over at the flight academy dorm, and who'd been found later when the hue-and-cry went up. Turned out *he'd* ended up as one of the victims.

The whole thing was giving Mark chills.

"This looks to me like it was done in a hurry," Di told him quietly; she was very pale, but very composed. "Like somebody was skimping on the rites for lack of time. Another thing—there's only *one* of those signature auras here; one of the weakest at that."

"Speculation?"

She rubbed eyes that had greenish circles beneath them, and suppressed a yawn. "That our five principals split up tonight, maybe because the four weak ones have finally accumulated enough power to cover their tracks for a limited time. My guess is that the stalking took longer than this one thought, and he or she had to finish up with a shorthand version of the proper sacrifice. Whatever power was lost by skimping was probably made up for by the number of victims."

"How many so far?" Mark asked Melanie Lee, who was in charge of the site nearest the gate.

"Six bodies, five sites," she said, distractedly. "We think that's all—it's not like anybody was trying to hide the bodies or anything. Amerine's had their people out checking the entire grounds since they realized that there was more than one victim. We think all this happened between eleven and one ack emma. We'll have to run some tests, but right now it looks like all six were offed within the same thirty-minute period."

"Which means it *had* to be more than one killer—just like we've been figuring," Mark said flatly. Melanie nodded, and turned back to her meticulous charting.

The Chief joined them at just that moment; it was fairly obvious that he was stressed—the cigar was lit, and he was sending up enough smoke to kill every mosquito within a mile.

"We got us a problem," he told Mark, "Them Amerine boys is raisin' holy hell about this. It's bad enough that four a' their stews an' a pilot bought it, but looks like the last stiff was some yuppie boy had no reason even *bein'* here—that's mighty bad publicity fer them, an' it don't look so good fer us, neither."

"We could *use* that, Chief," Mark replied, thinking furiously. "Look, half the department's had to deal with Amerine at one time or another—trying to get them to allow us on their sacred soil is like trying to get a bunch of old maids to look at a copy of *Hustler*. So—hit 'em back; it's *their* private property, as they've told us so often—it's *their* security that let these people on the grounds—killers and yuppies included. Since they tied our hands, let *them* take the rap."

"And even if the killers got in clandestinely, there's no way that businessman climbed over the wall—so *he*, at least, went right by their security. You might make sure the press *knows* that," Di chimed in. "Make sure they know exactly who was supposed to be in charge, here. You might drop a hint or two about how Amerine's thrown their weight around about sovereignty before this—and *now* they're trying to blame *us* for what *they* let in."

The Chief brightened a little. "That'll get 'em offen our backs, that's fer sure—"

"Chief!" Ramirez came pelting up, mostly out of breath from the long run to where the Chief's car was parked. "Chief, we got another one. White Rock Lake Park, burning car, unknown number of victims, but at least two. It's not a crash, the thing was set. They haven't been able to put it out yet, but it's homicide and no doubt about it."

"Aw shit—" the Chief spat. "Dammit, why *now*? Melanie, drop this 'un, get yer team on over there. Valdez, go hunt up Fred, get his team split an' send half on 'em over here—"

"I'll help at this site," Di offered. "I can finish the preliminaries now that Melanie's started them."

"I'll take that," the Chief answered instantly. "Boys say y'all know what yer doin'. Okay, Ramirez, let's roll."

By the time Mark returned with Fred and a second tech, Di had completed the preliminary layout work and the body had been taken away. Fred sighed with relief when he saw how much she'd accomplished, and proceeded to wade into the tedious inch-by-inch combing of the site.

"I could use you," he told Di, "But why don't you check the other four sites first, then come back here. By looking at all five you might catch something in your field—"

"No bad thought," she replied, "No bad thought at all. It won't take me long—"

"Go right ahead then; Valdez, you got a map, didn't you?" he asked, craning his neck around so that he could see Mark from where he was kneeling on the wet grass.

Mark nodded. "Yeah, no prob. We'll be back in—say half an hour."

"Good, 'cause that's when I'll really start needing you, Di."

The second site—the one he'd pulled Fred away from—was where they had found two victims together. And what the spouses of the two would have to say, Mark didn't want to find out—for it had been fairly evident that they'd been up to some serious fooling around before their murderer found them. Their clothing had been found tangled up with a couple of blankets nearby, and the various items of apparel showed no signs of having been removed by force.

The pilot hadn't even fought—no sign that they were even surprised. They might as well have been asleep or drugged—and Mark couldn't imagine two people being either out in the cold damp of the park area. Again there were no mutilations, but there *were* signs that the victims had been somehow rendered unconscious, dragged over to a nearby boulder, given floral decorations, then favored with a cardiectomy.

"Full ritual here, I think," Di mused. "But only one aura—this time it was the number one, the one I know is male. Let's get to the other three."

The third was like the second, except that the clothing *had* been cut off the poor thing; the Forensics team had found what was left of her uniform thrown under a nearby bush. The fifth site was exactly like the third. But the fourth—

The fourth girl had either *not* been surprised so totally, or had possessed a little more moxie than the others. She had fought back; used her purse as a weapon until the strap broke, then had struggled when seized and nearly torn herself loose. If her uniform had been a little less well-constructed, she might have succeeded in getting away. But the sleeve didn't *quite* tear off in her captor's hands, and she had been clubbed into insensibility.

But she hadn't been stripped; once again, she'd been thrown to the sidewalk, her clothing had simply been torn open and the heart removed. No decorations, no evidence of elaborate ritual; just like the first murder tonight.

And for once, they'd been given a break. She hadn't been searched by her murderer, either.

"Well, lookee here—" one of the Forensics men had managed to pry the girl's clenched fist open.

She was holding a tiny scrap of elaborately brocaded cloth—most probably torn from the garment of her killer. The bright colors seemed alive in the harsh floodlights.

Mark sucked in his breath sharply. Di glanced over at him.

"I take it you recognize this stuff?" she said.

"It *looks* like some of the material Sherry's been working with," he replied slowly. "Robert's been ignoring her work, so she's been showing it off to me. . . ."

"It's pretty distinctive," Di agreed. "And it certainly doesn't look like any fabric I've ever seen before. How much of this stuff does she sell?"

"Not a lot; it takes a long time to weave, and it's real pricey. She got the technique from some Indians, though, so she isn't the only one that knows how to create it." He turned to the tech. "What's the chances I can have this some time tomorrow for about four hours? Or—maybe a good photograph would be better."

"Photo shouldn't be a problem," the tech replied, scratching his bald head, "Seein' as y'all are s'pposed t' get pretty much what y'all need, an' y' been pretty reasonable-like. Reckon we c'n get y'all a nice color print—enlarged, an' everything. Say, pick it up fr'm us round 'bout two? Reckon we'll be done with it by then."

"That would be perfect," Mark replied, knowing that Sherry was always home mid-afternoons—and so Robert usually wasn't. Right now he'd rather not talk to Robert around Sherry. And she was always less nervous and more herself when he wasn't around.

"You ready to head back?" he asked Di.

She nodded, and they began cutting across the landscaped area between the paths. The sun was coming up, and even though it was gray and still overcast, they had no trouble seeing where they were going. The wet grass squelched under their sneakers, and the cuffs of Mark's jeans were getting wet and kept wrapping around his ankles. The tree trunks were gray and ghostly in the ground fog that was rising, and the air smelled more like a tropical rainforest than dry-as-dust Texas. It was going to be another hot day, and after the rain of last night, a humid one as well.

"That last was the second-strongest of the signatures," Di told him, sniffling a bit in the cold air. "And I got a *definite* feeling of 'female' this time. I'll tell you something else, *this* one doesn't need Number One anymore; she's a power in her own right. If she fought that girl hand-to-hand, it was either because she was too startled to think of using her powers, the victim had some defense of her own, or because she *wanted* to fight that way. She ought to have been able to stun her with a psi-bolt, unless the girl had natural shields."

"What happened to the hearts this time?" Mark asked, having a sinking feeling that he'd already guessed the answer, and not looking forward to finding out that his guess was correct. "The last time we found them with the body."

Di looked a little sick. "I hate to tell you this—but—

well, there's a lot of cultures that took hearts. And when they did—they generally—ate them."

The sun was well up by the time they finished at Amerine. They were both dead tired—but on a hunch, Mark headed, not for home, but for White Rock Lake Park.

The park had guards at the entrance, chasing most people off. The site itself had been cordoned off, but their IDs got them past the blockades with no fuss. The site was in a very public place—even though the park was supposedly closed to the public after ten, it was patrolled; *someone* should have seen the car coming in, or found it before it was set afire. But, as at Bachmann Lake Park, no one had. That alone made Mark very nervous; it was beginning to sound to him as if this, too, was going to turn out to be another of "their" cases.

They found that the Chief had left Ramirez in charge of this site; it wasn't much to get excited about—just a blackened hulk of a late-model BMW near one of the picnic shelters.

Ramirez stumbled over to them, his face gray with fatigue, his chin shadowed with stubble. "I dunno what you're doin' out here when you could be grabbin' some sleep, Cisco," he told Mark, yawning and shaking his head. "This don't look like one of yours at all—"

"What *do* you have?" Mark asked, clenching his jaw on a yawn himself, and beginning to want a second shower almost as badly as he wanted his bed.

"Four males, two front, two back; race and identity unknown, all probably offed earlier tonight. Whoever offed 'em shoved 'em in the car, then the car was set on fire; we found the empty gas can in the shelter. Car belongs to a Missing name of Ben Bronson—"

"This is one of ours," Di interrupted, flatly. She looked like she was coming to the edge of her energy, and was operating on nerve and guts alone. "Is everything still in place?"

"Yeah, we've been waiting for the damn car to cool down; took the Fire Department boys nearly an hour to

put the bastard out," Ramirez replied, looking somewhat taken aback. "You sure this is one of yours? Naw,
forget I asked. Shit, you mean now they're settin' fire to
'em too?"

"Why not?" Di said wearily. "They drowned the last
three."

Then she trudged off across to Melanie Lee, leaving
the two men behind. Mark was not inclined to follow;
first of all, he was too tired, and second, he'd been on a
homicide by incineration once before. If he never saw—
or smelled—another toasted corpse, it would be too
soon.

It was less than a half hour, and Di was back, looking
decidedly greenish.

"Well?" the two men asked simultaneously.

"Oh, it's ours; Melanie says they all got cardiectomy,
and there were some little fried bits of flower wreaths on
all of them. *I* would guess they had the full rites done on
them; just like the man at Bachmann Lake—except for
maybe the mutilations. I think the kills at Amerine were
to raise power so that they could perform *this* sacrifice
undisturbed. Ramirez, if I were you, I'd start looking for
a big flat rock somewhere in the park with bloodstains all
over it."

"I'm on it—" the detective shook his head wearily,
and headed over to the picnic shelter, where a group of
three uniformed cops were standing. He spoke with them
for a few moments; they nodded, and started off into the
park in three different directions.

"So this time they didn't clean up after themselves,"
Mark said, thinking out loud. "Probably figured on the
fire taking care of the evidence—and either forgot, or
didn't know that green plant stuff doesn't burn worth
shit."

"Could be," Di replied, shaking her head and blinking
hard, as if she was having trouble with blurring vision.
"Could also be they're getting enough power that they
don't care. And that scares me."

"I've got another guess—" Mark said, shifting from
one, tired, aching foot to the other, and wishing he could

sit down for a while. Or better yet, lie down for a while. "I bet that one of those four guys was our missing Bronson."

She nodded. "They won't know for sure until they match dental records, but *I'm* certain. The one on the passenger's side in the front seat was Bronson."

Mark cursed under his breath all the way home.

Mark was still feeling groggy as they pulled up to the gate at the Bear Creek apartment complex where Robert had moved his family in their newfound prosperity. *This* time (unlike the first time he'd come out here) he called ahead, so the guard had his name and waved him in—though not without the usual frown of disapproval at the battered old Ghia.

"I wish you'd warned me," Di said with a completely deadpan expression, "I'd have dressed for the occasion."

Certainly they were going to look as out of place once they stepped out of the car as the little Ghia did among all the BMWs, Mercs, and Porsches. Mark pulled into a slot between a Corvette and an antique Triumph and replied defiantly. "Be damned if I'm going to cater to *this* lot's delusions—"

"Whoa there, Magnum, I was just putting you on!" she said hastily, swinging out of the passenger's seat. "Look at it this way—from the tensions around here, I can promise you that this bunch isn't enjoying themselves or their work half as much as you are—or at least the way you do when you haven't the kind of pressure on you have now."

"Yeah, well—"

"I know; there's times I get jealous, too," she said softly. "When I look at something that's selling off the bookshelves and think—'hell, I've thrown out better writing than that.' Stay cool; you do more good in half a year than these hedonists will do in a lifetime, and that's what counts."

He managed to grin at her as they headed up the sidewalk to Robert's townhouse. "Like they say, money may not buy happiness, but it sure makes misery comfortable."

"It does that," she answered, as they paused on the flagstoned doorstep and Mark rang the bronze-framed doorbell.

Sherry must have been waiting for them; the heavy oak-finished door was opened almost before the echoes of the chimes died away.

"Mark!" exclaimed the slender blond who pulled the door open—then practically flung herself at Mark. "Dammit, Mark we have *missed* you!"

Mark felt his temperature rise a notch, and told himself sternly to stay calm. He kind of wondered, with a twinge of worry, what Robert had been doing to make her so happy to see him. He also wondered what Di was picking up.

At that point Sherry noticed that Mark wasn't alone, and pulled away from him, flushing, and betrayed her nerves by tucking a flyaway strand of hair behind one ear.

"Sherry, this is Di; a colleague of mine," Mark said hastily.

The slight hint of wariness faded from Sherry's expression, and she extended her hand with nervous friendliness. "Hi," she answered, "I'm glad to meet one of Mark's co-workers, finally."

"Not quite a co-worker," Di answered serenely. "I'm more of a PI. Mark and I met back in college, and when all this mess started up, he remembered that I specialize in weird cults, and got Dallas PD to bring me in."

"Deprogramming?" Sherry asked, with a hint of interest. More, maybe, than the question warranted.

"Among other things, sometimes," Di replied, looking at her oddly. Sherry flushed a little, and looked uncomfortable.

At that moment they were interrupted by a blond-haired ball of energy that flung itself at Mark's legs. "Markmarkmark!" the boy crowed.

"Heya!" Mark was rather grateful for the interruption; Di was handling the situation, but Sherry was obviously uneasy and off balance. He grabbed the giggling child and tossed him into the air. "How's my favorite dragon-slayer?"

"*Miss* you!" the child said, completely without shame. "Da won't tell me stories, an' he won't play wif me neither."

Mark gave the little rug-rat a quick hug and put him down. "Now, kidlet, your Da's a busy man. He's—"

"He don't wanta play wif me; he wants to play wif the Mean Ladies," the child retorted.

"Bobby!" his mother exclaimed, blushing a full crimson.

"Well, he *does* an' they *are*," Bobby insisted. He turned his attention to the one stranger in the group. "Who're *you?*" he demanded.

Di was obviously struggling to keep from laughing. "My name is Di, and I'm a friend of Mark's."

"Are you a cop too?" he said with intense fascination. "Like on TV? Are you like Cagney and Lacey?"

"Kind of. I knew Mark from a long time ago, and when Mark asked me to come help him, I did. And if you'll promise not to embarrass your mum again by calling your father's models the Mean Ladies, I have something for you."

Bobby considered the offer thoughtfully. "Okay," he decided.

"Then hold out your hand—"

He did, and she put a lavender-toned, eight-sided crystal the size of a walnut in his palm.

"That keeps monsters away," she said, absolutely seriously.

He was enthralled, his blue-gray eyes big and round. "*Really?*"

She nodded. "Cross my heart. Put it by your bed and you won't even *dream* about monsters, unless you want to."

He cocked his head to the right and looked up at her, as if trying to measure her sincerity. "I *like* Godzilla."

"Then if you want to dream about Godzilla, you will. But only monsters you like. Okay?"

"Okay!" He ran back inside, clutching his prize.

Sherry looked at her with a very bemused expression. "How on earth did you know he's been having nightmares? And what was that you gave him?"

Di shrugged.

"Mark said something about it, and I've worked with kids a bit. At his age, nightmares are pretty common, especially when the family is under stress—moving to a new home is a lot of stress to a little one," she replied with delicate tact. "Frequently you can reprogram kids that age to eliminate their own nightmaring by giving them a talisman, and it works especially well if what you give them is unusual enough. That was just a common fluorite crystal, but I figured it wasn't likely he'd ever seen one. They aren't the kind being sold as pendants, mostly because they generally aren't as pretty as that one."

"Well, if it works—I am going to be in your debt. He's been waking up screaming about once a night and Robert has been getting pretty tired of it," Sherry replied, waving them in. "Not that he's blaming Bobby—" she added hastily, "but—"

"It's okay, Sherry, we dig," Mark replied. "After a while it gets old."

"Exactly," she said, leading the way to the sunken living room, a room utterly unlike Mark's apartment. It looked like a *House Beautiful* ad, all fashionable beiges and creams, from the soft carpet to the velvet upholstery of the pit-group. "Oh Mark, Robert's home for a change —he didn't like what the lab did to the last set so he swears he's going to do all the developing himself from here on in. We got the new darkroom finished *just* in time."

She waved at a door at the farther end of the room as they settled into the living room. Mark recalled that the last time he'd been here, that had been an extra-large bathroom. There was a kind of design or glyph in hand-forged brass mounted on the door. It matched the obviously handmade (and expensive) brass lamps and occasional tables.

"Like the logo?" Sherry asked, with a certain amount of pride. "It's Aztec, it means 'Fire and Water.' That's the official name of the company. I think that glyph is our good-luck charm; ever since we started using it, we can do no wrong."

"Nice," Di said. "Where on earth did you find some-one to do that kind of metal work around here?"

Sherry shrugged. "Robert found an artist; he's good at getting things done nowadays. Well, what can *I* do for you?"

"We've got—" Mark began, when the door to the darkroom opened.

"I *thought* I heard your voice," Robert said genially, as Mark rose to meet him. His handsome, almost sculptured face was crossed with what seemed to be a genuine smile of welcome. Mark was gladder than ever that he hadn't given in to his longings and—

He'd have hated like hell to do anything that would have ruined that friendship. No matter how he felt about the way his friend was treating his wife, no matter how attracted *he* was to that wife, he still *liked* Robert.

"So, old buddy, what can we do for you?" Robert asked, when they'd finished exchanging greetings.

"This time it isn't your expertise we need, it's Sherry's," Mark said. "Got a fabric sample I want to see if she can identify. It's handmade; we're hoping she can place it."

"Oh well," Robert replied, glancing (Mark thought) a little uncomfortably at Di. "I can tell when *I'm* superfluous."

"Don't give me that—"

"No seriously, I have a lot of work I need to do. I hate to say hi and run, but—"

"If you *don't* get back in that darkroom, you aren't gonna be able to keep up the payments on this heap," Mark teased.

"Don't I know! Okay Sher, be nice for me—"

"No problem," she replied, wrinkling her nose playfully at him. He waved vaguely at them and disappeared back into the darkroom.

"All right, let's see this fabric sample," she said, turning back to them as they all sat back down again. Mark thought he detected a certain haunted quality to her eyes, but if so, she closed it off before he could be certain.

"It isn't really a sample," he said apologetically, handing her the big envelope he'd picked up at the Forensics lab. "It's a photograph. The sample is the only piece we've got, so the lab's hanging onto it like it was the Holy Grail."

"Right, I understand," she answered absently, sliding the photograph out of the manilla envelope. Her eyes went very wide with surprise.

"Recognize it?" Mark asked.

"I certainly do! It's Mestizo—only it's much finer work than I do. I work with bigger patterns and a coarser weave, but otherwise it's exactly the kind of thing I learned in Mexico. I'd say it was Chiapas, except that— see this line of figures, and this, and this?" She indicated the patterns as Di and Mark leaned over her shoulders. "Those aren't Chiapas patterns at all; in fact, I don't recognize them. But in general, well it's definitely Mex-Indian work. My bet would be that it's a renegade weaver; one using traditional techniques, but making up her own designs. That's supposed to make bad luck— but now and again somebody will say 'be damned to tradition' and chance it."

"What do you mean, that you use a coarser weave?" Mark asked.

"Well, come on into my workroom and I'll show you."

They followed her through the kitchen into what probably had been intended by the apartment designers as a third bedroom or a den. There was no carpet on the pale gold hardwood floor; the only furniture was a huge loom. But that loom was not in use; it wasn't even strung. Instead Sherry showed them a loom barely the size of a coffee table.

"You see?" she said. "This is a piece I'm doing for myself; a *huiple* and wrap-skirt with all the patterning in the weave instead of in the colors." She brightened as she stroked the finished fabric. "It was Robert's idea; it was the first time in a long time that he's shown any interest in my work. I've got the skirt done, the blouse is three-fourths finished. But look, this is the finest weave I've done yet, and you can see that my piece has only about half the number of threads per inch as the piece in the photograph."

Mark looked closer, and saw that she was absolutely correct. "So this couldn't have come from one of your outfits?"

She shook her head. "No, no way. I've only seen work like that once and that—" she faltered. "That was in Mexico," she finished flatly.

Her eyes flickered over to Di and back. Mark didn't miss the glance; neither did Di.

"If you don't mind, Mark," Di said then, "I'll get back to the car and start writing this up. It'll probably take me a while to put this into terms the Chief understands, so take your time."

"You don't have to leave—" Sherry began half-heartedly.

Di shook her head. "I'll think better in the car—and I mumble when I write. No problem, and it's a beautiful day."

"Then let me see you to the door," Sherry replied, obviously torn between relief and a desire to be the proper hostess.

Mark followed them as far as the living room, where he sank down into the luxuriously soft upholstery in one of corners of the pit. He couldn't help reflecting wryly on how out-of-place he looked, in his sneakers, jeans, and blue workshirt.

"So," he said, when Sherry returned alone. "Why don't you tell me a little about where you saw that kind of work."

Her face was closed and about as close to expression-less as Sherry ever got. "Well, it was on the trip where Robert met the girls. We were in Mexico City; Robert was working on spec for *TravelWorld*, and I was looking for examples of the kind of clothing I told you about. We were out at the pyramids when this young girl came up to us, trying to sell us silver jewelry."

Her brow wrinkled in puzzlement. "It was Lupe, of course; she's not the oldest of the girls, but she's the leader. She was wearing exactly that kind of weave, I think. The funny thing is that I *don't* remember much about that day, or the next. I think I might have gotten heat stroke, or something. I know that I was in a kind of fever; but I don't remember taking half the photographs or making a quarter of the charts that I obviously *did*. I do remember that Lupe loaned me more garments to copy while Robert took them out to pose in the ruins; that was what I was photographing and charting all day. But I really *don't* remember much about the things she was wearing, except that the figures in the weave were different from what she gave me."

"So—this stuff could, in fact probably *did*, come from Mexico City?"

To his surprise, she shook her head. "No, because I don't know where Lupe is originally from. She *could* be from up on the border around El Paso; her English is certainly good enough for that. It's really odd; I just don't know that much about the girls. It's that I really don't care that much, I guess. I—" She laughed, but it was obviously forced. "I resent them. And I just can't get past that. I guess I don't *want* to know more about them than I do; knowing about them would make them human, and I'd have to like them then."

"Sherry, why did you ask Di if she did deprogramming?"

Sherry blushed again, and bit her lip. "Just—I have these stupid ideas, sometimes. Like—sometimes it seems as if Lupe and the others have got some kind of strange hold on Rob that has nothing to do with sex. I can't help thinking that they've maybe gotten him tangled up in a peyote thing or something."

"He didn't look like or act like a druggie to me," Mark said, cautiously. "And I've seen more than my share."

"I know," she sighed. "I told you it was stupid. I think all kinds of nasty things about the girls; I'd like to think everything that's kerwhacky between us is *their* fault. But it isn't, and in my saner moments, I know it."

Mark was at a loss for words. He was saved from having to make a stupid reply by the sound of the front door opening and closing.

"That would be her highness now," Sherry said bitterly. "She never bothers to knock."

The rapid click of high heels on the tile of the entryway and hall preceded "her highness." Mark had no doubt who Sherry meant; his assumption was confirmed when one of Robert's four models prowled into view.

"Prowled" was the only appropriate word. Mark had seen women before who had been described as being graceful as a cat; this was the first one he'd ever seen who merited the description.

Lupe moved with all the lithe swiftness and controlled strength of one of the big hunting cats. Her black hair was confined at the nape of her neck in a simple knot; where Sherry was wearing little more than a bit of eye makeup and some lip-gloss, she was made up to within an inch of her life. And somehow Mark was irresistibly reminded of Indian warriors decorating themselves for combat. She had changed a great deal since she and her sisters had made those initial photographs—no simple folk costumes for *her*, not now. The skin-tight jeans she was wearing bore a top designer name over one hip; the sleeveless tee was silk, he'd bet on it. She was wearing a heavy silver necklace with odd designs incorporated into it; he rather wished he could see it a bit closer. It seemed to him that it looked a lot like the one Robert was wearing.

She was incredible, unbelievably sexy and attractive; skin so perfect it seemed almost poreless, vivid dark coloring, hair a thick fluid cascade of black silk. He could feel himself responding to her in spite of himself. She held herself with the poise of one born royal, and so aware of the fact that it had become unconscious awareness. Even that prominent nose was not a detraction— rather, it seemed that Sherry's nose (for example) was absurdly small by comparison.

The Queen of the Tigers, he thought, looking at her with mixed admiration and some emotion very like apprehension. *My God, poor Sherry! How can a lovely spirit compete with a body and face like that? She looks absolutely washed out next to this girl.*

"Sherry, señora, is Robert home?" the girl asked innocently. Her voice was low, and seemed to throb. Mark found his attraction to her increasing when he heard her speak, and he fought against it.

He managed to break the spell, at least in part—so he actually saw the split-second glance of hate she cast at him before turning a blandly sweet face towards Sherry.

He spared a second to catch a glance at Sherry himself. To his surprise, she was looking—bemused, was the only way he could put it. A little dazed. She showed not a hint of the resentment and anger she had expressed earlier. Instead she almost looked ensorcelled by the lovely model.

"He's in the darkroom," Sherry said slowly. "He asked me not to bother him."

"Ah well, in that case, we will wait for him at the studio, *si?*" She again cast a split-second glance of barely-curbed aggression at Mark. "*Buenos dias, señora.*"

And with that, she turned and glided back the way she had come.

"Now that was odd," Di said thoughtfully when they had left the apartment complex.

"What was odd?"

"First, *I* didn't see Lupe, but unless she made a really strange detour she'd have had to come right by me."

"Huh-uh, no mystery," Mark replied absently. "Sherry told me they live in the same complex; it's convenient for Robert."

"I bet it is," Di said flatly. "Still—I'm surprised I didn't at least see her at the front door. Well, the other odd thing was pretty minor—Robert is even more of a negative personality than you are."

"Gee thanks—"

"Sorry, that doesn't mean what it sounds like. A negative personality is one that attracts discarnate personalities and moves aside for them very easily. In other words, a medium. It has nothing to do with your strength of will, which is fine, thank you. It really doesn't have much to do with what makes you 'Mark Valdez'; it has everything to do with how strongly you and your physical body are linked in. In your case, not very. In Robert's case, even less so. That was why I put the shields on you in the first place right after we cleaned up the mess in Quasi's apartment; they prevent other personalities from forcing you out."

"Yeah I remember," he said, waiting for a light to change.. "You told me I was about as defenseless as a baby. That if you hadn't come along, that thing we called up would have moved right in and set up housekeeping."

"It would have, too. Although I will admit to deliberately trying to scare you so you'd give me consent to shield you." She grinned thinly.

"Well I'm damned glad you did," he replied, returning the grin, and accelerating into traffic. "There's been a couple times since I've felt something tapping on the door that I was pretty sure I didn't want to let in."

"Then I'm doubly glad. I like *you*, Mark. I'd rather not find somebody else in your body. Well, the third odd thing is that Robert seems to have shields on him that are just as good as the ones I put on you. They *feel* like they were set up internally—so either he's been learning something other than photography these last few years, or he's a natural."

"He must be a natural," Mark replied, thinking that she was right in saying that was odd. Robert was about the *least* mystical person he knew. "In all the years *I've* known him, he's never been interested in the occult."

"It's not impossible," Di said thoughtfully. "I've run into people shielded even tighter than he is that were doing the shielding unconsciously. Including a healer— which is *really* odd. So he isn't the weirdest natural I've run into, by a long shot. I just wish I could have gotten past those shields; it would have been useful to know how he *really* feels about Sherry. If he doesn't give a damn, we maybe could do something about the situation among the three of you—"

That cut a little too close to the quick. "Speaking of Sherry," Mark said hastily, "I've got a bit of a lead. She said she thinks she remembers that Lupe and the others were wearing brocades like that when they first met in Mexico City. So I'm going to take the pic to the Archeology and Anthropology Departments over at the university this afternoon."

"Sounds like we're splitting up, then," Di replied.

"Why?" he asked, surprised. "I thought you'd come with me—"

"If you can wait until tomorrow, fine. But this afternoon I have to get Aunt Nita talked into plugging me into the *brujiera* net. And like I told you, so far as the *brujas* are concerned, it's 'no men allowed.'"

"Oh." Mark thought about that for a while. "Okay, then I'll get hold of Charlie Mountainhawk and see if he's had a chance to get with his brother. We'll split up this afternoon, and get together tomorrow morning."

"If something doesn't happen first," Di replied, pessimistically. "This was just the first night; if the pattern holds, we've got two more to go."

· ELEVEN

As it happened, Mark didn't have to go looking for
Charlie Mountainhawk; Charlie was already looking for
him.

There was a message in his locker: *If you can come by
between noon and six, give me a buzz. Johnnie wants to
talk.*

He checked his watch: it was only four. He stopped by
the pay phone in the hall, plugged in a quarter, and
punched Charlie's number.

"Hello?" said a familiar, female voice with more than
a hint of wariness.

"Doreen?" Mark replied, holding his hand over his
free ear to cut out the noise from the people in the hall
behind him. "It's Mark Valdez. Charlie left a note—"

"Oh, Mark!" The tone warmed about twenty degrees.
"Hi, sorry to sound unfriendly, but we've been getting
crank calls. Charlie said you might be calling if you got a
chance. He and Johnnie are down in the garage, so why
don't you come on over?"

"I'll be there in about fifteen minutes, is that all
right?"

"Silly man." Doreen Mountainhawk chuckled. "You
know good and well you're welcome any time you choose

to show your face. Bring your appetite and stay for dinner. I'll put some more water in the stew."

It was Mark's turn to chuckle. "Sure, okay—but only because I know you'll make me feel guilty if I don't. When are you going to stop trying to fatten me up?"

"About the same time I stop trying to find you a wife. Now hang up the phone and get your tail over here!"

"Yes'm," he said obediently, and replaced the receiver.

He stopped at Dispatch to leave his whereabouts with Lydia, the little girl from Baton Rouge. As he'd more than half expected she gave him a sobering stare, fixing him with eyes the color of the darkest brown velvet imaginable, but said only "You-all be careful, Valdez. There's some folk out there got a serious anger wit' you."

He figured she would know. It was amazing how many sensitives were coming out of the headquarters woodwork since he began this case. "I am being careful," he replied. "But I've got a job to do, too—and damned if I'm going to let them keep me from doing it. Hear?"

She nodded, slowly. "I hear. Just be watchin' behind."

"And to all sides, and overhead," he responded. "I won't forget. I like my hide the way it is."

Charlie's apartment wasn't far, either as the crow flies or by road. It took him just about the fifteen minutes he'd told Doreen that it would—and then only because he'd checked his finances and stopped on the way for a baby gift.

"Hey, Cisco!" Charlie hailed him from the garage.

"Hey, Cochise!" he hailed back, pulling the Ghia in behind Charlie's orange VW bug.

"Better watch out," said a second voice from somewhere under the Beetle. "Don't park these two kraut cars too close together; it's springtime, and they might decide to mate. Then Charlie'll be stuck with a garageful of little orange safety cones."

As Mark got out, the owner of the second voice emerged from under the front end of the Bug; though he had grease smudges reminiscent of war paint on both cheekbones, there was no mistaking the family resemblance to Charlie. This young man, a bit thinner and a bit less muscular than Charlie, had to be Johnnie Mountainhawk.

Johnnie came around the car, wiping his hands on a rag. "Hi," he said, holding out his right, his expression cool and appraising. "I've heard a lot about you."

"Same here," Mark replied, taking the offered hand after shifting his package to his left.

Johnnie grinned. "If it was good, it was all the truth; if it was bad, it's all lies. Charlie, I think you're set for another year or so."

"My future offspring blesses you," Charlie laughed. "Because if I hadn't gotten those brake shoes replaced, Doreen was gonna kill me!"

"Speaking of Doreen—here," Mark said, handing Charlie his package. "Happy baby. It's an answering machine; best way I know of to discourage crank callers. For some reason they don't seem to take to the notion that they only have sixty seconds to make their point."

"Either that, or they don't like the idea that they're being recorded," Johnnie pointed out, visibly thawing a bit.

"Either, or. Doesn't much matter, so long as they quit," Charlie responded, obviously pleased. "Man, thanks. I hadn't even thought of using an answering machine, and those sickos are making Doreen real upset."

"Well I bet this discourages that," Mark answered. "*I* made the recording, my best 'I'm uh linebacker an' I like ta hear bones break' imitation. Anybody who gets past *that* really *wants* to talk to you."

Right after they hooked it up to the kitchen extension, the phone rang. Charlie checked his watch. "That just might be our spooks," he said. "They call about now—"

All four of them hovered over the machine expectantly. "This is the Mountainhawk residence," Mark's voice snarled after the third ring, pitched a good half an octave lower than he normally spoke, and sounding more as if he wanted to kill something than be answering the phone, even via recording. "They can't come to the phone right now, but if you'll leave your name, number, and brief message, they'll get back to you."

The machine emitted a tone; there was silence for a moment, then a high voice—either female, or young male—cursed briefly and softly, and the phone was hung up.

"That was them," Charlie said with satisfaction, as the machine rewound. "By damn, Cisco, it worked!"

Doreen threw her arms around Mark's neck and kissed his ear. He blushed.

"Aw, gosh, sheriff, 'tweren't nuthin'," he drawled.

"Well, that makes two we owe you," Johnnie replied. "So let's see if what I can tell you makes a down payment, all right?"

"Sounds good to me," Mark nodded, as Doreen shooed them all into the living room.

"Okay, let me tell you *where* I am in the scheme of things," Johnnie said as they all arranged themselves on the brown tweed couch. "I tend to be a moderate, but I'm also fairly well known to be a peacemaker, good at building compromises. The gods themselves know that if you get two different *families* together you're likely to have fights, much less tribes. So I hear a lot that most moderates don't. I hope you don't mind, but I'd rather *not* help you infiltrate, okay? If anyone figured out you were a ringer, we'd both lose."

Mark shrugged. "I can live with that, so long as you're willing to keep talking to me."

It was hard to tell, but he thought Johnnie looked relieved. "I'm in a pretty good position of trust, and I don't want to blow it. Especially since, because Granddad is a Medicine Man, I sometimes hear more from the mystics than your average moderate would."

"I take it that you *have* heard something disturbing?" Mark said, with one eyebrow raised.

Johnnie leaned forward on the couch, hands clasped between his denim-clad knees. "From *both* the radicals and the mystics. From the radicals I've heard about a new militant who calls himself 'Burning Water.' They claim he's got the charisma *and the cash* to build a new Indian army and literally take this area away from the whites by force of arms. From the mystics I have been hearing about a new man-god—"

He seemed to be groping for the appropriate term, so Mark tried to supply it. "An avatar?"

"Yeah, that's it, an avatar. They say he's going to somehow reconcile all the tribes, purify their spirits, and build a new Indian stronghold right here in Dallas—a spiritual *and* physical stronghold. And if you guessed he's called Burning Water, you guessed right."

Mark sat back, whistling. "Damn. Now how much of this is smoke-talk and how much is real?"

Johnnie shrugged. "Your guess is as good as mine. I can't prove anything one way or the other, since so far it's just talk and rumor; nobody *I* know has actually met this Burning Water or been recruited by him. Thing is, about half of the mystics are scared spitless—they don't want any part of this 'savior.' The rest of them are falling all over each other in anticipation. The rest of the moderates other than yours truly are figuring the radicals have had a little too much peyote, if you know what I mean. But—this is the catch—none of them have the connections I do because of Charlie, and nobody's put the whole picture together with the sacrificial murders."

"You buy Di's speculation that this and the killings are tied in?"

Johnnie nodded. "Shit, yes. If those killings don't have all the marks of sacrifices, I'll eat your Ghia. I've *always* figured Medicine Magic was for real; took Charlie a while, but he came around to it too. There's *plenty* of traditions that involve blood-sacrifice; it was usually animal, but there's nothing against making it the blood of your enemy. I just wish I had some proof, is all. You wouldn't find many of us shedding any tears over those fat cats getting theirs, but not even the wildest of us go in for drowning kids. That's *not* the way you do it—you *kidnap* the kids and turn 'em into Indians. Anyway, if you get any proof that ties the name 'Burning Water' in to the murders, I want to know about it. If nothing else, this guy is liable to get a lot of *us* blamed for what he's doing, and a lot of us killed, and there aren't enough of us as it is."

"I'll do my best," Mark said. "And thanks for what you've given me. To change the subject, what *were* those phone calls that they got Doreen so upset? I remember the last time you got a porn caller, 'Reenie just laughed at him until he hung up."

"Unfortunately, that *isn't* changing the subject," Charlie said soberly. "They just started this week, and they're part of the reason Johnnie said he'd give you a hand. It was always the same voice, and the same words. 'Tell Mountainhawk that he can't hide behind white man's magic forever. When Burning Water comes, he will have to choose—or die.'"

"Aunt Nita," Di said from the kitchen doorway, "I have a real big favor to ask of you."

Juanita Valdez turned from her sink of dirty dishes and looked at her appraisingly. "From the look on your face, I would say you do," she said, "and the dishes can wait for a moment."

She walked over to Di, drying her hands on her apron, and pulled out two of the chairs around the kitchen table. "Sit; it's easier to talk sitting down."

Di did as she was told, trying to formulate her words in her mind. "I need to find a *bruja*," she said finally. "I figured that you would be the best one to get one to talk to me."

Aunt Nita pursed her lips. "I don't patronize that sort of thing," she said reluctantly. "I *do* believe in certain powers and so forth—but *brujiera*—it's so—I don't quite know how to say it. It seems so loaded down with peasant superstitions."

Di nodded. "I understand. But it's beginning to look like this case Mark and I are on could well be tied in with the darker sort of *brujiera*; the kind that keeps people living in fear of the sorcerers even to this day, and not always just in remote little villages."

"I don't know," Aunt Nita replied hesitantly. "I just *don't* know."

"Aunt Nita, we've been trying to keep this out of the

papers, but do you know how many people have been killed by this bunch of lunatics just since I got here?"

She shook her head, dumbly.

"Sixteen," Di told her flatly. "Three of those were children—the three little ones they found in that cattle tank last month. And there were a half-dozen deaths before *that* murder that we know of."

The elderly woman straightened at that, and Di could sense the indecision leaving her.

"Well," she replied, after a long pause during which she was obviously thinking hard. "I personally don't believe in *brujiera,* but if I did, the first person *I'd* consult would be Marguerita, the woman that comes in to help me clean once a week. And it so happens that she's due tomorrow. I can have a word with her then."

Di fought down a feeling of triumph. They *still* had a long way to go before she could feel she'd accomplished anything.

Tom Beckerman usually went out running as soon as possible after dinner because he could lose himself and not have to think about the working day he'd just passed through. Unfortunately, right now *nothing* was going to drive his worries away, not even the endorphin-high of running.

No two ways about it; ever since they put me on project lead, I've been in a world of hurt.

He swung around the corner and into the parking lot of Five Banners Over Dallas, the big amusement theme-park. It was closed down for the winter, except on weekends, which was why he liked to run here. He couldn't get *in* the park, of course, but the landscaping around the fence was nice, there was a decent path worn there by the maintainance people, and there wasn't even a hint of traffic.

It wouldn't be so bad if those jerks supposed to be doing the programming had gotten off their thumbs and done some work instead of deciding to prove it couldn't be done in the time schedule I set. So what if I'm not a program-mer? No big deal to doing a decent project estimate.

He ran through the parking lot and crossed the grass, heading for a little space between two big evergreen bushes. He got himself slotted into the path, and increased his pace a little, trying to drive the useless worries out of his mind.

But the worries wouldn't go.

Is it my fault the machine was down so much? Is it my fault we lost half the old crew? I hired in twice as many new bodies—they should have been able to pick up the slack and then some! Programming is programming is programming.

He recalled with shame the retirement party they'd thrown for George Herschal this afternoon. George had been with the company since—forever. Since before computers. And toward the end of the party he'd taken Tom aside—

"Young'un," he'd said, in that good-ol'-boy accent of his, his arm lying heavily across Tom's shoulders, *"what you got is a people problem, he-ah. You don't know programmin', an' you don' know squat about how t' handle people. That wouldn't hurt you so much, I've seen leads manage with less'n you—but dammit, boy, you don't lissen t' them as knows what they're doin'! You done hit off more'n you c'n chew, an' the sooner you 'fess up an' let 'em put you back t' what you do good, the happier you're gonna be. You keep tryin' t' play boss-man when you ain't got what it takes, an' you gonna find you went an' painted yourself inta a corner fer sure."*

God, the humiliation.

The damp air was heavy, and seemed hard to breathe. He glanced up, noting that there weren't any stars visible. The sky was heavily overcast again tonight. Hopefully there wouldn't be a repetition of last night's monster storm. The path had dried out during the day, but another rain would make it a muddy mess and he'd have to use the street for a while. And if it began to rain now—Carole had told him not to go out running—

But shoot, that wasn't because of the weather, that was just because she was hysterical about all those people getting carved up. He snorted to himself. Women and their irrational fears. Nothing like that would ever happen to *him*. Most of that bunch had been bums, winos, street-gang punks. Probably the papers were making a big deal out of nothing. Probably the only two solid citizens that had gotten killed had been killed for their money. Nobody mugged a jogger. Everybody knew they never had any cash on them.

He rounded the first landmark that marked his half-way point, feeling the air weigh heavily in his chest, feeling none of the usual runner's euphoria. *Too bad one of those hadn't been my head programmer,* he thought wistfully. *Then I could have claimed that the entire team was too shaken up to work.*

He brooded on his problems as he continued to run, never noticing the shadows that were paralleling his course past the screening trees.

Mark had been forewarned, but it didn't make the scene any easier to handle. After one look, Di had turned pasty white, then headed straight for the nearest park ladies' room, and he didn't blame her.

The only good thing about this was that the Five Banners park was self-contained and more than adequately fenced. So there were no gawkers and journalists, and there had been no one at all in the park until the maintainance people had found the body.

If you could call it that. It was appalling.

The maintenance crew that had found the body had been carted off to the hospital to be treated for shock. So far as anyone could tell, they'd unlocked their entrance after checking the perimeter as they always did, and had found nothing out of the ordinary—certainly no signs of illegal entry. Then they'd gotten as far as the central plaza. . . .

As was getting to be routine (if such a thing could be called "routine"), there had been a cardiectomy. But not until after the victim had been flayed from his soles to his hairline. The heart was missing again; so was the skin.

The whole rite had been performed on a big flat rock right in the middle of the deserted park, next to the double-decker carousel. With the park closed for the winter and the maintainance people gone for the day, Mark figured you could have staged a sit-down orgy for five hundred and nobody would have noticed.

Of course, that didn't explain how the victim and his murderers got *inside* the park in the first place. The insurance company that covered the park was very unhappy; they had some pretty stiff rules regarding access to the place during off hours. Of course, the owners of the park were even less happy—this was supposed to be a place for fun, not mayhem. And since they ran their *own* security, they, like Amerine, had no one to blame but themselves.

To see the aftermaths of these things by floodlight had been bad enough—but to see it by the light of day made it somehow worse.

The coroner himself was on the scene, supervising the whole thing personally.

When Di got back, Mark came up behind him and tapped him on the shoulder, Di trailing along behind him, silent and still very pale.

"Got anything for me yet, Doc?" he asked.

The middle-aged, tough coroner looked more like a weathered old ranch hand than a doctor. It took a lot to rattle him—but by the pallor beneath his tan, this had rattled him good.

"A bit," he replied. "It ain't what you'd call pleasant hearing." He looked askance at Di.

"Fire away," Mark said, "I think I'm getting numb at this point."

"I'm part of the team, too," Di gulped. "I have to know eventually; it might as well be now."

"First thing is it looks like the poor bastard was gang-raped before he was skinned. Not what you're thinkin', not by men. By women."

Mark felt his jaw coming unhinged. "You have *got* to be kidding me!" he exclaimed. "A *guy?*"

The coroner nodded reluctantly. "Yeah, I know; it sounds impossible. But it can be done, and it leaves real distinct signs. It looks to me like it *was*. Second thing is it looks from the pattern of bloodstains and the condition of the corpse like they were real careful about how they got the skin off the poor SOB. What I'm saying is they literally skinned him alive. *Then* they cut his heart out."

Mark had thought he was numb, but his gorge rose at that. He was just as glad that they were taking the body away and he didn't have to look at it any more.

"And I got another update on the second lot of stiffs from night before last," the coroner added.

"Go ahead," Mark managed. Di nodded agreement.

"Ramirez found the rock, like you said he would. He found somethin' else; what was left of a bonfire, and we found bits of burned skin all over that rock. So it looks to us like they threw those four men into the fire, toasted 'em for a bit, pulled 'em out *still alive.* Then they tricked 'em out in their flowers and all, and cut the hearts out. Looks to us like throwin' 'em in the car and settin' it afire was just their way of cleanin' up afterwards."

He grimaced, shrugged, and got back to his crew.

The atmosphere got a little easier after they took the gruesome corpse away. While Di worked with the Forensics group and did a little discreet "checking" with a different set of investigative "tools," Mark took the opportunity to talk with the Chief.

This was the first time he'd ever been put in charge of anything on a case this major, even if it was only a two-man team, and while he wasn't precisely nervous—

Well, he wasn't precisely at ease with the idea either. So he buttonholed the Chief—*outside* the "official" atmosphere of the office—and went over everything they'd checked out so far, including his own solo legwork. This wasn't a class, after all; this was a damned serious case. He wasn't being graded. And there were people dying out here. The Chief had told them all, time and time again, that they were a *team* and should act like one—and Mark was not too proud to ask for advice—ever. Especially not from the man who had solved more big cases than Mark and all his buddies combined.

There *were* a few things he had to leave out, of course,

which was something of a pity, but he was surprised at the amount of ground they'd covered in the last four or five weeks.

"Have I missed anything?" he asked when he'd finished. "Left anything undone that you would have done?"

The Chief slowly shook his head. "Not by my reckonin'," he replied. "Yer doin' what I asked y'all t'do; m'nose tells me yer gettin' close. Closer'n we bin gettin', that's fer sure. Charlie's brother gonna git you in with them war-drummers?"

"We decided against it," Mark replied. "We don't want to flush *his* credibility; we might need somebody where he is again some day."

"Huh; yeah, could be. Jest keep in steady touch with him, okay? Otherwise play it as it lays, boy. Say, what was it Miz Di did t' rout that kraut t'other day? Heard somethin' 'bout that, but jest enough t' make me powerful curious."

Willing to change the topic of conversation now that he was fairly sure of the Chief's mind, Mark gave him a blow-by-blow account of Di and the German journalist. Before he was through, the Chief was laughing so hard his face was red and tears were squeezing out of his eyes.

"Oh *damn!*" he gasped. *"Damn,* I wish't I'd been there! That boy is one pain in the you-know; I bin prayin' fer an excuse t' bounce him out on his can, but he don't give me none. Lissen, you kin tell Miz Di fer me that I think she is one all-right gal. An' the next time she takes on Herr Fieber, I wanna be there. Front row seat, an' popcorn."

When Di returned to the house late that afternoon, Mark's aunt was waiting for her, and with her was a thin, sun-bronzed woman not too many years Juanita's junior.

"Diana, this is Marguerita Valdoza," Aunt Nita said quietly. "I took the liberty of telling her something about you, and something of what you need."

"I'm very pleased to meet you," Di replied with all the sincerity she could muster; not easy since she was about ready to drop. "Thanks, Aunt Nita; that makes things a lot simpler."

She held out her hand and the woman took it; her clasp was warm, firm, and dry. Di's immediate impression was of a woman who would brook no nonsense from anyone; and a woman of absolute and unwavering honesty.

Not an easy person to live with—but then, I don't have to live with her, she thought wryly.

The woman measured her with her eyes for a moment before replying. "Señorita Diana—I must tell you that I do not personally know anyone of the kind you wish to speak to."

"But you know someone who knows someone?" Di hazarded.

Marguerita shrugged. "So they claim. I have never seen the need for witchery—but there are those who believe. And those who believe are something shy of speaking to strangers. So I must send you through the maze; to my daughter-in-law, who has a friend, who—so I am told—knows a *bruja.*"

Di nodded. "I understand," she said. "And I know it's going to take time. This kind of thing always does."

For the first time the woman smiled. "Less, perhaps, than you might think," she said. "I am not known for my patience."

Marguerita took Di in tow, a slender yacht being bossed out of the harbor by a very expert tug. They traveled to her home, just on the edge of an area near where Athena lived. They went by bus—a form of transportation Di was becoming depressingly familiar with. Once at Marguerita's home, a place scoured so fanatically clean that Di suspected her of Dutch blood rather than Spanish-American, there was coffee—and, at length, a phone call—and again after a wait, an introduction to the daughter-in-law, Consuela.

Consuela was another, younger version of Marguerita. There was more coffee, and questions by Marguerita while Consuela listened and passed a silent judgment.

Eventually some signal passed between the two women, for Consuela became friendlier, and took her across the street to her own apartment.

There was *more* coffee (Di was rather glad she had a very high tolerance for caffeine) and another phone call, and at long last Di was passed into the hands of Maria Angelita Rosario.

This was not the end; like a pair of Inquisitors, both women plied her with questions, some of which seemed to have little or nothing to do with the problem she faced or the *bruja*. Di curbed her impatience, held her tongue, and answered them as clearly and with as much politeness as she could manage.

Finally the two women nodded to each other, rose from the table almost as one, and motioned to her to follow.

A walk of several blocks brought them all to the home of the *bruja*, a young widow, Theresa Montenegro. There the other two left her, after spending some time in a whispered discussion with the object of Di's search.

The widow was a tired-looking, faded slip of a woman, somewhat washed out by the black dress she wore. "You will come in, please, Miss Tregarde," she said, reluctantly, her voice as faded and tired as the rest of her. "I do not know that I can help you, but I will listen."

"Thank you," Di replied, preceding the *bruja* into the apartment, and finding herself in a room that had been intended as a living room and now was serving as a kind of place of worship.

Dominating one wall was an altar, thick with candles and statues of various saints, and surmounted by a statue of the Virgin. Despite the heat, every candle on the altar was lit, and the light reflecting from the gilded statues was a little dazzling. Beneath the altar was a padded kneeler, well worn.

There were a couple of benches at the end of the room opposite the altar; Theresa took a seat on one, and Di on the other.

Well, she's not as high-powered as Athena was, Di thought, after taking stock of the atmosphere, *But she knows what she's doing, and she's got the gift.* She took a moment to analyze the emotions emanating from the *bruja,* and was less pleased. *She's afraid. Dammit, I was hoping to avoid that. Is it me?*

She delved a little deeper, while the *bruja* appeared to be taking the same time to study *her.*

No, she decided. *It isn't me. But she is afraid. She doesn't want to talk to an outsider at all. There's some threat she perceives, and she thinks talking to me will draw its attention to her.*

"Señora Montenegro," she said, breaking the silence when it became apparent that the *bruja* would not do so, "I come to you in most urgent need of information. I have reason to believe that there is an evil *brujo,* a man of power, making blood-magic to give him strength. I think that only the power of *brujiera* or the knowledge held by the *brujas* will reveal him to me. I believe that it is *he* who has committed the murders that have the police so confused."

"You are working with the police, *si?*" the *bruja* asked in a thin voice.

"I am, yes," Di replied. "I am working with them as a favor to a friend, who is the nephew of the friend of Marguerita Valdoza and is himself a policeman."

"Ah." The *bruja* studied her for another moment. "I have no love for the police," she said, finally.

"Señora, it is not a matter of whether one loves the police," Di replied patiently. "It is a matter of whether or not one will allow this evil *brujo* to continue to kill. The police are only the means to remove him. It may become necessary to use other means, but for now, the police must be my means."

"Ah," the woman said again, and studied her worn, work-roughened hands. "I do not know, Miss Tregarde. I do not know that I can help you."

Substitute "can" for "will," and we're a lot closer to the truth, Di thought, curbing her anger at the woman's reluctance. *If I stay much longer—I am going to lose my temper; I know it. Damn. All right, I know where she lives—maybe I can find some leverage to use on her later.*

"I must go," she said, rising, the woman's eyes follow-

ing her. "Whether or not you can help me, I must do
what I can."

"I—" the woman began, then shut her lips firmly on
whatever she was going to say, and led the way to the
door.

"Will you just promise me this, Señora Montenegro?"
Di asked as she paused halfway into the outer hall. "Will
you promise me to *think* about what I have asked?"

The *bruja* bowed her head, as if taking on a heavy
burden. "*Sí*," she whispered. "That, I will promise."

Pablo had picked up the trail of the gringo witch as she
passed near the *barrio*. He was elated that she had come
to him; it would have been far more difficult to find her
in her own territory.

Even better, she was taking the bus; that made it
possible for him to follow her closely—if she had been
traveling about with the man, in his car, Pablo would
have had to borrow or steal a vehicle, and might well
have been far more obvious. As it was, he was just one
more Mestizo boy on the bus; a little quieter, more
well-behaved than most, but just a face in the crowd.

He would have thought she would stand out in that
crowd, but somehow she seemed to blur into it. He
decided finally that it was because of her magic; she was
blending in like the chameleons on a branch. That made
him wary; he knew it took Burning Water a great effort
and much power to keep their sacrifices hidden, yet this
witch was casually hiding herself as if the effort was
nothing. He understood the god's caution now in dealing
with her; until Burning Water came into his complete
power at the Great Sacrifice, it would be well to beware
even of such a negligible thing as this witch.

Especially when it appeared that she was not insignifi-
cant at all.

But the witch seemed preoccupied, buried deeply
within her own thoughts, as she sat hunched on her little
sliver of bus bench. Her chin was tucked down into her
jacket, and her collar up around her ears; her dark eyes
stared ahead of her without truly *seeing* much of what
was going on about her.

It came to Pablo then that she might well be working some of her magic; a thing not at all unlikely, now that he came to think about it.

His own magic was all borrowed, and he used it gingerly, as he would use an unfamiliar weapon. He feared to trigger something by coming too close, and so eased his borrowed magic only near enough to test the very edges of hers.

He recoiled at once, sensing powerful defenses, and alarms and traps behind the defenses.

So she *was* working magics. Best to leave her alone, then.

It was then, turning his vision from *within* to *without* that Pablo saw the strange blond man.

He certainly stood out on this bus, with his golden blond hair and his sunburned face. And there was no magic hiding *his* presence. Strangely enough the gringo witch did not seem aware of him—but he was certainly aware of *her*. He pretended to read a paper, but he never turned the pages, and Pablo knew within moments that this man was, as was Pablo, following the witch.

And that made Pablo very happy.

Helmut Fieber, journalist for *Der Tag,* was also very happy.

At first, after the strange madwoman had routed him with her maniacal speech and her supposed "fecal samples," he'd simply been relieved to escape from a potentially unpleasant situation. But after reflection, he had begun to wonder if he hadn't—as the Americans put it—"been had."

For he had seen this woman at or near the site of every murder since then—and yes, she *had* been working side by side with the coroner's Forensics team—

But she had never once departed with them. Rather, she left—and presumably arrived—with a young man. A young man who was never in uniform, but who Helmut had discovered was one "Mark Valdez." *Detective* Mark Valdez, to be precise.

And Helmut had more than once seen this woman in

consultation with the Chief of Detectives, Samuel Grimes. He had watched as the unapproachable, surly Grimes listened to her every word, and seemed to accord those words some weight and importance.

In short, this was no coroner's assistant.

So he had attached himself to her at the Five Banners park, and spent the entire day following her.

That had *not* been an easy task—and it had been made more difficult by the fact that this woman (surely, surely she must be at least a *little* mad) had either walked or taken public transportation. He had nearly lost her any number of times today; he was hot and very tired, and did not in the least understand why she was not in possession of a car like every other American. The buses were all hot, crowded, and smelled of things best not thought of. And those who used the buses were not the sort that Fieber would have associated with by choice.

He was uncomfortably aware that his blond hair and light skin were (and had been all day) attracting surreptitious attention from a great many people; on this bus, on other buses, on the street. This obsession with public transportation of the madwoman—it seemed very dangerous to him.

Only now do I begin to understand that man in New York, who shot those boys on the subway, he thought, trying to make himself as inconspicuous as possible. *I felt safer in Nicaragua.*

He could not understand why *she* was ignored, either; she surely looked as out of place as he did.

Perhaps, in her worn jeans and jacket, she did not look prosperous enough.

He began to regret his clothing choice of the morning. He *did* look prosperous. At least more than most of the rest of the bus riders.

Perhaps she will get off, soon, he thought hopefully, seeing her rousing from the inward-turned concentration she had been showing and display some signs of taking note of her surroundings. *If I can get her alone—more important, if I can find out where it is that she lives—all of this will have been worthwhile.*

To his immense relief, at that moment she pulled the wire to signal the bus driver to stop, and rose gracefully to her feet, using the momentum of the bus to propel her down the aisle to the front door.

He lurched to his feet and took the rear exit, hopping quickly down to the pavement and trusting the darkness of near-midnight to conceal the fact that he was behind her.

But she did not look to see if she was followed, merely strode off at her normal (albeit unnervingly) brisk pace.

Fieber was right behind.

Juanita Valdez had known all her life that she was "sensitive"; the Gift (as her grandmother had called it) ran in her blood. That Gift had saved the family time and time again from fire, flood, Indian raid—

It didn't save us from the greed of politicians—but then, I'm not certain that anything would have—

Tonight her Gift was warning *her* of danger. Her nerves were as tight as guitar strings, and had been so ever since sundown. She circled the house repeatedly, checking locks, checking windows, peering out into the darkness and watching for the shadow that should not be there, the movement where nothing should move—

And all for nothing. The locks were sound, the windows secure, and all outside the house was serene.

You old fool, she scolded herself. *Nobody is going to get in except your girls. Nobody is going to get in without a key! And the girls are all safely in their beds. Except young Di, of course, and she should be able to take care of herself.*

Those thoughts did not comfort; instead the feeling of danger grew with every passing minute. It got so bad that she turned out all the lights, the better to see what was going on outside—*and* to avoid betraying her movements to anyone who might be lurking out there.

Finally she felt her way to the kitchen and armed herself with the biggest cleaver she owned. That gesture, as futile as it might be, at least made her feel a little better.

Certain that she was being terribly foolish, and yet

unable to help herself, she set herself up as guard on the front door.

Great-grandmama must be grinning like a fox at me from her seat in Paradise, she told herself. *I am surely playing the senile old idiot. What's going to come at me anyway—bandidos? Pancho Villa? Renegades?*

Then she heard the rattle of a key in the lock, and froze.

Di wrenched the door open and closed it quickly behind her, double-locking it and throwing the security bolt. She was panting like a greyhound at the end of the race, and with good reason—she'd run the last six blocks to the boarding house.

From the moment she'd stepped off the bus she'd known she was in danger. At first she had simply acted normally—except for putting up full and battle-hardened shields. But nothing attacked—

Only the feeling of peril had grown, nearer and stronger with every minute, until she had found herself running as fast as she could for the relative safety of the boarding house and her tools. She'd hit the door and unlocked it so fast she hardly believed it, and had squirted inside as if she'd been oiled.

She heard a movement behind her and started to spin—then her empathic senses identified Aunt Nita, and she relaxed just a trifle; completing her turn, but without the urgency of self-defense.

Her eyes had already adjusted to the limited light in the hall. It did not surprise her to see that Aunt Nita had armed herself with a cleaver.

She cleared her throat. "So you feel it too—" she said; more of a statement than a question.

Aunt Nita nodded, slowly, the light from the streetlight outside glinting off the shiny blade of the cleaver. "Since sundown, and getting worse," she replied.

Di took a deep breath, willing her pulse to slow now that she was no longer running. "How about," she whispered, "if we make the rounds of the perimeter?"

Aunt Nita just nodded.

* * *

Although the feeling of danger had not faded, just having Diana with her made Juanita feel immeasurably better. *Somehow—anything I've missed she'll find. I'm not sure how, but—*

She followed in Diana's wake; the girl went first to the kitchen, to her faint surprise. She took a tumbler from the cabinet, filled it with water, then dumped the entire contents of the saltshaker on the kitchen table into it.

If I didn't know that she *knows what she's doing—*

Then Juanita almost voiced an objection, as the girl muttered something over the tumbler and traced little signs over it with fingers that moved more swiftly than the cloud-shadows racing across the moon outside. Then she remembered that the girl had promised *not* to compromise Juanita's beliefs—and that Di had weaponry that was—had to be—something other than purely physical. She bit the half-hearted protest back, and simply watched.

Starting with the kitchen, Diana began a circuit of the entire house, tracing little diagrams on each window and door with the salt-water mixture. She moved as surely as any cat in the darkness; moved as surely as if she had Juanita's own lifelong familiarity with the house and its contents.

Somehow Juanita was not terribly surprised to see those little diagrams glowing blue; nor that they continued to glow, very faintly, for a few seconds after they both passed.

When the circuit of the house was completed, Diana led the way, still in silence, to the darkened living room. There they sat, as quietly as it is possible for two living women to sit; Juanita clutching her cleaver so tightly her fingers hurt, Diana still holding that tumbler of saltwater as if it was both talisman and weapon.

It might well be both—Juanita thought—

Then the night was splintered by the shattering of glass.

"The back—" Diana cried, grabbing a poker from the fireplace beside her and racing for the kitchen.

Juanita ran right along with her—until they both

suddenly had an attack of good sense at the kitchen door and halted right there, listening for further sounds.

No sounds at all—

And—it's gone, Juanita realized suddenly. *The feeling of danger—it's gone.*

She steeled herself, transferred the cleaver to her left hand, and flung open the kitchen door with her right, flicking on the kitchen light as she did so.

There was a large blond man lying on his side across her kitchen table, sprawling half in, half out of the now-shattered west window.

He was staring at them both, from eyes that were nearly popping out of his head. He wasn't moving.

That was largely because he was very dead.

Juanita had not known until this moment that she was a brave woman. She put down the cleaver—noting, with a detached portion of her mind that her hand was not shaking at all—and followed Diana across an expanse of brown linoleum that now seemed as wide as the state of Texas itself.

The man was dripping blood all over her spotless kitchen table and floor, and another part of Juanita was outraged at the mess she was going to have to clean up. Now that they were closer, she could see that there was a gaping hole in his chest. Presumably his heart had been cut out—

It was a rational presumption, because she could easily see that a meaty lump of something vaguely heartlike and heart-shaped had been stuffed halfway into the man's mouth.

She jumped and nearly screamed as Diana cleared her throat.

"I think—" Diana said slowly "—that somebody is doing their best to scare me off this case." Her face hardened. "And it isn't going to work."

·TWELVE

THEY HAD BEEN EXPECTING—AND DREADING—ANOTHER massacre of some kind. It was practically inevitable, given the pattern that they had established.

But there was no way that they could have anticipated the scene they were called to in the early dawn hours at Possum Kingdom Park.

"Mark," Di choked, after one look, "I can't take any more of this."

Her face was so pale it was nearly transparent, and her eyes seemed to fill the upper half of it. Mark had a feeling that he was as green as she was pale. All of the horrors that had led up to this climax of the three-day cycle were totally eclipsed by the sheer *slaughter* that had been found this morning by the park-department employees whose duty it was to check the park over when they arrived for the day's work.

From the signs it appeared as though the park had been in use for some time as a transfer point for illegal aliens. There were half-a-dozen trucks parked in an orderly row, all cleverly set behind a screening of evergreens running as a windbreak on an island in the middle of the parking lot—evergreens that would just happen to hide them from patrols. Their painstaking arrangement argued for practice and much thought. All of the trucks were a mottled, dark green, further blending with the foliage, and all sported license plates from differing states. All of them were registered to families of migrant agricultural workers.

This didn't have the look of a "professional" people-smuggling job; it had more of the air of something that legal immigrants had concocted to get friends and family across the border.

It appeared that the illegals were taken across the border by some other means, then brought to the park and dropped off there, to be met by prearrangement. Probably each family (represented by a truck) took on three or four "new members," then headed on to another job. From there the new workers could slip into the migrant population almost invisibly.

It was a slick system; one that had probably been functioning for months, if not years, without detection.

Only—last night, the system had been used for someone else's purposes, and the migrants had walked into a trap. A death-trap.

There were nearly fifty bodies in the picnic area near the parking lot. Men, women—and children. Nearly *half* of the bodies were of children under twelve.

And there were parts missing. Hearts—and other things.

Di hadn't been able to bear more than a single glance. She took one look and buried her face in Mark's shoulder. He held her awkwardly, unable to give her any comfort at all. He attempted to deal with the scene, but he wasn't handling it much better than she was.

For that matter, neither was most of the rest of the Homicide team. They were somewhat used to death—but this went beyond their experience and worst nightmares.

The Forensics crew was coping, managing to do their job despite the horror that could be seen behind their deadpan expressions, but only with the help of the same emergency crew that had helped sort out the bodies after the last big air disaster at DFW. *That* lot was familiar with horror, and their steadiness helped to keep the Forensics folk from losing their own grip.

After several abortive attempts to face the carnage, all of which ended in her tears and failure, Mark sent Di back to the car; but he felt honor-bound to stay. She wasn't coherent enough for him to make out whether it was *just* the physical butchery that was getting to her, or something more. She looked on the verge of a breakdown—and he wouldn't let her risk one; he needed her too much.

But he also knew *he* must look like hell, because one of the parameds came over and patted his shoulder with clumsy encouragement.

"Hang in there, buddy," the stranger said, his own face stiff and his eyes dull, his blond hair lank with nervous sweat. "You get numb after about a half an hour, honest."

Something inside Mark winced at the idea. He didn't *want* to go numb—

And yet, at the same time, he did. It would almost be worth losing one's humanity to also lose the frustrated agony, the knife-edged guilt, the sheer revulsion caused by seeing human beings, *children,* reduced to so much butchered meat—

"How many?" he asked, his jaw clenched so hard it ached.

"Thirty-eight. And no sign that any of them fought, either. It's damned spooky, is all I can tell you. It's like they just laid themselves down for the knife—like another Jim Jones thing, you know?"

When Mark forced himself to go nearer to examine the bodies heaped in the center of the clearing behind the shelter, he discovered that the paramed was right. Even though every face he saw was a mask of terror, even though the expressions were distorted with a pain and fear he could only imagine, there were *no* signs of combat or attempts at flight on the part of any of the victims.

And that was more than just "spooky." That was unnatural, and it raised the hair on the back of his neck in a way that almost made him forget the blood and the mutilated bodies.

Now he was *drawn* to the actual sacrificial site by an urgency he could not deny. Behind the cement and wood shelter was a picnic table, the makeshift altarplace. There was thick, dry grass all about it, grass that was showing distinct signs of life after the rain of the night before. He knelt beside Jean in the grass and studied the site, studied the way the grass was trampled flat in places, studied the obvious trail—

Unable to believe what he thought he was seeing, he walked around to the opposite side of the site. It looked exactly the same—at least to his eyes—from there. He returned to Jean's side.

"No," he said flatly to her. "There is no way—"

"Tell me what *you* see," she replied. "I'm trying to decide if I've gone around the bend."

"It—no, it's too damned weird."

"Cough it out, dammit!" she snapped, a wild look of being near the edge herself stirring in the depths of her hazel eyes.

"It looks—it looks like they all lined up *here*—" He pointed to a nearly straight line of flattened grass at the edge of the parking lot. "—like they lined up like kids after recess. And then—then they came forward, one at a time—" He indicated the path that was clearly worn into the grass from the beginning of the flattened line, past the shelter, to end at the picnic table that had been used as the sacrificial altar. "—of their own free will—and—I *can't* believe it! Even if whoever it was had these people under guard, and the guards were armed with machine guns, *some* of them should have tried to break and run! But—"

"There's not a sign of it," Jean agreed, nodding, not losing a particle of that strange, fey expression as she turned to study the site once again. "I don't believe it either—but there isn't one single indication that anything else happened. They could have been zombies or robots—except that—those faces—"

She shuddered, and Mark shuddered in sympathy.

"They *knew* what was going to happen to them, and they marched up to their deaths anyway," she said. "Mark, it doesn't make any *sense!* Not even drugs or hypnosis could make people do that! It's like they were all under some kind of horrible, evil·spell."

"It *was* a 'spell.' Of control," Di said flatly. "They were controlled, from first to last. Like robots—only these robots knew what was going to happen to them."

She had managed to come out of the car and face the site once the bodies were all carted off to the morgue. By then nearly everyone had gone except Mark and Ramirez.

She passed a trembling hand through her hair, and bit her lip. "That's not all, Mark. This time the cult leaders haven't bothered to wipe out the traces of what they did. It's like they've gotten powerful enough to be contemptuous of me. . . ."

"Maybe," he replied. "Maybe not. They *could* be counting on the idea that they've scared you off. Hm?"

"*I don't know!*" She looked at him with haunted eyes. "That's the problem—I *don't know!*"

"Easy kid—" he soothed her as he would have soothed Treemonisha in a thunderstorm. "Tell me how you know they were controlled."

She crossed her arms tightly across her chest and hunched her shoulders in misery. "I can feel it," she said. "It's still here. They were—like in a nightmare where you try to run and can't." Her nostrils flared, like a horse scenting smoke. "I—I know how to do it, too—I could control two, maybe three people myself if I had to. I'd be more subtle, though." She closed her eyes in a spasmodic grimace of pain. "And I wouldn't do it if there were any other way. But *I* couldn't control thirty-eight. Not if my life depended on it."

"There were *five* of them," he reminded her, "and half of those thirty-eight were kids, and not too bloody likely to run away from their parents. That's seventeen adults to control, and you can bet they only used psi-coercion on the ones that were *likely* to bolt. Say, half of the seventeen. What does that bring the total down to?"

"Nine-ish." She gave him a look that said she wanted to hope that he was right, but was afraid to.

"*Less* than two each," he persisted, laying a hand on her arm, with a gesture he hoped would steady her. "Whatcha think, Pancho?"

Ramirez nodded thoughtfully. "Makes sense to me," he agreed, rubbing his chin. "I mean, I don't know squat about this stuff, but stands to reason if they were good enough to put the whammy on thirty-eight people, Di, they'd have squashed you like a bug last night."

"And they didn't," Mark asserted. "Did they."

"No—they didn't even try to hurt me or someone connected with me. They got that kraut reporter instead." She was standing a little straighter, and losing some of that haunted expression. "What's more, they didn't cross my protections; they didn't even try. Maybe they couldn't. Maybe I am still their equal. I think—you might be right."

Mark heaved a mental sigh of relief. "How 'bout we get away from here—get somewhere you can think?"

She nodded, and unfolded her arms. He took the hand nearest him and gave it a brief squeeze before dropping it.

"Look on the bright side," he said, guiding her toward the car with one hand lightly on her forearm. "We're clear for another three weeks—"

"Sure," she agreed somberly, as Ramirez parted from them to trudge across the worn asphalt to his own vehicle. "And then it begins again—*worse* than this."

Di had never been one to use drugs as a crutch—but she was glad of the emergency one-pill stash of Valium in her purse. She needed more than herb tea to calm her nerves after the revelations of this morning. It was dangerous to be tranked—but far more dangerous to be on a hair trigger and ready to break if someone sneezed. When the pill took hold it steadied her enough to cope, but left her still pretty well in control of psi-senses and shielding.

I daren't try a levinbolt—but hopefully I won't need to use one until after the pill wears off. Okay—reality check. She took a careful accounting of herself. *I'll be okay. I'm wired enough that it isn't making me fuzzy or shutting me down, just getting me a little unwired. But no more after this one wears off.*

She parted from Mark at headquarters, but only after giving him the address she was going to be seeking. If she didn't show up at the university by the time his appointment with Professor Jermaine came due—

Hopefully they wouldn't have to worry about that. But after last night, she was taking no more stupid chances.

She was headed once again for the *barrio* and the home of the *bruja*. And this time she was armed with more than mere words.

The bus was jammed full; noisy, hot, and full of diesel fumes. The fumes gave her a headache, and she was literally squashed up against the window. She leaned her forehead against the window-glass, unfocusing her vision and shutting her ears, and delicately probed at the minds around hers, looking for danger, for hidden enemies.

For there must have been one of those unknown enemies on the bus last night, following her—and she had been too inward-turned to pick him or her out of the crowd. She would not make that mistake again.

There was nothing and no one to set off her internal alarms. Not a hint of magic, not a trace of anything other than the normal flickers of almost-psi encountered in any crowd.

But that did not mean she dared relax her vigilance.

Ogoun told me to be wary; I didn't take the warning seriously enough. Some "warrior" I am! Oh André—I wish you were here—

She sighed, and rubbed the sweat-slick skin of her forehead between her eyebrows with her index finger. *If wishes were fishes we'd eat for a year. Thank the gods—I get off at the next stop.*

She reached up for the signal cord and managed to yank it without disturbing the old lady dozing in the seat next to her. The woman woke as she slid out, but only gave her a kind of half-smile, and settled back into her nap.

The driver glared at her as she passed him, as if he resented having to stop. She jumped down off the bus and the driver nearly closed the door on her heels, taking off again with a surly and completely unnecessary reving of the engine. She coughed and wrinkled her nose in the resulting cloud of fumes; her eyes burned and watered in the acrid smoke.

The *bruja's* apartment was not more than a few feet from the bus stop; but this time Di climbed the linoleum-covered stairs to the fourth floor alone. And found herself standing before the worn wooden door for the second time in less than twenty-four hours.

But this time—this time I'm prepared.

She knocked softly and heard the approach of footsteps on the other side of the door. Even if she hadn't heard the footsteps she'd have known there was someone there; the feeling of *presence* was that strong. She waited then, waited for several minutes, *feeling* eyes upon her.

I am not going away, señora, she thought grimly. *I'll park out here all afternoon if I have to.*

At length the door creaked open, slowly, reluctantly.

"Señorita," the widow said, her tone as flat and expressionless as her face.

"Señora Montenegro—" Di replied firmly, "I would not have chosen to disturb you, but many things have happened since last night that I think you must learn of."

Once again the widow led the way to the two benches in the room that held her altar—and the feeling Di got from her was still one of fear, with a faint hint of hope that something about the room would make Di go away.

It isn't going to work, Di projected. *I need you and I need what you know.* She settled onto the unforgiving seat of one of the benches, and the widow perforce took the other, reluctantly.

Then Di pulled the photos taken at Possum Kingdom Park out of her purse.

It took only one—the pictures supplied by the Forensics team were in full color and merciless in their detail. Señora Montenegro folded within seconds. Just the one picture did it—the one of the six-year-old girl still twisted in her death-agonies. . . .

The *bruja* moaned with anguish after that one glance, and pushed Di's hand away.

"No more—*por favor*—" she begged, her eyes filling with tears. "Señorita, you are right, I am wrong. Please, show me no more."

Di took pity on her, and shoved the rest of the two-dozen photos she had yet to display back in her purse. She was quite willing not to have to look at them again herself.

"So?" she said, making the word a demand for information.

The widow looked about her, furtively, as if she suspected unfriendly ears in her own living room. "There *is* a *brujo*," she said, almost too softly to hear. "A most evil *brujo*. He is calling upon ancient magic, forbidden magic. He has been among us since the Feast of the Resurrection."

"Last spring, then," Di translated. The widow nodded, fearfully, her black eyes still scanning the room. And she was using more than her eyes to scan for enemies, Di sensed.

"He has not sought followers—not until very recently. He calls upon those of the *indios,* the Mestizo—always of the pure, or nearly pure blood. He promises much power, and the magic that only death and blood can fuel. And they answer him; more every day, especially the young *bravos*." She twisted her hands together on her lap, the beads of her ebony rosary tangled in her work-roughened fingers.

"Why?" Di asked, baffled. "I can't imagine gang members going in for *that*. Not magic—"

The *bruja* shook her head. "Indeed, no, not *brujiera*. Not *my* way, the uncertain and slow—no, no. Not the magic that does not always answer to the caller. But this one—it is said that *his* magic does not fail, not ever. And it is said that he promises great things, a new age for those who will follow him; he promises that a day will come *soon* when he will call forth an army and they shall slay the oppressors with their new powers of magic and take the land back from them."

Di felt her eyes widening. *Good gods—that sounds exactly like the line Johnnie Mountainhawk told Mark about—*

The woman was continuing. "This is the last that I know—I have felt his power calling me, and it is like a sickness in the blood, like the craving for drug or drink. At first he took only the eager, but now—it may be that he can claim all of the old blood. It may be that the Mestizo *must* answer now, his power grows so great."

"Who is he?" Di asked the obvious question.

The *bruja* shook her head. "I have not answered to his calling, so I do not know what this *brujo* names himself. I only know that *my* magic tells me that he is all that he claims, I can feel it in the part of me that wishes to answer the calling. And one thing more—"

Di waited, while the woman took a deep breath and whispered the last bit of information.

"He has caused the word to be sent forth that he is nearly ready, this one. And the word is that the rising shall be within the next pair of months."

"This is a *remarkable* photograph, young man," the professor said, staring at Mark over the top edge of it. His white mane stood out sharply against the dark bindings of the books crammed into the bookshelf that ran floor-to-ceiling on the wall behind his desk. "Rather *too* remarkable."

Mark sighed. It had taken him most of the afternoon to finally get in to see Professor Jermaine, and now the man was treating him like he was some kind of fraud.

"Professor, you've seen my credentials—"

The crusty old fart waved a dismissing hand at him, and the little breeze he raised stirred some of the nest of papers spread untidily all over his desk. "Really, young man, don't you think I've had pranks played on me before? Of course your credentials *look* genuine; so does your badge. The more elaborate the hoax, the better the props—"

There was a slight, hesitant tap, and the professor's secretary poked her mousy head in the door. "Professor, a Miss Tregarde is here," she said diffidently. "She says you were expecting her with Mr. Valdez."

"You might as well show her in too," the irascible old man grumbled, setting the photograph down and shoving it across the desk to Mark. "Might as well have all the jolly tricksters in one place."

The secretary vanished; Di opened the door wider and strode through it, wearing a certain air of confidence. Mark heaved a sigh of relief that he didn't bother to conceal. Now that Di was here—he saw that she'd donned her "successful professional" suit, and realized that she had probably dealt with characters like Jermaine before this. She'd know how to handle this old SOB. Mark had been feeling sorely out of his depth.

"Professor Jermaine?" she began—then took a long look at the professor's rather cynical expression.

"Doctor Jermaine is convinced we're trying to play an elaborate April Fool's joke on him a couple months too early," Mark said sourly, taking back the color photo of the swatch of brocade.

She cocked her head to one side and her face went unreadable. Her stance changed entirely, became challenging. "Oh, really?" Her tone was as dry as the professor's. "And just *why* would we be playing a prank on him when *neither* of us are students here?"

"Heavens, *I* don't know," Professor Jermaine replied, a little flustered that she had gone on the offensive. "For all I know you've been hired by—"

"The Dallas police?" she interrupted sarcastically, crossing her arms and giving him a cynical glare of her own. "If you were *really* interested in finding out if we were on the level, all you'd have to do would be to have your secretary call Homicide. Obviously you aren't interested in anything except saving some of your precious time. Obviously you have no intention of helping us. Come on, Mark." She crooked a finger at him. "I think I can possibly talk Carolyn Reseune into identifying this for us. The photo should fax all right—"

"Carolyn Reseune?" The professor reacted to *that* name the way a bull reacts to a matador's cape. He rose abruptly out of his chair; his voice rose as he did. "*Doctor* Carolyn Reseune? Of Yale?"

Mark had started to leave his own chair, now he settled back, repressing a smirk. Di had the professor well and truly hooked.

"I don't know of any other Carolyn Reseune," Di replied acidly. "I know she's busy, but she knows me; she knows I don't waste my time or anyone else's on stupid pranks. I suspect she'll make some time for me."

"But—" The professor's voice rose another octave, as he protested the wisdom of her decision. "—she specializes in *Incan* work—she couldn't *possibly*—dammit, *give* me that photograph!" He leaned over the desk and snatched it out of Mark's hand.

Di fixed the professor with a needle-like stare. "Do I take it that you've changed your mind?"

The professor just grumbled, and rummaged in the clutter on his desk for a magnifying glass. Di took the chair beside Mark's without invitation, settling herself into it and taking a position that said as much in body language as a book the size of any of the tomes on the archeologist's desk could have. Everything, from the way her legs were crossed to the way she held her head, was a challenge; her whole posture was saying, "All right, you old fraud—prove to me you aren't wasting *my* time now!"

After a few minutes' scrutiny, he looked up from the photo, stabbing the both of them with a calculating glance of his own.

"Where's the garment this came from?" he asked, his voice full of sharp-edged overtones. "I need to see it!"

"I would say that only two people are likely to know that," Mark replied politely. *If Di is going to play "bad cop" I'm only too happy to play "good cop."* "The first is the owner, and the second is rather dead."

"And just why do you need to see it?" Di asked on the heels of Mark's statement, her tone still conveying impatience and annoyance.

"Young lady, the patterns woven into this scrap are patterns that have not been *seen* since the days of the Conquistadors!" he exclaimed. "No one—certainly no modern weaver—knows how to produce them! Great good God, no modern weaver *would* produce them even if they knew how, it would be sacrilege bordering on insanity to reproduce the sacred garments reserved for Tezcatlipoca and his priestesses! It could *only* bring the weaver and the wearer the worst of misfortune!"

"Who?" Mark asked, bewildered by the strange name.

"Tezcatlipoca," the professor repeated impatiently. And at Mark's look of blank incomprehension, translated, even more impatiently, "Smoking Mirror."

Mark shook his head, still not understanding.

"The Aztec god of war and warriors," the professor explained with a sigh of exasperation.

Mark could literally *see* the light go on inside Di's head, but didn't want to wait for enlightenment. "Look, I'm just a dumb cop," he replied, "Can you tell me more about this Smoking Mirror?"

"He was the especial god of the Aztecs and of their capital city," Professor Jermaine began, and visibly thawed at the intense interest in Mark's face. "His symbol was the 'tiger'—actually, the jaguar; *'el tigre'* is a misnomer. His sacred time of day was the afternoon—the descending sun. His particular feast took place in April, nearly the same time as our own Easter, but he permeated the entire sacrificial year and presided as chief priest over many of the other sacrifices in the person of a young man, a kind of Chosen One or avatar. This Chosen One in his turn was sacrificed at Smoking Mirror's feast, and resurrected again immediately in the body of another Chosen One. It was really a very unusual ritual for the Aztecs in that the Chosen One was quite often a volunteer, and at this particular sacrifice, which was the culmination of their ritual year, there was only the *single individual* as sacrifice instead of the multitude of victims normally put to the knife."

"Why was that?" Mark asked.

"Because the Chosen One was *literally* Tezcatlipoca

himself," the professor answered warmly. Mark's unwavering interest was obviously flattering to his ego. "He was treated all year long with all the honor and deference given the god—he was given four of the most beautiful virgins in the city to be his priestesses and handmaidens, and feasted and pleasured during his entire reign. So for the Aztecs, the man *was* the god, and the special god who had chosen them as his people."

"I thought the chief Aztec god was Quetzalcoatl," Di said slowly.

The professor shook his head vigorously. "A common misconception. Quetzalcoatl was the titular deity of the Toltecs, the people who preceeded the Aztecs in the region. The Aztecs incorporated Quetzalcoatl into their pantheon, but as Smoking Mirror's brother and subordinate; in fact, in their mythology, the Smoking Mirror is the Feathered Serpent's implacable enemy and his ultimate destroyer."

This was beginning to make more and more sense. *This Burning Water—he must have set himself up as a priest of this Tezcat—whatsis, and he's using the old Aztec rites mixed up with* brujiera. *If we can match the timing of these things, we'll have every correspondence we need for a positive match.*

"What kind of calendar were the Aztecs on?" Mark asked carefully.

"Nothing like ours," Professor Jermaine said. "They had an eighteen-month cycle, with each month being about three weeks long—twenty days, if you want to be precise about it. There were major and minor sacrifices at each month-end feast. Let's see, the last ones would have been—" he reached behind him without seeming to look and pulled a book down from the shelf and flipped it open. "—ah—about three weeks ago would have been the Feast of Tlaloc. The major sacrifice would have been children, mostly. Following that—in fact, it's only just over—was Xipe-Totec, the Flayed One."

"What *kind* of sacrifices are you talking about?" Mark asked. "I'd like more than generalities, if you would."

The professor raised an eyebrow. "They *aren't* for the

squeamish—" For the first time, he smiled. "Foolish of me—you *did* say you were from Homicide, didn't you. Well, the central sacrifice to Tlaloc was designed to determine how long it would be before the rains began; the priestess would paint the sacrificial children with rubber-tree sap, and the priest would hold them under water until they drowned. How many breaths it took for them to die would tell them how many weeks it would be until the rains."

Mark nearly exploded then and there—the details of the three drowned children had *not* been released to the press. There was no way the professor could have described their murders so accurately unless he was detailing some rite that really *had* existed.

The professor continued. "The next one, the Feast of Xipe-Totec, was one where the major sacrifice was flayed alive and the priest donned the skin and danced in it at every other sacrifice during the feast. Particularly grim, that one. Some sacrifices were half-burned before being killed, and the whole thing culminated in a kind of cannibal feast."

As the professor continued, Mark could hear Di muttering under her breath. "Aztecs!" she breathed angrily. "Why the *hell* didn't I think of Aztecs?"

He was a little stunned.

The professor consulted his book further, oblivious to her mutterings. "The next would be the second most important rite in the year, next to the sacrifice of Tezcatlipoca himself. And it's another one where the man-god presides personally."

He looked up at Mark, obviously wanting to be coaxed into revealing his erudition. Mark obliged him by leaning forward with an eagerness he did *not* have to feign, until he was sitting on the very edge of his hard chair.

"Yes?" he breathed encouragingly.

"Well, it's the Corn Goddess, and she bears several striking resemblances to John Barleycorn and the old Corn Kings," the professor said with unconcealed satisfaction. "She's a bit like Smoking Mirror in that she is supposed to die and be reborn. They would pick a woman who had borne at least one child—the fertility assured, as it were. Then they'd set her to weaving, making her own garments for her ultimate sacrifice. They had to be pure white, absolutely, no colored patterns at all, which for the Aztecs was practically unheard of. On the appropriate day Tezcatlipoca would present her to the multitude. Then with his own hand he would slay her—and he had to get as little blood as possible on the white of the garments. Then he would go into the temple and ceremonially flay the body—a little like the Xipe-Totec rite, except that the flaying was done after death, rather than before—then reappear clothed in her skin *and* her garments, denoting that the corn had gone into the earth and been reborn as the young corn plant. That it would be Tezcatlipoca that performed all this himself shows that it was considered almost as important a rite as Smoking Mirror's own."

Di shook her head. "All I ever knew about the Aztecs was the Feathered Serpent cult—"

"In the time of the Aztecs," the professor said firmly, "That's *all* it was; a cult. A very degraded and debased form of the Toltec rites. The Toltecs practiced a *kind* of blood-sacrifice, but it was their *own* blood they shed, like the priests of Cybele that castrated themselves, or the medieval monks who went in for flagellation until their backs bled. Shedding one's own blood was an act of will, of willingness to sacrifice one's own earthly self to one's higher self, and a kind of self-purification. When the Aztecs first arrived, they were *not* the powerful conquering army they later claimed to be; rather they were a rather barbarous, seminomadic tribe. Warlike, yes, but hardly capable of conquering the Toltecs."

"But—how could they take over?" Mark asked, now quite interested on his own.

"The simplest way of all; they insinuated themselves among the Toltec culture and conquered by subversion. You can trace that subversion by the gradual elimination of Quetzalcoatl as supreme deity and the substitution of

Tezcatlipoca, and by the way in which self-sacrifice was replaced by the sacrificing of others."

He warmed to the subject; this was obviously his own pet theory. "That was *why* the arrival of Cortez and his identification with Quetzalcoatl so alarmed and demoralized the Aztecs in general and the rulers in particular. The legends of Quetzalcoatl had always included a promise that he would return—and the Aztecs could *not* imagine him returning unless it was to conquer *them* as they had conquered the Toltecs. That might have been one reason why they never eradicated the Feathered Serpent cult—instead, they tried to *change* it so that it reflected *their* heritage. The writings, the records of the liturgy, had us puzzled for a long time; here were liturgical writings speaking of self-sacrifice and mercy, of self-abasement and peace—yet the actual rituals culminated in pain and agonizing death! *Then*, of course, we came upon the evidence that the Toltec had been absorbed into the Aztecs, that the Aztecs were *not* the first in the area, and everything became obvious."

"Professor," Di said when he paused for a breath, "Are there *any* extant sources here at the university for the original *Toltec* rites?"

He pondered her question for a moment. "Well—*my* specialty is the Aztec culture, so I'm only peripherally interested in the Toltecs they replaced—but I think we have a fair collection of codex reproductions and translations in the library stacks."

"I *need* to get at them," she said, urgently, locking her eyes with his.

He looked at her with mild surprise. "Is it that important?"

She nodded, slowly, grimly. "We can't tell you everything, professor, but it is *very* important. The two of us are assigned to the 'Texas Ripper' case."

He was rather taken aback. "Well—I never thought I'd see the day when the police needed the advice of an old pot-hunter. Here—" he rummaged in his desk for two slips of pink paper, then scribbled his name on both.

"—here are passes to the stacks for both of you. Am I right in assuming that madman the papers have been calling the 'Texas Ripper' has been using Aztec rites?"

It was Mark's turn to nod. "So closely that you inadvertently described things we didn't let out when you were talking about Tlaloc and—the one that sounded like 'Ziplock bag'—"

"Xipe-Totec," the professor answered, looking a bit stunned.

"And so far as we can tell, whoever this is has the timing down to correspond exactly to the Aztec calendar and no other."

Professor Jermaine could only shake his head. "If that is indeed the case—knowing what I know about the callousness and blood-thirst of the Aztecs themselves—I can only say, may God help you. Because you will need that help."

"Those bastards had me blocked but *good*," Di said as they left the building that held the professor's office. Her expression was still fairly neutral—but her eyes held a sullen, if suppressed, fury. "I never even thought of Aztecs, and it should have been obvious."

"Are you freed up now?" he asked anxiously.

She nodded. "Once I got shook loose, I shook everything off. I can see things now—it's like getting the keypiece of the jigsaw puzzle. Another thing, Mark, Johnnie Mountainhawk is right. The *bruja* told me about an Indian sorcerer that's calling for an Indian rebellion. *She* told me that she's felt his power, and she's something of a clairvoyant, enough to have identified the prime signature aura from the murders last night as *him*. She didn't know his name or what he calls himself—"

"Firm bet that it's Johnnie's Burning Water."

"That's a sucker bet if ever I heard one." She contemplated the stacks pass in her hand. "So what we have here looks like somebody setting himself up as the new priest of Tezcatlipoca; appropriate for a radical militant."

"Uh-huh, that's exactly what I thought," Mark agreed.

"Probably originally a *brujo*, then began researching the origins of the rituals as he became more militant and radical."

"*Then*, once he tapped into the *original* rituals, discovered that he had the equivalent of a magical tactical nuke if he could build up enough power and believers." She chewed her lip a little. "From what we heard in there, and what the *bruja* told me—Mark, she says the word on the street is that the sorcerer is going to make his move some time within the next two months."

"We don't have much time—"

"No. And my guess is that he's probably planning on timing his uprising with an attempt to manifest Smoking Mirror. If he can actually pull it off—he'll have more than a tactical nuke at his disposal, he'll have enough power to play with to enable him to affect the physical world in very profound ways."

"Like what?"

"Like—think what could be done if the head of a guerilla force could call a storm *and direct the lightning*. Wherever, whenever he wanted."

"Like a direct hit on the main power station. Say, Friday night at about seven. The city would be paralyzed, helpless."

"And then—you felt the Hunter-in-the-dark. You know how close it came to panicking *you*, and you were ready for it! Imagine all those helpless people trapped in the dark—then exposed to *that*. At a powerful enough level, he could make the Hunter physical enough so that even normals could perceive it and feel its hunger."

"Good God!" he exclaimed, stunned by the thought. "That would be like—yelling 'fire' at the circus!"

"Exactly so. Neither he nor the Hunter would have to *do* anything; people would kill each other in panic. By dawn the city would be depopulated." She shook her head. "Well, he's *not* there yet, and it's up to us to see he doesn't *get* there. I think we're going to have to split up again. To be brutally frank, love, you never were much of a scholar."

"No argument from me," he said agreeably, comfortably certain that she couldn't come to any harm in the university library—*especially* in the stacks, where entry was restricted. "Tell you what, why don't I see if I can get hold of Johnnie while you do your thing?"

"It's a deal," she nodded. "Come fetch me around seven?"

"Seven it is."

·THIRTEEN

THIS WEEK CHARLIE HAD BEEN SWITCHED TO FIRST SHIFT—
which meant he was home now. Mark pulled the Ghia up
to the first working pay phone he spotted, a booth nestled
in to the side of the bus shelter, figuring he'd better call
before he descended on his friends. He squinted into the
setting sun while the answering machine played its
recording at him. It was kind of unnerving to hear his
own voice snarling at him from the handset.

"Guys?" he said when the thing beeped at him. "It's
Mark Valdez. Can I—"

He heard the *click* of the receiver being lifted. "Mark?"
It was Doreen, and she sounded quite definitely shaken
up. "Mark, are you on your way over? Please tell me
you're on your way over!"

"Yeah 'Reenie—" he replied, straightening from his
slump, alarmed at the frantic tone of her voice. "What's
wrong? Is Charlie—"

"No, it's not Charlie, it's Johnnie, and I can't explain
it, you'll have to see for yourself. Only, please, Mark,
hurry!"

She hung up; he hardly looked to see if the handset
connected with the cradle—he just threw it in place, and
sprinted back to the Ghia, heart in his throat.

It was almost dark when he got there; the Mountainhawk apartment was clear across town from the university, and he'd bent more than a few laws to get there as quickly as he had. Doreen answered the doorbell almost as soon as he pushed it; he rather suspected she must have been lurking at the front hall, waiting. A cop's wife learns to cover her negative expressions pretty quickly, but there was panic in Doreen's eyes, raw panic, and bewilderment.

Before he could say or do anything, she just grabbed his arm and pulled him down the dark hall into the back bedroom, in so much of a hurry that she didn't even bother to flip on the hall light as she passed the switch.

The only light there was back *here* was coming from the overhead fixture, and only one of the three bulbs it held was working. They didn't use this room very often, and there wasn't much in the room; Mark had figured all along that they were going to save it for a nursery. About the only furniture was a massive cast-iron bedstead, an antique that they used for guests. It weighed a ton; Mark knew that only too well, since he'd helped wrestle it up here when they moved in.

His back still hurt when he thought about it.

The light was dim, but there still wasn't much to look at—the bed was still about the only piece of furniture. Charlie was sitting on the edge of it; shoulders hunched, head in hands, looking drawn and exhausted.

Johnnie Mountainhawk was on the floor beside the headboard, looking twice as exhausted. He leaned against the mattress, his head pillowed in the crook of one elbow, the other arm draped clumsily over his head. He was *handcuffed* to the bedframe, sagging against the pull of the cuffs on his wrists.

"What the *hell?*" Mark exploded.

Somewhat to his surprise it was Johnnie who answered him, opening eyes that had purple circles beneath them. "I asked him to cuff me, Mark. It was the only way I could keep from following the thing that was calling me."

"Huh?"

"There's this—thing in my head. It wants me to go to it. Every so often it drives me crazy and I start to answer—"

Mark flashed then on some of what Di had told him about her second meeting with the *bruja*; about how the woman had told her that Burning Water was calling everyone of Indian or Mestizo blood. Presumably what she had *really* meant was that he was "calling"—using psychic coercion—those who could "hear" him, those with psychic gifts of their own. Charlie was one of those, but Di had put him under shielding, so he was safe—

Gifts *tended* to run in families, though. It looked like Johnnie shared Medicine Power with his brother and grandfather. And Johnnie was *not* shielded.

So Johnnie was right up this bastard's alley.

Mark clenched his jaw. *Like Hell! Not without a fight from me! But*—

Was there anything he *could* do? Mark knew warding —but that was meant for a *place*, not a person. And he didn't know if warding would work against something that was not an attack or an attempt to invade.

"How long have you been fighting this thing?" he asked.

"Since last night; it comes and goes," Johnnie replied wearily. "Just a damn good thing for me I was here when it hit. When I went zombie Charlie tackled me and Doreen knocked me out. When I came to, I told 'em to cuff me. It's better now, but when Charlie went off to work I nearly dislocated my shoulder trying to get loose."

"Mark," Charlie spoke for the first time, "You've been hanging around that psychic chick for a long time. Can you get hold of her? Can *you* do anything?"

"I probably can't get to Di right now—she's in the stacks at the university library, and she won't get any messages until she comes back to the desk. Which is going to be hours from now. The way you look— Johnnie, I don't think we have that much time."

Johnnie nodded unhappily. "I feel like I'm standing at

the edge of a mental cliff; one or two more sessions and I may go bats permanently. But what about *you* doing something?"

"I'm thinking, I'm thinking." He tried to dredge up every fact he had picked up in the past few weeks since Di had started giving him theory-and-practice at his own request. "This—calling. I don't think it should be hitting you this hard. Di talked to a *bruja* this afternoon—*she* said Burning Water was calling in Indian and Mestizo psychics, but he wasn't getting to her *nearly* so strongly. Unless—unless they have a way of getting at you, specifically."

Okay, what laws could be applying here—Knowledge? Don't think so, nobody would know Johnnie that well, except maybe his own kin. That lets out the Law of Names too. And Words of Power; Cherokee is different enough from Aztec that the power words would differ. Synthesis and Identification are out; those are for acquiring power, not what's going on here. Balance; hardly. But—Association or Contagion—we might have an answer here.

"What's the chance somebody in that lunatic fringe that's been talking about the Great Red Hope could have gotten hold of something of yours or something that's been around you?" he asked Johnnie.

"Pretty good," he replied soberly. "I'm the original 'lose your head if it wasn't fastened on'; right, Charlie?"

"Worse, little brother—I see what Cisco's getting at. *You had a cold last week.* Remember?"

"Shit, yes! Scattering Kleenex behind me like snowflakes, and filling every wastebasket in town."

"I'd bet the Laws of Contagion and Association are in effect, here," Mark said. "'What was part of you is always part of you.' And given how strong the pull is on you, I'd put money on the notion that while they are casting a general call-in spell, they've added a specific on top of it for anybody they could get artifacts for that they wanted to recruit."

"How come *I* don't feel it?" Charlie asked, "Given

those phone calls and grand-dad's warnings, they want me pretty bad. It would have been pretty easy to get something of *mine*."

"*You're* shielded," Mark pointed out. "Johnnie's not. Besides, get him and they're bound to get you. No?"

"Yeah," Charlie replied sourly. "And much as I hate to admit it, if they called me up saying they had him, I'd act like any moron on the tube and go charging in after him."

"Mark, can you do *anything?*" Doreen begged.

"I'm still thinking." He closed his eyes. *Even if I could shield, and I can't, it probably wouldn't do any good because shields don't necessarily block what's already there and they've got a line to his mind alr—*

—wait a minute; hold that thought—

They've got a line to his mind already. They've got a line to his mind. A line—

Di said those lines are psychically tangible; they can be seen and felt at both ends. I wonder; Aztec magic and Cherokee magic are both Indian magic. Maybe I could use Cherokee to force Aztec to release one of Cherokee magical lineage, 'cause Aztec wouldn't have a real claim. And to sever a line—

You cut it. You cut a line—with an edged weapon, like Di cut the line between me and the thing in Quasi's living room. But it would have to be a magically charged weapon. I don't have one, and I'll bet Charlie doesn't know how to fire one up—

—fire one up. Fire one up. Fire!

"Charlie, do your folk have some way of starting a kind of *sacred* fire?" he asked, hoping that the answer would be in the affirmative.

Charlie gave him a strange glance. "Yeah," he said slowly.

Good; holy things always *have identical arcane counterparts, Di said. The act of blessing creates the counterpart.* "Okay; the sixty-four dollar question. Can *you?*"

"I—" He hesitated.

Mark could sympathize with the hesitation; he *was* an

outsider. But this wasn't the time for secrecy. "Look, you want me to help, or don't you?"

Charlie sighed. "Yes. I can."

"All right then. I'm going to tell you what to do, but *you're* going to have to do it. I'd like to do this myself; I can't, my talent isn't going to do any good here. You said you've got 'spirit vision'; okay, use it. I'm betting you're going to see a kind of line, or rope, or something like that, leading off in the direction Johnnie's being pulled—"

Charlie sat a little straighter on the edge of the bed, and stared at the general area his brother occupied. His eyes went unfocused and blank; his brow creased and Mark held his breath, afraid to distract him even a little.

"I—see it," he said slowly, in what was very close to a whisper.

"Good," Mark replied just as softly. "Now, this is what you're going to have to do. Charlie, you have to start one of your sacred fires and *burn through* that tie. Johnnie—*you* have to totally disavow any connection with whatever's on the other end of that tie—otherwise they'll just be able to reestablish it. That sounds easy—I can promise you that it won't be. It's going to take tremendous concentration—and the tie is as much physical as it is mental."

"Which means?" Johnnie Mountainhawk asked, shaking sweat-damp hair out of his eyes.

"I can't predict what the effect of burning the tie will be—I only know that there *will* be a physical side to it. We're going to try something I'm still a sorcerer's apprentice with, and I don't know what the side effects are."

"We all ready?"

Charlie nodded nervously; he had a single stick in his hand; fire licked sluggishly at one end. It was a makeshift torch made of a piece of two-by-four wrapped with oily rags. Doreen had had to turn off the smoke detectors after they'd set them off twice trying to get it lit. Charlie had *not* allowed Mark to actually watch the lighting of the sacred fire—he was rather touchingly relieved that Mark hadn't been offended.

"Johnnie?" Mark made the name a question, turning to where the younger brother sat, held to the bedframe by only one cuff. He was seated in the middle of a warded circle chalked on the carpet of the room, a circle Mark hoped would protect him from some of the unknown "side effects."

"About as ready as I'll ever be."

"Okay—" Mark looked from one brother to the other, and hoped he knew what he was doing "—let's do it."

Mark got up from the bed and seated himself on the floor behind Johnnie, within the circle. Charlie advanced on the (to Mark) invisible line, with no sign that he might be feeling that this was ridiculous.

That was exactly what Mark was hoping for—as Di had told him at least a hundred times—in magic, *belief* was half the power. Both Charlie and his brother *believed* in this; and as long as they believed, it would work.

He hoped.

Within seconds, he had proof that it *was* working.

As Charlie reached out with the smoking torch, it suddenly flared up; now it was a clear, steady flame nearly a foot tall, and colored a bright blue-white, like an oxyacetylene torch—and Johnnie screamed in mortal agony.

Mark moved with the speed of a striking tiger; grabbing the younger Mountainhawk before he could begin fighting the cuff, gripping Johnnie's shoulders, and holding him steady. "It's *not you*. Johnnie—it's *not you*. Deny what hurts! Say it! Say it!" He continued to hold Johnnie's shoulders as the young man fought the pain that blocked his voice, fought to concentrate—he was *willing* Johnnie to regain control, to deny that what was being destroyed and what it led to was or had ever been a part of him.

"It's—not—me." Johnnie gasped out each word, fighting around the pain that made the muscles of his neck stand out like bridge cables, and forced his back

and shoulders into an involuntarily arc. "It's—not—
mine!"

With that last word, Johnnie threw his arms wide—
and Charlie uttered a cry of triumph.

Charlie snuffed the torch in the bucket of water
Doreen had brought from the bathroom, as Johnnie
sagged back into Mark's hands and dropped his arms.
Then Charlie was on his knees beside his brother,
unlocking the cuffs.

And Mark knew that this time, in *this* battle, their side
had won.

Di was startled entirely out of the book she was
skimming by a sound—

—where no sound should be.

She suppressed the desire to sneeze; suppressed even
the sniff she *almost* made. She was alone in the stacks;
entirely alone, for the librarian had given her the only
key. Therefore there *could* be no one else here.

Except that the sound came again, soft, but unmistakable. A footstep.

Internal alarms shrilled, even as she was closing the
book, warning her of danger; deadly, and as near as the
next breath.

And something brushed against the edges of her
shields, testing them.

She set the book down on the metal shelf before her so
softly that she did not even disturb the dust, and stilled
even her breath, forcing her awareness and concentration into her senses and toughening her shields to one
step below battle-ready.

This was no place to meet danger; all about her were
the towering gray-metal bookshelves of the stacks, a
veritable maze of them. There was no room for her to
meet a physical attack, either close-in or a shooting
match—there wasn't enough room to use karate, and all
that metal made ricochets a dangerous probability.

But when she'd come in here, she'd followed one of
her favorite mottos—"know where all the exits are"—
almost without thinking about it. So she knew that to her

left and two rows down from this, at the very end of the row, there *was* an exit. It wasn't one of those that led into the library, though—it was one of the fire exits that led to the roof.

She heard a soft whisper of sound, as if someone had inadvertently brushed against the spine of a protruding book; it sounded nearer than the footstep had. That decided her.

Cursing the neccessity that had her wearing a suit instead of her usual jeans, she carefully slipped off her shoes and stowed them in her purse. Pulling the bag off her shoulder, she made a loop in the strap and slipped it over her wrist, closing her hand in a fist over the strap. Now she had a weapon of some reach; one that could, in fact, be slung with no little velocity into someone's face, if the need came. She eased her way along the bookshelf, stopping every time she came to a join and crouching to pass below line-of-sight, so that she wouldn't flicker the light that leaked between each bookcase. When she reached the end of the row, she crouched again to peer around it. She was *not* going to use her arcane abilities to probe ahead of her; not after that little brush by her shields. That would be as bad—and as stupid—as shouting her location. She had no illusions about avoiding a confrontation; she just wanted it to be on ground of *her* choosing.

The way was clear; she sprinted for the door, easing it open and shut again, then began the run up the staircase to the flat roof of the library.

The stairs were metal—and anyone in shoes was going to make a racket on them; even sneakers would make some kind of sound. She strained her ears behind her, but heard nothing by the time she reached the locked door that led to the roof.

The lock itself was no challenge; it wasn't even a deadbolt, it was the kind a kid could open with a credit card. Which was exactly what *she* did.

Unfortunately *this* door wasn't opened too often; its hinges shrieked in three separate keys, like three damned souls, and the screams echoed down the staircase and back up again with ear-piercing shrillness.

"Dammit!" she cursed, scooting through the door, then getting shoes and gun out of her purse and slamming the door behind her. *Well, he knows where I am now. Could have been worse, I guess. I could have set off an alarm, and gotten innocents into the line of fire.*

The tar-and-gravel-covered roof was *no* place for bare feet; she got her shoes back on and secured her purse around her waist by slipping it over her shoulders and cinching the strap like a belt. If it came to an arcane fight there were things she needed in there. . . .

It was a moonless night, but not dark; enough light was reflecting from the clouds and coming up from the streetlights for her to be able to see quite well once her eyes adjusted. She ran across the roof to a wind-turbine, one angled to the door, rather than straight ahead. Once there, she crouched in its slight shelter, and waited, gun in hand.

The door shrieked open; light poured from it. Something leapt out, almost too fast to make out—only that it was there one moment, and not there the next. It rolled into the shelter of another wind-turbine, and the door swung slowly shut of its own weight, seeming to scream even louder as it protested moving yet again.

Diana waited, gravel digging into her knee, but nothing happened.

Mexican standoff. In all senses, I suspect. Whose patience is better, buddy—yours, or mine?

She watched, and waited—and listened. There was no breeze tonight, so the only sound was coming from the air-conditioning plant behind the rooftop door and the elevator shaft behind them. Although *that* was enough; it covered just about any other sound anyone could produce, short of a gunshot or a shout.

After a considerable length of time had passed, a shadowy silhouette of a man rose from behind the structure, answering her question.

And as soon as he stood completely erect, his hands

began to glow with a flickering orange light. He stood there for a moment, as the light strengthened and steadied, then drew a glyph in the air that flared redly and hung there for a full minute.

A challenge. One she dared not refuse.

She replaced the gun in her purse, and pulled out two rings and a necklace by feel, donning them even as she stood and moved away from the shelter of the wind-turbine. By the time she stood in the open, *her* hands were glowing as well—although the light was blue-violet, rather than orange. She answered his glyph with one of her own; green. It remained in the air a fraction of a second longer than his.

She couldn't *read* the meaning of his glyph, but she doubted that he could read hers, either. It was just the formal prelude to a duel arcane; challenge, acceptance.

This was *not* the chief *bruja*; she could sense it in the crude qualities of his shielding and the simplicity of the glyph he had drawn. *But he might well make up for lack of technique with sheer, raw power—*

She raised her shields to full just as he let fly a levinbolt that bid fair to prove her guess was right.

Glory—that one's so strong it's in the visible *range!* she thought, startled. The bolt hit her shield and actually penetrated a good bit before she could deflect it, splitting it up into a shower of harmless—and quite non-arcanely noticable—sparks. She staggered back a little under the blow. *If he keeps that up, the normals are going to wonder who's shooting off fireworks up here!*

He evidently realized that himself, for the bolt that followed right behind it was apparent only to her Othersight. This one she did not deflect; she caught it and sent it hurtling back at him, following it with one of her own.

The first he captured and absorbed—

Damn. I was hoping he didn't know that trick.

The second staggered him, sent him stumbling back two or three steps before recovering.

He spread his hands wide, then clapped them together —and she had a split second to decide if the snarling thing with the head of a jaguar and the wings of a bird was an illusion or a real manifestation—

Because if she guessed wrong, the illusion could hurt her as much as the manifestation could, because she would *believe* it could.

But if she guessed that it was an illusion, and it was a manifestation—it could penetrate her shielding and ravage her before she could turn it. *If* she could.

It was the complexity of the thing that convinced her that it was a manifestation—one who accidentally let fly a levinbolt that fluoresced in the visible range would never be able to control, much less build, an illusion that was so complex she could count the scales on its tail—

All this she decided in a fraction of a second, and reacted with a manifestation of her own; calling out of her left-hand jade-set ring the ally that wore the guise of a golden Imperial Dragon, and pulling on the power-pole on her right-hand amber ring to give it strength.

The two creatures met in the space between the two magicians. As the dragon fastened its claws into the serpentine body of the jaguar-bird-snake, Di felt a moment's rush of relief that her guess had been right.

But the jaguar opened its jaws in a soundless squall of fury, and sunk foot-long fangs into the dragon's neck. *Di* (as she knew she would) was the one who felt the pain.

She willed power to her ally, enduring what seemed to be the lacerating of her own throat; pain so real that the unwary would put a hand to the neck and expect it to come away red with blood.

And that was another trap; for if she allowed herself to believe *that*—it would happen.

For this was what was tested in a sorcerer's duel of manifestations: the testing of control, the testing of will, and the testing of concentration were as important as the manifestations themselves.

The dragon had wrestled the jaguar-creature to the ground, and was gaining the upper hand. The jaguar-creature responded with long, desperate rakes of its claws, trying to reach the dragon's belly.

But the belly of an Imperial Dragon is as well-armored

as its back; the claws made no dent in the thick armor plates. The jaguar-creature bit at the dragon's legs, finding the weak place in the join of leg to body where there was no armor. Di bit back a cry of hurt and continued to will strength to her ally.

The jaguar twisted with the writhing of the dragon, trying to maintain its hold—and exposed its throat.

The dragon closed its jaws in a stranglehold on the jaguar's neck; and now the cat-snake-bird was no longer trying to attack, just escape.

Its struggles grew weaker—then ceased altogether.

The dragon threw back its head in a soundless roar of triumph, and vanished. The jaguar-creature faded out, dissolving slowly. Behind it, visible now, was the *brujo*, bent nearly double in pain and gasping for breath. Although he was scarcely more than a shadow, Di could *feel* his angry eyes on her. *Her* dragon would fight again, though the power she had expended to give it strength was gone until she could recharge the amber of her right-hand ring—but *he* had lost a valuable ally *and* a great deal of stored power.

In fact, he had lost enough so that the outcome of the duel was forgone, unless he had something extraordinary up his sleeve.

He did.

A gun.

Breaking the one and only rule of a duel arcane—*no physical weaponry.*

It was the glint of the streetlights on the blued metal of the barrel that warned Di, and just barely in time. She flung herself frantically back into the dubious shelter of her wind-turbine as his first shot rang out.

It ricocheted off the metal of the turbine, whining. Di fumbled in the purse at her waist for her own gun, and winced as a second shot rang out—

—and the magician crumpled to the asphalt of the roof.

Maybe Mark *wasn't* primarily a sensitive, but he figured he'd have had to be headblind altogether to miss the fireworks going on up on the roof of the library. A paranormal display like *that* could only mean one thing: Di had gotten cornered and forced into a magic duel.

Good God, that's the second *one this evening!* he thought in amazement, even as he whipped the Ghia into a parking space with a shriek of tires and a horrible stench of burned rubber. *Where are these guys* coming *from?*

Theoretically the fire escape that led from the roof couldn't be reached from the ground—but that was theory, and as any cop would, Mark knew better. Before too many minutes had passed, he was easing himself up the metal structure as noiselessly as he could.

Maybe she won't need me— he told himself, *—but then again maybe she will. Might and right don't necessarily mean squat if the other guy decides to break the rules.*

The battle was mostly wasted on him; when he poked his nose over the edge of the low parapet surrounding the roof, all *he* saw were some amorphous swirls of colored light that were twining and twisting about each other in the space between the two magicians, and the back of a strange man. The guy near him was slowly doubling over in what looked like pain, though; and Di (at least he *thought* the shadow over on the other side of the roof was Di) wasn't, so he figured it must be going her way. Then the orange swirl sort of flattened out, the gold-colored one flared up, and vanished. And Mark saw the man before him reaching under his coat.

God damn! *I sure called that one!* he thought, as his own hand went for *his* piece, drew, and fired almost simultaneously with the stranger.

The man dropped like a stone—

And—that was wrong; Mark hopped up onto the roof and walked slowly toward the body, sorely puzzled.

I shot to wing *him, not ice him! My aim isn't that badly off!*

"Mark!" came a cry bright with relief and joy from the far side of the roof. He waved absently and advanced on the unmoving body.

Better be careful—he might be faking—

But no—

As Di came pelting up, he prodded the body—indisputably a body, there was *no* sign of life—with his toe.

"Damn—I didn't *mean* that," he said slowly, hardly aware that he was speaking.

Di was already on her knees beside the body. She did something then that she seldom *ever* did—she called up light—a ball of *visible* light—in the palm of her hand.

"You didn't *do* that," she said, finally. "Look for yourself."

And he did so, seeing with amazement what she had seen in the few moments before campus security came pounding up the staircase with a flashlight and she hurriedly extinguished the light.

There was *one* bullet-wound. In the gun-arm of the corpse.

And it showed no sign of blood whatsoever.

"Right," Mark said into the receiver, and hung up the phone.

He turned to Di, who was nursing a double Scotch, stretched out in one of his flip-chairs, which was half unflipped into a lounger.

"Seems I won't be facing a board in the morning after all," he said, not at all sure of what he was feeling, but quite sure that he wanted exactly what Di was drinking. He reached for the bottle on the stereo shelf and another glass, and poured himself one.

"Why?" she asked bluntly.

"Because I shot a corpse. Nothing in the rules covers that."

"You *what?*" she exclaimed, sitting bolt-upright—and not spilling a single drop of Scotch.

"I shot a corpse. The guy I shot—he wasn't American, he wasn't legal, and he wasn't alive when I shot him. Mexico City police say he was buried six months ago, Immigration says they have no records on him, and Forensics says he was cold meat when my bullet hit him. So I'm off the hook."

She stared at him, looked at her glass, took a *large* swallow, and stared at him again.

"Nobody's going to be saying anything about it," he continued. "It's too bizarre. The official word is that this one gets filed with the little green man cases and forgotten. The campus fuzz is former Fort Worth PD—he's agreed to keep his mouth shut. The Chief is *entirely* weirded out."

"That makes two of us," Di replied. "Zombies, I know; they're natural, and they're mindless. In no way would a zombie be able to handle magic on his own. This is a new one on me."

She settled back onto the backrest, crossing her arms —at least so much as holding the glass would permit— and took another large swallow.

"I'm still thinking," she said, finally. "I've been thinking ever since the professor shook my memories loose. You know the old phrase, 'What goes around, comes around?'"

"Yeah," he said, "I thought it was new, though."

She shook her head. "Old as the hills. Older. You know, arcane things, magic things, never just *stop*. They echo, sometimes for centuries. And—there's too much going on for all of this to be coincidence. Too damned many coincidences are piling up on top of each other. Like—was there any real reason for *you* to get interested in the Texas Ripper?"

"No," he replied, after taking a long moment to think. "Not really; I just felt like I needed to be in on it and I pushed real quietly until I got put on it."

"There's stuff going on here that has *got* to be echoes," she said. "And I would bet my hand that a lot of it ties in to you. It just feels that way."

Instead of denying that, Mark thought about it. "You know," he answered reluctantly, "I hate to say this, but I think you're right. It *does* feel that way."

"I have a proposition."

"Shoot."

"Your Prime is mediumism. There's a corollary to that—mediums very frequently are *quite* good at past-life regressions—"

"What, Bridey Murphy?" he laughed. "Come *on*—"

She shook her head. "Let's leave poor Bridey out of this; it was a very *un*scientifically done study, and unfortunately it's thrown a pall over the whole notion. I've done some work along those lines that was a lot better, so I'm inclined to have it incorporated into *my* belief system. Thing is, I'll also keep an open mind on it—while I believe in recycling, I'm also willing to believe that what the regressed subjects are picking up is the memories of strong-minded individuals in the akashic record."

"The who?"

"Remember that I told you that there's another kind of collective memory—one that *does* go back to the caves?"

He nodded.

"That's the akashic record. You will also recall, I think, that I told you that *I* can't get at it without a whole elaborate song-and-dance act. And even then I'm not very good at it. Mediums, on the other hand, are—or else they're good at past-life regression. You pays your money, you takes your choice; the important thing is, it works the same no matter which you believe."

"So? Are you asking me—"

"To be the *victim*. I'm convinced this all dates back to the last days of the Aztec Empire. I'd like to regress *you* because I'm convinced you've got a former incarnation back then—or get you accessing the akashic record, whichever you prefer—and find out what the hell happened back then that links this all together."

He considered the proposition. It had a lot of merit.

"Any chance I could get—ah—*stuck* back there?"

"Not in my hands," she said. "I've done this too many times."

"Okay," he said, secretly a bit pleased that *she* was calling on *him* for help. "You're on."

The god was not pleased. Chimalman cowered beneath the lash of his anger. The metaphor was *not* figurative; although his anger would leave no *physical* signs, she felt the agony of one having the skin flayed from her back.

Finally his anger cooled enough to end the punishment.

"I told you to leave the witch *be*," he rumbled, sitting back into the furs of his throne. "I told you that if she drew too near, that you were to *kill* her, not challenge her!"

"Lord—"

"Five times a fool you are! Once—to be so proud as to leave your marks upon the last sacrifice. Twice—to decide that *you* were wiser than I, that the power of the sorcerers we have trained was greater than hers. Three times—to take the *best* of those *without my leave*, and goad him to challenge the witch. Four times—to *fail* to kill the witch when she began to win! And *five times*—to allow her to regain her memories and her mind!"

"Lord—"

"It was only by sheer good luck that I discovered what you had done and broke the spell that held him in life before they could question him!"

"Yes, Lord." Chimalman groveled a little more.

"Now it is too late; she is alerted, and we, *we*, are not strong enough to challenge her at her full strength." He brooded for another long moment, and his eyes glowed red with anger. Chimalman cowered, and awaited the descent of the sorcerous lash again.

"We must lie quietly; very, very quietly. In fifteen suns comes the sacrifice of the Corn Woman; that will bring us to full power, enough to defeat the witch. Until then there must be *nothing* to arouse her suspicion or her wrath." He stared down at the cowering handmaiden. *"Nothing!"*

"No lord," she quavered, trembling. "Nothing."

·FOURTEEN

It took a week before they both felt ready to try the regression. Di needed to recharge after the duel arcane—badly. Although she hadn't let on, she'd been running on pure nervous energy until the moment Mark dropped her off at his Aunt Nita's.

She'd slept twenty-four hours straight, and so deeply that even her alarm clock going off in her ear hadn't awakened her.

After that she'd spent the next three days not only replacing the energy she had depleted, but bringing herself up to maximum energy charge. *Then* she'd spent three days in near-total isolation—"meditating," she'd said. Mark figured it was more complicated than that—but he also figured it was something along the line of religious secrets and had no wish to pry. One thing he did know: she'd spent at least part of those three days closeted with some of the Xeroxes she'd made at the university library.

Finally she'd gone over his apartment from top to bottom, first physically and non-arcanely cleaning the place (for which he was profoundly grateful), then purging it magically. She was taking no chances on *anything* going wrong—

And Mark wasn't feeling like arguing with her. After all, it was going to be *his* psyche on the line.

They decided that Mark's living room would be their "sanctuary" for the regression; it was where he felt the most comfortable and secure. Di could ward just about any place, so Mark's sensibilities took precedence.

"Scared?" Di asked Mark, easing herself down onto the carpet beside him.

"A little," he admitted, trying to find the most comfortable reclining position he could on the flip-chair which had been stretched out its entire length. Di had warned him that this was what he'd *better* do, since he might be spending a long time that way. "I've never been hypnotized before."

She half laughed. "That's what *you* think."

He twisted his head around so that he could see her; she was sitting in a very relaxed lotus position just behind the "pillow" of the chair. "What's that supposed to mean?"

"My turn at confession. I've had you under at least half a dozen times, my friend. Only I didn't tell you I was hypnotizing you; I told you I was putting you through a 'relaxation exercise.' You're such a good subject that after the first time all I had to do was use the trigger phrase on you, and *pop*"—she snapped her fingers, a rueful smile on her lips "—you were gone to na-na land."

He remembered those "relaxation exercises" quite vividly—they had all been times when she had needed his particular talent and he'd been spooked, too nervous (and, frankly, scared) to cooperate properly. "Spooked" was an appropriate term, since all six times they'd been checking out buildings Di had certified as genuinely haunted, and she had been unable to get the haunt to "move on," as she put it.

He felt a little betrayed. "Why didn't you tell me that was what you were doing?" he asked, hurt. It wasn't so much that she'd hypnotized him—because he could account for nearly every second of the time he'd been "under." It was that she had not told him the truth.

"Mark, you were the only reliable medium I had, and those weren't abstractions or Hollywood special-effects, those were *people* we were trying to help; trapped, unhappy *people*. Dead people, but still people. If I'd even mentioned the word 'hypnosis' back then, you'd have freaked on me. You still thought all hypnotists were children of Svengali. And you'd make a damned ugly Trilby."

"Okay, I'll admit I was a bit irrational. It still wasn't right," he complained, trying to read her eyes.

"I agree," she replied, and he had no doubt that she was feeling a certain amount of guilt. "And I'm sorry. I'm not immune to making mistakes, moral or otherwise. If I had it to do over, I wouldn't have pulled that trick on you; it wasn't fair at all. Will you accept my apology?"

"Yeah," he said, after a while. "You did what you thought you had to do, I guess."

"And there are times when my sense of proportion is a bit skewed. Still want to go through with this?"

"More than ever." He grinned up at her. "Now that I know you had me in your power before this, and didn't take advantage of me."

"Don't count on it," she grinned back. "The tapes will only cost you a small fortune. Okay, are you ready?"

"All systems go," he answered, getting himself back into his comfortable position.

"Meadowsweet, lycopodium, knotweed."

"Who are you?"

Cuauhtemoc heard the voice in his head without fear; it was odd—but he somehow knew that it meant him no harm, just as he somehow knew his name was also "Mark," although that was nothing like his name now, and that in that time-to-come he was not seven, but much older and a wise warrior. So he answered the voice without taking his attention from the spectacle before him.

"Cuauhtemoc, son of Nanautzin, a potter." Then,

because that seemed too little to say about the kindest, bravest father in all of Tenochtitlan, he added, "Son of the best potter in all the world!"

The voice chuckled. "Well said, Cuauhtemoc. What is the year, and the place?"

"The year is Three House, in the Fifth Month, the Feast of Tezcatlipoca," he answered politely. The voice in his head gasped a little. "We are, I am, in Tenochtitlan, in the plaza before the Great Temple of Tezcatlipoca."

"What do you see before you?"

He described for the voice (poor, blind voice, not to be able to see the most beautiful place in all of the wide world) the plaza in which he was standing. To both sides and behind him was a throng of Azteca, brilliantly garbed in their very best. They had gathered, hoping with fading hope that the Great One would descend truly at the climax of this rite, descend and save his people. Their thin, sun-darkened faces were full of equal hope and fear. The bright colors of their festival costumes, red and yellow, blue and white and green, were dulled and smutched a bit by the smokes and fires that had plagued the city daily. Even now there was smoke on the wind, and beyond the chanting of the priests you could hear the screaming and the sound of fighting on the causeways to the city.

His mother's hand was warm on his shoulder as he told the voice of the immaculate stone-paved plaza, shining white in the blinding sun before him, the equally dazzling pile of the pyramid atop which rested the beautiful temple itself. "The temple of Tezcatlipoca is the most beautiful temple in the city—now," he concluded—and his voice faltered a little at the memory of the evil omen.

"Was there another that was more beautiful?" the voice prompted.

He began to nod; then, remembering that the voice was blind, answered. "Yes—the Great Temple, the twin temple of Huitzilopochtli and Tlaloc, the place called

Tlacatecan. It burned, of itself. It was a terrible omen, though no one knew what it meant, then."

"What did it mean?"

"The coming of the Terrible Men, the ones led by the man who said he was Quetzalcoatl. He lied," the boy said defiantly, although he knew very well that his elders were divided on the subject. "There were other omens, too. There was a fire in the sky in the year Twelve House, then the temple burned. Then the sun struck a blow to the temple of Xiuhtechutli. That was all before I was even born. Then there was a fire that ran from sunset sky to sunrise sky, while the sun itself was still shining. Then in the year of my birth the lake boiled up and flooded the whole city, and there was a spirit-woman that ran through the streets, weeping and saying that all must flee. Then a bird with a mirror in its head, all covered with feathers the color of ashes, came to the emperor and showed him fearful things. Then there was a man in the city with two heads. I myself saw him," he added, self-importantly.

"I don't doubt you," the voice replied gravely. "Those are fearful omens."

"Then the Terrible Men came," he said, sadly. "That was why my brother—"

"Yes?" the voice prompted.

"That was why my brother became Tezcatlipoca. He said that if the Great Sacrifice was given by one who *chose* to become the god, that the god would *have* to answer and save us. My mama cried." *And so did I*, he added, without speaking the words aloud.

"That was very brave of him."

"Yes," he replied, secretly wishing that his brother had been a little less brave. There had been no shortage of volunteers. But his brother had said scornfully that most of *those* only wished to trade a probably painful death in combat for a year of pleasure and a quick, nearly painless death. "Even the emperor said so. The emperor is very afraid. He thinks the Most Terrible Man *is* Quetzalcoatl; but even if he *is*, and I know he cannot be, the Feathered

Serpent is not as strong as Smoking Mirror. I know this, for are we not stronger than the Elder People? The Smoking Mirror is *our* god, and he is my brother, and when the Great Sacrifice is made, he will rise up from the altar and he will kill *all* the Terrible Men and their emperor who is *not* the Feathered Serpent!"

There were tears running down his cheeks now, tears of passion—and the loss he dared not confess, for was his brother not greater than the emperor? Was he not the savior of his people? Was such a sacrifice a reason for tears?

"Hush, hush—" the voice soothed. "Tell me what you know of the Terrible Men, what they have done to your people."

"They have taken Moctezuma; they hold him prisoner. They killed many, many people and they have burned up all the country beyond the lake," he told the voice, trying not to be afraid. "They tried to take the city, but we drove them out. I helped. I carried water and arrows to the soldiers."

"Where are they now?"

"All around the lake. They have demons that make a noise and throw round stones, and more demons, huge, with two heads and four legs and voices like trumpets, and they stop everybody who comes on the causeway from the city. They have tried to come back, but we have stopped them." The procession came into view just then, and the boy craned his neck, intent on being the first to catch sight of his brother.

"What are you seeing?"

"It is the procession!" he answered, excitedly. "I see the priests—now the handmaidens—there! There is my brother! He is playing his flutes, and he doesn't look the least, tiniest bit afraid! But—"

"Is something wrong?"

"He—" the distant figure seemed very pale, and not entirely steady. "He—nothing. He is going up the pyramid."

"Tell me."

"He is playing, he has a servant with all the clay flutes he has played this year, and he is climbing the pyramid and breaking each one after he has played it a little—"

There was no doubt about it, the distant youth staggered as if he was drunk.

"Go on."

"There is something wrong—" Panic edged the boy's voice.

"What?"

"I don't know!" The notes of the song quavered now, and it was not a deliberate trill. "I think—I don't know! He *can't* be sick! He's the god, gods don't get sick!"

"How, sick?"

"The Terrible Men—there was a sickness, with spots—"

"'Mission control to Mark,'" said the voice, "Mark, what is he talking about?"

"Measles," the boy heard his mouth saying, though he was too worried about his brother to find it strange that another spirit should use his mouth. "The Spanish brought measles with them; it wiped out hundreds, maybe thousands, and it's at epidemic levels right now."

Just then the youth, so small, so fragile on the great stone stairs, stopped halfway up the pyramid. He set his hand to his head, swaying, and dropped the flutes he was carrying. And as they shattered, he himself dropped to the stone, cried out—and stopped moving.

The boy screamed—echoing the screams of the thousands gathered around him, the screams of his mother as her fingers dug into his shoulder—

"'All systems, red alert!' Mark, take over!" the voice ordered; firmly, but calmly.

Mark found himself looking out of the eyes of the seven-year-old boy, observing, but unable to affect what was happening. Yet at the same time, he was in total control of *himself*. It was a very eerie feeling; like living in a movie.

"What's happening?"

"Looks like about half the people here are heading for the exits, screaming their heads off," he said, surveying the crowd about him as the boy stood in frozen paralysis. The boy's attention was still on his brother, but Mark found he could bend his own attention on whatever happened to be in the boy's field of vision. "The rest are just falling to the ground and having hysterics."

"Not surprising; that must be the worst of all possible omens. What are the priests doing?"

He looked toward the distant pyramid and distantly felt the boy's anguish. "They're dragging the body up to the altar, but I think the kid is already dead."

"Go forward a few weeks—"

He found himself kneeling in the dirt with a rope so tight around his neck that it nearly choked him, one of hundreds of young boys roped together in a chain of sheer misery. He was filthy, sore, and weary, and utterly without hope. There was a place on his shoulder that throbbed and felt burned; he *knew*, with the boy's knowledge, that the Spaniards had branded him there with the mark of a slave. He knew also that his father was dead, his mother a suicide rather than face a fate in Spanish hands. The once-great city was in smoking ruins; about a hundred feet away from him was one of the Spaniards. He wrinkled his nose in distaste; he could smell the filthy, greasy, unwashed mercenary from where he knelt.

Uppermost in the boy's mind was the hope that *this* man would not want *him*. The man was known to have a taste for young boys. And that was the only hope the boy had; all the rest was despair.

"What does the boy know about the aftermath of the sacrifice?"

"The priests and the sorcerer-priests were unable to take the living heart from the sacrifice, and right after that the Spaniards made their final assault on the city," he said, after scanning the memories. "But the priests swore that it wasn't the end; they cursed the Spanish and their faithless allies who had deserted them and gone over to the Spanish side; they said that since the cycle was left unfinished, it would hang over the invaders like a balanced stone, and that one day it would fall."

"Things left unfinished have a way of doing that," said the voice. "Okay, Mark—'there's no place like home.'"

He sat up, blinking. His mouth was dust-dry, and every muscle was stiff. "Wow—"

"Double wow," Di answered, handing him a glass of ice water. "That's one of the clearest regressions I've ever encountered."

"God, it was like watching a movie—when it wasn't like being there." He shook his head, trying to sort out the distracting double-memories.

"Now we know how *you're* tied into this," she said thoughtfully. "I *knew* it couldn't be coincidence. Did you pick up anything on your way out?"

He considered all the slowly fading impressions, and grabbed what he thought was the most important. "It seems like that Burning Water guy—I mean, the *brujo*-activist, here and now—and the guy that was my brother are the same person," he said, carefully. "I don't know, that's just what it feels like. Like, that was something *he* has to complete, too. But that's crazy! That would mean that he's going to let his own people sacrifice *him!*"

"Maybe crazy, maybe not," she answered slowly. "The original felt very strongly that a voluntary sacrifice would bring the god to save his people. Every tradition I've ever worked with agrees that a consensual sacrifice has enough power to work literal miracles—including your *own* tradition, my friend."

Days, weeks, even hours ago, that might have disturbed or even angered him, her lumping Calvary in with pagan traditions. Now, after having just spent several hours as someone who believed as passionately in the truth of *his* gods as any fervent Catholic, Mark could not find it possible to be offended.

"So, you think they're going to try to complete what was interrupted?"

She nodded. "Uh-huh. And going for the same results, I'd bet—given what he's been doing with the activists and the *brujos*. So; what's that tell us?"

"He's probably Mexican," Mark said, after thinking.

"Or at least he *came* from Mexico; probably around April of last year, since that's when the first animal mutilations started."

"He probably *isn't* an illegal alien," Di frowned, thinking out loud. "That would hamper his movements too much, I think. Which means—"

"Customs will have a record on him!" Mark said in triumph. "Di, we've *got* him!"

"Next time I say the show's over before we've got it in the bag, shoot me, won't you?" Mark said in disgust, shoving a pile of papers away in complete frustration. "I mean, how long have we been at this?"

"Two weeks," Di replied wearily, reading another set of Customs records while she sipped her tenth cup of coffee for the day. "We're no closer than we were when I regressed you. And it's almost time for the next cycle. This is day one; you can bet there'll be blood tonight."

"What one was that?" Mark asked, wondering if there was some way they could pinpoint and stake out a probable victim.

"The—Corn Goddess thing. You know, mature woman, white outfit—"

"Right; pick a woman. Could be any female in the city over the age of thirteen. Shit." He glared at the pile of file folders. "Look at this—everybody and his brother was down there visiting Mexico about that time. Even Robert."

There was a crash of crockery, and Mark spun, startled. "Di—are you—"

She was staring at him, the shards of the cup at her feet, sitting so rigid and straight it looked like somebody had jabbed her with a needle in the rear. "Robert—" she said slowly. "Before April—nothing. After April, the hottest photographer in Dallas. Before April, living in a roach-motel; after April, living like a *god*. A *god*, Mark. And those four gorgeous models of his—entirely at his beck and call, serving only *him*."

"My god—the four handmaidens? And—we've always been like brothers—my brother—"

She reached down beside her chair and dove into a satchel of Xeroxes from some of the university books, and began to dig frantically through them.

She pulled out the one she wanted, and skimmed it while Mark sat paralyzed. "Oh gods—" she moaned, "Mark, the other common name for Smoking Mirror is *Burning Water*—and look at this!"

She thrust a page with a sketch from one of the codexes at him. On it was a glyph he'd seen before, on the door to Rob's darkroom.

One of the simple hieroglyphs of Tezcatlipoca, the caption read, *the hieroglyph of Fire and Water, or Burning Water*.

"My god—" Mark choked out. "It all fits, god help me, it all fits!"

"Robert and Burning Water are the same—the channel for Tezcatlipoca. That would account for those shields I sensed on him, and why he didn't much want to stick around me. *And* why his model avoided me; the deity could probably keep me off the scent, but there'd have been no way I wouldn't have sensed what *she* was. Mark, there's no other answer at this point."

"My god." He *thought* his mind was going in circles; it wasn't—it was putting facts together too fast for him to follow. He only knew what was happening when it presented him with the answer to his earlier question.

"Oh my god—Sherry—"

She didn't need prompting.

"Oh *gods*—" she groaned. "The Corn Goddess—"

Sherry set the last stitch into the snowy *huiple*, knotted the thread and cut it. Her hands fell away from the completed work. The blouse lay on her lap, finished at last, and she could only stare at it, dull-eyed.

Okay, it's done. It's beautiful, no doubt about it; my best work to date. Now what? God, talk about all dressed up and nowhere to go—

The thing had come to completely dominate her life over the past couple of weeks, an obsession that strengthened every time Rob asked about it. She even had dreams of weaving. This last week she'd put off all her commissioned work, put off her clients, just so she could work on *this*—

And for what? Why had she *done* this? What on earth had possessed her?

"Sherry?"

The voice startled her out of her wits. She jumped and let out a little yip, half scream and half gasp, despite the fact that the voice was achingly familiar.

"Rob!" she snapped, twisting in her straight-backed chair to face the door, "I've *asked* you a million times not to sneak up on me tha—"

She bit the rest of the sentence back when she saw that Robert wasn't alone. That he'd brought all four of his models with him, ranged behind him like acolytes with a priest, faces expectant.

"Is it done?" he asked, ignoring what she had said completely, and nodding at the *huiple* in her lap.

"Uh-huh," she replied, listening for the sounds of Bobby rattling around in the kitchen, and not hearing him. "Where's Bobby? He should be home from school by now."

"I told him to go to his grandmother's after school today," Robert said softly. "You and I need to—talk."

Before she could react to that statement, he turned to Lupe and said—*something*—to her. It wasn't Spanish, that was for sure. Whatever he said, it was in some guttural language *Sherry* had never heard before, and it sounded like an order.

It *was* an order. Lupe smiled, threw a glance of veiled triumph at Sherry, bowed to Robert—and turned to lock the door of the workroom just behind her.

That tore it. Now *they* were taking over *her* territory, *her* space. That was *it*, she wasn't going to stand this charade another moment!

Sherry leapt to her feet, hot with anger. "Now just one *damn* minute here! What the hell do you think you're do—"

"*Be still.*"

Sherry blinked—and found herself sitting meekly back in her chair, clutching the *huiple*.

She took a good look at him—and realized that *this* wasn't the Robert she knew and loved anymore.

She looked at the girls, and they were looking at her the way Bobby looked at an ice-cream cone.

"Robert—" she faltered.

Their expressions didn't change, and she felt her throat choke with fear at the sight.

She had had nightmares about this. This was obviously her worst fear come home to roost. Whatever those girls had gotten Robert into had him good now—and for some reason they wanted *her* as well. Or else they wanted her dead.

And she'd just thought she was being jealous and irrational!

Her head reeled, but she managed to hold to just enough calm to think a little. Without a single backward glance she abandoned seven years of marriage and all her new-won prosperity. If she could get out with Bobby and her life—

"Look, Robert," she pled shamelessly, "Whatever you want, you can have. Anything but Bobby. You can have a clean divorce, I won't contest, just leave me my workroom stuff and a little furniture, and a college trust fund for Bobby. No alimony, no child support, we can do fine—"

"I don't want a divorce, Sherry," he said in that deadly, gentle tone. "I want something far more from you."

She had a sudden, panicked vision of herself as the center of some kind of weird, orgiastic ceremony, and then flashed on Lupe holding a knife over her—and stood up so abruptly that the chair overturned. She backed away from them, stumbling over the chair; moving slowly, whimpering a little with fear. "Please, Robert, you know I never hurt you, no matter what you did to me!"

"Sherry—" He followed her.

She ran right up against the wall and flattened herself to it.

"Sherry—*look at me!*" he ordered, seizing both her arms.

She did, completely unable to disobey the command in his voice.

She felt dizzy—almost as if she were being drugged. His eyes were—strange. Depthless. Glowing? It felt as if she was falling into them. And she couldn't—didn't want to—look away. Or escape. Her knees went weak, and she couldn't move.

"Listen to me Sherry—" he slid his hands down her arms, took both her wrists in his hands, and pulled her back into the center of the room, where Lupe was setting her chair back upright. Some tiny corner of her mind screamed at her to resist, to fight—but her body wouldn't obey her, and the rest of her mind was drowning in Robert's eyes.

He pushed her down into the chair; once there, she couldn't move.

"This is true, what I'm going to tell you," he said, with a power Sherry could almost touch behind his words. "When the Spanish came to Mexico, the greatest nation, the greatest *empire*, in the New World was the Aztec empire. They *could* have stopped him, but he lied to them, and told him that he was a god that was supposed to return, Quetzalcoatl. By the time they found out differently it was almost too late."

"But—" she heard herself saying, as if in a dream, "they lost—the Aztecs—"

"There was one rite, the Tezcatlipoca sacrifice, that *would* have saved them if they had been able to complete it. It would have brought Burning Water down on the heads of the defilers and He would have crushed them like the insects they were!"

There was no doubt about it. Robert's eyes *were* glowing, down in the depths of them. A sullen, smoldering red.

"But those bastards brought more than guns with them; they brought disease, diseases the Azteca had no defenses against. The intended sacrifice died of that disease on the very steps of the temple pyramid. The cycle could not be completed; the door was closed to Smoking Mirror, and he could not save his people. Until now."

She shook her head, not understanding his words.

"I am Robert. But since last April, I am also Tezcatlipoca. We, my handmaidens and I, have begun the cycle again—but *this* time, it will be completed. When it is complete, Tezcatlipoca will be freed to enter this world in full power, and we will drive the interlopers back into the sea, giving the land back to the ones to whom it belongs!"

She believed him. She *had* to believe him; his will overwhelmed hers and crushed it to dust.

"But you don't need *me*—"

"I *do* need you, Sherry. I am asking you to agree to what I, Robert, have already sworn to: to sacrifice this pitiful shell so that Tezcatlipoca can return and liberate his people." His voice was still gentle, but now it was persuasive. Very persuasive. "The sacrifice tonight must be a woman, a mature woman in the fullness of her beauty who has borne a child. And she must have made the garments she will wear at the rite with her own hands—and they must be completely white, without ornamentation."

Lupe laid the *huiple* and wrap-skirt she had just finished on her lap. She felt her hands clutching the fabric involuntarily.

"Yes," Robert/Tezcatlipoca said. "Yes. Think, Sherry. Think what a little thing it is. Such a small thing, one life, in the light of all the suffering it would end. For the good of the people. Sherry. Think how much it would mean to those who suffer, who *have* suffered for so very long . . . fated to be the lowest of the low ever since the cursed Spaniards came. Everything was taken from them, they've been made hardly better than slaves. *You* can give it all back to them, Sherry."

He was *so* persuasive, and his eyes were so compelling.
She felt herself nodding.

The Ghia screamed into a parking place just outside
the apartment complex; they were *not* going to warn
Robert by pulling up to the townhouse. Instead, they
pulled into the *un*guarded subdivision that abutted it,
then found a place where houses screened the thick
adobe wall that divided the subdivision from the complex. They weren't worried about being spotted; it was
almost rush-hour time and this was yuppie territory.
Both spouses were about to hit the Twenty-Mile Parking
Lot, aka the Dallas–Fort Worth freeway, any kids were
in after-school care, and that held for both sides of the
fence.

The whole of the way here Di had been muttering
something under her breath, eyes closed in complete
concentration—words like nothing Mark had ever heard
before, yet which had a tantalizing air of familiarity. But
he'd been too busy breaking every traffic law on the
books to get to the townhouse—if Di was going to call
something up, he wasn't about to stop her, but he also
wasn't going to be much help either. So he'd stuck to his
driving, and let her do her thing—

The wall around the complex was of fake adobe, a
good twelve feet tall and a foot thick—daunting to
punks, maybe, but not to Mark, who regularly worked
out on the Academy obstacle course. Nor did it provide
any barrier to Di—for when he pulled himself up onto
the top, and turned to offer her a hand up—he found
that she was already beside him.

He nodded, then, and they dropped down together
with similarly soft *thumps*, finding themselves on the
service road behind the complex.

Together they slipped onto one of the sidewalks
threading the complex, headed toward Robert's townhouse, strolling casually as if they belonged here, until
they reached the last townhouse block before his. *Then*
they took to the bushes planted all along the walls,
sprinting across any open spaces one at a time like

commandos, ending up at the outer rear corner of Robert's place.

"Let me check the front to see if Rob's car is there," he said, as they eyeballed the back for signs of life in the privacy-fenced patio.

Di grabbed his arm before he could slip off. "Mark—I want to take the shields off you. Now."

"Why?"

"Because—I'm going to try something, to bring in help—but it's going to need a physical body if it comes. It can't be mine; I'll have to handle the girls."

"Which leaves me." Mark didn't entirely like the notion. "What if Tezli-whatsis decides he likes me better than Rob?"

"He can't switch; not until Robert is dead."

"You think. Are you sure you *have* to do this?" he asked, still not happy. He *liked* being under shields; he didn't want to give them up, not now, not under fire.

"Shit, *I'm* not sure it's even going to do any good!" she replied, looking just as unhappy as he felt. "It's an outside chance at best; I'm not sure I read the rite correctly, I'm not sure I *did* it correctly a week ago, I'm not sure I recited the right invocation in the car, and I'm not sure it's going to work at all even if I did everything perfectly. But we're dealing with powerful stuff here; one hell of a lot more powerful than *I* can handle—go ahead, test the water; even *you* ought to be able to feel it—"

He closed his eyes and imagined himself extending a cautious mental "hand" toward the townhouse—and pulled it back a lot faster than he'd extended it.

"Something—there, and not there." He shivered. "Weird, even by your standards. And *strong*."

"Exactly. *He's* up there, and manifesting through Robert. The only way he could be stronger would be if he didn't need a vehicle. In no way am I going to be able to hold off a god! Mark—please—"

"Okay," he sighed. "Take 'em off."

Mark had been shielded for so long, he'd forgotten what it "felt" like to be unshielded.

It felt naked, was what it felt like. Open to every little thing that blew by. A house with all the doors and windows standing wide. *Come on in, sit right down, make yourself at home, help yourself to the family silver—*

"Okay," Di told him. "Go—"

He slipped around the corner, bending low to stay under the windows; he peeked around the next corner at the assigned parking slots. The car *was* there, and so was Sherry's. He sprinted back.

"We're go."

They kept to the shrubbery, edging their way behind its concealment, until they made the edge of the privacy fence itself. A quick eye to the cracks showed there was no one on the patio, and there didn't seem to be anyone in the kitchen beyond. This fence was a mere six feet tall, but it did not have the wide top that the exterior adobe fence had. Di took one look and shook her head at him. Mark got himself over; then, with a cautionary glance at the patio door, slid over to the gate and let Di inside.

The patio door led into the kitchen—and it was not locked. Which was just as well; if it had been, Mark had been quite prepared to pick it, or if that took too much time, shoot the damn thing open.

They eased it open enough to squeeze through, and froze as they heard voices.

Di looked to Mark for guidance.

"We'd better rush them," he whispered. "It sounds like they're moving toward the front door. Anything I should do to kick off this 'help' you said you've called?"

"Pray," she said, grimly. "Just—pray. It doesn't matter to who; it'll get where it needs to go."

With his shielding off he could *feel* the weirdness and the strength of it, and he was coldly afraid. He couldn't think of anything—just as on that long-ago Halloween night. Not so much as a "Hail Mary."

So he did now what he'd done then—as he charged through the kitchen and dining room and on into the living room (grateful for all the times he'd been here, so that he knew the layout of the place), he put everything he could spare into a single, simple cry for help.

He hit the carpet of the living room in a roll, and came up behind the back of the sectional sofa with his gun drawn and trained on the astonished group headed for the outer hallway.

Sherry was toward the front of the group, dressed (Mark's heart plummeted) in the white outfit she'd been working on all this time. He'd been hoping that he and Di weren't right in their guess.

Behind her were the four priestesses, two on either side, wearing perfectly ordinary clothing. Bringing up the rear was Robert.

But when the man turned, and Mark saw his eyes, he knew there wasn't much of Robert there anymore.

"Freeze!" Mark barked. "Rob, don't try me. You know I never aim at what I don't intend to hit."

Behind him, he could hear Di gliding into the room—without shielding he could *feel* her too; like a bright flame at his back. Before him, Robert laughed softly.

"Go ahead," he mocked. "Shoot. You won't get very far."

Then he made a short rush toward Mark—and reflex took over. He fired three times.

And he heard the bullets hit something with an audible *clang*—and saw them hang in midair a foot in front of Robert's chest for a moment, then fall to the carpet.

Robert laughed again, and gestured, and Mark discovered that *he* couldn't move.

"You won't manage that trick with *me*, Burning Water," Di's voice rang out behind him, high and clear. Then, before any of them could react, she vaulted the sofa—into, then out of the pit group—then leapt for the group of five women, tearing an unresisting Sherry out of their hands and shoving her out of the way behind her. The moment Di's hands were free of Sherry, she had both of them raised before her, and Mark could not only sense the shields she'd raised about her and Sherry, he could *see* them—like some kind of special effects forcefield in a sci-fi movie.

The girls recovered quickly, and raised shields of their own. Within a heartbeat the living room began to resemble the kind of battle a special effects man would sell his soul to reproduce—fiery balls and lances of colored light licking out and exploding against the shields in showers of sparks, an occasional weirdly shaped and half-seen critter tearing into one side or the other before one of those blasts of light could take it out. Only two things would the effects man have to complain about. First, that there was nothing visible happening when the weaponry connected; just a gasp of pain from the recipient, or the momentary weakening and dimming of the shield. Second, that the entire battle was soundless except for grunts of effort or gasps of pain.

After a few moments during which he was too confused to make out much, Mark began to get a clearer idea of what was happening. Robert had not yet joined in—and Di was holding her own, but just barely.

If Robert decided to pitch in—

He glanced at Robert as the fight began to work away from Robert and back nearer to where Sherry sat dull-eyed and unseeing beside the couch. He saw Robert frown; he saw Robert start to raise *his* hands.

If Rob joined in, Di was doomed. And so were Sherry and himself.

And Mark again remembered Di's admonition to pray.

This time he wasn't distracted by having to make a dive for cover; he sent every bit of what he had winging outward in that inarticulate call for help.

If he could have fallen, he would have; dizziness made the room spin and start to go black. This was a replay of the strange, disorienting vertigo he'd begun to feel that Halloween when the *thing* had set eyes on him, only *much* stronger, much more intense. Once a private plane he'd been in had gotten caught in turbulence and began to spin out of control; this was like that, only the plane was *him* and he didn't have the controls—

Suddenly everything steadied, as if a giant, gentle hand had caught him and was supporting him. He still couldn't see—but he felt a—a *presence*. Like the bright flame that was Di, only *more* so.

Your pardon for the intrusion, little brother, the presence said/felt/thought in his mind. *But you called; is it permitted?*

What the hell am I supposed to say? he thought, confused. All Mark could think of was old vampire movies. *Uh—enter freely and of your own will?*

My thanks.

Now he could see and hear—but when he tried to raise his gun, he discovered that he could not act. It was uncannily like what had happened when he was doing the regression with Di; he was an observer in his own body.

As his hands holstered the gun, Mark saw with relief that Robert had not yet completed whatever action it was that he had intended to take.

"Brother—" said his mouth—

But it was not *his* voice coming from that mouth.

Robert started, and pivoted to face him, a look of utter incredulity on his face. Mark's body rose, and stood facing him, completely relaxed, completely confident, radiating serenity.

Mark managed to notice that the battle with the four priestesses had now gone from pyrotechnics to a battle of wills: the four grouped together, holding each other's hands; Di alone, feet slightly apart, hands clenched at her sides—both sides staring silently at each other with eyes locked.

He turned his attention back to Robert. The man's expression was one of surprise, disbelief, and something Mark couldn't identify.

"Your time is past, my brother," the voice said gently.

Robert flushed with anger. "And yours is not?" he spat.

"Both yes and no."

Robert was gone now. There was no trace of Mark's old friend in the figure that faced him/them.

Burning Water sneered. "I see you haven't given up ambiguity. Still the philosopher—"

"As *you* still seek war and conflict, and turn your back on other solutions. Brother, this man you hold, you have some right to—he is yours by consent, and twice. And the four priestesses. But *this* man—the other women—

no. No. Choose another Corn Woman, brother. Or choose another way."

Burning Water snarled, and his face twisted into something very like a cat's snarling mask. "Your way? *Never*. I destroyed you once, *brother*—"

"Yet I continue to return." Mark felt his lips smiling.

Then he felt the presence within him turn a fraction of its attention back on him, as if it had forgotten that he was still there and only just now remembered the fact. He could feel its regard; it was a great deal like being caught in the tropical sun at high noon. It was warming, and dazzling, but too bright and intense to bear for long.

Then he heard himself speaking again, but his lips were shaping strange, guttural words that sounded faintly familiar, but not familiar enough for him to guess what was being said.

If he could have flushed, he would have. It was frustrating and a little shaming; he felt as if he was a kid again, and the adults in the room had just switched to a code so he wouldn't be able to eavesdrop!

Whatever was going on, both entities were still arguing. The argument finally ended when Mark's controller suddenly gestured peremptorily toward the group still engaged in their psychic duel in the far corner of the living room.

The four priestesses went glaze-eyed, and froze. Di blinked, shook her head; then swiveled, hands in the guard position, to face Mark.

He had no notion of what she saw there, but she relaxed completely.

She shook herself all over, gave a great sigh of evident relief, then made a strange little bow and said something hesitantly in that odd guttural tongue, of which Mark only understood the word "Quetzalcoatl."

That was enough for him to figure out just who he was sharing his body with. He didn't feel *quite* so badly then at being left out. . . .

The entity sharing his mind replied to her salutation, but not with voice. Mark could actually feel the thoughts reaching toward Di, although he could not touch them, nor read them himself.

She made a sour face, but didn't protest, although he could tell from her expression that she would have liked to. Instead she stepped reluctantly away from the four handmaidens.

Robert beckoned, anger written in every muscle-twitch. The four women seemed to wake partially from their trance, and answered his summons, gathering around him with bewilderment, confusion, and a little fear in their eyes.

Robert snapped something at them, and they headed for the door, still acting a bit glazed. Then, Robert stalked towards the couch, and Sherry—

Mark fought the entity controlling him, then; fought in sheer rage and panic.

Dammit, no! he shouted at the entity. *You said he has no right to her! I won't let you give her away, damn you! Not Sherry—*

But Robert only seized his wife by the arm, yanked her to her feet, and shoved the half-conscious woman straight at Mark. "Take her and be damned to both of you," Robert snarled in English, as Mark's arms caught and held her gently.

He realized then that it was *his* arms catching her; the entity Quetzalcoatl had relinquished most of the control to him, only remaining watchfully in the back of his mind.

Robert snarled something else, then—and Quetzalcoatl took back just enough control to reply—

Then Robert was striding angrily out of the room, into the hall, slamming the front door behind him so hard that the whole apartment shook.

And like an omen, the bronze glyph of "Burning Water" fell from the darkroom door and shattered on the tiles of the doorstep where the carpet ended.

For a few moments more, Mark was held by the entity within him; able to support the now completely unconscious Sherry, but unable to do anything else.

Then, with a rush very like great wings of light sweeping all about him, it was gone, leaving only a sense of deep peace behind.

But with it went ninety percent of his energy.

He sagged against the couch, the weight of Sherry in his arms now more than he could cope with. He managed to haul her ungracefully over the back of it and down onto the couch cushions where she curled up on her own into a sleeping position, and then did not move again except for her steady breathing.

That done, he suddenly remembered that his quarry was getting away.

He stumbled toward the front door; Di intercepted him before he could get there and caught his arm. Weakened as he was, she was more than a match for him.

"What the *hell* do you think you're doing?" he cried, too damned tired to muster anger, and trying to pull out of her grasp. "Those—those *things* have murdered nearly a hundred people, and they're getting away!"

She collapsed to the floor—looking just as exhausted as he was—and let go of his arm. "That's the price Tezcatlipoca demanded for letting us go," she said, wearily. "Enough time to get away. When Sherry wakes, we can set the dogs on him, but not before."

He stared at her, totally aghast.

"Mark, I don't *like* it any better than you do," she snapped. "It sure as hell wasn't the way I figured things would turn out. I thought we'd either win or lose—and win *or* lose, I thought we'd get this stopped for good. I told you once that if I went, I'd take this thing with me—I felt Burning Water beginning to make his move, and I was getting ready to do a really spectacular kamikaze act when your visitor arrived. And I never expected him to work this thing out to a damned draw!"

"Well, the hell with that!" he growled, and headed for the door—

And literally bounced off an invisible barrier at the entrance to the hallway, landing flat on his rump.

"What I figured," he heard Di sigh from across the room, and saw that she was pushing at what was probably a similar barrier, trying to get at the designer phone on the table next to the dining room door.

"*Shit!*" he cursed, seeing no way out of it.

She looked over at him, and favored him with another of her rueful smiles.

"Gods," she told him, "have a habit of enforcing their bargains."

". . . so I guess they figured we'd finally fingered them," Mark concluded, "Since by the time we got there, they were gone and Sherry was just coming around after they'd knocked her out."

Sherry hadn't remembered a thing, so that was the story he and Di had concocted between them, claiming their arrival time at Robert's apartment for a good six hours after the actual confrontation.

"Aw *hail*," the Chief swore. "We got an APB on 'em, but ah doubt it'll do much good." As always, when angry, his accent had thickened. "They're prob'ly halfway t' Tee-ah-joo-wana by now."

"Probably, since Rob had more than enough cash to *buy* his own plane, and there's more little private airports around here than fleas on a hound," Mark agreed. "Well, at least we've seen the last of them—and you *have* got a perp. They practically confessed by heading out."

"Yeah, they did, an' that's how ah'm gonna handle it," the Chief replied, still mad as hops. "But they got two more afore they went. Gawddammittall!"

"Oh *hell*," Mark groaned.

"At least we *think* they got 'em; ain't found no bodies yet, but the husband and the ex are hollerin' up a storm. Two broads," the Chief said, totally disgusted. "An' both of 'em pokin' their noses inta places ain't nobody with the sense God gave a mosquito would go." He threw down two pictures that looked to have been cropped and enlarged from vacation photos; one of a post-middle-aged woman with dead-white skin and overly black (obviously dyed) hair, the other of a younger woman with round glasses and brownish hair the length of Di's, tied back with a scarf. "*That* 'un, that one's fr'm Frisco," he said, pointing his cigar at the second. "She was cruisin' th' *barrio* fer Godssake! Her ol' man says she was looking fer *folk music*." The Chief's expression spoke volumes about what he thought of that. "T'other idiot's a touristo too—fr'm KC. She was—you ain't gonna believe this, boy—lookin' fer a *gay bar*. Th' ex says she was suppose'ta meet a friend'uv hers, what useta be a tenant. Gawdawlmighty! How th' *hell* are we suppose'ta keep damnfools from gettin' killed by their own damnfoolishness?"

"I dunno, Chief," Mark sighed. "I dunno. Sometimes I think it's a losing battle."

He looked over the makesheets, and suppressed an hysterical desire to laugh.

Living with Sherry had certainly given Robert a very distorted view of women. And Tezcatlipoca wouldn't know any better, either.

Robert was used to having a wife *with child*, and one who handmade all her own clothing. That, naturally, had made her perfect for the sacrifice. And there was no reason for him to suppose all women were less domestic than Sherry, *despite* the fact that Robert had worked for the fashion industry.

Both of the women abducted had disappeared while wearing all-white outfits—and since neither of them were the least virginal, he figured Tezcatlipoca expected that *one* of them, at least, should have had a child.

In point of fact, neither had.

And neither was at all likely to have *made* her clothing, since the younger one was wearing a bargain-basement ripoff of one of Sherry's designs, made in Mexico and bought just that afternoon—and the other had been gowned by Calvin Klein. . . .

DFW; it all begins and ends here, Mark thought, as he and Di scouted for empty seats in the waiting area.

"Well, did you get *any* research done?" Mark asked Di, while the gate agent announced the delay of her flight.

"Believe it or not, yes," she said with a certain weary content. "Between all that Mexican and Indian stuff we waded through and your darling aunt, plus spending all that time hauling around Dallas and Fort Worth, I have plenty for a linked family series. Just a matter of getting it organized and doing the outlines—I have most of what I need in my head."

"Thank God for small favors," he replied, giving up on finding a seat; he fed the paper-vending machine next to them with the last of his coins and extracted the afternoon newspaper from its bowels.

"Which one?" she asked impishly. "God, I mean."

"Jehovah, the Almighty," he replied serenely. "I've decided I'm perfectly happy with a masculine deity that operates on a solar schedule, Catholic style. And I'm equally happy to let anyone else choose differently."

"*Good*," she replied with a sincerity no one could doubt. "That's all I've ever hoped for. Quick—two chairs!"

They scrambled for them before anyone else could grab them, and settled in. Beyond them, a cold winter rain lashed at the window and the tarmac beyond.

"Look at that beautiful rain," she said, nodding at the drippy gray sky beyond the glass.

"Never thought *I'd* be happy to see cold rain again," Mark confessed. "Now—every time it gets warm in midwinter I'm going to have nightmares."

"Don't blame you; the heat wave sure moved out when Burning Water and company did, didn't it?"

"You figure they were causing it?"

"Uh-huh. No doubt in my mind. Can I have some of that?" she asked, setting her carryons down.

He handed her most of the paper, reserving to himself the only two important sections—the sports and comics.

They slumped into the hard plastic chairs that no one could be comfortable in, and perused quietly—until Di made a choking noise.

Mark looked up, startled. "What—"

She pointed to a tiny article on the bottom of page five.

Mexico City. Associated Press. American photographer Robert Fernandez was found murdered today on the tip of the Pyramid of Tlaloc, it read. *Fernandez, who was known throughout the fashion world for his photographs of four young Mexican models recently was named as a suspect in the mass slayings in Dallas and Fort Worth attributed to the "Texas Ripper." He fled the country with his models, and until now his whereabouts have been unknown. He is also suspected of having ties to the radical Indian movements and to a cult that he apparently founded among the radicals. This cult apparently advocated terrorist-type activities, which may have been the goal of the murders, and his death has been attributed to those activities. The whereabouts of his four models are still unknown. Fernandez is survived by his wife, Sherry, and a son, Robert Junior.*

"So they went through with it anyway," Mark said softly. "I wondered—when we found both those women skinned—"

"They must have been hoping that a flawed sacrifice would do anyway." Her face was very quiet. "I could almost feel sorry for him; he was trapped in so many ways by the past. . . ."

"Yeah," Mark said softly, sadly; remembering a friend, and a brother.

"Mark, don't you think you'd better go to Sherry? She's *got* to have been notified; surely she needs at least a shoulder."

"She's gotten a lot stronger and a lot more mature in the last six weeks. And besides, I'm playing that very cool," Mark replied. "If she needs me, she'll call me. It's touchy enough, what with me being the cop that fingered him."

"Hm. If this were one of my novels, there'd be an instant happy ending. It would turn out not be as touchy as you think," Di replied thoughtfully, her eyes shuttered. "Let's see, how would I plot this—maybe I'd give you a quicky reading, a surface scan of Sherry's psyche—"

"I—" he hesitated.

"Then—then I'd tell you something comfortable—like—that a good part of her standoffishness was guilt on *her* part; half of her feeling like she still should be loyal to Robert, half wanting desperately to go to you. Then I'd point out that now she won't have to deal with that—now she can get her mourning over with, and come to you without the guilt. And I'd tell you that's what she'll do. Bingo, all better, everybody in love, or at least in bed."

"Right—" He snorted. "Too damned easy—and too damned convenient."

"Love, you're learning. No free lunch, and the happy endings aren't guaranteed."

"I don't suppose you have any deathless wisdom at all?"

She sighed. "Not a bit; I have no more idea what's in her mind than you do, and if I did, I probably still wouldn't tell you, because the information wasn't mine to give. We may be the good guys, but we don't get to ride off into the sunset with the significant other of our choice. You go back to try to deal with a lady as fragile as a glass unicorn right now, and I go home—"

"To what?"

She grimaced. "A hatful of work, a man who can't understand why I won't make a commitment to him when he knows I care for him, and a good friend who's dying by inches."

"No happy endings."

"No happy endings. Does Sherry remember anything?"

He shook his head. "Not a damned thing. Her memory is that the girls roped Robert into a weird pro-Indian cult, probably involving drugs, and *that* was the reason for his personality change, and the things he did."

Di shrugged. "I won't swear to you that Quetzalcoatl didn't play some tricks with her memory to make it easier for her to cope. How's she *really* been doing these past few weeks?"

"Better than I expected, all things considered. You said one thing that *was* true, this makes an end to it for her. And I suppose that's the end of it for us, too."

"Huh," she said thoughtfully, looking out of the window in front of her, but obviously not seeing the plane pulling into the gate. "They failed this time, or I'd feel it. So now—"

"So now, what?"

"Now I only wonder who the *next* one is."

AFTERWORD·

I APOLOGIZE TO ANY TRUE DEVOTEE OF AZTEC CULTURE FOR taking some liberties (sometimes extreme) with the Quetzalcoatl/Tezcatlipoca mythic cycles for the sake of the story. I plead poetic license. For the curious, it is likely that the sacrifice to Tezcatlipoca was *indeed* interrupted in exactly the way I quote—it *is* known that the sacrifice was aborted, and it happened in such a way that it was a terrible omen, and that there was a measles epidemic raging in Tenochtitlan at the time.

The omens that I quote preceding the invasion of the Spaniards are also noted in the chronicles of the times.

For those interested in Aztec mythology, I offer the following as excellent sources:

Burland, Cottie. *The Gods of Mexico.*

———. *Montezuma, Lord of the Aztecs.*

Carrasco, David. *Quetzalcoatl and the Ironies of Empire.*

Davies, Nigel. *The Aztecs, A History.*

Duran, Diego. *Book of the Gods and Rites and the Ancient Calendar.*

Lafaya, Jacques. *Quetzalcoatl and Guadalupe: The Formation of Mexican National Consciousness.*

Radin, Paul. *Sources and Authenticity of the History of the Ancient Mexicans.*

Sejourne, Laurette. *Burning Water: Thought and Religion in Ancient Mexico.*

Vaillant, George. *The Aztecs of Mexico.*

Weaver, Muriel Porter. *The Aztecs, Mayas, and Their Predecessors.*

Wolf, Eric. *The Valley of Mexico.*

And finally, please, *please* do not ask me to actually *pronounce* any of the Aztec names! I had a hard enough time keeping them spelled right!

—Mercedes Lackey
January 1988